I0831338

HIDDEN AND VISIBLE REALMS

TRANSLATIONS FROM THE ASIAN CLASSICS

HIDDEN AND VISIBLE REALMS

Early Medieval Chinese Tales of the Supernatural and the Fantastic

COMPILED BY

LIU YIQING

EDITED AND TRANSLATED BY

ZHENJUN ZHANG

COLUMBIA UNIVERSITY PRESS

New York

Columbia University Press wishes to express its appreciation for assistance given by the Wm. Theodore de Bary Fund in the publication of this book.

Columbia University Press
Publishers Since 1893
New York Chichester, West Sussex
cup.columbia.edu

Library of Congress Cataloging-in-Publication Data

Names: Liu, Yiqing, 403-444, author. | Zhang, Zhenjun, editor, translator.
Title: Hidden and visible realms : early medieval Chinese tales of the supernatural and the fantastic / compiled by Liu Yiqing ; edited and translated by Zhenjun Zhang.
Other titles: You ming lu. English | Early medieval Chinese tales of the supernatural and the fantastic | Chinese tales of the supernatural and the fantastic
Description: New York : Columbia University Press, 2018. | Series: Translations from the Asian classics | Includes bibliographical references and index.
Identifiers: LCCN 2017050419 (print) | LCCN 2017059537 (ebook) | ISBN 9780231547055 (electronic) | ISBN 9780231187169 (cloth)
Subjects: LCSH: Tales—China—Translations into English. | Paranormal fiction, Chinese—Translations into English. | Fantasy fiction, Chinese—Translations into English. | Tales—China—Translations into English. | GSAFD: Fantasy fiction.
Classification: LCC PL2666.L55 (ebook) | LCC PL2666.L55 Y813 2018 (print) | DDC 895.13/24—dc23
LC record available at https://lccn.loc.gov/2017050419

Cover design: Noah Arlow

In memory of

Zhao Qiping 趙齊平 *(1934–1993)*

and

Wu Xiaoru 吳小如 *(1922–2014)*

CONTENTS

ACKNOWLEDGMENTS

This project started over a decade ago when I was working on an earlier project, *Buddhism and Tales of the Supernatural in Early Medieval China: A Study of Liu Yiqing's* Youming lu, though I translated most of the pieces more recently. During the course of finishing this book, I received help from my teachers at the University of Wisconsin-Madison and colleagues at St. Lawrence University.

I am grateful to Professors William Nienhauser and Victor Mair for their careful reading of my introduction and their valuable suggestions. I am indebted also to my colleagues Sid Sondergard and Roy Cardwell for their many helpful suggestions about the chapters they read over. In addition, I would like to thank my daughters, Yuxi and Kaixi (Jennifer), who read this book as the first readers as well as proofreaders.

A special debt is due to Jennifer Crewe, Christine Dunbar, Christian Winting, and Leslie Kriesel at Columbia University Press for their kindness and sincere help in the process of reviewing and editing my manuscript, as well as to the two anonymous reviewers for their invaluable comments and suggestions.

This volume is published in memory of my teachers at Beijing University: Professor Zhao Qiping, my academic advisor, and Professor Wu Xiaoru.

ABBREVIATIONS

AGM	*A Garden of Marvels.* Honolulu: University of Hawai'i Press, 2015.
BKLT	*Bai Kong liutie* 白孔六帖. 2 v. Taibei: Xinxing shuju, 1969.
BTSC	*Beitang shuchao* 北堂書抄. 2 v. Taibei: Wenhai chubanshe, 1961.
CCT	*Classical Chinese Tales of the Supernatural and the Fantastic.* Bloomington: Indiana University Press, 1985.
CLEAR	*Chinese Literature: Essays, Articles, Reviews*
CXJ	*Chuxue ji* 初學記. 3 v. Beijing: Zhonghua shuju, 1961.
FYZL	*Fayuan zhulin jiaozhu* 法苑珠林校註. 6 v. Beijing: Zhonghua shuji, 2003.
GXSGC	*Guxiaoshuo gouchen* 古小說鉤沉. In *Lu Xun quanji* 魯迅全集. Beijing: Renmin wenxue chubanshe, 1973.
HJAS	*Harvard Journal of Asiatic Studies*
KYZJ	*Kaiyuan zhanjing* 開元占經: Beijing: Zhongyang bianyi chubanshe, 2006.
LLZS	*Chongkan zengguang fenlei Leilin zashuo* 重刊增廣分類類林雜說. 15 v. No. 1219 of *Xuxiu siku quanshu* 續修四庫全書. Shanghai: Shanghai guji chubanshe, 2002.
LS	*Lei shuo* 類說. Beijing: Shumu wenxian chubanshe, 1988.
SBBY	*Sibu beiyao* 四部備要
SBCK	*Sibu congkan* 四部叢刊
SLFZ	*Shilei fu zhu* 事類賦註. Beijing: Zhonghua shuju, 1969.
SSXY	*Shishuo xinyu* 世說新語
SSJ	*Soushen ji* 搜神記. Beijing: Zhonghua shuju, 1979.

ST	*Selected Tales of the Han, Wei and Six Dynasties Periods*. Beijing: Foreign Languages Press, 2006.
TPGJ	*Taiping guangji* 太平廣記. 10 v. Beijing: Zhonghua shuju, 1961.
TPYL	*Taiping yulan* 太平御覽. 4 v. Beijing: Zhonghua shuju, 1960.
YWLJ	*Yiwen leiju* 藝文類聚. 2 v. Beijing: Zhonghua shuju, 1965.
YML	*Youming lu* 幽明錄

TERMS REGARDING WEIGHTS AND MEASURES

dou 斗, a decaliter
hu 斛, bushel, 10 *dou* before the Tang dynasty; 5 *dou* since the Song dynasty
sheng 升, pint, 1/10 of *dou*
jin 斤, catty, half a kilogram
liang 兩, tael, 1/10 of *jin*
dan 石, bushel, 10 *dou*
yi 鎰, 24 *liang*
chi 尺, foot
cun 寸, inch, 1/10 *chi*
duan 端, 20 *chi*
fen 分, 1/10 *cun*
li 里, half a kilometer, or approximately one-third of a mile
zhang 丈, pole, 10 *chi*, approximately 3 1/3 meters
pi 匹, bolt [of cloth]

CHRONOLOGY

Shang	ca. 1554–1045 BCE
Western Zhou	ca. 1045–771 BCE
Eastern Zhou	770–256 BCE
Spring and Autumn Period	770–476 BCE
Warring States Period	475–222 BCE
Qin	221–207 BCE
Western Han	206 BCE–8 CE
Xin	9–25 CE
Eastern Han	25–220
Three Kingdoms	220–280
Wei	220–265
Shu	221–263
Wu	222–280
Western Jin	265–316
Eastern Jin	317–420
Southern and Northern Dynasties	386–589
Southern Dynasties	420–589
[Liu] Song	420–479
Southern Qi	479–502
Southern Liang	502–557
Southern Chen	557–589
Northern Dynasties	386–534
Northern Wei	386–534
Eastern Wei	534–550

Western Wei	535–556
Northern Qi	550–577
Northern Zhou	557–581
Sui	581–618
Tang	618–907
Five Dynasties	907–960
Northern Song	960–1126
Southern Song	1126–1279
Yuan	1279–1368
Ming	1368–1644
Qing	1644–1911

INTRODUCTION

The appearance of *zhiguai* 志怪 (accounts of anomalies), or "tales of the supernatural," was an important cultural phenomenon in the history of China. Liu Yiqing's 劉義慶 (403–444) *Hidden and Visible Realms* (Youming lu 幽明錄) was one of the most important *zhiguai* collections in early medieval China, or the Six Dynasties 六朝 period (220–589). This collection is distinguished by its varied contents, elegant writing style, and fascinating stories, and by the fact that it is among the earliest collections that were heavily influenced by Buddhism. Besides the traditional themes that appear in the genre of *zhiguai*, many new themes bearing Buddhist beliefs, values, and concerns appear here for the first time. In addition, *Hidden and Visible Realms* was not one of the collections of miraculous tales written by Buddhists for laymen, intended to assist in propagating Buddhism,[1] such as the *Records of Manifest Miracles* (Xuanyan ji 宣驗記) or the *Signs from the Unseen Realm* (Mingxiang ji 冥祥記). Instead, it was miscellaneous in nature, drawing mainly on folklore that was widely spread throughout society. In this lies its unique value for the study of the cultural history of Chinese Buddhism. For these reasons, *Hidden and Visible Realms* deserves to be read by anyone interested in this era and in the rise of Buddhism.

---

1. Which Lu Xun 魯迅 (1881–1936) called *Shishi fujiao zhishu* 釋氏輔教之書. See Lu Xun, *Zhongguo xiaoshuo shilue* 中國小說史略, 39–42.

THE *ZHIGUAI* TRADITION AND THE *YOUMING LU*

The *zhiguai* tradition is rooted in the pre-Qin 秦 period of China. Early individual records of anomalies were included in the historical texts. When they were separated from history and spread independently, the *zhiguai* as a genre emerged.[2] This explains why some scholars consider *zhiguai* a branch of history.[3] *Zhiguai* collections first appeared independently as early as the Warring States period.[4] The genre developed during the Han 漢 dynasty, flourished during the Six Dynasties, and continued until the end of the Qing 清 dynasty.[5]

During the Han, Wei 魏, and Six Dynasties period, a variety of collections appeared in large numbers. According to their contents, Li Jianguo 李劍國 classifies the *zhiguai* collections into three categories: 1) records of anomalies associated with specific sites, such as the *Comprehensive Charts of Terrestrial Phenomena* (Kuo di tu 括地圖) and Zhang Hua's 張華 (232–300) *A Treatise of Curiosities* (Bowu zhi 博物志); 2) miscellaneous biographies, such as Liu Xiang's 劉向 (ca. 77–6 BCE) *Biographies of Exemplary Immortals* (Liexian zhuan 列仙傳) and Wang Jia's 王嘉 *Uncollected Records* (Shiyi ji 拾遺記); and 3) miscellaneous records of anomalies, such as Chen Shi's 陳寔 (104–187) *Records of Marvels Heard* (Yiwen ji 異聞記) and Cao Pi's 曹丕 (220–226) *Arrayed Marvels* (Lieyi zhuan 列異傳). The last category flourished during the Six Dynasties period, and Gan Bao's 干寶 (fl. 335–349) *In Search of the Supernatural* (Soushen ji 搜神記) and Liu Yiqing's *Hidden and Visible Realms* are the most important and famous ones.[6] It can also be useful to divide *zhiguai* collections based

2. See Li Jianguo 李劍國, *Tang qian zhiguai xiaoshuo shi* 唐前志怪小說史, 1–85.
3. See Liu Yeqiu 劉葉秋, *Wei Jin Nanbeichao xiaoshuo* 魏晉南北朝小說, 21.
4. *Suoyu* 瑣語 [Minor sayings], for example, is considered "a book of phenomena concerning divinations, dreams, deviations and anomalies, and physiognomic techniques from various realms" 諸國卜夢妖怪相也. See Li Jianguo, *Tang qian zhiguai xiaoshuo shi*, 92.
5. Cf. Li Jianguo, *Tang qian zhiguai xiaoshuo shi*; Inglis, *Hong Mai's Record of the Listener and Its Song Dynasty Context*; Zeitlin, *History of the Strange*; and Leo Tak-hung Chan, *The Discourse on Foxes and Ghosts*.
6. Important studies of Six Dynasties *zhiguai* include Li Jianguo, *Tang qian zhiguai xiaoshuo shi*; Wang Guoliang 王國良, *Wei Jin nanbeichao zhiguai xiaoshuo yanjiu* 魏晉南北朝志怪小說研究 and *Liuchao zhiguai xiaoshuo kaolun* 六朝志怪

on their relationship to religion: those collections that tend to especially promote a single religion or religious idea, such as the *Records of Manifest Miracles*, *Signs from the Unseen Realm*, and *Biographies of Exemplary Immortals*; and those that do not, including *In Search of the Supernatural* and *Hidden and Visible Realms*.

Almost no *zhiguai* collection survives in its original form.[7] Fortunately, however, from the fourth century forward important *zhiguai* were widely quoted in the *leishu* 類書, reference works arranged by category, which have become invaluable sources of early *zhiguai*. Lu Xun's *Collected Lost Old Stories* (Guxiaoshuo gouchen 古小說鉤沉), a monumental work first published in 1938, was the earliest attempt to extensively recompile early *zhiguai* collections from the quotations in the *leishu*.[8] Today it is still the most important text for *zhiguai* studies.

The Nature of Zhiguai *as a Genre*

The term *zhiguai* first appears in the early Daoist classic *Zhuangzi* 莊子 (ca. 320 BCE) and was later used as the title of several supernatural tales collections during the Six Dynasties period. *Zhiguai xiaoshuo* 小說 (fiction) was first mentioned by Duan Chengshi 段成式 (803–863) of the Tang (618–907).[9] But as early as the Six Dynasties, Yin Yun 殷芸 (471–529)

小說攷論; Campany, *Strange Writing*; Liu Yuanru 劉苑如, *Shenti, xingbie, jieji: Liuchao zhiguai de changyi lunshu yu xiaoshuo meixue* 身體、性別、階級—六朝志怪的常異論述與小說美學; Xie Mingxun 謝明勳, *Liuchao zhiguai xiaoshuo yanjiu shulun: Huigu yu lunshi* 六朝志怪小說研究述論：回顧與論釋; and Zhenjun Zhang, *Buddhism and Tales of the Supernatural in Early Medieval China*.

7. Two works, Liu Jingshu's 劉敬叔 (fl. early fifth century) *Yiyuan* 異苑 [A garden of marvels] and Xie Fu 謝敷 (fl. mid–late fourth century) and Fu Liang's 傅亮 (374–426) *Guangshiyin yingyan ji* 光世音應驗記 [Responsive manifestations of Avalokitesvara], are considered by some scholars as original texts. See Campany, *Strange Writing*, 78–79 and 68–69.
8. Lu Xun completed his recompilations of 36 lost works of pre-Tang literature in 1911, and one year later his preface on *Guxiaoshuo gouchen* was published in the first (and only) issue of *Yueshe congkan* 越社叢刊, but it was not until after his death that the work itself was published, as part of the first edition of *Lu Xun quanji* 魯迅全集 [Complete works of Lu Xun] in 1938. See Lu Xun's preface with annotations, in *Gujixuba ji* 古籍序跋集, 3–5.
9. Duan Chengshi, "Self Preface," in *Youyang zazu* 酉陽雜俎, 1.

named his tale collection (which includes numerous strange tales) *xiaoshuo.*

Zhiguai were widely viewed as historical works during the Tang dynasty, and many pieces of *zhiguai* are included in the official histories compiled in this period. Around twenty tales from *Hidden and Visible Realms*, for example, are included in the *History of the Jin* (Jin shu 晉書), compiled by Fang Xuanling 房玄齡 (578–648). The bibliographic treatise of *History of the Sui* (Sui shu 隋書), compiled by Wei Zheng 魏徵 (586–643) in the early seventh century, includes *zhiguai* texts under the category of history in a section devoted to works labeled "miscellaneous biographies" (*zazhuan* 雜傳). Other works in this category are accounts of local worthies, exemplary types of people, group biographies of famous families, and hagiographies of religious practitioners and immortals. Even though the compiler(s) views the contents of some of the works in this category as absurd or doubtful, he still believes that all of the works are histories. This reflects how contemporary people regarded the *zhiguai* genre.

This situation changed during the Song dynasty. In the bibliographic treatise of the *New History of the Tang* (Xin Tangshu 新唐書), compiled by Ouyang Xiu 歐陽修 (1007–1072) and Song Qi 宋祁 (998–1061), *zhiguai* is included under fiction (*Xiaoshuo*) instead of history. Ming dynasty scholar Hu Yinglin 胡應麟 (1551–1602) considers *zhiguai* to be one of the six categories of *xiaoshuo* in his classification system. Of course, the term *xiaoshuo* can be confusing because its original meaning in Chinese tradition was "minor talk," a kind of gossip,[10] similar in nature yet not equivalent to the modern concept of fiction.

Following Hu Yinglin, modern scholar Lu Xun classifies Six Dynasties tales into two genres: *zhiguai* and *zhiren* 志人 (records of people).[11] While *zhiren* works are mainly anecdotes of notable figures, *zhiguai* is

10. Hu Yinglin classified *xiaoshuo* into six categories: 1) *zhiguai*, 2) *chuanqi* 傳奇 (transmission of marvels), 3) *zalu* 雜錄 (miscellaneous records), 4) *congtan* 叢談 (collected talks), 5) *bianding* 辨訂 (documented sources), and 6) *zhengui* 箴規 (exhortatory writings), among which only the first three are narrative in nature. See Hu Yinglin, *Shaoshi shanfang bicong* 少室山房筆叢, 29. 374.

11. Lu Xun, "Zhongguo xiaoshuo de lishi de bianqian" 中國小說的歷史的變遷, in his *Zhongguo xiaoshuo shilue*, 274–79.

"the generic name for collections of brief prose entries, primarily but not exclusively narrative in nature, that discuss out-of-the-ordinary people and events."[12]

Lu Xun believes that, differing from the much later Tang tales, the Six Dynasties *zhiguai* were not consciously created; he argues, "The men of that age believed that although the ways of mortals were not those of spirits, nonetheless spirits existed. So they recorded these tales of the supernatural in the same way as anecdotes about men and women, not viewing the former as fiction and the latter as fact."[13] However, he still considers the two genres, *zhiguai* and *zhiren,* the earliest forms of Chinese *xiaoshuo,*[14] and the term *xiaoshuo* is used here as "fiction" in a modern sense, which was defined a century ago.[15] Lu Xun's above argument has become authoritative and influential in China since the publication of his book. Western scholars such as Kenneth DeWoskin upheld it by claiming that the Six Dynasties *zhiguai* constitute the "birth of fiction" in China.[16]

This conventional view on *zhiguai* has been challenged by more recent scholarship. In his *Strange Writing* and later works, Robert Campany argues that the major feature of *zhiguai* is "historical," not "fictional,"[17] and that considering *zhiguai* as "made up" is "misleading." His argument is supported by the following evidence: 1) early medieval *zhiguai* compilers saw their enterprise as a branch of history; 2) both these works' narrative forms and their generic suffixes incorporated into their titles (*ji* 記, "records"; *zhuan* 傳, "traditions"; and *zhi* 志, "accounts") were drawn from classical historical writings; 3) the verb used in metatexts to name authors' activity connotes

12. See Kenneth DeWoskin's entry on "Chih-kuai" in William H. Nienhauser, Jr., ed., *The Indiana Companion to Traditional Chinese Literature*, 2nd ed., 280. For a more detailed discussion of the genre of *zhiguai*, see Campany, *Strange Writing*, 21–32.
13. Lu Xun, *Zhongguo xiaoshuo shilue*, 29; Yang Hsien-yi and Gladys Yang, trans., *A Brief History of Chinese Fiction*, 45.
14. See Lu Xun, *Zhongguo xiaoshuo shilue*, 29–44.
15. Cf. Ming Dong Gu, *Chinese Theories of Fiction*, 17–42.
16. See DeWoskin, "The Six Dynasty *Chih-kuai* and the Birth of Fiction," in Andrew H. Plaks, ed., *Chinese Narrative*, 21–52.
17. "Anomaly accounts are predominantly, then, in their style, format, and temporal setting, historical." See Campany, *Strange Writing*, 178.

"collect" or "stitch together," not "fabricate"; and 4) their compilers were attempting to understand the subtle workings of the actual unseen world, not to invent a new fictional world from their own imagination.[18]

In this vein, whether the Six Dynasties *zhiguai* can be viewed and studied as fiction or folklore becomes an issue. In a book review on Xiaohuan Zhao's *Classical Chinese Supernatural Fiction: A Morphological History* (Lewiston, NY: The Edwin Mellen Press, 2005), Kang Xiaofei remarks, "Recent works on *zhiguai* by historians of Chinese religion and literature have recognized *zhiguai* as a special form of historiography. The genre can no longer be taken as mere fiction or folktales."[19]

Sarah M. Allen goes even further. Contrary to the conventional view of Lu Xun and his followers, she considers neither Six Dynasties *zhiguai* nor Tang tales (*chuanqi* 傳奇) fiction.[20] Her rationale is that "there is no evidence that the writers of these tales conceived of them in terms of a 'making' of something new that is associated with fiction; rather, the process of composition, in the few instances when we can find one articulated, is that of collecting material and filling in gaps in an incomplete record."[21]

Opposite opinions exist. Scholars such as William Nienhauser and Ma Zhenfang 馬振方 believe that fictionality exists not only in early medieval *zhiguai* but also in the pre-Qin texts.[22] Ming Dong Gu even says that Lu Xun "evidently underestimated the intelligence of [the] Six Dynasties period" by saying that "people of the Six Dynasties period were not engaged in consciously creating fiction, because they treated the events of ghosts and those of men as the same; both kinds were regarded as real events."[23] Daniel Hsiah argues that "one does not have to be conscious of doing something to do it": "While one can agree that writers such as Yuan Zhen 元稹 (779–831) or Bai Xingjian 白行簡 (ca. 776–826) were not consciously writing fiction in the modern

18. Campany, "Introduction," in his *A Garden of Marvels*, xxiv–v.
19. See Kang Xiaofei's book review in *Journal of Chinese Studies* 47 (2007): 514–17.
20. Allen, *Shifting Stories*, 1–15.
21. Allen, *Shifting Stories*, 1.
22. See Nienhauser, "Origins of Chinese Fiction," 191–219; Ma Zhenfang 馬振方, *Zhongguo zaoqi xiaoshuo kaobian* 中國早期小說考辨.
23. Ming Dong Gu, *Chinese Theories of Fiction*, 38.

sense, this does not necessarily mean that what they wrote was not fiction."[24]

Starting from Lu Xun's view on *zhiguai*, scholars clearly go opposite ways, fiction or history. Both interpretations of *zhiguai* have their own evidence and rationales, but neither is able to beat the other side.

In fact, early Chinese fiction and history are too close to be distinguished absolutely from each other. I have observed that the earliest authors/collectors of *xiaoshuo* were historians, the earliest novels were "unofficial history," and the narrative structure, elements, and skills of Chinese *xiaoshuo* were all derived from historical writings. Mimesis of history is the most prominent national feature of traditional Chinese fiction; thus valuing reality (尚實), a standard by which to evaluate historical writings, is also one of the major standards for evaluating fiction in the history of China. However, there are numerous fictional depictions in official history, which have been frequently criticized by historians, and it is common to see *zhiguai* tales in an official history.[25] In addition, neither the *zhi* (account) nor *ji* (record) in the title of *zhiguai* guarantees that it is purely historical, because even much later writers such as Pu Songling 蒲松齡 (1640–1715) still named his book *zhiyi* 志異 (accounts of marvels), and nobody would venture to deny the fictional creativity in his works. If we use the evidence Campany used (to deny the *zhiguai* as fictional works) to evaluate all traditional Chinese fiction, including such masterpieces as *Dream of the Red Chamber* (Honglou meng 紅樓夢), also known as *Records of a Stone* (Shitou ji 石頭記), none of them should be considered fictional.

Andrew Plaks observed many years ago, "Any theoretical inquiry into the nature of Chinese narrative must take its starting point in the acknowledgement of the immense importance of historiography and, in a certain sense, 'historicism' in the total aggregate of the culture."

24. See Daniel Hsiah's book review of *Shifting Stories: History, Gossip, and Lore in Narratives from Tang Dynasty China*, in *Chinese Literature, Essays, Articles, Reviews* 37 (2015): 202.

25. See Zhang Zhenjun 張振軍, "Shi bai xueyuan shuolue: jianlun Zhongguo chuantong xiaoshuo de shizhuan tezheng" 史稗血緣說略：兼論中國傳統小說的史傳特徵, 93–99; also included in *Chuantong xiaoshuo yu Zhongguo wenhua* 傳統小說與中國文化, 3–19.

"Since both history and fiction are engaged in the mimesis of action, it is often difficult to draw the line neatly between the two."[26]

Thus, in order to study *zhiguai* in different perspectives at ease and avoid the impossible task of defeating others, perhaps a better solution for the debate on the nature of *zhiguai* would be to stop trying to draw such a neat line.

The Nature of Zhiguai *as a Cultural Phenomenon*

The nature of *zhiguai* as a cultural phenomenon is also significant, and it is closely related to the compilers' sources. Gan Bao says in his "Preface to *In Search of the Supernatural*," "I inspected the previously recorded [stories] in old books and collected the lost anecdotes of the time."[27] This is a clarification of the sources of the *zhiguai*: besides selecting stories from a variety of earlier texts, the compilers recorded local folktales that were widespread at that time as well as stories directly told by individuals. For this reason, *zhiguai* stories are often considered to be from oral tradition and related to popular culture.[28]

However, some scholars disagree with this assumption. Robert Campany, for example, argues in his *Strange Writing:* "authors (of anomaly accounts), with few exceptions, must have drawn mostly on written documents as opposed to oral sources."[29]

Campany's observation on the sources of *zhiguai* is probably true for the genre as a whole, but it is clear that some collections of the third category of *zhiguai* (miscellaneous records of anomalies), such as *In Search of the Supernatural, Hidden and Visible Realms,* and *A Garden of Marvels* (Yiyuan 異苑), are among the "few exceptions." According to

---

26. Plaks, "Toward a Critical Theory of Chinese Narrative," in *Chinese Narrative: Critical and Theoretical Essays*, 311–12.
27. 考先志於載籍, 收遺逸於當時. See Gan Bao, *Soushen ji*, 2.
28. As Karl S. Y. Kao says, "Originating mainly in folk traditions, the CK [*chih-kuai*] narratives are legends and stories associated with popular culture and reflecting the belief systems of the people." See "Introduction" in Kao, ed., *Classical Chinese Tales of the Supernatural and the Fantastic*, 4.
29. Campany, *Strange Writing*, 178. In a footnote to this statement on the same page, he adds, "There are oral-based items, as will be seen below, but they account for only a small fraction of the total corpus."

Li Jianguo's research, less than one-quarter of the tales in *Hidden and Visible Realms* are taken from older books.[30] Most pieces appear for the first time in the collection and are mainly about current events of the Jin and the Song periods. Therefore the whole book reflects a strong sense of the time in which it was written/compiled. In addition, the majority of tales in *Hidden and Visible Realms* are anecdotes about scholars, commoners, Buddhist monks, and laymen living in this period.[31] Many of these pieces could be considered records from people of the compiler's local community as well as part of oral tradition.[32] The cases of *In Search of the Supernatural* and *Hidden and Visible Realms* are fairly similar in this regard. Thus the *zhiguai* accounts were not necessarily devoid of "folklore" tracts.

Significance of Zhiguai*: Why Should They Be Read?*

The *Analects* (Lunyu 論語) says, "The topics the Master did not speak of were prodigies, force, disorder, and gods,"[33] indicating Confucius's prioritization of mundane practicalities and neglect of the supernatural. The fact that almost all the *zhiguai* collections were lost soon after their compilation can be taken as an indication of their status in Confucian culture. Then, why did *zhiguai* exist and why were they circulated?

It seems easy to find the motive behind and aim of a *zhiguai* collection if it is explicitly promoting Buddhist or Daoist teachings, but it is harder to know the aims of the collections with miscellaneous contents that were compiled by general intellectuals, though some compilers might have been followers of Gan Bao, who himself claimed he was attempting "to make clear that the way of spirits is not a fabrication."[34] As mentioned above, tales of the supernatural were viewed as history

30. For examples of tales from prior collections, see the discussion about the resources and authorship of the *Youming lu* in chapter 1 of Zhenjun Zhang, *Buddhism and Tales of the Supernatural in Early Medieval China*, 40–54.
31. Li Jianguo, *Tangqian zhiguai xiaoshuo shi*, 357.
32. "Husband-Watching Stone" 望夫石 (8. 234) and "Peng E" 彭娥 (8. 235) in this collection are good examples of this. According to their authors, these stories were from folklore.
33. 子不語怪力亂神. See Lau, *The Analects of Confucius*, 88.
34. 發明神道之不誣. See Gan Bao, "Preface," in *Soushen ji*, 2.

in ancient China. Their historical value, the fact/event, is beyond doubt an important factor behind their circulation.[35]

Many scholars also read *zhiguai* for entertainment. For instance, Tao Qian 陶潛 (365–427), the compiler of the *Sequel to* In Search of the Supernatural (Soushen houji 搜神後記), writes in a poem:

> I skim through the "Story of King Mu"
> and view the pictures in the *Classic of Seas and Mountains.*
> A glance encompasses the ends of the universe—
> where is there any joy, if not these?[36]

Both the "Story of King Mu" and the *Classic of Seas and Mountains* he mentions in the poem are noted early *zhiguai.* Since Tao Qian loves *zhiguai* so much, the purpose of his compiling the *zhiguai* collection, the *Sequel to* In Search of the Supernatural, was most likely entertaining himself as well as his readers. Gan Bao addresses a similar idea in his preface to *In Search of the Supernatural:*

> I will count myself fortunate if in the future curious scholars come along, note the bases of these stories and find things within them to enlighten their hearts and fill their eyes. And I will be fortunate as well to escape reproach for this book 幸將來好事之士, 錄其根體, 有以遊心寓目, 而無尤焉.[37]

Gan Bao addresses readers of his *zhiguai* collection as "curious gentlemen" (好事之士), indicating that curiosity, or interest, was at least one of the major reasons for the circulation of the *zhiguai* texts. In

35. Sarah Allen claims in her study of *zhiguai* and *chuanqi*, "The exchange of information in narrative form was a more important motivation behind the production, reception, and reservation of most of these tales than aesthetic enjoyment of tales as 'literature'" (*Shifting Stories*, 25). But this may not necessarily be true.

36. 覽周王傳，流觀山海圖。俯仰終宇宙，不樂復何如！ James Robert Hightower's translation, "On Reading the Seas and Mountains Classic," in Mair, ed., *The Columbia Anthology of Traditional Chinese Literature*, 82–83.

37. Gan Bao, "Preface," in *Soushen ji*, 2. This translation is from DeWoskin and Crump Jr., *In Search of the Supernatural*, xxvii.

other words, readability (the quality to attract curiosity) of the works is essential to their survival. Gan Bao also directly talks about his motivation for collecting and reading *zhiguai*—"youxin yumu" 遊心寓目, rendered by DeWoskin and Crump as "enlighten their hearts and fill their eyes." It may also be rendered as "set their minds wandering by filling their eyes,"[38] referring to the free and relaxed state of mind in the process of enjoying literary works, instead of observing historical events or obtaining information.

Additionally, in ancient China collecting and reporting anomalies to the authorities was considered essential to governance,[39] undoubtedly another reason for the circulation of *zhiguai*.

In recent years, "historical" reading of *zhiguai* has become popular. An indication is the appearance of a model of reading local religious culture through medieval *zhiguai*. The pioneering work is Glen Dudbridge's *Religious Experience and Lay Society in T'ang China: A Reading of Tai Fu's Kuang-i chi*,[40] and the most recent works include Campany's *Making Transcendents: Ascetics and Social Memory in Early Medieval China*, Dudbridge's *A Portrait of Five Dynasties China: From the Memoirs of Wang Renyu (880–956)*, and probably my own *Buddhism and Tales of the Supernatural in Early Medieval China: A Study of Liu Yiqing's* Youming lu.[41]

In the preface to his selected *zhiguai* collection, *A Garden of Marvels*, Campany lists four reasons to read the *zhiguai* texts in view of history: 1) these texts offer unparalleled material for the history of Chinese religion, as well as evidence that there was religion beyond the great tradition (elite religion) and their specialists;[42] 2) these texts—especially the ones in narrative form—provide many glimpses of aspects of ordinary social life and material culture that can be hard to discern from other surviving evidence; 3) *zhiguai* texts preserve

38. Cf. Cai Meghan, "The Social Life of Texts," 32.
39. See Campany, *Strange Writing*, 101–59.
40. Dudbridge, *Religious Experience and Lay Society in T'ang China*.
41. Campany, *Making Transcendents*; Dudbridge, *A Portrait of Five Dynasties China*; and Zhenjun Zhang, *Buddhism and Tales of the Supernatural in Early Medieval China*.
42. Erik Zürcher depicts elite Buddhism ("Court Buddhism" and "Gentry Buddhism") as the "Great Tradition" and popular Buddhism as the "little tradition." See his "Perspectives in the Study of Chinese Buddhism," 161–76.

anecdotes about individuals and events known from more formal histories and often throw new light on them; 4) they are worth reading precisely because they were not inventions of a few individuals but instead artifacts of many people's exchange of stories and representations.[43]

It is clear that Campany highlights the value of *zhiguai* as unofficial writings in the study of religions and history, but he neglects their literary value because he does not consider them literary works. While agreeing with Campany's insightful arguments, I would like to add two more reasons to augment his list: the *zhiguai* texts provide samples of early fictional works for the study of Chinese fiction; and the *zhiguai* texts—especially those possessing a complete plot—are enjoyable to read.

Traditional Anomalies in Zhiguai*: Toward a Classification*

Strictly speaking, *zhiguai* differ from the supernatural and fantastic literature in the Western tradition in many ways,[44] but they share at least one commonality: an "otherness" in contrast to this human world and the general, mundane ways we perceive it. This is also the most prominent feature of the anomalies (*guai*) in *zhiguai*.

Anomalies in *zhiguai* can be classified into numerous types, and all are rooted deeply in ancient Chinese culture. Below are some of the

43. Campany, *A Garden of Marvels*, xxxviii–xli.

44. Based on Karl Kao's observations, tales of the supernatural and fantastic in Chinese tradition differ from their Western counterparts in three ways: 1) in the Chinese tradition, the distinction between the supernatural and fantastic is mainly based on the nature of the "facts" recorded, instead of the author's creative perception; 2) in the West the fantastic is distinctly a later product than the supernatural in literary history and was a product of an uneasy, "pulverized" consciousness resulting from the loss of faith in the unity of man and nature; 3) the Chinese supernatural and fantastic never engage in the experience of alienation from nature and rarely inspire horror, nor are they tormented by any indeterminacy in the character's or the reader's attitude toward the supernatural manifestation in the human world that characterizes the Western fantastic. See "Introduction" in his *Classical Chinese Tales of the Supernatural and the Fantastic*, 1–4.

important ones found in the *zhiguai* collections of the Wei and Jin periods,[45] with examples from *Hidden and Visible Realms*.

1. Other Species (*Yilei* 異類): The Supernatural Beings

a. Deities (*shen* 神): rooted in ancient Chinese religion and developed in Daoism. In the Daoist deity system, the highest gods include The Most High Lord Lao (*Taishang laojun* 太上老君), The Grand Jade Emperor (*Yuhuang dadi* 玉皇大帝), and the Heavenly Sovereign of Original Beginning (*Yuanshi tianzun* 元始天尊; after the Six Dynasties). At the lower level, there are local deities everywhere. There are also netherworld deities. The head of the netherworld was originally the Emperor of Heaven. Beginning in the late Warring States period this figure was replaced by the Lord of the Underworld (*Dixia zhu* 地下主), which was replaced by the Governor of Mount Tai (*Taishan fujun* 泰山府君) during the Eastern Han dynasty.[46]

b. Ghosts (*gui* 鬼):[47] derived from the belief that a person becomes a ghost after death 人死曰鬼 ("Jifa" 祭法 of *Liji*).[48] "Gongmeng" 公夢 (Master Gongmeng) of *Mozi* 墨子 says, "The old sage kings all took ghosts and spirits as numinous gods, who bring calamities or good fortune."[49] An entry from the seventh year of Duke Zhao 昭公 (534 BCE) in the *Zuo zhuan* 左傳 says, "When an ordinary man or woman dies a violent death, the *hun* 魂 and the *po* 魄 are still able to attach to

45. For a typology of the *guai* phenomena, cf. Kao, *Classical Chinese Tales of the Supernatural and the Fantastic*, 4–16.

46. Yu Yingshi 余英時, "Zhongguo gudai sihou Shijieguan de yanbian" 中國古代死後世界觀的演變, 123–43; Xiao Dengfu 蕭登福, *XianQin LiangHan mingjie he shenxian sixiang tanyuan* 先秦兩漢冥界和神仙思想探源, 168–75; and Pu Muzhou 蒲慕洲, "Muzang yu shengsi—Zhongguo gudai zongjiao zhi xingsi" 墓葬與生死—中國古代宗教之省思, 206–12.

47. Karl Kao calls it "necromantic communion." See his *Classical Chinese Tales of the Supernatural and the Fantastic*, 7–8.

48. *Liji zhengyi*, in Ruan Yuan 阮元 (1764–1849), ed., *Shisanjing zhushu* 十三經註疏, 46. 1588.

49. Sun Yirang 孫詒讓 (1848–1908), *Mozi xiangu* 墨子閒詁, 12. 275.

people and thereby act as an evil apparition."[50] In the "Ming gui" 明鬼 (Illustration of ghosts) chapter (B), Mozi gives two examples.[51]

While in early texts the ghosts always seem to have supernatural powers and therefore inspire awe in people, the portrayal of ghosts in the Six Dynasties *zhiguai* is quite different: the ghosts are shown not only in their divine aspect but also in those aspects that resemble human beings. In the noted story "Zong Dingbo" 宗定伯 from *Arrayed Marvels*,[52] the ghost is not horrible at all and is even inferior to human beings. In some ghost stories, ghosts are full of human emotions. *Hidden and Visible Realms* includes most kindly ghost mothers (#125, 128, and 154), extremely caring ghost fathers (#115 and 124), a most filial ghost child (#9), and a very caring ghost friend (#7).

c. Monsters (*yao* 妖) and goblins (*jing* 精): animistic phenomena.[53] The original meaning of *yao* was anomaly, resembling the *guai.* After the Qin and Han, however, its meaning changed to demon, spirit, or goblin. Ge Hong's 葛洪 (283–343) *The Master Who Embraces Simplicity* (Baopu zi 抱朴子) says, "As for all the old creatures, their spirits can change into the form of a person, so as to dazzle and delude man's eyes."[54] Demons and goblins in earlier texts are generally hideous and evil, yet in the *zhiguai* some of them become beautiful girls to seduce men. Many love stories between spirits and men are included in volume 1 of this collection, "The Wonder of Love."

d. Immortals (*xian* 仙): derived from the Daoist classics, *Laozi* 老子 and *Zhuangzi* 莊子, and from the theory of immortals of the Qin and Han.

50. *Zuo zhuan zhushu* 左傳註疏, 764; *Sibi beiyao* version (Zhonghua shuju, n.d.), 44. 8a.

51. One is about King Xuan 宣 of Zhou 周 (r. 827–780 BCE), who unjustly killed his vassal, Du Bo 杜伯, whose spirit later shot and killed King Xuan. The other is about Duke Jian 簡 of Yan 燕 (414–370 BCE), who unjustly killed his vassal, Zhuang Zi Yi 莊子儀; later (the spirit of) Zhuang killed Duke Jian with a red stick. See Sun Yirang, *Mozi xiangu*, 8. 139–43.

52. See Lu Xun, ed., *GXSGC*, 255–56. For an English translation, see Ding Wangdao, ed., *100 Chinese Myths and Fantasies*, 87–89.

53. Cf. Karl Kao, *Classical Chinese Tales of the Supernatural and the Fantastic*, 8–9.

54. 萬物之老者, 其精悉能假託人形, 以眩惑人目. See Wang Ming 王明, ed., *Baopuzi neipian jiaoshi* 抱朴子内篇校釋 [The master who embraces simplicity with collations and explanations], 300.

Exclusive/specialized collections include Liu Xiang's *Biographies of the Exemplary Immortals* and Ge Hong's *Biographies of the Divine Immortals* (Shenxian zhuan 神仙傳).

2. Other Spheres (*Tajie* 他界): The Realms Beyond the Human World

a. Heavens (*tiancao* 天曹): the realm of gods and deities, as well as the dead. Those found in *Hidden and Visible Realms* are the Northern Dipper (#68) and the heaven for the dead (#162).

b. Underworld (*difu* 地府): the realm of the dead. The indigenous Chinese netherworld includes both the heavens and the underground. Those realms located under earth include Yellow Springs (*Huangquan* 黃泉), the Land of Darkness (*Youdu* 幽都), and Mount Tai (*Taishan* 泰山). From about the eighth century BCE, the term "Yellow Springs" began to be used in historical and literary writings to denote the home of the dead.[55] The term "Land of Darkness" first appears in the "Yaodian" 堯典 chapter of the *Book of Documents* (Shangshu 尚書).[56] Around the end of the first century BCE the belief in Mount Tai as the location of the netherworld arose.[57] It was also in the Eastern Han period that the ghost state of Fengdu 酆都 appeared in Daoist scripture.[58] The motif of the "netherworld adventure"—in which the soul departs from the body in a temporary death—is an important one that appears in more than ten stories in *Hidden and Visible Realms* (see chapter 5).

c. Immortal Land (*xianjing* 仙境): the realm of immortals. The idea that there are immortal lands overseas appeared in the late Warring States

55. Yu Yingshi, "Zhongguo gudai sihou Shi jieguan de yanbian," in his "Zhongguo sixiang chuantong de xiandai quanshi," 123–43; Yu Yingshi, "O Soul, Come Back! A Study in the Changing Conceptions of the Soul and Afterlife in Pre-Buddhist China," 363–95.

56. "[Emperor Yao] ordered Heshu to dwell in the North, [a place] called *youdu* (Dark Headquarters)" 申命和叔，宅朔方，曰幽都. See "Tang Kao" 湯誥 of Shangshu. See *Shangshu zhengyi* 尚書正義, 8. 21b, in Ruan Yuan, *Shisanjing zhushu*, vol. 1.

57. See Maeno Naoaki 前野直彬, "Meikai yugyo" 冥界遊行, 38–57; Yu Yingshi, "Zhongguo gudai sihou Shi jieguan de yanbian,"123–43; Yu Yingshi, "O Soul, Come Back!"

58. See Luan Baoqun 栾保群 and Lü Zongli吕宗力, eds., *Rizhilu jishi* 日知錄集釋, 30.

period, when the belief in immortality was in vogue. Depictions of immortal lands, including the Three Islands, Ten River Islets, Ten Grand Caves, Thirty-six Small Caves, and Seventy-two Daoist Paradises, became a fascinating part of *zhiguai* collections, such as the *Records of the Ten River Islets* (Shizhou ji 十洲記), *Records of Penetration Into the Mysteries* (Dongming ji 洞冥記), *Biographies of Exemplary Immortals*, and *Biographies of the Divine Immortals*. The first story featuring the "immortal land adventure" motif is "The Tale of Hanzi" 邗子 in the *Biographies of Exemplary Immortals*. In the tales of "Liu Chen and Ruan Zhao" 劉晨、阮肇 (#1) and "Huang Yuan 黃原 Encounters Miaoyin 妙音" (#14) from *Hidden and Visible Realms*, the element of encountering fairy maidens is added. The tale of Liu and Ruan became the most influential one, and allusions to it appear in numerous literary works of later times. Another tale, "Dragon Pearl" (#64), is also an immortal land adventure, in which the protagonist obtains immortal ambrosia instead of love.

d. Exotic Territories (*shufang yiyu* 殊方異域): Mythical exotic territories appeared in *The Classic of Mountains and Seas* (Shanhai jing 山海經). Qu Yuan's 屈原 (c. 340–c. 278 BCE) "Summons of the Soul" ("Zhaohun" 招魂) also depicts exotic territories, for example, "O soul, come back! In the east you cannot abide. There are giants there a thousand fathoms tall, who seek only for souls to catch, and ten suns that come together, melting metal, dissolving stone."[59] In the *Records of Penetration Into the Mysteries*, various exotic territories are described as Daoist paradises.[60]

3. Cross-Boundary Oddities

a. Omens (*zhao* 兆)—messages from other species. *The Classic of Changes* says, "Heaven sent down patterns, from which things auspicious and inauspicious are seen" 天垂象,见吉凶.[61] This theory was enhanced during the Han dynasty in Dong Zhongshu's 董仲舒 (c. 179–c. 104 BCE) theory of "mutual correspondence between heaven and man" (*tian ren*

59. See Hawkes, trans., *The Songs of the South*), 224.

60. For a study of the other world in *zhiguai*, see Ye Qingbing's 葉慶炳 "Liuchao zhi Tang de tajie jiegou xiaoshuo" 六朝至唐的他界結構小説, 7–28.

61. "Xici 繫辭, A," see Li Daoping 李道平, *Zhouyi jijie zuanshu* 周易集解纂疏, 606.

ganying 天人感應) and the prognosticatory apocrypha (*chen wei* 讖緯) that came into vogue during the reign of Emperor Cheng (32–7 BCE) and Emperor Ai of Han (6–1 BCE).[62] In *Hidden and Visible Realms,* omens are numerous, including strange items (#37, #50), air (#206, #208), creatures (#42, #55), comets (#47), illusions (#33, #48), and dreams (#29; #211, #219, #232, #233).

b. Thaumaturgy (*shushu* 術數)—the quest into the other spheres. As indigenous Chinese magic arts, the activities gathered under thaumaturgy originated in the Warring States period (465–221 BCE) and included astrology, divination, necromancy, geomancy, alchemy, and communication with the dead and transcendent beings.[63] Some of them can be seen in *Hidden and Visible Realms* (#69, #221, #230–231).

c. Metamorphoses—the demonstration of supernatural power. Metamorphoses are found in Chinese myth.[64] The most famous one is the *jingwei* 精衛 bird, carrying twigs and stones from the west mountain to fill up the East Sea. In *zhiguai* collections there are a lot of metamorphosis stories, such as those in *Hidden and Visible Realms*: #51, #56, #70, #72, and #76.

d. Trafficking between humans and supernatural beings. The most popular theme is affairs between men and goddesses and spirit girls.[65] It is found in the "Nine Songs" (Jiuge 九歌) in the *Songs of the South* (Chuci 楚辭) and appeared in *zhiguai* after the Warring States period, when belief in immortals became popular.[66] Quite a few tales featuring this motif can be found in chapter 1 of this book (#1, 10, 14, 18, 19, 20, and 24).

---

62. See Feng Youlan 馮友蘭, *Zhongguo zhexueshi* 中國哲學史, 497–573.
63. See Karl Kao, *Classical Chinese Tales of the Supernatural and the Fantastic*, 9; and Wang Yao 王瑤, *Xiaoshuo yu fangshu* 小說與方術, 85–110.
64. Cf. Yue Hengjun 樂衡軍. "Zhongguo yuanshi bianxing shenhua chutan 中國原始變形神話初探, 159–72.
65. For a study, see Zhang Zhenjun, *Chuantong xiaoshuo yu Zhongguo wenhua*, 87–107.
66. For the origins of this motif, see Zhang Chang 張萇, "Luelun Gudai xiaoshuo zhong de renshenlian gushi" 略論古代小說中的人神恋故事, 94–99.

e. Interactions of humans with humanized beasts: including animals understanding human words or speaking in human words (#199–200), animals' revenge for being killed by human beings, and animals' repayments of debts of gratitude to human beings (see chapter 6). The earliest story about an animal's repayment of a debt of gratitude to a human is found in pre-Qin China: the famous "Pearl of Marquis Sui" (Suishi zhizhu 隋氏之珠).[67] As a narrative motif, however, it did not become popular until the Six Dynasties period, when Buddhism had been transmitted and widely spread in China. Thus the flourishing of stories about animal retribution in Chinese tales was most likely stimulated by Buddhist culture. Besides similar stories from Buddhist sutras, which should be considered the originating source for the motif in China, many ideas evident in the tales—such as animal release and the prohibition against killing creatures—come from Buddhist beliefs. Traditional non-Buddhist Chinese views on animals support a human exceptionalist worldview, in direct opposition to the doctrine of Buddhism, and are definitely not a supportive factor for the flourishing of stories illustrating interactions on the same moral footing between human beings and animals.[68]

4. Human World Oddities

a. Legendary figures: including those possessing extraordinary courage, virtue, or skills. Examples include heroic men (#59, #137, #213) and Taoist magicians (#227–228, #230–231).

---

67. "The Pearl of Marquis Sui" is frequently mentioned in pre-Qin texts, such as "Rangwang" 讓王 of *Zhuang zi* 莊子 and "Jie Lao" 解老 of *Hanfei zi* 韓非子. The detailed story is recorded in later works. It is said that the Marquis of Sui, a nobleman of the Warring States Period, saved a wounded snake, and in return the numinous snake found a large bright pearl from the river and gave it to the marquis. See Gan Bao, *Soushen ji*, 20.238.

68. Traditionally, the human-animal difference was portrayed in China thusly: animals possess physical power, while humans are endowed with a sense of morality and ritual propriety. Those who failed to reciprocate propriety were considered by Mencius as not being different from birds and beasts. For a detailed study on this topic, see Sterckx, *The Animal and the Daemon in Early China*, 88–92.

b. Strange creatures: including those with odd shapes, features (#177–178), or feelings (#192–93).

c. Natural wonders: including legendary mountains (#236) and stones (#75, #235, #237), strange springs (#240–241), and marvelous trees (#260–261), etc.

d. Other marvels: such as flying cash (#35) and becoming pregnant through a dream (#28).

New Anomalies Evident in Hidden and Visible Realms

Besides traditional anomalies seen in prior *zhiguai* collections, many new anomalies appear in *Hidden and Visible Realms.*

1. *Karmic retribution*. The concept of retribution, or *bao* 報, is deeply rooted in Chinese culture. As a moral concept, it is found in the *Lao zi* and *The Classic of Odes* (Shi jing 詩經). As a religious concept, heavenly retribution, it can be traced back to the Shang and the Western Zhou. Demonic retribution, a combination of heavenly and ethical retribution, appeared as early as the *Zuo zhuan*. As it continuously spread in orthodox historical writings, it became a popular theme in the *zhiguai*. In *Hidden and Visible Realms,* this theme in many stories becomes blurred because the demonic figure is not directly evident, showing a tendency of intermingling with the Buddhist notion of retribution, *xianshi bao* 現世報 or "retribution in this life" (#121–122). Most importantly, stories with explicit Buddhist flavor, such as those featuring the themes of retribution for killing creatures and animals' repaying debts of gratitude (#184, 187, 189–190) as well as those featuring Buddhist karmic retribution (#215), appear in the collection in large numbers.[69]

2. *Reincarnation*. "Biography of Lu Wenshu" (Lu Wenshu zhuan 路溫舒傳) in *History of the Han* says, "The dead cannot be revived, while the disconnected cannot be reattached."[70] Early Daoists insisted that

69. See Zhenjun Zhang, "From Demonic to Karmic Retribution," 267–287; also included in Zhenjun Zhang, *Buddhism and Tales of the Supernatural in Early Medieval China*, 82–106.

70. 死者不可復生, 斷者不可復屬. Ban Gu 班固 (32–92). *Han shu* 漢書, 51. 2369.

everyone has only one life and cannot be reborn after death.[71] But rebirth is at the core of Buddhist teachings. "A Ghost Nurtures a Child" (#153) is about a ghost who has already been punished in hell and temporarily lives in the realm of ghosts, but later is reborn into the world of human beings. "Prince of Anxi's 安息 Three Lives" (#215) provides a vivid picture of karmic retribution through transmigration: a man must repay what he owed in his previous life. The three lives of the hero are retold in this story, and the hero himself knows what he did in his previous lives.

3. *Buddhist concepts of hell.* The most striking difference between Chinese indigenous concepts of a netherworld and the Buddhist hell is that the latter is a place for the dead to be judged through court trials.[72] "Zhao Tai 趙泰 Travels in Hells" (#175) is among the earliest examples of netherworld trials in Chinese literature: there everyone receives a trial after death, and, according to what they did when they were alive, each receives different treatment. Another striking feature of the Buddhist hell that differentiates it from Chinese indigenous concepts of a netherworld is that it involves physical torture. The earliest literary depictions of the multitude of physical tortures in Buddhist sutras are seen in *Hidden and Visible Realms* ("The Shaman Shu Li" 舒禮, #170).[73] New images of the afterlife were also created. In "Zhao Tai Travels in Hells," for example, a passage describes the "city of receiving transformation" (*shou bianxing cheng* 受變形城) where punishments are mainly based on the Five Precepts, showing a distinct Buddhist origin.

4. *Buddha as a savior.* The traditional savior of China is heaven. In *Hidden and Visible Realms,* Buddha appears as a new savior in "Zhao Tai Travels in Hells" and "*Raksasas*" (#98).

---

71. 人居天地間，人人得一生，不得重生也。" "人人各一生，不得再生也。" See Wang Ming, *Taiping jing hejiao* 太平經合校, 72. 298 & 90. 340.

72. For the depiction of such court trials in Buddhist sutras, see Zhu Tanwulan 竺曇無蘭 (Dharmarājan), trans., *Fo shuo tiecheng nili jing* 佛說鐵城泥犁經 [Buddha Preached Sutra on Iron City Hells]; *Zhong Ahan jing* 中阿含經 [Mādhyamāgama; Medium Length Āgama-sutra], *juan* 12.

73. Cf. Daigan Matsunaga, *The Buddhist Concept of Hell.*

5. *Buddhist ghosts*: Ox-headed and *raksasas*. Among these Buddhist demons, the *yecha* (*yaksa* or *yaksha*, Japanese *yasha*) was probably the first to appear in Chinese literature.[74] This demon was originally part of a class of nature ghosts or demons in Hindu mythology.[75] In *Hidden and Visible Realms*, the creature with the head of an ox and the body of man in "Shu Li" is an image from Buddhist sutras. Another Buddhist ghost, a *raksasa* (male), or *raksasi* (female), first appears in this collection (#98, "*Raksasas*").[76]

6. *Buddhist magical arts*: seen in self-mutilation (#223, "The Buddhist Nun") and predicting events in the future (#216, "Futu Cheng 佛圖澄, the Western Monk").

7. *Lord of the Northern Dipper* (*Beidou* 北斗) *as a Daoist savior* (#107, "Northern Dipper Saves Mr. Gu 顧 from Demons").

8. *Chengfu* 承負, *or "the transmission of burdens."* In "He Bigan" 何比干 (#203) the offspring of the He family became rich and honorable not because of their own good deeds, but because of those of their ancestors. The main idea in this story may have an indigenous Chinese origin. In the *Scripture on Great Peace* (Taiping jing 太平經), the concept of *chengfu* maintains that the evil deeds of a man may bring calamities to his offspring, while his good deeds may bring them good fortune.[77]

---

74. See "Gao xin" in Wang Jia, *Shiyi ji*, in Wang Genlin 王根林, *Wei Jin Liuchao biji xiaoshuo daguan* 漢魏六朝筆記小說大觀, 497–98.
75. In the mythology of India, *yaksa*, or *yaksha*, is "a class of generally benevolent nature spirits who are the custodians of treasures that are hidden in the earth and in the roots of trees. . . . Yakshas were often given homage as tutelary deities of a city, district, lake, or well. Their worship, together with popular belief in nagas (serpent deities), feminine fertility deities, and mother goddesses, probably had its origin among the early Dravidian peoples of India. The yaksha cult coexisted with the priest-conducted sacrifices of the Vedic period, and continued to flourish during the Kusana period." See *Encyclopedia Britannica*, 12: 806.
76. Li Jianguo said that this is perhaps the first time that a Buddhist demon appeared in Chinese literature (*Tangqian zhiguai xiaoshuo shi*, 362), but he missed the *yaksas* in *Shiyi ji*, which he himself considers to be prior to the *Youming lu*.
77. Wang Ming 王明, *Taiping jing hejiao*, 22–23.

However, Tang Yongtong 湯用彤 (1893–1964) and others suspect that this is a mixture of indigenous Chinese and Buddhist retribution.[78]

9. *Detached dream soul*: found in "Pang E 龐阿 and His Infatuated Lover" (#3). This is the earliest depiction of a detached dream soul in Chinese literature.

THE COMPILER OF THE COLLECTION

Traditionally, *Hidden and Visible Realms* has been attributed to Liu Yiqing, nephew of Liu Yu 劉裕 (r. 420–422), the founder of the Song dynasty (420–479). The document that first lists *Hidden and Visible Realms* under Liu's name is the bibliographical treatise *History of the Sui*,[79] the only extant[80] treatise of this kind, compiled after the *History of the Han* and before the bibliographical treatises the *Old Tang History* (Jiu Tang shu 舊唐書) and *New Tang History*. All three accounts consider Liu Yiqing the compiler of *Hidden and Visible Realms*.[81]

Modern scholars tend to see Liu Yiqing as an editor instead of the sole compiler. Lu Xun says in his *A Brief History of Chinese Fiction*: "The *History of the [Liu] Song* says that Yiqing had little gift in writing himself yet that he assembled men of letters from near and far. Then, it is possible that the books attributed to him were all compiled by multiple hands."[82] Lu Xun is referring not merely to *Hidden and Visible Realms* but to all the works attributed to Liu Yiqing, which amount to 225–276

78. Cf. Zhenjun Zhang, *Buddhism and Tales of the Supernatural in Early Medieval China*, 96.
79. See Wei Zheng 魏征 et al., *Sui shu*, 33. 980.
80. Wei Zheng added a lot of entries concerning books already lost in his own lifetime, but still extant in 523 CE when Ruan Xiaoxu 阮孝緒 (479–536) finished his catalogue of the palace library of the Liang dynasty, *Qi lu* 七錄 [Seven records], a book still extant in Tang times. Cf. Liu Xu 劉昫 (877–946), *Jiu Tang shu* 舊唐書, 46.2011, and Ouyang Xiu 歐陽修 (1007–1072) and Song Qi 宋祁 (998–1061), *Xin Tang shu* 新唐書, 58.1498. Thus, for many books written between the Han and Tang dynasties the bibliographical treatise of *Sui shu* has become the only record of their very existence.
81. Liu Xu, *Jiu Tang shu*, 46. 2005; Ouyang Xiu and Song Qi, *Xin Tang shu*, 59. 1540.
82. Lu Xun, *Zhongguo xiaoshuo shilue*, 67.

volumes (*juan*),[83] and it is known from his biography that he summoned many writers and scholars to his service. So it is likely that Liu compiled those books, including *Hidden and Visible Realms*, with the assistance of his contingent of writers and scholars. In any case, it is fair to say that Liu Yiqing played an important role in the compilation of *Hidden and Visible Realms.*

The *History of [Liu] Song* (Song shu 宋書) by Shen Yue 沈約 (441–513) presents the life of Liu Yiqing in the chapter on imperial kinsmen (chapter 51), which offers the most detailed accounts of his life and career.[84]

Liu Yiqing was born into a royal family at Pengcheng 彭城, the modern city of Xuzhou 徐州, Jiangsu, in the first year of Emperor An 安 of Jin 晉 (403). His father, Liu Daolian 劉道憐 (368–422), was Prince Jing 景 of Changsha 長沙;[85] Liu Daolian was also the younger brother of Liu Yu, founder of the Song. Liu Daolian had six sons, and Yiqing was the second. In the eighth year of Yixi 義熙 (412), when Yiqing was ten years old,[86] his uncle Liu Daogui 道規 (370–412), the youngest brother of Liu Yu, died and was posthumously enfeoffed as the Prince of Linchuan 臨川.[87] Daogui had no sons, so Yiqing was made his heir.[88]

As recorded in his biography in *History of [Liu] Song*, Liu Yiqing was put in key positions when he was still young. At the age of thirteen (415), Yiqing inherited the title of Duke of the Southern Commandery 南郡公 and was appointed as Executive Assistant, but he did not take

83. See Xiao Hong 蕭紅, "*Shishuo xinyu* zuozhe wenti shangque" 《世說新語》作者問題商榷, 9.

84. Shen Yue, *Song shu* 宋書, 51. 1475–80. His biography in the *Nan shi* 南史 [History of the southern empires] is a simplified version. For a detailed account of Liu Yiqing's life and works, see Zhenjun Zhang, "Observations on the Life and Works of Liu Yiqing," 83–104; see also *Buddhism and Tales of the Supernatural in Early Medieval China*, 20–43.

85. The seat of Changsha Commandery was at modern Changsha city, Hunan. See Tan Qixiang 譚其驤, *Zhongguo lishi dituji* 中國歷史地圖集, 4. 26.

86. This is based on the traditional Chinese method of counting years or *sui* 歲. He was nine years old based on the modern Western standard.

87. The seat of Linchuan Commandery was Linru 臨如, west of modern Linchuan County, Jiangxi. See Tan Qixiang, *Zhongguo lishi dituji*, 4. 25–26.

88. See *Song shu*, 51. 1474.

up the post, likely due to his young age. The following year, he accompanied Liu Yu in Liu's attack on Chang'an 長安. After returning in 419 he was awarded the posts of Bulwark-General of the State and Governor of Qingzhou 青州 but again did not take up the post, and then he became Army Commander of Yuzhou 豫州 and Governor of Yuzhou. Yiqing was also made the Governor of Shouyang 壽陽 in the same year.[89]

In the first year of the Yongchu 永初 period (420), when Yiqing was eighteen, he inherited the title of Prince of Linchuan 臨川 and was offered the post of Palace Attendant. After this, he stayed in the capital, Jiankang, for ten years. During this period as the Palace Attendant, his first four years at the capital, his life was stable and peaceful.

After Emperor Wen 文, Liu Yilong 劉義隆 (407–453), ascended to the throne, Liu Yiqing's life changed dramatically. In the first year of the Yuanjia 元嘉 period (424), he was transferred from one position to another. He became Cavalier Attendant-in-Ordinary, then Director of the Palace Library, then Minister of Revenue and Governor of Danyang 丹陽.[90] After several moves, however, in the sixth year of the Yuanjia reign period (429) Yiqing took up the highest position he would hold during his life, Left Vice Director of the Department of State Affairs, which was second in the government only to the Director of the Department of State Affairs. Surprisingly, Yiqing stayed in that position for only two years before his request of resignation was accepted.

The cause of his resignation is puzzling. According to his biography in *History of [Liu] Song*, Venus had impinged on the Right Upholder, a bad omen. Yiqing was afraid that there would be a calamity and thus requested a transfer to the provinces. Emperor Wen 文帝 tried to dissuade him, but Yiqing insisted.

89. *Song shu*, 36. 1072. The region under the jurisdiction of Shouyang is not clear. Zang Lihe 臧勵龢 says that the prefecture was established in the Southern Qi 齊 dynasty, and it was in modern Sichuan; see his *Diming dacidian* 地名大辭典, 1085.

90. See Shen Yue, *Song shu*, 51. 1475.

Having left the capital, Yiqing became the Governor of Jingzhou 荊州 in 432, and he remained in this position for seven years (432–439).[91]

In the sixteenth year (439) of Yuanjia, Yiqing became the Governor of Jiangzhou 江州, another strategic location. The following year (440), however, he was transferred and became the Governor of Southern Yanzhou 兗州. Yiqing stayed in Yanzhou for three years before he returned to the capital in the twentieth year of Yuanjia (443) and died the next year at the age of forty-two.[92]

Liu Yiqing has been noted for his talent in literature. His biography in *History of [Liu] Song* indicates that "He was addicted to few things, [yet] he loved literary writings," and "Although his literary works were not numerous, he was good enough to be a representative of the royal house." The biography also notes that his talent was respected by others, including Emperor Wen: "When Taizu 太祖 (Emperor Wen) wrote to Yiqing, he often weighed his words carefully again and again."[93]

During Yiqing's tenure as the Governor of Jingzhou, he displayed an obvious interest in literature. According to his biography in the *History of [Liu] Song,* during this time he wrote the *Biographies of the Previous Worthies in Xuzhou* 徐州 in ten volumes and the *Comments on the Classics.*[94]

Liu Yiqing was also noted for gathering notable scholars of his time. When he was governing Jiangzhou, he invited the well-known writer Yuan Shu 袁淑 (408–453) to be the Administrative Advisor of his guarding troops; and he also promoted Lu Zhan 陸展 (d. 454), He Changyu 何長瑜 (d. 446), and Bao Zhao 鮑照, who all made beautiful literary works, to titles of accessory clerks.[95] Literary activity, including the patronage of talented literati, appears to have provided Liu Yiqing with some degree of solace, as well as protection against political maneuvering.

91. Shen Yue, *Song shu*, 51. 1476.
92. Shen Yue, *Song shu*, 51. 1480.
93. Shen Yue, *Song shu*, 51. 1477.
94. Shen Yue, *Song shu*, 51. 1475–80.
95. Shen Yue, *Song shu*, 51. 1477.

In his later years, Liu Yiqing devoted himself to Buddhism and spent a prodigious amount of money supporting Buddhist monks. A passage from his biography reads:

> As he had appointments to a succession of provincial frontier positions, he did not have the faults of luxuriance and extravagance. It was only in his later years that supporting Buddhist monks caused him tremendous expenses. He was a good rider when he was young, yet when he had grown older, he did not ride a horse anymore because the road of life was so hard.[96]

This passage indicates that Liu Yiqing's devotion to Buddhism was related not only to the social background in which Buddhism was flourishing but also to his personal life and experience.

As a prince and high-ranking official, Liu Yiqing was said to have been upright, honest, and attentive to the people under him, though his political career was far from dazzling. As a lover of literature, however, he was unexpectedly successful. While his talent in writing was recognized by his contemporaries and his gatherings of talented literati became anecdotes in his own time, it was his compilations, especially the *New Account of Tales of the World* (Shishuo xinyu 世說新語) and *Hidden and Visible Realms,* that earned him a place in the history of Chinese literature and culture. Tragically, Liu Yiqing's interests in literature and Buddhism were likely due to conflict in the royal house and his own unsuccessful political career.

Concerning Liu Yiqing's works, his biography in the *History of [Liu] Song* says that when he was in Jingzhou he also wrote the *Comments on the Classics* (Dianxu 典敘).[97] Besides, his biography in Li Yanshou's *History of the Southern Empires* (Nan shi 南史) adds two works: *New Account of Tales of the World* in eight volumes and *Jilin* 集林 in 200 volumes. The bibliographical treatise of *History of the Sui* includes *Records of the Famous Men South of the Jiang* (Jiang zuo mingshi lu 江左名士錄) in one volume; *Records of Manifest Miracles* in thirty volumes; *Hidden and Visible Realms* in twenty volumes; *Minor Sayings* (Xiaoshuo 小說) in ten volumes; and

96. Shen Yue, *Song shu*, 51. 1477.
97. Shen Yue, *Song shu*, 51. 1475–80.

An Anthology of Liu Yiqing, the Prince of Linchuan (Linchuan wang Yiqing wenji 臨川王義慶文集) in eight volumes.[98]

None of Liu Yiqing's works was transmitted intact. Though there is a problematic version of the *New Account of Tales of the World,* the rest have all been lost. Two of his shorter prose pieces can be found in the *History of [Liu] Song* and another in the *TPYL* (Taiping yulan 太平御覽).[99] Yan Kejun 嚴可均 (1762–1843) also collected the remnants of three of Liu's rhapsodies from various collectanea.[100] Additionally, there are two extant poems.[101]

As for the fictional works attributed to Liu Yiqing, none survives in the original form. Only those passages cited in other books or collectanea are available today. The *Records of Manifest Miracles* was lost at an early date; it exists only in thirty-five quotations, collected by Lu Xun from various collectanea.[102] *Hidden and Visible Realms* experienced the same fate. *New Account of Tales of the World* is the only collection that exists as a whole book, but modern scholars believe it deviates from the original version.[103]

---

98. See Wei Zheng, et al., *Sui shu*, 33.980; Liu Xu, *Jiu Tang shu*, 46.2005; and Ouyang Xiu and Song Qi, *Xin Tang shu*, 59.1540. Though there has been debate concerning the authorship of some of these works, such as *Shishuo, Youming lu*, and *Xiaoshuo*, by and large, scholars accept their attribution to Liu Yiqing. The *Xiaoshuo* listed here is, however, tricky, because there is also a work by the same title by Yin Yun 殷芸 (471–529). Since almost all the other bibliographies attribute *Xiaoshuo* to Yin Yun, this caused confusion. Xiao Hong, for example, considers the record of Liu Yiqing's *Xiaoshuo* in *Sui shu* to be a mistake. Actually, it seems there are two collections with the same title. For this reason, commentators refer to Liu's collection as the "*Xiaoshuo* of Mr. Liu" 劉氏小說, so as to distinguish it from Yin Yun's *Xiaoshuo.*
99. In Li Fang et al., ed., *Taiping yulan*, 703. 3267b.
100. Yan Kejun, ed., *Quan shanggu sandai Qin Han sanguo liuchao wen* 全上古三代秦漢三國六朝文, 3. 2496–97.
101. See Lu Qinli 逯欽立, ed., *Xian Qin Han Wei Jin Nanbeichao shi* 先秦漢魏晉南北朝詩, 2. 1202.
102. Lu Xun, *Guxiaoshuo gouchen*, 547–60. An account of this book can be found in Gjertson's *Miraculous Retribution*, 20–22.
103. See Fan Ziye 范子燁, *Shishuo xinyu yanjiu* 世說新語研究, 122–206. Modern translations of *Shishuo xinyu* include: Bruno Belpaire, *Anthologie chinoise des*

A BRIEF HISTORY OF THE TEXT

As stated above, *Hidden and Visible Realms* is not mentioned in Liu Yiqing's biography in the *History of [Liu] Song,* yet it is listed in the Miscellaneous Biographies (*zazhuan* 雜傳) category of the bibliographical treatise of *History of the Sui* in twenty volumes[104] and listed in the bibliographical treatise of the *Old Tang History* and *New History of the Tang* in thirty volumes.[105] This collection was not included in later histories, suggesting that it was lost in the Song dynasty. Based on the fact that the *TPGJ* (Taiping guangji 太平廣記), which was compiled in the Northern Song 北宋, included many stories from *Hidden and Visible Realms,* it is probable that this book was lost in the Southern Song 南宋 period, perhaps when the royal house moved southward in 1127.

After the Song, there is no evidence that *Hidden and Visible Realms* was ever seen as a whole and complete book. Fortunately, a large number of tales were preserved in quotations in some *lei shu* or collectanea such as *TPGJ* and *TPYL.*

Selections of the Text

Many compilers of *xiaoshuo* selected tales from *Hidden and Visible Realms.* The ones still extant are as follows:[106]

1. Selection of tales in the *Classified Tales* (Lei shuo 類說).[107] Compiled by Zeng Zao 曾慥 (1091–1155) of the Southern Song dynasty and includes six tales from *Hidden and Visible Realms.* Two of these narratives, the

---

5e et 6e siecles; Mather, *A New Account of Tales of the World*; and Makoto Mekada 目加田誠, *Sesetsu shingo*, 3 v..

104. Wei Zheng, et al., *Sui shu*, 33. 980.

105. Liu Xu, *Jiu Tang shu*, 46. 2005; Ouyang Xiu and Song Qi, *Xin Tang shu*, 59. 1540.

106. For detailed information on the selections and recompilations of the *Youming lu*, see Zhenjun Zhang, "A Textual History of Liu Yiqing's You Ming Lu,": 87–101; see also *Buddhism and Tales of the Supernatural in Early Medieval China*, 44–60.

107. Zeng Zao, *Lei shuo*, 11.189ab. On the textual history of *Lei shuo*, cf. Dudbridge, *The Tale of Li Wa*, 7–10.

second tale about "Yang Hu" 羊祜 and the fourth one about "Xi Kang" 嵇康 (223–262), are not found in other sources.

2. Selection of tales in the *City of Tales* (Shuo fu 說郛).[108] Compiled by Tao Zongyi 陶宗儀 (fl. 1360–1368) during the Yuan-Ming transition and transmitted in manuscript form until 1927, when it was printed in Shanghai by Hanfen lou 涵芬樓. It includes four tales from *Hidden and Visible Realms* in volume 66. The first three, including the one concerning Xi Kang, are from *Classified Tales*. The last one, which is a story about Yuan An 袁安 (d. 92), is from volume 137 of *TPGJ*.

3. Selection of tales in the *Re-collated City of Tales* (Chong Jiao Shuo fu 重校說郛).[109] Compiled by Tao Ting 陶珽 (fl. 1610) and first printed in 1646 by Wanwei shan tang 宛委山堂. It includes eleven tales from *Hidden and Visible Realms*, all collected from *TPGJ*, but the last tale, "Yu bao" 魚報, is mistakenly attributed to *Hidden and Visible Realms*. According to *YWLJ* and *TPGJ*, this tale is from *Records of the Three Qin* (Sanqin ji 三秦記).[110]

4. Selection of tales in the *Grand Spectacle of the Five Dynasty Stories* (Wuchao xiaoshuo daguan 五朝小說大觀).[111] This was first published in Shanghai by Saoye shanfang 掃葉山房 in 1926. This edition of *Hidden and Visible Realms* is just copied from the *Re-collated City of Tales*.

5. Selection of tales in *Old Fiction* (Jiu xiaoshuo 舊小說).[112] This was compiled by Wu Zengqi 吳曾祺 (b. 1852) and first published in 1914. It includes seventeen tales.[113] All the tales are from *TPGJ* and other collectanea, and also included in Lu Xun's *Collected Lost Old Stories*.

108. *Shuo fu* (in 100 *juan*; Shanghai: Shangwu, 1927), 3.6b (rpt., Taibei : Xinxing, 1963, 50a).
109. (*Chongjiao*) *Shuo fu* (in 120 *juan*; Siku quanshu edition): 117A.12a–15a.
110. See Ouyang Xiu, ed., *Yiwen leiju*, 84.1438, and Li Fang et al., eds., *Taiping guangji*, 276.2174.
111. *Wuchao xiaoshuo daguan*, 1. 107–9.
112. Wu Zengqi, *Jiu xiaoshuo*, Collection A2.155a–161a.
113. Wu Zengqi, *Jiu xiaoshuo*, Collection A2. 155a–61a.

Recompilations of the Text

Besides the above selective editions, there are a few exhaustive compilations of *Hidden and Visible Realms* that attempt to provide a comprehensive edition. They include:

1. Recompilation in the *Series Books of Secret Room Linlang* (Linlang mishi congshu 琳琅秘室叢書). Including 158 tales, this work was compiled by Hu Ting 胡珽 (1822–1861). This is the first attempt to recompile the entire *Hidden and Visible Realms*. Except two tales, the tale about Wang Daizhi 王逮之 and the ghost (page 6a) and the tale of "Ran shi" 燃石 (Burning stone; 53a),[114] all these narratives are included in Lu Xun's edition of *Hidden and Visible Realms*.

2. Recompilation in the *Collected Lost Old Stories* (Guxiaoshuo gouchen 古小說鉤沉).[115] Lu Xun completed his recompilations of thirty-six lost works of pre-Tang literature in 1911, and already one year later his preface to *Collected Lost Old Stories* was published in the first (and only) issue of *Yueshe congkan* 越社叢刊. But it was not until after his death that the work itself was published, as part of the first edition of *Complete Works of Lu Xun* (Lu Xun quanji 魯迅全集) in 1938.[116] It was believed that this version was compiled on the basis of the above-mentioned *Series Books of Secret Room Linlang* edition of Hu Ting,[117] but he enlarged his edition of *Hidden and Visible Realms* by adding quotations from *YWLJ* (Yiwen leiju 藝文類聚), *TPGJ*, *TPYL*, *SLFZ* (Shilei fu zhu 事類賦註), and other encyclopedias, collecting all together a total of 265 tales.

Lu Xun mistakenly includes two pieces that are not from *Hidden and Visible Realms*. Tale 257 about mole crickets does not specify a source.

---

114. The source of the first tale is unknown; the second tale in Wu Shu's (947–1002) annotations to his *Shilei fu* [Rhapsody of classified matters], 7.144, is cited from *Yi zhi* [Records of the strange]. This may explain why Lu Xun did not include them in his edition of *Youming lu*.
115. *Guxiaoshuo gouchen*, 351–436.
116. Cf. Lu Xun's preface with annotations in *Gujixubaji*, 3–5.
117. Wang Guoliang, "Youming lu chutan," 171, note 3, says that it includes all of the 158 tales from the *Linlang mishi* version. However, the two tales already mentioned were rejected by Lu Xun.

But the *TPYL* volume 948 and *TPGJ* volume 473 both say it comes from *Sequel to the Record of the Strange* (Xu Yi ji 續異記). Tale 217, a story about how Jia Yong lost his head, is also spurious, because the same story cited in all the extant editions of the *TPGJ* does not give its source.

In addition, Lu Xun intentionally includes three tales (63, 64, and 258) that are attributed to *New Account of Tales of the World*. In a note regarding tale 63, he says, "The present edition of *New Account of Tales of the World* does not include this tale, and when the collectanea of the Tang and Song quote from *Hidden and Visible Realms*, they sometimes also say that this is from *New Account of Tales of the World*." He does not explain why the *New Account of Tales of the World* is used as a substitute for *Hidden and Visible Realms*. The problem is that the tales attributed to the *New Account of Tales of the World* are numerous, not limited to these three. If what Lu Xun says is true, all the other tales might also be from *Hidden and Visible Realms*.

There are at least two excluded tales found in the *Classified Tales*, and one (the tale about Xi Kang) found in the *City of Tales*. It seems Lu Xun consulted neither *Classified Tales* nor *City of Tales*. In *Chrestomathy of Illustrations and Writings, Ancient and Modern* (Gujin tushu jicheng 古今圖書集成), there is another tale that he overlooked.[118]Maeno Naoaki has pointed out that the versions of the collectanea Lu Xun used might have been inferior ones. He also points out some problems regarding editions and punctuation.[119] It seems Lu Xun did not have an opportunity to examine the Ming manuscript version of *TPGJ*. Besides, citation errors are many.[120] However, in the most popular *Collected Lost Old Stories* edition in *Complete Works of Lu Xun*, published by Renmin wenxue chubanshe (1973), almost all of those errors have been corrected.

118. "Mu ke" 木客, Chen Menglei 陳孟雷 (b. 1651–1752) et al., eds., *Gujin tushu jicheng*, 514. 37a. Li Jianguo noticed this tale many years ago. See his *Tang qian zhiguai xiaoshuo shi*, 357.

119. Maeno Naoaki, *Chūgoku shosetsu shi ko*, 197–211.

120. Chen Guishi 陳桂市 has listed some of them in his unpublished M.A. paper. Chen listed those tales to which Lu Xun failed to give a source, but actually they can be found in extant collectanea such as *Taiping guangji* and *Taiping yulan*. Chen also pointed out some mistakes in sources and errors in volumes of books cited in *Guxiaoshuo gouchen*. See Chen Guishi, "Youming lu Xuanyan ji yanjiu" 幽明錄、宣驗記研究, 37–43.

Thus this edition is still the best so far in terms of its accuracy and reliability.

3. The edition published by Zheng Wanqing 鄭晚晴.[121] This collection was compiled on the basis of the *Collected Lost Old Stories* edition, but it rearranged the order of the tales according to their contents. All the tales are divided into six categories, and each tale is given a title. Nine tales are added and eleven appear in the appendix. The total number is 284. The detailed annotations are generally useful as well.

Unfortunately, this collection has fatal problems. First, the standard of selection, especially for the added tales, is problematic. By following Lu Xun, Zheng adds sixteen tales attributed to *New Account of Tales of the World*, yet he puts five of them in the text and the rest in the appendix. Most importantly, the Zheng edition is generally unreliable because of its numerous errors, including missing words, wrong volume numbers (and titles) of sources, incorrect punctuation, and groundless additions and corrections.

NOTES ON THIS NEW RENDITION AND RECOMPILATION

Differing from all the prior editions of *Hidden and Visible Realms,* this is not only the first complete English rendition of the collection with an introduction and annotations but also a recompiled edition and the most comprehensive version of the book.

1. This recompiled version of the collection includes all 265 tales in Lu Xun's *Collected Lost Old Stories* edition, though the two mistakenly included items, tales #217 and #257, and the three items attributed to *New Account of Tales of the World*, #63, #64, and #258, are moved into the appendix.

2. The sixteen added tales in Zheng Wanqing's edition (five in the text and eleven in the appendix), attributed to *New Account of Tales of the World,* are also included in the appendix.

121. Zheng Wanqing, *Youming lu.*

3. Three tales that are not included in the *Collected Lost Old Stories* edition but included in the Zheng Wanqing edition (two from *Classified Tales*, one from *Chrestomathy of Illustrations and Writings, Ancient and Modern*) and one that I have newly found from *A Collection of Dunhuang Transformation Texts* (Dunhuang bianwen ji 敦煌變文集) have been added. The total number of tales here is 285 (264 in the text and 21 in the appendix).

4. All stories are classified into eight categories, and each of them is given a title.

* * *

Below are my notes on the translation and sources used:

1. The major source used in this translation is Lu Xun's *Collected Lost Old Stories* edition of *Hidden and Visible Realms*, in volume 8 of *Complete Works of Luxun* (Renmin wenxue, 1973), 353–436. In order to provide a reliable and accurate rendition, I have also consulted other major sources such as *TPGJ, TPYL, YWLJ, BTSC, FYZL*, and *SLFZ*.

2. Since the Zheng Wanqing edition of *Hidden and Visible Realms* is unreliable (as stated above), when occasionally using a piece from Zheng's collection because it is more informative and complete, I have compared it against the *Collected Lost Old Stories* edition and other sources to make sure it is accurate.

3. Footnotes are provided on cultural and literary context, historical figures and events, as well as some important terms and variants in major sources.

4. For the convenience of readers who wish to locate the Chinese text, major sources used are given in parentheses at the end of each tale. Following the abbreviation of a book title, the first number indicates the volume while the second indicates page(s). But the first number after *GXSGC* is the tale number in the *Collected Lost Old Stories*, instead of the volume number.

5. Besides the translations of some forty tales in my *Buddhism and Tales of the Supernatural in Early Medieval China* (Brill, 2014), other prior English

renditions of selected tales from *Hidden and Visible Realms* are found in the following three publications: eight in Karl Kao, ed., *Classical Chinese Tales of the Supernatural and the Fantastic* (Bloomington: Indiana University Press, 1985), 137–50; ten in Yang Xianyi and Gladys Yang's *Selected Tales of the Han, Wei and Six Dynasties Periods* (Beijing: Foreign Languages Press, 2006), which was previously published in 1958 and again in 1990 as *The Man Who Sold a Ghost: Chinese Tales of the 3rd–6th Centuries*; and twenty-five in Robert Campany, trans., *A Garden of Marvels* (University of Huwai'i Press, 2015), 107–19. For the convenience of readers, a list of tales from this collection that have been rendered into English is included at the end of this book.

HIDDEN AND VISIBLE REALMS

1

THE WONDER OF LOVE

1. LIU CHEN AND RUAN ZHAO[1]

In the fifth year of the Yongping reign period (58–75) under Emperor Ming of the [Eastern] Han Dynasty (25–220), Liu Chen and Ruan Zhao, natives of Shan County,[2] went together to Mount Tiantai to gather paper mulberry bark;[3] there they got lost and could not return home. After

1. This is a story of traveling to the land of the immortals, an enduring motif since the late Han, when the idea that immortals exist in the mountains and islands over the seas entered popular culture. Yet this piece is perhaps the most frequently quoted example among all the classical tales of the supernatural in the Six Dynasties. "Mr. Liu" 劉郎, "Mr. Ruan" 阮郎, and "Liu and Ruan" 劉阮 all became allusions in numerous poems, dramas, and fiction in later times. Besides the archetypal theme of fairy encounters, the "otherness" indicated by the setting on Mount Tiantai, literally "Heavenly Terrace," and the story's unique concept of time, in which one day in fairyland is equivalent to a year in the human world, were probably additional reasons this tale became so fascinating to Chinese people, especially the literati, in later generations. For studies of the lands of immortals, see Li Fengmao 李豐楙, *Xianjing yu youli: shenxian shijie de xiangxiang* 仙境與遊歷: 神仙世界的想像.
2. Shan 剡 County, present-day Sheng 嵊 County, Zhejiang.
3. Tiantai 天台, the mountain noted for its connections with Daoism and Buddhism in modern Tiantai County, Zhejiang.

thirteen days, they had exhausted all of their provisions and were starved almost to death.

From a distance they saw a peach tree bearing much fruit on top of the mountain, but the cliffs were steep, the stream deep, and they could not find a path leading up to the top. They climbed by grabbing the kudzu vines, and thus they were eventually able to get to the top. After they each ate several peaches, their hunger ceased and their bodies were filled with energy.

They went back down the mountain and scooped up water with cups, intending to wash their faces and rinse their mouths, when they saw some turnip leaves, which were extremely fresh, being swept downstream from the mountain's interior. Then a cup that contained sesame seeds mixed with yellow millet drifted down as well.

"Judging from this, we know someone's residence is not far from here!" Liu and Ruan said to each other. So they dove together into the water, swam upstream two or three *li,* and were able to cross the mountain before climbing out of the large stream.

By the stream were two girls of wonderful natural endowment and matchless beauty. Upon seeing the two men wade ashore with the cup in hand, they smiled and exclaimed, "Mr. Liu and Mr. Ruan caught the cup that we set adrift!"

Liu Chen and Ruan Zhao did not know them, yet the two girls called them by their surnames, as if they were all old friends. Thus they were delighted to see one another.[4]

The three characters *Qu gupi* 取穀皮 (gather paper mulberry bark), not found in *FYZL*, are added from *TPYL* 41 and 967. *Gu* 穀, also called *chu* 楮, *gou* 構, or *gupiteng* 穀皮藤 (*Broussonetia papyrifera* or paper mulberry), is a kind of shrub in the family *Moraceae*, widespread in central and southern China. Its bark fiber has been used to make high-quality paper and cloth. Its root and bark are still used as herbs. See Xie Zongwan 謝宗萬, ed., *Quanguo zhong-caoyao huibian* 全國中草藥匯編.

4. For *xinxi* 忻喜 (be delighted), *FYZL* (31) reads *er xi* 而悉 (be acquainted with).

"Why do you come so late?" the two girls asked. Then they invited the two men into their home.

Their house had a roof of bronze tiles.[5] By the south and the east walls stood two large beds, both draped with crimson silk curtains. On each upper corner of the curtains, bells in gold or silver hung. By the head of each bed, ten servant maidens stood.

An order [from the two girls] was passed down [to the maids], saying: "Mr. Liu and Mr. Ruan have just scaled mountains and valleys. Although they have just eaten the carnelian fruits, they are still weak and tired. Hurry up and cook something for them!"

The foods they cooked were millet with sesame seeds, dried goat meat, and beef; all were delicious. When Liu and Ruan were finished eating, wine was laid out, and a crowd of girls approached. Each of them held three or five peaches in their hands, smiling and saying to the two girls, "Congratulations on the arrival of your bridegrooms!"

Music was played while they drank to their hearts' content. Liu and Ruan were filled with both happiness and apprehension. Once it was dark, each of them was ordered to sleep on one of the curtained beds, and the two girls went to sleep together with them for the night. The voices of the girls were gentle and sweet, making both men forget their worries.

Ten days later, Liu and Ruan intended to go home and made a request to do so. The two girls said, "You've already come here, and it was your fated fortune that led you here. Why do you still want to return?" Thus they remained there for half a year. When the climate, grass, and trees all indicated that it was the spring season, hundreds of birds were chirping and singing. This made the two men harbor even more sadness, and they earnestly pleaded to return. The girls replied, "If you are still tied to sinful, worldly cravings, then what can we do!" Consequently, they summoned thirty or forty girls, who had showed up previously, to gather and play music. Then all of them escorted Liu and Ruan together, showing them the way to return home.

5. *TPYL* (41.195) reads *tongwa* 筒瓦 (tube-shaped tiles).

By the time they came out of the mountain, their relatives and old friends had all passed away, the town and their residences had been changed, and there was no one left who knew them. Making inquiries, they found their seventh-generation grandsons, who had heard that their ancestors once entered the mountain and were lost, unable to return. During the eighth year of the Taiyuan reign (383) of the Jin dynasty (265–436), Liu and Ruan suddenly left again, and nobody knew where they had gone.

(*GXSGC*, #38. 361–62; *FYZL*, 31. 967–68; *TPYL*, 41. 194b–95a)

2. THE GIRL WHO SOLD FACE POWDER[6]

There was once a very rich family that had only a single son. The parents doted on the boy and were excessively indulgent with him. Once when the boy was wandering in the market, he saw a beautiful young girl selling face powder. He fell in love with her but found no means to express his feelings. Pretending to buy face powder, he went to the market every day. Upon purchasing the powder, he would leave without a single word.

Gradually, the girl became deeply suspicious. The next day, when the boy came again, she asked, "After buying this powder, what are you going to do with it?"

The boy replied, "I love you, and I didn't dare tell you. Yet I always desire to see you. By buying this powder, I am able to view your lovely face. That is all."

The girl became upset, yet was deeply touched as well, so she promised him a private meeting. The time was set for the following evening.

That evening, the boy was quietly lying in his room, waiting for the girl's arrival. Once it was dark, the girl arrived as expected. The boy was extremely overjoyed. He held the arms of the girl and cried, "My long-cherished wish will now be fulfilled!" He jumped in excitement—and thereupon died.

---

6. This is a touching love story written in an elegant style. It has been selected in almost all the selected collections of Chinese tales of the supernatural.

The girl was seized with anxiety and fear, not knowing what to do. Consequently she fled, returning to the powder store the next morning.

At breakfast time, the parents of the boy were surprised that he had not yet gotten up. When they went to look at him, they found that he was dead. As his corpse was about to be put into a coffin and brought to the graveyard, they opened his bamboo suitcase and found more than one hundred packets of face powder in different sizes, all piled together.

The mother of the boy exclaimed, "It must be this face powder that killed my son!" Then they went to the market and purchased face powder everywhere they found it.

Upon reaching the girl, by comparison they found that her method of tamping the powder into packets matched what they had seen previously at home.[7] Thus they seized the girl, demanding, "Why did you kill our son?"

Hearing this, the girl sobbed, and told them the whole truth. The parents didn't believe her, so they brought a lawsuit against her to the court. The girl said, "Why should I still care if I go on living! I beg to see the corpse once more, to mourn for him." The magistrate granted permission for her request.

She went directly to the boy's home. Embracing the corpse with her arms, she wailed, "I'm so unlucky that things happened like this! If after death your soul is still present, what regret could I possibly have!?"

Suddenly, the boy was revived. The girl told him everything that had happened; they subsequently became husband and wife, and their sons and grandsons proved very prosperous.

(*GXSGC*, #203. 410; *TPGJ*, 274. 2157)

7. *Shouji* 手跡 here indicates "the way the girl packs a packet" instead of "fingerprint."

3. PANG E AND HIS INFATUATED LOVER[8]

In Julu Commandery,[9] there was a man by the name of Pang E who was handsome and carried himself well. The Shi family of that same commandery had a daughter who took a liking to him after she chanced to see him from the inner quarters of her house. Not long thereafter, Pang E saw this girl coming to pay him a visit.

Pang E's wife was a very jealous woman, and when she heard this, she ordered her maidservant to tie up the girl and send her back to the Shi family. However, when they were halfway there, the girl transformed herself into a wisp of smoke and disappeared.

Thereupon the maidservant went straight to see the Shi family and told them about this. The father was shocked and said, "My daughter

8. This is the earliest work featuring the detached-soul motif in Chinese literature. After "Pang E," the motif of the detached soul grew increasingly widespread. The best-known examples are the tale "Lihun ji" 離魂記 [Record of the detached soul] by Chen Xuanyou 陳玄祐 (fl. 779) of the Tang and the drama *Qiannu lihun* 倩女離魂 [Qiannu's soul detachment] by Zheng Guangzu 鄭光祖 (fl. 1294) of the Yuan (1279–1368). For a study of this motif, see Zhenjun Zhang, "On the Origins of the Detached Soul Motif in Chinese Literature," 167–84; see also his *Buddhism and Tales of the Supernatural in Early Medieval China*, 205–21.

In Chinese religion, a person has two souls, the *hun* soul and the *po* soul. The earliest depiction of the duality of souls in a Chinese text is found in an entry from the seventh year of Duke Zhao 昭 (534 BCE) in the *Zuo zhuan* 左傳. There the *hun* 魂 soul was defined by Zichan 子產 (d. 522 BCE) in connection with the *po* 魄 soul. Kong Yingda 孔穎達 (574–648) comments: "The spirit that attaches to the body is the *po* soul, the spirit that attaches to the vital energy is the *hun* soul" 附形之靈為魄，附气之神為魂 (*Zuo zhuan zhushu* 左傳註疏, in Ruan Yuan 阮元, *Chongkan Songben shisanjing zhu shu* 重刊宋本十三經註疏, 764; *SBBY* version [Zhonghua, n.d.], 44. 8a). Ge Hong's 葛洪 "Lun xian" 論仙 [On immortals] in *Baopu zi* 抱朴子 [The master who embraces simplicity] says, "People, whether worthy or stupid, all know that souls exist in their body. And when his/her *hun* soul or *po* soul departs, the person will be sick; when both his/her *hun* soul and *po* soul leave, the person will die" 人無賢愚，皆知己身之有魂魄. 魂魄分去則人病，盡去則人死. See Wang Ming 王明, ed., *Baopuzi neipian jiaoshi* 抱朴子內篇校釋, 19–20.

9. Julu 巨鹿, present-day Jin 晉 County, Hebei.

has never even stepped outside this house. How can you spread such slander as this?"

From then on Pang E's wife took even more care to keep an eye on him. One night she came across this girl again in the study, whereupon she herself tied her up and took her back to the Shi family.

When the father saw her he stared dumbfoundedly and said, "I just came from inside and saw the girl working with her mother. How could she be here?" He then ordered a maidservant to call the girl to come out. As soon as the girl came out, the one who had been tied up previously vanished like smoke.

The father suspected that there must be an abnormal reason for this, so he sent the mother to ask the girl about it. The girl said, "Last year I once stole a glance at Pang E when he came to our house, and ever since then I have felt confused. Once I dreamed that I went to visit Pang E, and when I reached the entrance to his house, I was tied up by his wife."

Mr. Shi said, "How could it be that there are truly such strange matters as this in the world! Indeed, whenever one's sincerest feelings are affected, the spirit will manifest itself in mysterious ways. Thus the one who disappeared must have been her *hun* soul."

After this, the girl made a vow that she would never marry. Some years later, Pang E's wife suddenly contracted a terrible illness, and neither doctors nor medicines were able to save her life. Only then did Pang E send betrothal gifts to the girl and make her his wife.

(*GXSGC*, #222. 417; *TPGJ*, 358. 2830)

4. DREAM ADVENTURE INSIDE A CYPRESS PILLOW[10]

The curator of the temple at Lake Jiao owned a cypress pillow for more than thirty years.[11] In the back of the pillow there was a small crack. While traveling on business, a man of the county named Tang Lin passed by the temple to pray for good fortune. The curator said to him, "You are not married, right? Then you may place your head on the pillow, near the crack."

The curator asked Lin to enter the crack. [Once inside] Lin saw a vermilion gate, through which appeared jade palaces and gemmed terraces, all surpassing any in this world. He met Grand Marshal Zhao, who arranged a marriage for him. Lin begot six children, four boys and two girls. He was appointed the Assistant of the Imperial Library, and not long after promoted to the position of Gentleman of the Palace Gate.

Inside the pillow, Lin had never thought of returning home; yet consequently he got into trouble because of his transgression and disobedience.

The curator asked Lin to come out, and [once he did] he saw the pillow he had seen previously. Lin said that he had spent several years inside the pillow, but in fact it was only a short while.[12]

(*GXSGC*, #251. 428–29; *BTSC*, 134. 233b)

---

10. This unique tale is considered the prototype of the noted dream adventure motif in Chinese literature. This motif became popular from the Tang dynasty (618–907), and the most famous Tang tale featuring this motif is Shen Jiji's 沈既濟 (c. 750–c. 800) "Zhenzhong ji" 枕中記 [The world inside a pillow]; an English translation of it, by William Nienhauser, can be found in Y. W. Ma and Joseph S. M. Lau, eds., *Traditional Chinese Stories*, 435–38. Later literary works that follow this model include: the dramas *Huangliang meng* 黃粱夢 [Yellow millet dream] by Ma Zhiyuan 馬致遠 (1260–1325), *Handan meng* 邯鄲夢 [Dream of Handan] by Tang Xianzu 湯顯祖(1550–1617), and the story "Xu Huangliang meng" 續黃粱夢 [Continuation of millet dream] by Pu Songling 蒲松齡 (1640–1715). Cf. Zhenjun Zhang, "A Fantastic Dream World: New Literary Motifs and Buddhist Culture," in *Buddhism and Tales of the Supernatural in Early Medieval China*, 175–190.
11. Lake Jiao 焦, Lake Chao 巢湖 in Anhui.
12. A variant of this story is found in *TPGJ* 283 (credits *YML*) that reads:

    In the era of the Song 宋 dynasty [420–479], there was a cypress pillow—some say a jade pillow—with a small hole in it at the Jiaohu

5. THE GOD OF RIVERS MARRYING OFF HIS DAUGHTER[13]

In the [Liu] Song reign period (420–479), Shangxiang Lake was to the south of Yuhang County.[14] In the middle of the lake a dyke was built. Once, a man riding a horse and leading three or four attendants went to watch a play, then drank wine in Chen Village. Being somewhat drunk, they went back home. It was very hot, so the man dismounted from his horse, entered the water, and slept by pillowing his head on a piece of stone. His horse then broke its bridle and ran back

---

> 焦湖 Temple. At that time, Yang Lin 楊林, a businessman from Shanfu 单父 County, went to the temple to pray [for good fortune]. The sorcerer of the temple asked him: "Would you like to marry well?" Lin replied: "I would be fortunate to do so." Right then the sorcerer sent Lin to approach the pillow, and therefore Lin entered into the hole. Consequently he saw a red tower with a gemmed garret. Grand Marshal Zhao was inside, and he married his daughter to Lin. She had six sons, and all of them became secretaries in the imperial court. After several decades, Lin had no intention of returning. Suddenly [one day] he felt as if he had awakened from a dream, [and found he] was still at the side of the pillow. Lin was sad for a long time.

Taiping huanyu ji 太平寰宇記 126 credits this story to *YML* as well as *SSJ*. But it begins with "In the Song Dynasty," indicating that it was not from *SSJ*; furthermore, it does not exist in the extant version of *SSJ*. But Li Jianguo deleted the first line, "In the era of the Song dynasty," by saying that it was most likely added by the compiler of *TPGJ*, and then included this story in his *Xinji Soushen ji* 新集搜神記, 53–54. It is hard to say which of the two versions is earlier.

13. Love between man and spirit, ghost, or demon is a long-standing theme in Chinese tales. This is a moving story, especially its ending. What is unique in this tale is that the father becomes the go-between, and he even forces the young man to marry his daughter. In the next tale, however, the father go-between was not as lucky as the father in this story because his great effort in marrying off his daughter failed. The man in that story seems not as flexible as the young man in this one, and that might be the cause of his death.
14. *TPGJ* (295. 2350) reads *Shang hu* 上湖 for *Shangxiang hu* 上湘湖.

    Yuhang 餘杭 County, the area between present-day Lin'an 臨安 and Hangzhou 杭州, Zhejiang. See Tan Qixiang 譚其驤, *Zhongguo lishi dituji* 中國歷史地圖集, 4. 27–28.

home. His attendants all ran after the horse, and as it grew dark they still had not come back.

When the man awoke, it was about sunset. He could not find his horse and attendants, but he saw a girl around sixteen or seventeen arrive, who said, "This girl bows to you again! It is about sunset and this place is going to be truly terrifying. What are you going to do here?"

"May I ask your surname?" the man asked back. "Why do you suddenly greet me here?" Then he saw a teenager around the age of thirteen or fourteen, who appeared extremely intelligent, arriving in a new carriage followed by approximately twenty people. The teenager summoned the man to ascend into the carriage, saying, "My father wants to see you for a moment."

So they turned the carriage around and left. On the way, they saw torches continuously. Soon they saw city walls, towns, and residences. As soon as they finally arrived, they entered the town and walked into the hall of an official residence with a banner hanging above with an official title on it,[15] which read, "God of Rivers."

After a short while, he saw an officer around thirty years old who looked like a painting, with numerous attendants and guards. Happily they sat face to face and the officer ordered wine to be set out and meat roasted, saying, "I have a daughter who is fairly smart.[16] I intend to let her serve you with a broom and a dustpan."[17]

Knowing that this officer was a god, the man dared not refuse and go against his will. Then an order from the god was sent down: to prepare everything and everyone to be ready for the wedding of the Gentleman of the Interior. The reply was that everything was ready. The bridegroom was sent a single-layer silk garment, a double-layer garment, a fine silk skirt, a gauze shirt, a pair of pants, a pair of shoes, and a pair of slippers; all of them were fine and nice. In addition, he was sent ten young attendants and several dozen maids. The girl was

---

15. *GXSGC* made a mistake in punctuation: 進庭事上，有信幡 should be 進庭事，上有信幡. *TPGJ* reads without the *shang* 上 (295. 2351).
16. Following *TPGJ*, *po congming* 頗聰明 (295. 2351).
17. *Gei jun ji zhou* 給君箕帚 (let [her] serve you with a broom and a dustpan) means to marry you as your wife.

about eighteen or nineteen, and she was gentle and beautiful. Then they finished the wedding.

Three days later, the bride and bridegroom visited their parents. On the fourth day, the officer said, "Since there is a time limit according to the rites, he should be sent away." With a golden cup and a small musk bag as gifts, the girl bid farewell to her husband and they parted in tears. In addition, she gave him ten thousand cash and three volumes of pharmaceutical prescriptions, saying, "You can spread beneficence with these." Again she said, "Ten years from now I will be here to welcome you back."

The man returned home and was reluctant to marry other girls. He left his relatives and became a Buddhist monk. Among the three volumes of prescriptions he got, one was the *Classic of the Pulse*, one was the *Prescriptions of Decoction*, and one was the *Prescriptions of Pill*. He traveled around with them to cure and save people, and all of them showed marvelous effects. Later, when both his mother and elder brother became old, he returned home, married, and became an official in the court.

(*GXSGC*, #252. 429–30; *FYZL*, 75. 2220–21; *TPGJ*, 295. 2350–51)

6. ZHEN CHONG AND THE LOCAL DEITY

Zhen Chong of Zhongshan State,[18] styled Shurang, was appointed magistrate of Yundu.[19] When he arrived at Huihuai County,[20] a man suddenly came to inform him: "The son of the local deity would like to call on you." In a moment the visitor arrived, and he was young and handsome.

After they sat down and exchanged greetings, the young deity said, "My father sent me here since he admires your fame and wants to claim ties of kinship with your noble house by giving my younger sister in marriage. For this reason I came to inform you of his wish."

18. Zhongshan 中山 State, modern Ding 定 County, Hebei.
19. Yundu 雲杜 County; its seat was northwest of modern Mianyang 沔陽 County, Hubei. *TPGJ* reads *Yunshe* 雲社, a mistake due to the similar shape of the graphs.
20. Huihuai 惠懷 County; its seat was west of Mianyang County, Hubei.

Zhen was astonished, saying, "I have passed my prime, and besides, I have a wife already. What reason is there for such a proposal?"[21]

The son of the local deity said again, "My younger sister is young and her beauty is matchless. Certainly she wants to have a good match. How can you refuse?"

Zhen replied, "I am an old man and currently have a wife. How could I allow myself to violate regulations and transgress against propriety?"

They argued back and forth several times, but Zhen did not change his mind at all. The son of the local deity looked angry, saying, "My father will certainly come himself. I'm afraid that you will not be able to go against his will."

As soon as the young deity left, Zhen saw people wearing kerchiefs and holding whips on both banks of the river. They marched in good order and were followed by many attendants.

Soon, the local deity arrived in person with honor guards before and after him like a hegemon. He rode in a carriage followed by several carriages with dark-green banners and red trim. The girl rode in an open carriage with several dozen silk wind screens, and in front of her were eight maids, all wearing embroidered gowns such as Zhen had never seen.

Then they pitched a tent on the bank next to Zhen and spread a mat. The local deity stepped out of his carriage and sat on a white woolen rug by a low table. He brought with him a jade spittoon and a tortoiseshell towel holder, and he held a white flywhisk in his hand. His daughter, however, was at the east bank, with eunuchs holding white whisks on both sides of the carriage and maids in front. The local deity directed his sixty or so assistant officers to sit in front, then ordered music to be played. All the musical instruments were like colored glaze.

The local deity said to Zhen, "I have a humble daughter, yet she is dear to my heart. Because of your lofty morality and good reputation,

21. *Ci yi* 此議 (this proposal), originally *cili* 此里 (理, reasoning), is corrected according to the handwritten edition of the Ming dynasty (see *TPGJ*, 318. 2522).

I desire to claim ties of kinship with you in marriage. Therefore, I have sent my son to thoroughly express such an intention."

Zhen replied, "I am old and emaciated; I have a wife, and furthermore, my son has grown up. Even if I covet your honorable offering, I would not venture to accept it."

The local deity said again, "My daughter has just turned twenty. She is kind, beautiful, and possesses all of the Four Virtues. Now she is on the bank. Don't make trouble anymore—just go through with the wedding, please!"

Zhen declined him resolutely. Thinking that he might be an evil demon, Zhen drew his sword and laid it on his knees to resist him with death, without talking to him anymore.

The local deity was enraged, so he ordered two three-color striped tigers to be summoned, which opened their crimson mouths, roared as if the earth was splitting, and leaped directly at Zhen. This was repeated several dozen times. Zhen kept up his resistance until dawn.

Unable to do anything with Zhen, the local deity withdrew. He left a pull cart, along with several dozen people, to wait for Zhen.

Therefore, Zhen moved to Huihuai County to live. The cart and the people who waited for Zhen arrived at his door again. Among them, a man wearing a single-layer garment and kerchiefs bowed to him, yet he stopped there and was not able to go forward.

Zhen stayed there for more than ten days before he dared to leave. He saw two people wearing kerchiefs and holding whips arrive at his home. No more than a few days after he arrived home, his wife became ill and died.[22]

(*GXSGC*, #208. 411–13; *TPGJ*, 318. 2522–23)

22. The original graph 歸 (return) is a mistake of 婦 (wife) because of the similarity of their forms. Here I follow *GXSGC* instead of the Zhonghua edition of *TPGJ*, because the latter changes the original character into *ran* 染 (contract) based on the Ming dynasty hand-copied version and the correction does not make as much sense—based on that correction, the one who died becomes Zhen instead of his wife.

7. A GHOST MATCHMAKER

Both Ma Zhongshu and Wang Zhidu were natives of Liaodong Commandery,[23] and they were close friends. Zhongshu died first, and the next year he showed up physically and told Zhidu, "Unfortunately I died too early, yet you have always been in my heart. Considering that you don't have a wife, I should get a wife for you. By the twentieth day of the eleventh month, she will be sent to visit your home. You need only to clean your house, set up a bed and mat, and wait for her."

On that day, Zhidu secretly cleaned his house, when a strong wind blew and the day became as dark as night. When it was about evening, the wind stopped. Suddenly a red curtain set itself up in the bedroom.

Zhidu opened the curtain and looked inside. He found in the bed a woman who was attractive and dignified. Lying there, she was just able to breathe. All his cousins were startled and terrified; none of them dared to approach her. It was only Zhidu who was able to go see her.

In a short while, the girl got up and sat. Zhidu asked, "Who are you?"

The girl replied, "I am a native of Henan Commandery.[24] My father is the governor of Qinghe.[25] My wedding is approaching, but I don't know why I suddenly appeared here."

Zhidu told her all about the intention of his late friend. The girl said, "It must be Heaven that allows me be your wife." Thus they became husband and wife.

[The girl's father] went to visit Zhidu's home and was greatly delighted. He also thought that it was Heaven who offered his daughter to Zhidu, thus he offered her to him as well. The couple begot a boy, who later became the Governor of Nanjun.[26]

(*GXSGC*, #220. 416–17; *TPGJ*, 322. 2553)

23. Liaodong 遼東 Commandery, located to the east of the Liao 遼 River.
24. Henan 河南 Commandery; its seat was Luoyang 洛陽, Henan.
25. Qinghe 清河 Commandery; its seat was located at modern Qinghe County, Hebei.
26. Nanjun 南郡 Commandery; its seat was Jiangling 江陵, Hubei.

8. THE GIRL ONE SAVED BECOMES HIS WIFE

A man of Qu'e,[27] whose name has been forgotten, once returned home from the capital. It was almost dark, yet he was not able to reach his home. Furthermore, it started raining, so he lodged in a large house.

When the rain stopped and the moon was bright, he saw from a distance a woman arriving at the house and staying under the eave, sighing in despair.

Consequently she untied the rope from her waist and hung it on the upper corner of the house, trying to hang herself. It seemed that there was someone on the eave who was pulling the rope.

The man of Qu'e secretly cut the curling rope, and he cut toward the upper part of the house as well. Then he saw a ghost running toward the west.

Toward dawn the girl was just revived, yet she was able to speak. She said, "My home is just ahead, not far from here." So the man took her home and told her parents what had happened.

Probably it was heavenly fate that made it so. Thereupon the parents married their daughter to him as his wife.

(*GXSGC*, #188. 406; *TPYL*, 766. 3401b–02a)

9. THE MARRIAGE THROUGH CATCHING A GHOST

At the end of the Shengping reign period (357–361) of the [Eastern] Jin (317–420) dynasty, an old man of Guzhang County had a daughter who lived with him deep in the mountains.[28] Guang of Yuhang proposed that the girl become his wife yet was refused.[29]

Later when the old man contracted an illness and died, his daughter went to the county seat to buy a coffin. Halfway there she met Guang. The girl told him everything. She said, "I am pressed by poverty. If you can go to my home to guard my father's corpse, when I

27. Qu'e 曲阿, modern Danyang 丹陽, Jiangsu.

28. Guzhang 故章 (鄣) County, modern Anji 安吉 County, Zhejiang.

29. Yuhang. See note 14 in this chapter.

return I'll be your wife." Guang promised her. The girl said, "In our pig-pen there is a pig; you may slaughter it to feed the helpers."

When Guang reached the girl's home, he heard inside the room only the sounds of clapping and dancing. Guang broke the fence, seeing that many ghosts in the hall were toying with the old man's corpse in their hands. Guang grabbed a stick, shouted, and entered the gate. All of the ghosts left. Guang guarded the corpse and fetched the pig to slaughter.

When night came, he saw an old ghost who stretched his hand to beg for meat. Thereupon Guang grabbed his arms. The ghost was not able to escape, and Guang held his arms tighter and tighter. He heard from outside the ghosts yelling together, "This old slave is greedy for food, and now he must be very happy."

Guang told the old ghost, "It must be you who killed the old man. You may return his soul immediately, then I'll let you go; if you don't, I'll never release you."

The old ghost said, "My sons killed the old man." Then he called his sons, "You may give it back to him."

Gradually the old man was revived. Accordingly, Guang released the old ghost.

When the girl arrived with a coffin on a cart, they met in astonishment and sorrow. Thereupon Guang took the girl as his wife.

(*GXSGC*, #93. 379–80; *TPGJ*, 383. 3052)

10. THE MARRIAGE OF LIFE AND DEATH[30]

Mazi, the son of the Governor of Guangping Commandery named Feng Xiaojiang,[31] once dreamed of a girl around the age of eighteen or nineteen. She said, "I am the daughter of Xu Xuanfang, the previous

30. This piece is among the earliest works featuring the motif "Revival of a Ghost Wife." A variant version with almost no difference is found in volume 8 of Liu Jingshu's 劉敬叔 *Yiyuan* 異苑 [A garden of marvels]. A longer version of this story is found in volume four of the *Soushen houji* 搜神後記 [Further records of an inquest into the spirit realm], and it was included in Karl S. Y. Kao, ed., *Classical Chinese Tales of the Supernatural and the Fantastic*, 130–32. Noted works following this model include the famous Ming drama *Mudan ting* 牡丹亭 [The peony pavilion] by Tang Xianzu (1550–1616).

31. Guangping 廣平 Commandery, southeast of modern Xingtai 邢臺, Hebei. See Tan Qixiang, *Zhongguo lishi dituji*, 4. 51.

governor, and unfortunately I died young. It has been four years. I was wrongly killed by a ghost, yet according to the record of my life span, I should live to the age of over eighty. Now I am allowed to revive, return [to the mortal world], and be your wife. Would you like to marry me?"

Mazi dug up the coffin, opened it, and looked inside; the girl had already revived. Thus they became husband and wife.

(*GXSGC*, #205. 411; *TPGJ*, 276. 2181–82)

11. MR. XU'S REGRETFUL ENCOUNTER WITH THE CELESTIAL GIRL[32]

In Jingkou there was once a Mr. Xu,[33] whose home was fairly shabby. He often picked up floating firewood by the Yangzi River.

One day, all of a sudden, he saw a row of boats coming, which covered the whole river. The boats directly entered the river mouth and berthed near Xu.

A messenger was sent to him, saying, "Now the celestial girl is going to be the wife of Mr. Xu."

Xu went into the corner of his house to hide, refusing to come out. His mother, brothers, and sisters all encouraged him; then he came out reluctantly.

Before he reached the boats, the maids were ordered in advance to draw a bath for Mr. Xu in another room. The water was fragrant and could rarely be found in this ordinary world. Xu was given a garment of red silk, yet he only accepted it out of fear. He kneeled down at the end of the bed that night, without the courtesy of greetings and interactions between a man and a woman.

The girl then sent him out.[34] Xu gave her back the garments that she had bestowed on him and then withdrew.[35]

32. Among the love stories between men and spirits in Chinese narratives, this piece is fairly unusual. The young man was so shy and so cowardly, and the heavenly girl was so heartless and so mean.
33. Jingkou 京口, modern city of Zhenjiang 鎮江, Jiangsu.
34. The Ming dynasty handwritten edition reads 女怒，遣之使出, "The girl became angry and drove him out."
35. *Qi zhi* 乞之, "give her [stuff] back."

The whole family, young and old, all blamed and abused him severely. Consequently, he died with sighs of regret.

(*GXSGC*, #206. 411; *TPGJ*, 292. 2326)

12. DAUGHTER OF THE RIVER GOD

Wu Kan, a minor official of Yangxian County,[36] had a master south of the stream. Once when he crossed the river in a short-head boat, he saw a five-colored floating stone in the river. He grabbed it and put it on the head of his bed. When night came, the stone became a girl who said that she was the daughter of the god of the river.

(*GXSGC*, #166. 400; *BTSC*, 137. 255b; *TPYL*, 52. 254b)

13. THE GOLDEN JAR AS A GIFT[37]

The daughter of Cui Maobo of Qinghe County was betrothed to the son of the Pei family. Before the appointed time for the wedding arrived, the girl suddenly died. Holding a golden jar with the capacity of about two liters, the girl directly arrived and stood in front of Cui's bed, bestowing the jar upon Cui.

(*GXSGC*, #185. 406; *TPYL*, 758. 364b)

14. HUANG YUAN ENCOUNTERS MIAOYIN

During the Han dynasty, Huang Yuan, a native of Taishan Commandery,[38] opened his door one morning. Suddenly he saw a black dog sitting outside the door, guarding his home completely like a dog that he raised. Yuan tied the dog with a leash to hunt with his neighbors.

36. Yangxian 陽羨, modern Yixing 宜興, Jiangsu.
37. A more detailed account of Cui Maobo is found in *TPGJ* (324. 2574), yet no source is provided.
38. Taishan Commandery, modern Tai'an 泰安 County, Shandong.

Around sunset, he saw a deer. Then he released the dog. The dog ran very slowly. Yuan ran after it with all his strength, yet could never reach it.

After running for several *li,* they reached a cave. After entering it for more than a hundred paces, Yuan suddenly saw a smooth thoroughfare where scholar trees and willows were planted on both sides, surrounded by fences. Following the dog, Yuan entered a door where stood several dozen houses with windows, all filled with girls who were beautiful in appearance and wore colorful garments. Some of them were playing zithers, and others were playing chess.

When he arrived at the northern pavilion, there were three rooms with two maids on duty, and they looked as if they were expecting someone. Seeing Yuan, they smiled at each other, saying, "This is Miaoyin's husband who was led by the black dog." One of them stayed; the other entered the pavilion.

A moment later, four maids came out, saying, "Lady Taizhen let us inform Mr. Huang: 'There is a girl who is not yet fifteen, the age a girl has her hair pinned up, but she is fated to be your wife.'"

When it was dark, they led Yuan into the inner quarter. Inside, there was a hall facing south. In front of the hall there was a pool. In the pool there was a terrace. At each of the four corners of the terrace there was a one-foot-deep cave. Inside the cave, curtains and mats were illuminated by light. Miaoyin was gentle and attractive. Her maids were also beautiful. After the wedding was finished, they feasted and lived together like old friends.

After several days, Yuan intended to return home temporarily to inform his family of what had happened. Miaoyin said, "The ways of human beings and the spirits are different. Intrinsically we could not stay together for long."

The next day, she untied her jade pendant and gave it to him as a gift, and parted with him. By the steps where they parted, she was in tears. "Since there might be no chance for us to meet again, my love and adoration have become even deeper. If you still miss me, when the first day of the third month comes, you may fast, take a bath, and make sacrificial offerings to me."

The four maids sent Yuan out the door and saw him off. In half a day he arrived at his home, yet it seemed that he was in a trance. Whenever the appointed time arrived, he often saw a curtained carriage flying in the air.

(*GXSGC*, #46. 364–65; *FYZL*, 31. 968–69)

15. THE SILVER CHAIN AS A GIFT

In the third year of the Yixi reign period (405–418) of the Eastern Jin dynasty, Xu Qi, a native of Shanyin,[39] went out of his home and saw a girl who was extremely beautiful. Qi untied the silver chain on his arm and gave it to her as a gift. The girl said, "I am so moved that you come to bestow this on me." Then she gave Qi a green bronze mirror, and consequently they became a couple.[40]

(*GXSGC*, #135. 392–93; *BTSC*, 135. 241b & 136. 246a; *TPYL*, 812. 3608b)

16. A PINNED PAINTING

At Jiangling, Gu Changkang (348–409) fell in love with a girl.[41] After returning home, Changkang missed her endlessly. So he painted a picture of the girl and pinned it to the wall with a hairpin, but the place where the hairpin pierced was exactly her heart.

[At her place] the real girl walked for ten *li*, then felt a pain in her heart as if it was pierced, and she could not walk forward anymore.[42]

(*GXSGC*, #111. 385; *TPYL*, 741. 3288b)

39. Shanyin 山陰, modern city of Shaoxing 紹興, Zhejiang.
40. This story is also included in volume 6 of *Yi yuan*.
41. Jiangling 江陵, modern Jingzhou 荆州.

    Gu Changkang 顧長康, named Kaizhi 愷之, was a famous painter, calligrapher, and poet of the Eastern Jin. His biography is found in Fang Xuanling 房玄齡 (578–648), et al., eds., *Jin shu* 晉書, 92. 2404–06.
42. The biography of Gu Kaizhi in *Jin shu* includes this story with a happy ending as follows: "Kaizhi therefore expressed his feelings to her, and the girl yielded to him. Thus he secretly took the hairpin out, and the girl healed" (*Jin shu* 92. 2405).

17. THE GIRL PICKING CHESTNUTS

Lü Qiu of Dongping Commandery was wealthy and handsome.[43] One day when he reached the Qu'e Lake by boat,[44] he encountered wind and was not able to go forward.

After mooring beside the wild rice stems, he saw a young girl picking chestnuts on a boat, whose whole body was covered by lotus leaves. Thereupon he asked, "Aren't you a ghost? Why are your clothes like this?"

The girl looked at him in fear, replying, "Haven't you heard? 'Wearing a lotus coat with melilotus girdle, quickly he came and quickly departed'?"[45] Yet she showed fear on her face. Turning over and tidying her boat, she left hesitantly.

Qiu shot her from a distance and then obtained an otter. The boat of the former girl was full of clover fern, white wormwood artemisia, algae, and the like.

Qiu saw an old lady standing on the shore, as if expecting someone. Seeing the boat passing, she asked, "Did you see the girl who was picking chestnuts on the lake?" Qiu replied, "She is not far behind us." Then he shot the old woman and obtained an old otter.

Those who lived around the lake all said, "On the lake there has been a girl picking chestnuts, whose beauty surpasses that of other girls. Sometimes she went to someone's home. Those who became her lovers are numerous."

(*GXSGC*, #169. 401–02; *YWLJ*, 82. 405–06)

18. THE SEDUCTION OF A SWAN SPIRIT

In the Yuanxing reign period (402–404) of Emperor An of Jin, a man over twenty had not yet married. But his eyes had never glimpsed beautiful girls, and he had not engaged in immoral conduct.

---

43. Dongping 東平 Commandery; its seat was at modern Dongping County in Shangdong.
44. Qu'e 曲阿, see footnote 27 above.
45. These two lines are from the "Shao siming" 少司命 [Lesser master of fate] in Qu Yuan's 屈原 "Jiuge" 九歌 [Nine songs]. See Hawkes, trans., *The Songs of the South*, 112.

Once, when the young man was working in the field, he saw an extremely beautiful girl, who said to him, "I heard that you consider yourself a man of Liu Ji's type;[46] have you ever enjoyed meeting a girl in the mulberry?"[47] Then the girl sang a song. The color of the young man's face slightly changed.

Later the young man met her repeatedly. He asked her surname; she replied, "My surname is Su, my name is Qiong, and my home is in Tuzhong."[48]

Then he invited her to his home to enjoy the happiness of love. Unexpectedly, his younger brother entered and hit the girl with a stick. Immediately the girl became a female white swan.

(*GXSGC*, #147. 395–96; *TPGJ*, 460. 3768)

19. FEI SHENG'S AFFAIR WITH A WILD CAT SPIRIT

Fei Sheng of Wu County was the innkeeper of Nine *Li* Inn.[49] Once, when it was about dusk, he saw a girl coming out from the outer wall of the city, wearing white clothing and crying. She entered the embankment, weeping, toward a new tomb. When it was dusk the girl could not enter the city; thus she took lodging at the inn.

When night arrived, Sheng plucked his lute and urged the girl to sing. The girl said, "I am still in mourning. Don't laugh at me." The voice of her song was extremely seductive; it went,

The essence and vital energy interact in silence,
my descending is likely my fate.
Alas, what a good match I have met,
let me entrust my happiness to the dream of tonight.

---

46. Liu Ji 柳季, a man of Lu 魯 State in the Spring and Autumn period, also called Liu Xiahui 柳下惠, who had the fame of not behaving improperly even when a beauty sat in his arms.
47. "Sangzhong" 桑中 [Mulberry field] is a poem in the *Shijing* 詩經 [The classic of odes] that depicts a girl's rendezvous with her lover. a mulberry field later became the place of lovers' secret meeting.
48. Tuzhong 塗中, "in the mud."
49. Wu 吳 County, present-day Suzhou 蘇州.

The middle of the song went,

Jade Girl Chenggong followed Yiqi,
Goddess Lanxiang descended for Zhang Shuo.
Let's believe our affair is predestined,
and enjoy the sweet love tonight.

The end of the song went,

Waiting for our wind-cloud meeting,
expecting the wandering this evening.
Our spiritual interaction has not been long,
yet a feeling in our hearts intertwined.

Then they slept together.

At dawn, when Fei Sheng was leaving, he looked back, saying, "I am going to the Imperial Inn." Then the girl was terrified—a hunter had arrived. A pack of hunting dogs entered the room and killed her by the bed, where she became a big wild cat.

(*GXSGC*, #180. 404; *TPYL*, 573. 2588b–89a)

20. CHANG CHOUNU ENCOUNTERS A RIVER OTTER SPIRIT

Chang Chounu of Hedong Commandery[50] made his home in Zhang'an County,[51] making a living by picking cattails.

Once he brought a little boy to pull cattails, and they lodged in an empty farmhouse in the evening. Around dusk, he saw a girl who was extremely beautiful. Riding in a small boat loaded with water shield

50. Hedong 河東 Commandery, the area centered around present-day Xia 夏 County and north of the city of Sanmen xia 三門峽, Henan. See Tan Qixiang, *Zhongguo lishi dituji*, 3. 35. Its seat was located at modern Yongji 永濟 County, Shanxi.

51. Zhang'an 章安 County, located southeast of modern Linhai 臨海 County, Zhejiang.

plants, she directly approached Chounu, asking for lodging. Taking liberties with her, Chounu put out the fire and slept with her.

Smelling the scent of fish and touching her extremely short fingers, he cautiously suspected that she was a demon. The girl already knew what the man thought, so she requested to leave, and became an otter.[52]

(*GXSGC*, #170. 402; *TPYL*, 999. 4421a; *YWLJ*, 82. 1407)

21. CHICKEN TONGUE FRAGRANT GUM

The clerk of Yongxing County of the Song,[53] Zhong Dao, was newly recovered from a serious illness. His desire for love doubled.

Previously he loved a girl from the White Crane Fair. Until this moment, he was still thinking of her. Unexpectedly, he saw the girl coming with her clothes flying up and down, and then he stayed together with her intimately. After that the girl came several times.

Once Dao said, "I really want some chicken tongue fragrant gum." The girl said, "What an easy thing to do!" Then she took out a handful of gum pieces and gave them to Dao. Dao asked her to chew the gum together. The girl replied, "My smell is always fragrant, so I do not rely on this."

When the girl went out the door, a dog suddenly saw her and bit her to death. It turned out that she was an old otter, and the gum was her excrement. Suddenly Dao felt that she was stinking and dirty.

(*GXSGC*, #249. 428; *TPGJ*, 469. 3862)

22. GUO CHANGSHENG

During the Yuanjia reign period (424–454),[54] the Chao family of Taishan Commandery,[55] whose ancestor was the magistrate of Xiang

52. This tale was credited also to *Zhenyi zhi* 甄異志, likely Dai Zuo's 戴祚 (fl. late fourth century). *Zhenyi zhi* 甄異傳, by *TPGJ* (468. 3861).
53. Yongxing 永興 County; its seat was located west of modern Xiaoshan 蕭山, Zhejiang.
54. *TPYL* (580. 2617b) reads Yongjia 永嘉 (307–312) [of Jin] for Yuanjia.
55. Taishan Commandery, located in modern Tai'an 泰安, Shandong.

County,[56] lived at Jinling.[57] Once, a maid of the family went woodcutting and someone ran after her, and it seemed they were exchanging greetings. Consequently, they had an affair.

The man returned with the maid, lived there, and did not leave. Fearing he would make trouble, whenever night came the Chao family let the maid go outside. They heard him singing and talking with the maid. People in the family, old and young, all heard them. He did not allow anyone to see him. The only one who could see his physical form was the maid. Each time enjoying feast and wine with the maid, he would play a bamboo flute and sing a song. The song went:

This leisurely night is quiet and lonely,
my long flute is loud and clear.
If you want to know who I am,
my surname is Guo and name Changsheng.

(*GXSGC*, #68. 371; *YWLJ*, 44. 794; *TPGJ*, 324. 2574; *TPYL*, 580. 2617b)

23. THE DEMON AT FANGSHAN INN

Ding Hua of Dongyang Commandery went out of the town,[58] lodging at the Fangshan Inn. On the islet by the inn, the Gentleman Cavalier Attendant Liu had just experienced his mother's death, and he returned from the capital where he had buried her.

At night, suddenly a woman introduced herself to Ding Hua, saying, "Little Liu suffers from a sore, and I heard that you can cure it. That is why I have come." Hua asked her to come closer, and he saw that she was sedate and beautiful, followed by several maidens. Hua ordered his servants to prepare sumptuous courses.

---

56. Xiang 相 County, established in Liu Song, was in the area of modern Xuzhou 徐州, Jiangsu.
57. Jinling 晉陵, modern city of Changzhou 常州, Jiangsu.
58. Dongyang 東陽 Commandery was established in Wu of the Three Kingdoms period, and its seat was in modern Jinhua 金華, Zhejiang (Tan Qixiang, *Zhongguo lishi dituji*, 25–26).

When their drinking was at its height, the woman sighed, saying, "Our gathering tonight will no longer let me have the name of chastity." Ding Hua said, "You have great virtue, how could you care about this aged man?" Then the woman asked the maiden to get a *pipa*,[59] and she played it and sang as follows:

I heard of your great fame long ago;
today we meet at Fangshan Pavilion.
Even though your body is decrepit,
still you are delightful to me.

She put the *pipa* on her knee, embraced her head with her arms, and sang:

Though the appearance of this woman is humble,
it is my will to make you my husband.
Tender affection is seen in our pleasant meeting,
wish that our hearts be knotted for thousands of years.

Her voice was sweet and charming—it caused one to swoon with admiration.

Then Ding ordered his servants to turn off the lights, and they expressed their love together. At dawn, the woman suddenly disappeared. The clerks said that there used to be demons in this pavilion.

(*GXSGC*, #225. 418; *TPGJ*, 360. 2855)

24. CHUNYU JIN'S MARRIAGE WITH A WILD CAT GIRL

In the Taiyuan reign period (376–396) of Jin, Chunyu Jin, who lived in front of the Waguan Monastery,[60] was young and pure. When he saw

59. A lutelike four-stringed instrument with pear-shaped sounding box and fretted fingerboard.
60. Waguan 瓦官 Monastery, one of the oldest monasteries in Nanjing, built in the second year of the Xingning 興寧 reign (364) of Eastern Jin.

his guest off to the south of the City of Stone,[61] he met a good-looking girl and liked her, and so he visited her. When their feelings became harmonious, Jin brought her to the northern corner of the city, where they made love and then parted.

They planned another meeting, intending to become husband and wife then. The girl said, "With a husband like you, I would not have any regrets until death. But I have many brothers and my parents are both alive. I should ask my parents."

Then Jin requested the girl's maid to ask her parents, and her parents also nominally promised him. Accordingly the girl ordered the maid to fetch one hundred *jin* of silver and a hundred *pi* of silk to help Jin with the wedding. Over quite a long time, she raised two children.

Chunyu Jin was about to assume the position of Director of the Palace Library. The next day the attendants dealing with carts and horses came to summon him. Carts, horses, as well as musicians were arranged in front of and behind his cart.

A few days later, a hunter passed by and looked for Jin, leading several dozen dogs. The dogs entered abruptly and bit his wife and children. They all became wild cats, and the silk, gold, and silver were merely grass, bones of dead people, and mock strawberries, etc.

(*GXSGC*, #126. 390; *FYZL*, 31. 990)

25. CHEN ADENG

A native of Juzhang County was returning home after visiting the wildness of the eastern suburbs.[62] At dusk, he had still not reached the gate of his own home. Seeing that there was a light by the side of the road, he went to put up for the night.

There was a little girl who did not want to stay together with a man, so she called another girl, her neighbor, to accompany her. At night they played *konghou*, an ancient harp, together.

61. "The City of Stone" was built in the capital of Wu 吳 in the Three Kingdoms period (220–280), and since then it has become Moling 秣陵 (or Jianye 建業) and modern Nanjing 南京.

62. Juzhang 句章 County, modern Ningbo 寧波, Zhejiang.

At dawn the man thanked the girl before leaving, and he asked her name and courtesy name as well. The girl did not reply. Instead, she plucked the strings and sang,

> The unbroken vines from the kudzu,
> one is loose while one is tight.
> If you want to know my name,
> My surname is Chen and name Adeng.[63]

(*GXSGC*, #45. 364–65; *TPYL*, 573. 2588b; *BTSC*, 106. 92a)

---

63. *TPYL* (884. 3928b) credits this tale to *Soushen houji* 搜神後記, which adds the following at the end:

> The next morning he walked beyond the eastern outer wall of the city, where an old lady was selling food in the food store. This man sat there temporarily and told her what he had seen last night. The old lady was startled, saying, "This was my daughter who died recently and was buried outside the outer wall of the town."

TPGJ (316. 2504) erroneously credits this story to *Lingguai ji* 靈怪集, a much later work by Zhang Jian 張薦 (744–804) of the Tang dynasty.

2

A GARDEN OF MARVELS

26. LORD OF MOUNT LU

During the reign period of Sun Quan (r. 222–252),[1] the south sent an official to present a hairpin made out of rhinoceros horn. Passing by Lake Gongting, the official went to the temple of the Lord of Mount Lu to pray for good fortune. The deity sent down an order to request the hairpin, and the hairpin container was just in front of the deity.

The official kowtowed, saying, "This hairpin is intended for the emperor. I have to piteously beg your mercy."

The spirit replied, "Before you enter the City of Stone,[2] it will be returned to you." Thus the official left.

When the official arrived at the City of Stone, a carp three feet long jumped into his boat. The official cut open its belly and obtained the hairpin.

(*GXSGC*, #53. 367; *TPYL*, 688. 3071a & 936. 4160b)

1. Sun Quan 孫權, styled Zhongmou 仲謀, was the founder of the state of Wu 吳 (222–280) during the Three Kingdoms period (220–280).
2. The City of Stone, the capital of Wu. See footnote 61 in chapter 1 for more information.

27. EXCHANGING HEADS AND FACES

Jia Bizhi of Hedong was called Yier in his childhood.[3] Both of these names have been checked against his family genealogy. During the Yixi reign period (405–418), he was an adjutant in the government office of Langye.[4]

One night he dreamed of a man who had an acned face with whiskers, a big nose, and upward-looking eyes. The man asked him, "I admire your appearance, and I want to exchange my head with you. Is this acceptable?"

Bi replied, "Each person has his own head and face. How could one tolerate such an outrage?"

The following night he had the same dream again, and he was disgusted with it. Thus he promised to exchange heads in his dream.

When he got up the next morning, he himself did not realize what had happened. However, people all ran away and hid in surprise, saying, "Where did this man come from?"

Being frightened, the Prince of Langye sent someone to summon the man to have a look. When Bi arrived, the Prince of Langye saw him at a distance, stood up, and went back to the inner court.

Bi did not realize anything abnormal until he found a mirror and looked at himself. Then he returned home. All the members of his family went inside the room in a panic, and women ran away to hide themselves, saying, "Where did this strange man come from?" Bi sat down, spent quite a while telling his family his story, and sent someone to inquire at the prefecture; they then believed him.

Later, he was able to cry with half a face while the other half smiled. His two legs, hands, and mouth each could hold a pen and write at the same time. The meanings of the words were all good. This was truly marvelous. Otherwise, the rest of his life remained the same as before.

(*GXSGC*, #140. 393–94; *YWLJ*, 17. 312; *TPYL*, 364. 1676b; *TPGJ*, 276. 2183 & 360. 2852)

3. For Jia Bizhi 賈弼之, *TPYL* (364. 1676b) and *TPGJ* (276. 2183) read Jia Bi 賈弼. Hedong, see footnote 50 in chapter 1.
4. Langye 琅邪 Commandery was located north of modern Linyi 臨沂 in Shandong. See Tan Qixiang, *Zhongguo lishi dituji*, 3. 51.

28. PREGNANCY IN A DREAM

At the beginning of the Xianhe reign period (326–334) of Jin, Xu Jing had a long trip. He dreamed of sleeping with his wife and she was pregnant. The next year when he returned home, his wife gave birth to a baby as expected. What had happened later was just like what he said.

(*GXSGC*, #85. 377; *TPGJ*, 276. 2182)

29. REPORTING DEATH THROUGH A DREAM

Qin Jia (ca. 130–ca. 170) of Longxi Commandery,[5] styled Shihui, was a talented handsome man.[6] His wife, Xu Shu, was also noted for her talent and beauty.

During the reign of Emperor Huan (147–167), Jia went to the city of Luo as an official under a ministry, and Shu returned to her mother's home. While lying in bed during the day, Shu started to cry; the tears covered her face.

Surprised, her elder sister-in-law asked her for the reason. She replied, "I have just seen Jia [in a dream], and he said himself that he died of an illness in a hotel in Jinxiang. Neither of the two attendants have left. One is keeping vigil beside the coffin while the other is sending a letter to our home. He will arrive at noon."

All of the family were terrified. When the letter arrived later, everything was like what had been told in the dream.

(*GXSGC*, #42. 363; *TPYL*, 400. 1850a)

30. DRY CHOLERA

Zhang Jia of a certain commandery previously had kinship with Cai Mo (281–356), the Minister of Education [of Jin], and he lodged in Cai Mo's

5. *Longxi* 隴西 [commandery] is a traditional designation refering to the area west of Long Mountain, including present-day Tianshui 天水 and Lanzhou 蘭州 in Gansu and Long County in Shanxi.

6. Qin Jia 秦嘉 (courtesy name Shihui 士會) was a poet and official, Gentleman of the Palace Gate, of Eastern Han. His extant poems include the "Zeng fu shi" 贈婦詩. His wife, Xu Shu 徐淑, was also a talented poet.

home.[7] After a short trip of a few nights' duration, he did not return on time.

While Mo was sleeping during the day, he dreamed of Jia, who said to him, "During my short trip, I was suddenly infected with a disease. I suffered from abdominal bloating and was unable to vomit or discharge. After I died, the host put me in a coffin and sent me to the grave."

Facing him, Mo wept in grief.

Jia said further, "My illness is called dry cholera, which of course can be cured. But no one knows the remedy; therefore it caused my death."

Mo asked, "How is it cured?"

Jia replied, "Get a spider, break its legs alive, and swallow it. Then one will be healed."

After Mo awoke, he sent someone to the place Jia had traveled and examined it, and found that he was really dead. He asked the host and found out that the illness and the time all matched the dream.

Later, there were people who were infected with dry cholera; Mo tried the prescription, and thereupon the illness was cured.

(*GXSGC*, #78. 374–75; *TPYL*, 743. 3296a, 948. 4208a; *TPGJ*, 276. 2181)

31. THE TEMPLE OF DENG AI

The Temple of Deng Ai (197–264) [8] was in Jingkou,[9] and onto its ruin a thatched hut was built. Sima Tian (265–420), the General Pacifying

7. Cai Mo 蔡謨, styled Daoming 道明, was Minister of Education of Eastern Jin from 342 but was accused of having neglected his duty and was degraded to a commoner in 350. His biography is found in *Jin shu* 晉書, 77. 2033–41.

8. Deng Ai 鄧艾, styled Shizai 士載, was a general of the Wei State during the Three Kingdoms period (220–280). He was the General Governing the West and governor-general in charge of military affairs in Long-you (Shanxi and Gansu) in 256, but while accompanying Zhong Hui 鐘會 (225–264), the general of Wei, on the expedition against Shu 蜀 (221–263) in 263, he was unjustly implicated in Zhong's attempted rebellion and was executed with his sons. See Chen Shou 陳壽 (223–297), *Sanguo zhi* 三國志, 28. 775–83.

9. Jingkou 京口, present-day city of Zhenjiang 鎮江, Jiangsu.

the North of the Jin,[10] dreamed of an old man who said to him, "I am Mr. Deng. My house fell down and was ruined. Would you please repair it for me?" Later, Tian visited the place. He knew it was the Temple of Deng Ai, and therefore he built a tile-roofed house there for the old man.

During the Long'an reign period (397–402), one day a man had an affair with a girl on the seat of the spirit memorial tablet. A snake came, crawled around them four times, and then left. The family of the girl ran after and found it. They prayed with wine and meat at the temple; thus, the impending trouble was removed.

(*GXSGC*, #60. 369; *TPGJ*, 318. 2521)

32. A MAN FROM EARTHENWARE

A scholar, surnamed Wang, sat in his studio. A man sent a visiting card to meet him, which read "Shu Zhenzhong."[11] After the man had visited and left, Wang suspected that he was not human.

Having searched for the meaning of the name on the visiting slip, he read, "He is a man in the earthenware west of my house."

He asked people to dig there and they truly found a bronze statue more than a foot tall in the earthenware.

(*GXSGC*, #182. 405; *TPYL*, 606. 2728a–b)

33. AN ILLUSION

In the region of Yangzi River and Huai River,[12] there was a woman who was by nature greedy and indulged in fantasy day and night. Once,

10. Sima Tian 司馬恬, styled Yuanyu 元瑜, was a member of the Jin royal house. He has been the General Pacifying the North and the governor of Yanzhou 兗州 and Qingzhou 青州. He also inherited the title of Prince of Qiao 譙.
11. The name Shu Zhenzhong 舒甄仲 consist of seven characters, 予舍西土瓦中人, "a person inside the earthenware west of my residence."
12. The region of the Yangzi 揚子 and Huai 淮 rivers refers to the area between the Hui River and the Yangzi River in Jiangsu and Anhui provinces.

she got drunk. The next morning when she got up, she saw two little boys behind the house who were extremely fresh and clean, like the young officials in the palace. Therefore the woman intended to embrace them in her arms. But suddenly they became brooms. The woman fetched them and put them on the fire.

(*GXSGC*, #230. 419–20; *TPGJ*, 368. 2927)

34. ASHES OF THE EON FIRE

Emperor Wu (r. 140–87 BCE) of the Han dug the Kunming Lake. When they reached the extremely deep place, there was no longer earth, but all black ashes. No one of the emperor's court knew what it was, so they inquired of Dongfang Shuo (154–93 BCE) about it.[13]

Shuo said, "I am stupid, not possessing enough knowledge to know it. You may ask the foreign monk from the west." Since Dongfang Shuo did not know, the emperor felt it would be difficult to get the answer.

During the time of Emperor Ming (58–75) in the Later Han (25–220),[14] a foreign monk came to Luoyang. Someone thought of Dongfang Shuo's words and asked him. The foreigner replied, "The Buddhist sutra says, 'When an eon in the heaven and earth is about to finish, then there is a disastrous fire. These are the remains of an eon (*kalpa*) fire."

Thus people knew that Dongfang Shuo's words were correct.

(*GXSGC*, #262. 433–34; *Wenfang sipu*, 5; *SSJ*, 13. 162)

13. Dongfang Shuo 東方朔, styled Manqian 曼倩, was a noted scholar-official, necromancer, and court jester under Emperor Wu (140–87 BCE) of Han. He was noted for his humor instead of his knowledge. His biography can be found in Sima Qian 司馬遷 (145–86? BCE), *Shiji* 史記 [The Grand Scribe's records], 126. 3205–08; and Ban Gu 班固 (32–92), *Hanshu* 漢書 [History of the Han], 65. 2841–74.

14. "Ming" was added according to *Soushen ji*, 13. 162. Cf. Zheng Wanqing, *Youming lu*, 1. 22–23.

35. FLYING CASH

Huang Xun, a native of Hailing,[15] previously lived alone in poverty.

Once a gust blew scattering cash to his home. The flying cash bumped against his piles of fencing and landed all over the place; Xun picked up all of it.

Thereupon he became extremely wealthy, and his wealth grew to several dozen millions. Consequently, he became famous in the area north of the Yangzi River.

(*GXSGC*, #177. 403; *TPYL*, 836. 3735a, 472. 2166b)

36. FEI DAOSI

In the seventh year of the Yixi reign (405–418), Fei Daosi of Dongyang Commandery took a wife,[16] and they loved each other. When the bride combed her hair, Daosi teasingly drew out her silver hairpin and placed it on the cabinet above the door frame.[17]

(*GXSGC*, #137. 393; *BTSC*, 136. 247b)

37. QIAN CHENG

During the reign period of Sun Quan (r. 222–252), Qian Cheng of Wuxing once lay down for a long daytime nap.[18] While he was unconscious, both sides of his mouth oozed two liters of liquid.

His mother, in fear, called him to wake him. He said, "Just a moment ago I saw an old man who was feeding me with roasted tendon. It is a shame that I still had not finished eating when you woke me up."

---

15. Hailing 海陵 County, present-day Taizhou 泰州, Jiangsu.
16. Dongyang, see footnote 58 in chapter 1.
17. It seems this is a incomplete story, posing a challenge to readers.
18. Wuxing 吳興 County, present-day Huzhou 湖州, Zhejiang. Wuxing Commandery was also in present-day Huzhou.

Cheng was originally weak and thin, but after this happened he became famous for his strength, with his official title reaching Commander of the Mobile Imperial Guards.[19]

(*GXSGC*, #55. 367; *TPYL*, 398. 1840)

38. ZHANG MAODU

When Zhang Maodu (ca. 376–ca. 442) of the Wu Commandery was the Governor of Yizhou,[20] someone suddenly claimed that the court had sentenced Xu Xianzhi (364–426),[21] Fu Liang (374–426),[22] and Xie Hui (390–426) to death.[23] Consequently, this news was widely spread.

Zhang questioned the man, "You rumor maker! On what basis did you say that?" The man replied, "In fact, there was no basis. I said that in a trance." Zhang punished him with a whip, and the news stopped spreading.

Later, however, the news was proved to be correct.[24]

(*GXSGC*, #239. 422; *KYZJ*, 113. 775)

---

19. Translation of Wu'nan du 無難督 (監).
20. Zhang Maodu 張茂度, named Yu 裕, was the Governor of Yizhou 益州 in the first year of the Yuanjia reign (424) of Emperor Wen 文 (r. 424–453) of Song. Wu 吳 Commandery: its seat was in present-day Suzhou. Yizhou covered the area of modern Sichuan and Hanzhong 漢中.
21. Xu Xianzhi 徐羨之, Chief Overseer of the Department of State Affairs, Minister of Education, and Governor of Yangzhou 揚州 of the [Liu] Song. His biography is found in Shen Yue (441–513), *Song shu*, 43.1329–35; Li Yanshou, *Nan shi*, 15.432–35.
22. Fu Liang 傅亮, Director of the Department of State Affairs of the Song. His biography can be found in *Song shu*, 43.1335–41, and *Nan shi.*, 15.441–43.
23. Xie Hui 謝晦, the Governor of Jingzhou of the Song. His biography is found in *Song shu*, 44.1347–62.
24. This was one of the terrible palace coups d'état that occurred frequently throughout the history of imperial China. The original heir selected by Liu Yu (r. 420–422), Emperor Wu 武 of the Song, was his eldest son Yifu 義符, who was only 17 years old when his father passed away. Because Yifu was fond of idling about instead of governing, Xu Xianzhi (Chief Overseer of the Department of State Affairs), Fu Liang (Director of the Department of State

39. DISPELLING ACCUMULATED DISTRESS WITH WINE

Emperor Wu of the Han saw a creature that resembled an ox liver. After entering the earth, it stayed motionless. The emperor asked Dongfang Shuo about it. Shuo replied, "This is the air of accumulated distress. Only wine can dispel distress. Now if you pour wine onto it, it will disappear immediately."

(*GXSGC*, #28. 358; *BTSC*, 148. 324a)

40. YANG HU SUFFERED FROM HEADACHES[25]

Yang Hu (221–278) suffered from headaches, and someone had him treated.[26] Hu said, "On the third day after I was born, my head was facing the northern door. Feeling the wind blow against me, I worried about it very much, but I could not speak. Since the origin of the illness is so long ago, it is impossible to cure."

(*LS*, 11. 189a–b)

41. QIN MIN

To the south of the city of Xiangyang lived Qin Min.[27] By nature he was extremely filial. After his parents died, he wailed with bloody tears for

Affairs), and Xie Hui (Governor of Jingzhou) decided together to dethrone him and enthrone Yilong 義隆 (r. 424–453), the third son of Liu Yu. Only two years after Yilong ascended to the throne (426), however, he executed Xu, Fu, and Xie. See Shen Yue, *Song shu*, 5. 74.

25. This piece was not included in Lu Xun's *Guxiaoshuo gouchen* edition of *Youming lu*. It is added from Zeng Zao, *Lei shuo* [Classified tales], 11.189ab.
26. Yang Hu 羊祜, styled Shuzi 叔子, Jin vice-president of the Imperial Secretariat and governor-general of military affairs in Jingzhou. See *Jin shu* 34. 1013–25.
27. Xiangyang 襄陽, present-day Xiangfan 襄樊, Hubei.
    For *Qin Min* 秦民, *TPYL* reads *Qin Min mu* 秦民墓, "Qin Min's tomb."

three years. Someone chanted the poem "Thick Tarragons" for him.[28] Having heard of its meaning, everyone could not help but weep.

(*GXSGC*, #183. 405; *TPYL*, 616. 2770a)

42. A TURTLEDOVE ENTERS ONE'S ARMS

In Chang'an there was a man surnamed Zhang.[29] During the day, when he was in his room, a turtledove entered, standing on the ground across from his bed. Zhang disliked it. He untied the belt of his shirt and made a vow to the gods, saying, "Turtledove! If you come to bring me calamity, perch on the dust receiver (screen) over the bed; if you come to bring me blessings, enter my arms."

The turtledove flew up and down, but finally entered his arms. He stretched his hand to feel it, but could not touch it. However, he got a golden belt hook there, and he treasured it.

From then on, his sons and grandsons became prosperous.

(*GXSGC*, #35. 360; *CXJ*, 27. 646; *TPYL*, 811. 3604b)

43. CRESCENDOS OF MUSIC AFTER DEATH

Xie Chi, the Governor of Linchuan Commandery of the Jin,[30] heard crescendos of music at night. His older brother Xie Zao said, "Night symbolizes the netherworld. The music is not worth thinking of now. It will appear in your afterlife." When Xie Chi died, he was bestowed the position of Changshui Commandant, and the crescendos of music were added to the funeral.

(*GXSGC*, #155. 398; *TPYL*, 567. 2563a)

---

28. "Liao E" 蓼莪 [Thick tarragons; Mao #202], a poem from the *Book of Poetry* one of the five Confucian classics. It expresses the grief of a man who wanted to repay the favor of his parents yet they had died already. See Legge (1815–1897), trans., *The Book of Poetry*, 350–52.
29. Chang'an 長安, modern Xi'an 西安 in Shanxi.
30. Xie Chi 謝摛, Eastern Jin Governor of Linchuan 臨川 Commandery, modern Fuzhou 福州, Jiangxi.

44. THE MAN OF ANDING

During the time of the Northern Expedition against Yao Hong (387–417),[31] a man from the Anding Commandery,[32] surnamed Wei, returned to his home state, arrived at the capital, and lived in the home of his relatives and friends.

At that time there was social unrest, and a guest from Qi called on him. Wei said, "Even though I can avoid worries [about the disturbance] now, both my body and spirit are tired. I have no strength at all. I had intended to make a bowl of thick soup but could not do it. It is indeed extremely miserable!"

At night, when he was sound asleep, a messenger came and knocked at the door, saying, "The officer is giving you cash."

Startled, Wei immediately went out the door and beheld one thousand cash outside. Furthermore, he saw an official wearing a black silk cap with headdress, holding a tablet, standing with his back toward the door.

Wei called upon his host to meet the official together. By the time his host came, the official had left. Thus Wei fetched the money and used it.

(*GXSGC*, #153. 397; *TPGJ*, 321. 2547–48)

45. THE PORTRAIT IN TAIWU PALACE

During the time under Shi Hu (r. 335–349),[33] the head of one of the portraits of the worthies in the Taiwu Palace suddenly sank into his shoulders.

(*GXSGC*, #90. 378; *TPYL*, 885. 3933a)

---

31. Yao Hong 姚泓 was the last emperor of the Qiang 羌 State, Later Qin 秦. After Later Qin was conquered by Liu Yu, he was delivered to the Jin capital of Jiankang and executed. See his biography in *Jin shu*, 119. 3007.

32. Anding 安定 Commandery, centered around modern Jingchuan 涇川, Gansu. See Tan Qixiang, *Zhongguo lishi dituji*, 4. 55.

33. Shi Hu 石虎, the third emperor of the Later Zhao 趙 (328–351).

46. THE LORD OF THE RIVER

Emperor Xiaowu of Jin (r. 373–396) was once enjoying the cool under the northern window of the palace,[34] when he saw a soaked man in a white kerchief and yellow silk shirt. The man introduced himself, "I'm the deity of the Hualin Garden pool, named Lord of the River. Should you treat me kindly, I will bless you."

At that time the emperor was drunk, and he drew the knife that he often wore at his waist and threw it at the deity. The knife hit the air and met nothing.

The deity said in anger, "You did not receive me as a good man, I should let you know the reason for what is happening!"[35]

After living for a short while longer, the emperor suddenly passed away. Everyone said that it was the spirit who caused his death.

(*GXSGC*, #134. 392; *TPYL*, 882. 3919b; *TPGJ*, 294. 2343–44)

47. A COMET

At the end of the Taiyuan reign of the Jin (376–396), a comet was seen. Emperor Xiaowu disliked it immensely.

That evening, when the emperor was drinking in the Hualin Garden, he raised a cup to toast the star, saying, "Comet, I urge you to drink a cup of wine. Even since ancient times, when has there been a Son of Heaven who lived for ten thousand years?"

While grabbing a cup to drink together with the star, the emperor passed away.

(*GXSGC*, #132. 392; *KYZJ*, 88. 642)

34. Emperor Xiaowu 孝武 of Jin, Sima Yao 司馬曜, was the ninth emperor of Eastern Jin.

35. Zheng Wanqing (*Youming lu* 47) mistakenly punctuates 令知所以。居少時而暴崩 for 令知所以居。少時而暴崩.

48. ZHOU CHAO'S WIFE

At the beginning of the [Liu] Song, Zhou Chao of Yixing Commandery was the commander under Xie Hui (390–426) at Jiangling.[36] His wife, Nee Xu, was at home. At night, from a distance, she saw a house in which there was a light, the head of a dead person was on the ground, and blood was pouring. She was startled, but the house vanished right then. Later, Zhou Chao was sentenced to death.[37]

(*GXSGC*, #233. 420; *TPYL*, 885. 3933a; *TPGJ*, 141. 1015–16)

49. YUE XIA

In the ninth year of the Yuanjia reign (424–453), Yue Xia of Nanyang was once sitting inside, when he heard someone in the air urgently calling for him and his wife, not ceasing until midnight. He was greatly startled and terrified.

Several days later, when his wife was returning from the backyard, all her clothes were suddenly drenched in blood.

Less than a month later, both Yue Xia and his wife died.

(*GXSGC*, #243. 423; *TPYL*, 885. 3933b; *TPGJ*, 360. 2856)

50. A COFFIN CART

During the Yuanjia reign, Wang Zhi of Taiyuan was initially appointed the Governor of Jiaozhou.[38] When he went out in a cart, he heard a clang in front of it and saw a coffin cart on the way; yet the rest of the people could not see it. After arriving at Jingzhou, he died immediately.[39]

(*GXSGC*, #244. 423; *TPGJ*, 360. 2856–57)

---

36. At that time, Xie Hui was the governor of Jingzhou; its seat was Jiangling (modern Jingzhou). See footnote 23 in this chapter for Xie's bibliographical information.
37. In the third year of the Yuanjia reign (426), Emperor Wen of Song launched an expedition against Xie Hui. Both Xie Hui and Zhou Chao 周超 were sentenced to death.
38. Jiaozhou 交州, modern Guangdong and Guangxi.
39. Zheng Wanqing, *Youming lu* (50) mistakes *wang* (died) for *zhi* (stop).

51. MEAT BECOMES FROGS

Sima Xiuzhi (d. 417) once sent civil and military officials along with more than several thousand people to pick up his family.[40] When they reached Nanjun it was windy, so they anchored their boats and went on land to cut firewood. Seeing that there was several hundred *jin* of meat, they cut and took some away. After returning, they cooked the meat in a pot. When the water was about to become hot, all the meat became several thousand frogs.

(*GXSGC*, #151. 396–97; *BTSC*, 145. 306b–07a)

52. AN ABNORMAL TURTLE

During the Yixi reign period (405–418) of the Jin, when Fan Yin governed the Nankang Commandery,[41] a clerk of Gan County told him the following.

Previously, when the clerk entered the mountain to cut wood for fuel, he got two turtles, each as big as a two-inch plate. The firewood he cut was still not enough, when he saw two trees growing side by side. Thus the clerk put the turtles on their sides between the two trees and continued cutting firewood. When he had moved far away from the turtles, it began to rain. He did not feel like fetching them again.

Twenty years later, the clerk reentered the mountain. He saw the shell of one turtle had dried, but the other was still alive. The middle part of its body between the trees was around four inches while the two ends were about one foot, resembling the shape of a saddle.

(*GXSGC*, #138. 393; Zheng, *YML*, 3. 62; *TPGJ*, 472. 3885–86)

40. Sima Xiuzhi 司馬休之 was the governor of Jingzhou at the end of Eastern Jin. In the eleventh year of the Yixi reign (415), Liu Yu attacked Jingzhou; Xiuzhi was defeated and fled to Later Qin. When Liu Yu exterminated Later Qin, Xiuzhi died on his way to Wei.

41. Nankang 南康 Commandery; its seat was in Gan 贛 County, modern Ganzhou 贛州, Jiangxi.

53. ZHUGE ZHANGMIN

After Zhuge Zhangmin (d. 317) became wealthy and noble,[42] within approximately a month, or several dozen days, he woke up startled at night and jumped around as if battling someone.

Once staying overnight with him, Mao Xiuzhi was stunned at this.[43] Mao could not understand his behavior but watched him for a long while.

Zhangmin told him, "This creature is extremely strong. Nobody could control it except me."

Mao asked, "What creature was it?"

Zhangmin said, "I only saw a fairly black creature. Its arms and feet could not be clearly distinguished. Recently it came on several nights, and I fought with it. Naturally, I have been startled and terrified."

In the house, snake heads were seen at the ends of all the pillars and rafters. Zhangmin ordered some people to tie knives onto sticks to cut them; the snake heads disappeared when the blade came near yet emerged again when the knife moved away.

Finally, they wrapped all the ends of the pillars and rafters with paper, but it seemed that something was rustling inside the paper, resembling the sound of crawling.

(*GXSGC*, #150. 396; *TPYL*, 885. 3933b)

54. THE BLACK OX

When Huan Xuan (369–404) lived at the National Residence of Nanjun,[44] he went out to call on Yin [Zhongkan], the Governor of Jingzhou.[45] At

---

42. Zhuge Zhangmin 諸葛長民 was an impoatant general of Eastern Jin and the governor of Qingzhou 青州 and Yuzhou 豫州. He joined Liu Yu's expedition against Huan Xuan 桓玄 (369–404) but was killed by Liu in the ninth year of Yixi 義熙 (413).
43. Mao Xiuzhi was the Commander Pacifying the West of the Liu Song.
44. Huan Xuan was the son of Huan Wen (312–373), the notorious usurper of the Jin. He was enfeoffed the Duke of Nanjun 南郡.
45. *TPGJ* reads 晉商仲堪曾從桓玄行 (Shang Zhongkan of Jin once traveled along with Huan Xuan).

Huxue he met an old man with a bizarre appearance who drove a black ox. Then Huan exchanged the horse he rode for the ox.[46] On the back of the ox he reached Lingling Brook, when all of a sudden the ox ran exceptionally fast.[47] Therefore he stopped to water it. The ox entered the river directly and did not come out. Huan sent people to guard the river for several days, but the ox had disappeared.[48]

(*GXSGC*, #119. 387; *TPYL*, 900. 3995a–b; *TPGJ*, 360. 2850)

55. XI HUI

At the beginning of the Long'an reign (397–402) of Emperor An, inside the home of Xi Hui (d. 398),[49] a native of Gaoping and the Governor of Yongzhou,[50] a creature resembling a lizard suddenly appeared. Each time it came, it would knock at the door first; then there would be several of them, and the lights would be extinguished. Xi's sons and daughters, old and young, were all seized by terror. When they told Xi Hui about this, he was incredulous. But in a short while the creature came again.

In the second year of the Long'an reign, Xi Hui had a different point of view on Yin Zhongkan's scheme,[51] and he set forth to the capital. On the way, he was killed along with his sons.

(*GXSGC*, #143. 394–95; *TPGJ*, 360. 2851)

---

46. *TPGJ* reads 堪即以所乘牛易而取之 (Right then Kan replaced it with his ox).
47. For 至寧陵駛非常, *TPGJ* reads 至寧陵溪，牛忽駿駛非常. Here the rendition follows *TPGJ*.
48. For the last sentence, *TPGJ* reads 堪心以為怪，未幾玄敗，堪亦被誅戮焉 (Kan felt it was strange. Soon afterward Xuan was defeated and Kan was also excecuted).
49. Xi Hui 郗恢, styled Daoyin 道胤, was Governor of Yongzhou 雍州 in Eastern Jin.
50. Yongzhou 雍州, eastablished by Emperor Xiaowu (r. 372–396) of Eastern Jin at Xiangyang 襄陽, modern Xiangfan in Hubei.
51. Yin Zhongkan, the Governor of Jingzhou. He opposed the government of Sima Daozi 司馬道子 (364–403) as the regent and planned to attack the capital with Wang Gong 王恭, Governor of Qingzhou and Yanzhou 兗州, and Huan Xuan, Governor of Guangzhou 廣州. Xi Hui disagreed with them.

56. THE TRANSFORMATION OF A WHITE DOG

When Wang Zhongwen was the Assistant Magistrate of the Henan Commandery,[52] he lived in Goushi County.[53] Returning at night one day, he passed by a big marsh. Glancing back, he saw a white dog behind his cart. It was lovely, so he intended to call and take it.

All of a sudden, the dog transformed into the shape of a human being, resembling the deity statue used in funerals. It sometimes walked forward and sometimes reversed, as if intending to step onto his cart.

Zhongwen was in a great panic. When he had run to his residence and grabbed a torch to look, it had already disappeared.

More than a month later Zhongwen was on the path with his servant when he saw the dog again. Both Zhongwen and his servant fell prostrate and died.

(*GXSGC*, #160. 399; *TPGJ*, 141. 1014–15)

57. THE MESSENGER OF HEAVEN

When Liu Bin was in the Wu Commandery as governor,[54] by riding the wind and rain at night, a woman of Lou County suddenly arrived at the seat of the commandery in a trance.[55] She felt that she had left home for a little while, which was only long enough to cook a meal, and her clothes were not wet at all.

At dawn she was on top of the door of Liu's residence, requesting to converse by saying, "I am the messenger of Heaven. As governor, it is proper for you to get up and meet me, then you shall become extremely

52. Henan 河南 Commandery; its seat was in Luoyang 洛陽.

53. Goushi 緱氏 County belonged to Henan Commandery; its seat was in modern Yanshi, Henan.

54. Liu Bin 劉斌 was one of the associates of Liu Yikang 劉義康 (409–451), the Prince of Pengcheng 彭城 of the [Liu] Song. In the thirteenth year of Yuanjia (436) he was appointed the governor of Wu 吳 Commandery (seat in present-day Suzhou 蘇州, Jingsu).

55. Lou 婁 County; its seat was in present-day Kunshan 昆山, Jiangsu.

rich and noble; otherwise, calamities will certainly befall you." Liu asked where she came from, but she herself did not know.

About twenty days later, Liu was truly put to death.[56]

(*GXSGC*, #193. 408; *TPYL*, 885. 3933b; *TPGJ*, 360. 2856)

58. THE MONSTER IN YU JIN'S HOME

The mother of Yu Jin, a native of Xinye County,[57] was ill. While the three brothers were taking care of their sick mother, suddenly they heard the strange sound of dog fighting coming from the front of the bed. All of their family came to look, yet no dogs were seen. They only saw the head of a dead person on the ground, blood still on it, and the two eyes still blinking.

The family was seized with terror. They took the head out at night and buried it in the backyard.

The next morning when they went to look, the head had come out and was above ground again, with the two eyes still blinking.

They buried it again, but it surfaced again the next morning. Then they put a brick under the head and asked someone to bury it. It did not rise anymore.

A few days later, their mother passed away.

(*GXSGC*, #224. 418; *TPGJ*, 360. 2849–50)

59. GE ZUO AVERTED THE ABNORMAL

Ge Zuo was the Governor of Hengyang under the Wu (222–280).[58] Within the territory of his commandery there was a huge raft stretched across the river, which could cause demonic and abnormal phenomena. The commoners established a temple for it. When travelers prayed and

56. When Emperor Wen suspected Yikang in 440, as Yikang's associate Liu Bin was put to death.

57. Xinye 新野 County, modern Xinye, Henan.

58. Hengyang 衡陽 Commandery, the area west of modern Changsha 長沙, Hunan (Tan Qixiang, *Zhongguo lishi dituji*, 3. 33–34).

offered sacrifice, the raft sank into the water; otherwise, the raft would float up and thus damage the boat.

Ge Zuo was about to resign from his official position, so he gathered many axmen and was going to remove the burden of the people. During the night before the planned date of destroying the raft, voices of people in the river like the sound of roaring waves were heard. When Zuo and the axmen went to look, the raft had been moved. It drifted along the river for several *li* and stopped at a bend.

Since then there have never been disasters of boats capsizing or sinking. The people of Hengyang erected a stone tablet in honor of Ge Zuo, which reads, "Averting the abnormal by your upright virtue [instead of prayer], the divine wood was removed."

(*GXSGC*, #56. 368; *TPGJ*, 293. 2331)

60. A GIFT OF DATES

Wang Zhongde (d. 438) of Taiyuan experienced chaos when he was a child.[59] To avoid foreign robbers, he lay in the grass without eating a single grain for three days. Suddenly, someone stroked his head and called him, saying, "You may get up to eat dates." Then Wang awoke. In a glance he saw a child four feet long, who disappeared immediately. There was a small bag of dried dates in front of him. After eating the dates, he regained his strength a little, and then stood up.

(*GXSGC*, #201. 409; *TPYL*, 965. 4282)

61. THE WOODEN STATUE SHOOTS AN ARROW

When Sun En raised the rebellion (399–402),[60] Wuxing was in turmoil.[61] To seek refuge, a man suddenly entered the temple of Marquis

59. Wang Zhongde 王仲德, named Wang Yi 王懿, was General Governing the North during the Yuanjia reign of Liu Song. His biography is in *Song shu*, 46. 1390–93.

60. The Sun En 孫恩 Rebellion was a religious-led antigovernment movement that occurred in 399–402. Sun believed in Wudou mi 五斗米 [Five-bushel millet] Daoism.

61. Wuxing, see footnote 18 above in this chapter.

Jiang.[62] As soon as he came through the door, the wooden statue [of Marquis Jiang] shot an arrow at him and he died immediately. All the travelers and temple guards witnessed this scene.

(*GXSGC*, #149, 396; *FYZL*, 6. 203; *TPGJ*, 293. 2330–31)

62. HAN GUI

Han Gui of Guangling,[63] styled Xingyan, battled Chen Min's younger brother at Xunyang when Chen Min became a rebel.[64]

After returning to his camp, he was about to dismount from his horse when he felt that his whip seemed heavier. He saw a green silk bag, inside which was a short letter, attached to the tip of the whip, yet nobody knew where it had come from.

He opened and looked at it. It was the *Sutra of Spells by Buddha*, written on aged paper,[65] which has been heard frequently in the world.

(*GXSGC*, #173. 402; *TPYL*, 359. 1653b & 704. 3142a)

63. ZHAO LIANG

Zhao Liang of Henan went to Chang'an together with scholar Zhu, his fellow townsman. When they reached the territory of Xin'an,[66] they found it constantly raining.

Having exhausted their provisions, they said to each other, "Where can we get good food?"

---

62. The temple of Jiang Ziwen 蔣子文, Commandant of Moling 秣陵 (modern Nanjing) 尉 at the end of Eastern Han. For how Jiang became a deity, see *SSJ*, 5. 57–60, and DeWoskin and Crump, Jr., *In Search of the Supernatural*, 5. 53–6.
63. For Gui 晷, *TPYL* (704. 3142a) reads Lue 略. Guangling 廣陵, present-day Yangzhou 揚州, Jiangsu.
64. Chen Min 陳敏 occupied the Wu and Yue 越 during the reign of Emperor Hui 惠 (290–306) of Jin. Xunyang 尋陽, administrative seat Chaisang 柴桑, was southwest of present-day Jiujiang 九江, Jiangxi.
65. Translation of "gu guzhi Fo Shenzhou jing" 故穀紙佛神咒經.
66. The three characters, Ji Xin'an 及新安 (west of Luoyang), are added according to *BTSC* 142.

Within a moment, a cooked meal with soup appeared before them. Both of them were astonished and dared not eat. Then a human voice said, "Just eat. Don't be suspicious."

The next morning, the two men said again, "Where will we get good food once more?" Immediately, a nice meal appeared before them again.

Consequently, they arrived at Chang'an, and no calamities befell them.

(*GXSGC*, #167. 401; *TPYL*, 849. 3796b; *BTSC*, 142. 292a)

64. DRAGON PEARL[67]

During the Han dynasty, in the city of Luoyang there was a cave. Its depth was unfathomable. A woman who harbored murderous intention said to her husband, "I have never seen this cave." Even though it was against his own inclination, her husband accompanied her to see it. As soon as they arrived, the woman pushed him down into the cave, and after quite a long while he reached the bottom. The woman later threw food into the cave, seemingly offering sacrifice to him.

While suddenly falling, the man was in a trance. After a long time, he regained consciousness. He got the food and ate it, so his strength grew a bit.

Being flustered, he searched for paths and found another cave, and he crawled forward to approach and enter it. The path in the cave was rugged and zigzagged. After he had walked several *li,* it became a bit brighter. Consequently, he found broad and flat ground.

After walking more than one hundred *li*, he felt what he stepped on was dust, and smelled the fragrance of round-grained nonglutinous rice. He ate the rice, which was fragrant and delicious, not merely killing the hunger. So he packed some of the rice as his provisions, and walked along in the cave eating this food.

When the cave came to an end, he passed a path filled with a mudlike substance, the smell of which resembled the dust he had encountered

67. This is another story of traveling to the land of immortals. The marvels in the immortal land here are not beautiful fairy maidens, but rare treasures like the dragon saliva and dragon pearl.

previously. Again he got some of it and left. He walked very far, and the mileage was hard to clearly count. He constantly walked toward the direction that was bright and broad.

When he had eaten all that he brought with him, he reached a big city. The city walls were built in good order; the palaces were magnificent; the terraces, pavilions, and residences were all decorated with gold foil. Though there was no sun or moon, they were brighter than the natural light from the three sources of light [the sun, the moon, and the stars]. The people there were all thirty feet tall. They wore silk garments and played unique music, which was never heard in this world.

Then the man pleaded [for food] sadly. A tall man asked him to go forward. Following the order, he walked ahead, and passed nine palaces that were exactly the same. When he arrived at the last palace, he was suffering from hunger.

The tall man pointed to a huge cypress tree, which was about one hundred arm spans around, in the yard. Under the tree was a goat. He was asked to kneel down to stroke the goat's beard. He first obtained a pearl, and the tall man grabbed it. The pearl he got when he stroked the goat's beard for the second time was grabbed again by the tall man. When he got the third one during the subsequent stroke, the tall man asked him to eat it himself. Then he was able to cure his hunger.

He asked the names of the nine palaces, pleading to stay there and not leave. The tall man replied, "Our ruler said that you cannot stay here. After returning home, you may ask Zhang Hua (232–300),[68] who should be familiar with this place." The man then continued walking along the cave, and consequently he was able to come out in Jiaozhou.[69]

Six to seven years after his return, he came back to Luo. He visited Zhang Hua and showed him the two items he had obtained. Hua said, "The substance like dust was saliva of the Yellow River dragon, the

68. Zhang Hua 張華 was the Minister of Works of the Jin and the author of *Bowu zhi* 博物志 [A treatise on curiosities]. He was considered the most knowledgable in his time.

69. Jiaozhou, see footnote 38 above in this chapter.

mud was mud from Kun Mountain,[70] and the immortal at the nine palaces is called the Grand Master of Nine Palaces. The goat was a dimwitted dragon. The first pearl you got enables one to live as long as heaven and earth if he or she eats it, the second is able to prolong one's life span, and the third one may be eaten just as food."

(*GXSGC*, #62. 369–70; *FYZL*, 31. 966–67; *TPYL*, 803. 3567b & 920. 4004a–b; *TPGJ*, 197. 1476; and *SLFZ*, 9. 191)

65. THE MIANYUAN POOL

At the end of Jin, Huang Zu waited upon his parents with sincerest filiality.[71] When his mother was critically ill, he greeted and kowtowed to guests in the yard. In a short while, the Milky Way in the sky was seen broad and bright. An old man, carrying a child and holding a suitcase, announced his own arrival and offered two pills of medication for his mother to take. Suddenly her illnesswas gone. Accordingly, the old man stayed and lodged there.

During the night, five-colored clouds above the office touched the sky, and the sound of a zither and songs were clear and beautiful. Huang Zu went to see the old man and found him sitting in a square tent. At each of the four corners and the top of the tent there was a goose-egg shaped big pearl, dazzling with bright luster. The old man said, "In the third month of the year, you may come through the Yellow River."[72]

While traveling at the appointed time, Huang Zu saw a gate entitled "Gate of Goodness and Good Fortune." Inside it was a pool called Mianyuan Pool, in which lotus leaves as big as carriage wheels floated.

(*GXSGC*, #154. 397; *TPYL*, 699. 3120b & 999. 4420a)

---

70. Kun 昆 Mountain refers to Kunlun 崑崙 Mountain. Legend has it that the goddess of Kunlun is Queen Mother of the West.

71. For Jin mo Huang Zu 晉末黃祖, *TPYL* (699. 3120b) reads Jin Zhu Huangzu 晉朱黃祖.

72. Chinese people believed that the source of the Yellow River was connected to the Milky Way in Heaven.

66. CANDY FROM THE IMMORTAL

During the Taiyuan reign (376–396) period of Eastern Jin, Wang Yin, Zu Anguo, Zhang Xian, and others traveled by boat. They met an immortal who granted them three lumps of candy, which were as large as the *bilun* coin and two *fen* in thickness.[73]

(*GXSGC*, #130, 391; *TPYL*, 852. 3805a)

67. WHITE-HAIRED OLD MAN

During the Taiyuan reign of the Jin dynasty, when Gao Heng was the Governor of Wei Commandery,[74] he garrisoned in the City of Stone.[75] His grandson Yazhi was in the horse stable, saying that a deity had come down.

The deity, who called himself "White-Haired Old Man," walked with a radiant stick that illuminated the whole room. Together with Yazhi, he lifted his body lightly and walked on the air. They arrived in Jingkou at dark and returned at dawn.

Later, Yazhi and his father were wiped out by Huan Xuan.[76]

(*GXSGC*, #127, 390; *TPGJ*, 294. 2341)

68. LORD OF THE NORTHERN DIPPER

In the period of Wu Kingdom (222–280), there lived an old woman who had once "died" of an illness at the age of nine. She died in the early

73. *Bilun* 比輪 was a kind of round coin.

74. Gao Heng 高衡 was a general of Eastern Jin and Governor of Wei Commandery. In Western Jin the seat of Wei 魏 Commandery was located at Ye 鄴, modern Linzhang 臨漳 County, Henan. During Eastern Jin, Wei Commandery was temporarily established at Xiangyang 襄陽 instead of Jianye (as depicted here).

75. The City of Stone, see footnote 61 in chapter 1.

76. As Zheng Wangqing (*Youming lu*, 154) notices, this ending differs from the depiction in *Jin shu* (84. 2192), which reads, [劉敬宜] 與廣陵相高雅之具奔慕容超 . . . 旬日而玄敗 ([Liu Jingyi] and Gao Yazhi, the Magistrate of Guangling, both fled to Murong Chao to seek shelter. . . . About ten days later, Xun was defeated).

morning and revived in the evening. She said that she had seen an old woman who held her by the arm and flew to an audience with the Lord of the Northern Dipper. There was a dog as big as a lion, with deep eyes, crouching inside the balustrade of the well. The old woman told her that it was the dog of the Lord of Heaven.

(*GXSGC*, #57. 368; *SLFZ*, 8. 154)

69. MASTER CHEN XIANG

Master Chen Xiang was a native of Wucheng County, Wuxing Commandery.[77] He first saw the Buddhist sutras, and consequently he learned the Daoist arts of ascending the clouds. When he was in a studio of this human world, he heard the unique music that was clear and far-reaching and smelled the wonderful sweet fragrance.

(*GXSGC*, #100. 382; *FYZL*, 36. 1155)

70. A MAN TRANSFORMS INTO A HERON

A Daoist priest of Eastern Ba Commandery,[78] whose name has been forgotten, strived constantly to serve the Way. One day, he entered his room to burn incense, when the wind came and it began to rain. His family saw a white heron emerging from the room. When the rain stopped, the Daoist priest had disappeared.

(*GXSGC*, #196. 408; *TPYL*, 925. 4109b)

77. Chen Xiangzi 陳相子, "Master Chen Xiang," is not found in other texts. Wucheng 烏程 County (modern Huzhou, Zhejiang)was the seat of Wuxing 吳興 Commandery.

78. Badong 巴東 Commandery, administrative seat in modern Fengjie 奉節, Sichuan.

3

THE SPECTACLE OF MONSTERS

71. RETURNING SHOES

In the first year of the Taining reign (323–325) of the Jin, a man of Yuhang surnamed Wang—his forename has been forgotten[1]—went to a first-class hotel. When passing by a Buddhist temple, he entered it to beg for good fortune. After leaving, he noticed he had lost his shoes.

Since he had already walked five or six *li*, he did not feel like going back again to fetch them. But a person in white came after him, saying, "My superior sent me to return these to you." The person then transformed into a swan and flew into the field.

(*GXSGC*, #83. 376; *TPYL*, 697. 3111a)

72. THE MAIDSERVANT PINA

The maidservant of Wei Qianzu of Shangyu County,[2] called Pina, was beautiful. Xu Mi liked her. Then a rat showed up with Pina's appearance, approached Mi, and secretly slept with him. In doubt, Mi stroked her four limbs with his hands, and he felt them become smaller and smaller. Then the girl changed into a rat and fled.

(*GXSGC*, #228. 419; *TPGJ*, 440. 3588)

1. Yuhang, see footnote 14 in chapter 1.
2. Shangyu 上虞 County, present-day Shangyu in Zhejiang.

73. STRING MUSIC AND SONGS UNDER THE RIVER

Emperor Wu of the Han feasted with the entire body of his ministers in the Endless Palace.[3] He was about to eat broomcorn millet meat soup when he heard someone say, "This old vassal would like to appeal at the risk of his life." Yet his physical form was not seen. After searching for quite a while, the emperor saw an old man eight to nine inches tall on the roofbeam. His face was red and wrinkled, and his beard and hair were hoary white. Walking with a stick and a bent back, he looked extremely old.

The emperor asked him, "What is your surname? Where do you live? What are you suffering that you come to appeal to me?"

The old man came down along a pillar, put down his stick, kowtowed to the emperor with his head to the ground, yet kept silent without speaking a word. Then he lifted his head to look around the room, lowered his head to point at the emperor's feet, and suddenly disappeared.

Seized by shock and fear, the emperor did not know what to do. He said to himself, *Dongfang Shuo must know of him*.[4] Thus he summoned Dongfang Shuo and told him what had happened.

Shuo said, "His name is Zao, the spirit of rivers and woods. In the summer he dwells in the deep forest, and in the winter he dives in the deep river. Your majesty frequently built palaces and houses by cutting down what he takes as residence. For this reason he came to appeal, and that is all. That he lifts his head to look around the room and lowers his head to point to your feet indicates 'This is enough'; he hopes that Your Majesty's palaces and rooms are enough from now on."[5] The emperor was touched, and thereupon he stopped palace construction.

Later, when the emperor went on an inspection tour to the Huzi River,[6] he heard string music and songs coming from the bottom of

3. *Yu qunchen* 與群臣, "with the entire body of his ministers," was added based on *BTSC* (144. 305a) and *TPYL* (886. 3837a). *Weiyang gong* 未央宮, "Endless Palace," was a palace of the Han located at modern Xi'an, Shanxi.
4. Dongfang Shuo, see footnote 13 in chapter 2.
5. In Chinese the graph *zu* 足 means "foot" and "enough" as well.
6. Huzi 瓠子 River is in Puyang 濮陽 County, Henan.

the river. The old man who had been on the beam and several teenagers appeared in red garments and white belts with extremely bright ribbon. All of them were eight or nine inches in height. One of them, a bit more than one foot tall, came out by lightly walking on the surface of the water, his clothing not wet at all. Some of them carried musical instruments.

The emperor had just started eating, but he stopped for this and asked them to sit in a row in front of the dining table.

The emperor asked, "I heard someone playing music under the water. Was that for me?"

The old man replied, "Previously this old vassal appealed at the risk of his life. Luckily, because of Your Majesty's favor, which is comparable to the favor of heaven and earth, the axmen were stopped immediately, and we were able to keep our residences intact. Being overjoyed, we therefore privately celebrated with music ourselves."

The emperor asked, "Could you please play music for me?"

"We especially brought musical instruments, how would we dare not to play?" was the answer. The tallest man then played strings music while singing, and the song went,

> The virtuous Heaven and Earth sent down a message that was
> most human;
> taking pity on souls in the netherworld, they stopped the axmen.
> Having kept our cavernous residences which shelter our bodies,
> we wish you live ten thousand years, the Son of Heaven!

The volume of the song was not different from that of human beings. It was clear and loud, circling the beam for a long time. Furthermore, two people played music with a vertical bamboo flute and a zither. The sound of their playing matched well and their tones were harmonious.

Delighted, the emperor raised a cup and toasted them: "This unworthy man is not good enough to accept your kind offering."

The old man and others all stood up to kowtow and receive cups of wine. Each of them drank several liters, yet none was drunk.

The old man presented the emperor with a purple spiral shell, inside which there was a substance of the consistency and appearance of ox fat.

The emperor asked, "I'm not knowledgeable, and do not know what it is."

The old man replied, "Dongfang Shuo knows it."

The emperor said, "You may send me some more precious and unique things."

The old man looked back and asked for the treasure of the cave to be fetched. Receiving the order, a man dove to the bottom of the deep pool and returned in moments. He brought back a large pearl, several inches in diameter, with a brightness matchless in this world. The emperor enjoyed playing with it very much. The old man and the others, however, suddenly disappeared.

The emperor asked Shuo, "What is the substance inside the purple spiral shell?"

Shuo replied, "It is the marrow of river dragons, which makes one retain good skin color when one puts it on his or her face; in addition, if a pregnant woman uses it, her delivery would certainly be easy."

By chance there was a woman who was suffering a difficult delivery. They tried the marrow on her, and it had a divine effect. The emperor put it on his face, which then became more lustrous.

The emperor asked again, "Why is this pearl called a cave pearl?" Shuo replied, "At the bottom of the river there is a cave, several hundred *zhang* deep. Inside it there is a red clam that produces pearls. Therefore it is called a cave pearl."

The emperor not only deeply admired the story but also was convinced by Shuo's unique knowledge.

(*GXSGC*, #31. 358–60; *TPGJ*, 118. 822–23; *TPYL*, 886. 3937a; *YWLJ*, 84. 1438; & *BTSC*, 144. 305a)

74. A BLEEDING BOARD

In the Yixi reign period, on the Nie Lake of Jiangsheng County,[7] a board appeared unexpectedly. It was several feet wide, more than twenty feet long, and stayed constantly on the river. The water chestnut pickers and

7. Jiangsheng 江乘 County; its administrative seat was in modern Gourong 句容, Jiangxi.

fishermen used it to cross the river themselves. Later, when several people rode on it entering the lake, someone tried to cut it and blood oozed from it. Subsequently, the board sank and several people were drowned.

(*GXSGC*, #139. 393; *TPYL*, 767. 3403a)

75. STONE MIRRORS

By the Gongting Lake and next to the mountain[8] there were several stones. Each was shaped like a mirror, and so bright that people's faces could be reflected; thus they were called stone mirrors.

Later, when a traveler passed by, he singed one of them with fire. As a result, it was no longer bright, and the man became blind.

(*GXSGC*, #17. 357–58; *TPYL*, 717. 3179b)

76. A DOG DEMON

A year after Wen Jinglin of Taiyuan,[9] director of the palace library of Jin, had died, his wife, Nee Huan,[10] unexpectedly saw him returning. They stayed and slept together, yet he was reluctant to see men. When the son of his older brother came to see him, he opened the window slightly, exposing his face to meet the boy. Later he exposed his real shape while drunk; it turned out that he was the yellow dog of the neighbor. Then he was killed.

(*GXSGC*, #159. 398–99; *TPGJ*, 438. 3564)

---

8. Gongting 宮亭 Lake is part of Poyang 鄱陽 Lake in Jiangxi, so named because of the Gongting Temple at the foot of Mount Lu 廬山.
9. Taiyuan 太原 Commandery, western part of modern Shanxi 山西 during Western Jin. Its administrative seat was present-day Jinyang 晉陽. See Tan Qixiang, *Zhongguo lishi dituji*, 3. 39–40.
10. For Huan 桓, *GXSGC* mistakes it as Bo 柏.

77. A COCK SPIRIT

In the Dai Commandery,[11] there was an inn that was often haunted and could not be lodged in. Once a few strong and brave young scholars walked and sang along the street, intending to stop and lodge there. The clerk of the hotel tried to stop them. The young men said, "We ourselves can dispel this." So they lodged and ate at the inn.

At night, a ghost appeared playing a five-holed flute with one hand, seemingly almost unable to hold the flute. The young men became impatient; they laughed, saying, "You have only one hand. How can you cover all the holes? Let us play it for you." The ghost said, "You think I lack fingers?" Then it stretched out its other hand, which had several dozen fingers.

The young men knew that the ghost could be attacked; thereupon they drew their swords to cut it, and they got an old cock, its followers all chicks.

(*GXSGC*, #181. 405; *TPGJ*, 461. 3784; *TPYL*, 580. 2617b)

78. THE GIRL IN FUNERAL GARMENTS

In the Jianwu period of Jin (317–318), Feng Fa of Shan County was transporting his goods.[12] Having lodged by a reed dyke at night, he saw a short, white-skinned girl in funeral garments, asking for a free ride.

The next morning, when the boat was about to set off, the girl said she would go shortly to fetch her luggage. After she left, Fa lost one bolt of silk. The girl brought two bunches of hay and placed them in the boat. Something similar occurred more than ten times, and he lost ten bolts of silk.

Fa suspected that she was not human, so he tied up her feet. The girl said, "Your silk is in the grass over there." Then she transformed into a big egret. Fa boiled it and ate it. Its meat was not very delicious.

(*GXSGC*, #79. 375; *TPGJ*, 462. 3791)

---

11. Dai Commandery 代郡, the area from Yanggao 陽高, Shanxi, to Wei 蔚 County, Hebei. Its administrative seat was at modern Wei County, Hebei.
12. Shan 剡 county, see footnote 2 in chapter 1.

79. A BAT

At the beginning of the [Liu] Song dynasty, in Huainan Commandery a creature kept removing people's chignons.[13] The governor, Zhu Dan, said, "I know what the creature is now." He then purchased a lot of gum and smeared it over the walls.

At night, a bat as big as a chicken fell onto the gum and could not free itself. After the bat was killed, the trouble stopped. When people went to look, beneath the hooked curtain there were several hundred chignons.

(*GXSGC*, #236. 421; *TPYL*, 946. 4199b; *TPGJ*, 473. 3900)

80. LOSING KNOTTED HAIR

In the ninth year of the Yuanjia reign period (432), an attendant of Ming Yizhi, the adjutant of the General Conquering the North,[14] had a terrible nightmare. Yizhi went to wake him in person. The attendant could not respond for quite a while, and furthermore, he had lost his knotted hair. After three days he awoke, saying that three people had held his feet and one had tied his hair. Suddenly he dreamed of a Buddhist monk,[15] who gave him a pill resembling the seed of a tung oil tree and asked him to eat it with water. When he awoke, the pill was in his hand. He took it and then recovered.

(*GXSGC*, #242. 423; *TPGJ*, 276. 2185)

13. Huainan 淮南 Commandery; its administrative seat during Eastern Jin and the [Liu] Song period was located in Huyang 湖陽 County, present-day Dangtu 當塗 County, Anhui.
14. The General Conquering the North refers to Liu Yigong 劉義恭 (413–465), the Prince of Jiangxia 江夏. In the ninth year of the Yongjia reign, he garrisoned Guangling (present-day Yangzhou) as General Conquering the North and Governor of Southern Yanzhou 兗州.
15. In the Six Dynasties period (220–589), *daoren* 道人 frequently referred to a Buddhist monk.

81. AN ALLIGATOR SPIRIT

Cai Xing, a native of Jinling,[16] suddenly became crazy. He sang and chanted intermittently, and frequently talked to and laughed with the air as if with several people.

Someone said, "Whose daughter should I marry?"

Another one responded, "There are already many families."

Late at night, people suddenly heard the voices of more than ten people sending something into villager Liu Yuzhi's home.

When Yuzhi drew a knife and dashed out his door, he saw a black man who cursed him, saying, "I am the governor of lakes and I am visiting you. Yet you intend to kill me?" Then he asked his partners, "Why don't you help me?"

Yuzhi raised his knife and cut them wildly; in the end he obtained a big alligator and a fox.

(*GXSGC*, #229. 419; *TPGJ*, 469. 3865–66)

82. A MALE FOX

When Xi Zaochi (d. 383) worked as the Recorder of Jingzhou,[17] he once went out hunting with Huan Wen (312–373), the posthumous Emperor Xuanwu.[18] Seeing a yellow creature, he shot it, and it immediately died. It was an old male fox, with a crimson silk sachet tied to its foreleg.

(*GXSGC*, #109. 384; *TPYL*, 704. 3142a)

16. Jinling 晉陵, modern Changzhou 常州, Jiangsu.
17. Xi Zaochi 習鑿齒, styled Yanwei 彥威, was a historian of Eastern Jin and the author of *Han Jin chunqiu* 漢晉春秋 (History of Han and Jin).
18. Huan Wen 桓溫, styled Yuanzi 元子, was the son-in-law of Emperor Ming 明帝 of the Jin. At first he was the Governor of Jingzhou; later he wielded power arbitrarily as the *Da sima* 大司馬 (Commander-in-Chief). He schemed to replace the Jin himself, but died before he succeeded. After his son Huan Xuan (369–404) temporarily usurped the Jin throne in 403 as the emperor of Chu 楚, he was posthumously honored as Emperor Xuanwu 宣武帝. His biography can be found in *Jin shu*, 98. 2568–83.

83. A DEER SPIRIT

Xie Kun (281–323),[19] a native of Chen Commandery,[20] once lodged at an inn where many people had been killed. At the end of the fourth watch, someone in yellow yelled, "Please open the door, Youyu!" Kun asked him to stretch his arm through the window; thereupon the person gave him his wrist. Kun pulled it with all his strength. The arm was broken off, allowing the person to escape.

The next day, when Xie Kun looked at it, it turned out that it was the front leg of a deer. Following the traces of blood, he caught it.

(*GXSGC*, #65. 371; *CXJ*, 29. 715)

84. A SNAKE SNORES

Xue Zhong, a clerk of Guiji Commandery and a native of Mao County,[21] was allowed a vacation during which he returned home.

When he arrived, it was night and the door of his house was closed, and he heard the snore of a man from his wife's bed. Zhong called his wife, and she took quite a while to get out of bed.

Before his wife completely opened the door, Zhong approached her with a knife, asking, "Who is the drunk man?"

His wife was startled, declaring persistently that there truly was nobody there.

Zhong's house had only one door. He searched thoroughly yet found nothing. Then he saw a big snake hidden in the corner of the bed, with the bad smell of a drunkard. Zhong cut the snake into pieces and discarded it into the backyard ditch.

---

19. Xie Kun 謝鯤, styled Youyu 幼輿, was the Governor of Yuzhang 豫章 and a noted unconventional scholar during the Eastern Jin dynasty. See *Jin shu*, 49. 1377–79.
20. Chen 陳 Commandery, the area of modern Zhoukou 周口, seat in Huaiyang 淮陽, Henan; Chen Commandery was established temporarily at Hefei 合肥 in the fifth year of the Xianhe 咸和 reign (330) during Eastern Jin.
21. Guiji 會稽 Commandery during the Han covered the modern southern part of Jiangsu and western part of Zhejiang. It covered only the area of modern Shaoxing 紹興 and Ningbo 寧波 in Zhejiang during the Jin and Southern dynasties.

    Mao 鄮 County, east of modern Ningpo, Zhejiang.

Several days later the wife died. A few days after that, Zhong died as well, but he was revived after three days.

He said that at the beginning of death, someone put fetters around his neck and brought him to an official residence where he met an official.[22]

The official asked, "Why did you kill someone?"

Zhong replied, "I did not kill anyone, indeed."

The official said, "You cut someone into pieces and threw the dead body into your backyard ditch. Who was that?"

Zhong said, "It was a snake, not a person."

The commandery governor realized his mistake in astonishment, saying, "I often took him as a spirit. Yet he ventured to rape another's wife as well as groundlessly launch lawsuits against others." He ordered his attendants to summon him, and the clerks brought a man wearing a flat-top cap. The governor questioned him and accused him of raping Zhong's wife and sentenced him to jail.

Zhong was then sent back.

(*GXSGC*, #198. 409; *TPYL*, 934. 4151b)

85. THE MONK ZHONGZUO

Zhongzuo, a monk of the Northern Monastery of Wu Commandery,[23] was lying in his room when a rat came out from a pit, saying that Zhongzuo would die in a few days.

Zhongzuo summoned his servant and ordered him to buy a dog. The rat said, "I will not be afraid of it. If you let a dog enter through this door, you will definitely die."

In a short while, a dog arrived as expected. Zhongzuo then told his servant in a low voice, "Tomorrow hire someone to bring twenty buckets of water here."

---

22. For 有神人将重到一官府, *TPYL* reads 有人梏将重到一官府.
23. Beisi 北寺, Northern Monastery, refers to the Bao'en si 報恩寺 at the northern suburb of Suzhou, the seat of Wu Commandery. It was built by Sun Quan, the emperor of Wu (222–280), during the Three Kingdoms period to show his gratitude toward his mother.

The rat had already known of this and said, "Stop! You want to fill my den with water? My den connects to everywhere."

They poured water into its den for a whole day, yet obtained nothing.

Secretly, Zhongzuo asked his servant to hire more than thirty men. The rat said, "I'll go up to live on the roof of this house. What can you do to me?" When the thirty men came, the rat was on the roof.

Zhongzuo's servant was named Zhou. The rat said, "Zhou has stolen two hundred thousand cash, and he will desert you and flee." Later when Zhongzuo checked his storage, he found that what the rat said was true, and the servant had also fled.

When Zhongzuo had to do business, he closed his door and told the rat, "You are making me rich. Now I have a long trip. Please diligently guard my house, allowing nothing to be lost."

At that time, Huan Xuan urgently forbade killing oxen in Nanzhou.[24] Zhongzuo loaded several dozen thousand cash,[25] secretly purchased ox skins, and returned to the east. After he sold them, he obtained two hundred thousand cash. When he returned, his house was still closed. Nothing was gone, and the rat had vanished as well. Then he became very wealthy.

(*GXSGC*, #117. 386–87; *YWLJ*, 95. 1659; *TPYL*, 885. 3933a & 911. 4037b–38a; and *TPGJ*, 440. 3586–87)

86. THE RAT HAT

During the time of Prince Qi of the Wei,[26] Wang Zhounan of Zhongshan was the magistrate of Xiangyi County.[27] A rat suddenly emerged

24. For Huan Wen, *YWLJ* (95. 1659), *TPYL* (911. 4037b) and (440. 3587) all read Huan Xuan.

25. Zheng (3. 82) takes it as *shu chuan* 數船 (several boats) of cash. Yet both *YWLJ* and *TPYL* read *shuwan* 數萬錢. Even though the Ming edition of *TPGJ* reads *shuchuan* 數船, but no *qian* 錢 follows it.

26. Prince of Qi 齊 refers to Cao Fang 曹芳 (r. 204–254), the third emperor of Wei 魏. He was enthroned when still a child, so the administration was shared by Cao Shuang 曹爽 (d. 249) and Sima Yi 司馬懿 (179–251). In 254 he was demoted to his original title, Prince of Qi.

27. Xiangyi 襄邑 County, present-day Sui 睢 County, Henan.

from its den and said, “Zhounan, you will die on a certain date.” Zhounan did not respond.

When that day arrived, the rat changed its attire and came out with an official hat, handkerchief, and black clothing, saying, “Zhounan, you will die at noon.” Zhounan still did not respond, and the rat entered its den again.

At noon, the rat came out again with the official hat and handkerchief, saying, “Zhounan, you don’t respond; what should I say?” After finishing, it fell down and died, and its clothes and hat disappeared.

Zhounan approached and looked at it. It was just a rat, no different from others.

(*GXSGC*, #52. 367; *TPGJ*, 440. 3586)

87. THE RAT OF QINGHE

Each time a governor of Qinghe Commandery arrived to assume his post,[28] he would die immediately.

When the new governor arrived and went to the restroom, a tiny man, three inches tall and wearing an official hat and black clothing, told him, “You will die on a certain day.”

The governor did not respond, yet was extremely unhappy. He urged his clerk to be the host [to prepare for his funeral]. Outsiders felt it was fairly strange.

At noon on the day of his assumed death, when the governor went to the restroom, he saw the tiny man he had seen previously, who told him, “You will die today at noon.” He repeated his words three times, yet the governor still did not respond.

Then the tiny man said, “You should speak yet you do not. I, this rat, shall die on your behalf.” Then it fell down to the ground and appeared as big as a pig. Thus the commandery became peaceful.

(*GXSGC*, #227. 419; *TPGJ*, 440. 3587)

28. Qinghe 清河 Commandery; its administrative seat was in modern Qinghe County, Hebei.

88. THE FOX SPIRIT

The servant of Dai Miao of Wuxing,[29] surnamed Wang, had a young and beautiful wife, but the second younger brother of Dai Miao had approached her intimately.

The servant privately harbored resentment and anger, and he told Miao everything, saying, "Your second younger brother did this. It was extremely impertinent. I'd like to hear what you have to say."

When Miao questioned his brother about this, his brother cursed bitterly, saying, "Where was such a thing! It must be a demon or ghost." He ordered Miao to kill it.

At the beginning, the servant dared not hit the man [with his wife], and he reconfirmed the agreement seriously and clearly with Miao.

Later, when the man came again, the servant closed the door and intended to tie him up with a rope. Then the man became a big fox and dashed out the window.

(*GXSGC*, #195. 408; *TPYL*, 912. 4041a)

89. A ROOSTER'S TRANSFORMATION

Zhu Zong of Linhuai Commandery had just experienced the disaster of his mother's death,[30] and he constantly lived away from home. His wife was ill, so he went back to see her.

The woman said, "Due to the importance of your mourning, there is no need for you to return so many times."

Zong replied, "Since the torment occurred, when have I come back home?"

The woman said, "You have come back numerous times."

Knowing then that she was a demon, Zong ordered his wife's maid, "When she comes [into the room] again, close the door and catch her."

When she came, Zong immediately went to look. The creature could not escape, and it suddenly became an old white rooster. Through

29. Wuxing, see footnote 18 in chapter 2.

30. Linhuai 臨淮 Commandery covered ten counties south to the Huai River during the Jin dynasty; its seat was in modern Xuchi 盱眙 County, Jiangsu.

investigation, Zong discovered it was his family's rooster. He killed it, and then the anomaly vanished.

(*GXSGC*, #261. 433; *TPGJ*, 461. 3784)

90. ESCORT CHEN

In the morning of a certain day during the Yonghe reign period of Jin (345–356), Chen Xu, a resident of Xincheng County,[31] heard someone knocking at the door, and the man introduced himself, saying, "I am Escort Chen." Then there was the sound of a cart and horses, though their physical shapes could not be seen.

The man entered directly and called the host to talk together, saying, "I should come here and lodge in your home to bring you good fortune." He then ordered Chen Xu to arrange a bed and curtain for him in the house.

Sometimes people visited him, praying for blessings by fasting and offering wine and gifts, and what he predicted was all proven. Each time people offered him wine and food, he asked them to kowtow and sent them behind the curtain, and nobody was allowed to open it and look inside.

There was a person who suspected that Escort Chen was a fox or something similar. Taking advantage of being near him when kowtowing, this person tried to grab him. The creature retreated to the back of the bed, saying with fury, "How dare you suspect and test me!" The person then felt a severe pain in his heart. The host kowtowed on his behalf to apologize, and after quite a while Escort Chen's anger subsided. After that nobody dared offend him.

Chen Xu's entire family suffered no misfortunes, had no trouble, and benefited from everything they did. Besides this, everything went on as usual.

(*GXSGC*, #91. 378; *TPGJ*, 294. 2340)

31. Xincheng 新城 County, west of modern Fuyang 富陽, Zhejiang.

91. THE TRANSFORMATION OF A WILD CAT

During the reign of Lord Haixi (r. 366–371),[32] a man's mother passed away. Since his family was poor, he had no money for a funeral. Therefore he moved his mother's coffin deep into the mountain. Keeping filial love in mind, he started building a tomb by the side of the mountain and worked ceaselessly day and night.

One day when it was about dark, a woman, holding her son in her arms, came to lodge there. When night came, the filial son still had not finished his work. The woman urged him to sleep several times before she finally fell asleep by the fire. It turned out that she was a wild cat, holding a crow in her arms. Consequently the filial son killed her and discarded her in a back pit.

The next day, a man came to inquire, "My wife and child walked here yesterday and lodged in your place at night. Where are they now?"

The filial son said, "It was only a wild cat, and I have already killed it."

The man said, "You killed my wife, how could you say that she is a wild cat? Where is she now?"

Thereupon they reached the pit together, the wild cat had become a woman who died in the pit.

The man then tied the filial son up and sent him to the authorities, and he was supposed to pay for the woman's death with his life. The filial son told the magistrate, "This is indeed a demon. Should you bring a hunting dog here, you will see it is a demon."

Thus the magistrate asked, "Could this be distinguished by a dog?" The answer was, "A wild cat is by nature afraid of dogs, but a dog cannot distinguish [a cat or human] as well."

Accordingly, the magistrate released a dog. Thereupon the man became an old wild cat and was killed. Looking at the woman, they found she had become a wild cat again.

(*GXSGC*, #104. 383; *FYZL*, 31. 989–90)

32. Lord Haixi 海西公, Lord Haixi, refers to Sima Yi 司馬奕, Emperor Fei 廢帝 of Eastern Jin, who was dethroned by Huan Wen in 371.

92. THE ANOMALY OF HIDDEN RABBIT

During the time of the Grand Marshal Huan Wen,[33] an adjutant sat awake at night. Suddenly he saw a rabbit hidden between the ridgepole and beams, opening its eyes and snapping its teeth at him. It was extremely terrifying.

When the rabbit approached closer, the adjutant drew his knife to cut it. He saw his knife exactly hit the rabbit, yet, on the contrary, it hurt his knee and blood streamed down. He felt this was extremely strange, so he asked his family to hide all the knives and he himself never went near them.

Later, when he suddenly saw the rabbit again, his mind was confused and he grabbed a knife to cut it. Because of the wound subsequently inflicted upon himself, he became exhausted. Luckily, the knife was not sharp, so he did not die. This happened twice and then stopped.

(*GXSGC*, #110. 382; *TPYL*, 907. 4023b; *TPGJ*, 359. 2847–48)

93. THE "RECEIVING CLOUD" PREFECT

In the front yard of Dong Qi, a native of Jingzhao Commandery,[34] there was a big tree with good shade.

During a continuous heavy rain one day, Dong Qi was at home alone. A clerk notified him, "The Receiving Cloud Prefect has come." Then Dong saw the prefect.

Wearing a towering hat, the prefect was eight feet tall and called himself Regional Earl. "My third son has outstanding talent. He should be a friend of yours."

The next day, Qi felt something had changed under the tree: each day after dusk there would be a young boy approaching him to talk, play, or ask for food and drink. This lasted for half a year; Qi's vital energy became strong, and no member of his family had an illness.

33. *TPGJ* reads 穆帝末年桓溫府. . . Huan Wen, see footnote 18 in this chapter.

34. Jingzhao 京兆 Commandery was established during the Wei and Jin periods, covering the area around Xi'an. It was temporarily established at Xiangyang (modern Xiangfan) during Eastern Jin.

Later when Qi went to a villa, his three servants escorted him, saying, "The timber of your tree is useful. We intended to sell it, yet you have never listened to us. Let's cut it together today." Qi approved. The deity also vanished from then on.

(*GXSGC*, #226. 418–19; *TPGJ*, 415. 3380–81)

94. A DIVINE TREE

Behind the home of Chen Qingsun, a native of Yingchuan,[35] there was a divine tree. Numerous people went to it to pray for blessings, so a temple was built there, named the Heavenly Spirit Temple.

Qingsun had a black ox. The spirit said in the air, "I like this ox. If you don't offer it to me, I'll kill your son on the twentieth of next month!" Qingsun replied, "One's life is destined. It won't be determined by you." When that day arrived, his son really died.

The spirit said again, "If you still don't offer it to me, I'll kill your wife in the fifth month." Again Qingsun refused. When the time arrived, his wife died as well.

Again the spirit came and said, "If you don't offer the ox to me, I'll kill you in the autumn." Qingsun still didn't give it to him. When it was autumn, he did not die.

The ghost then came to apologize, saying, "As a man, your heart is upright, thus you receive great blessings. I hope you will not mention this to others—if Heaven and Earth heard of it, my crime is not a minor one. The fact was that I met a tiny ghost, so I was able to work as a clerk under the Controller of Fate. I saw the dates of your son's and wife's deaths; therefore, in order to obtain food I cheated you. I deeply hope that you will forgive me. The record shows that you will live to eighty-three years old, and your family is living with good fortune. Even ghosts and spirits will assist you. I will also serve you." Then the sound of kowtowing was heard.[36]

(*GXSGC*, #161. 399; *TPGJ*, 318. 3522)

35. Yingchuan 潁川 Commandery; its administrative seat was in modern Xuchang 許昌, Henan, during Western Jin.

36. Qisang 稽顙, *kowtow*.

95. THE HEAD OF A DEITY STATUE

A resident of Lubai Village of Guangling saw ghosts and demons every night.[37] Their shapes were different, but all were ugly and hideous. Those who were cowardly would not dare approach them.

The villagers suspected there must be a reason for what he saw. Ten men gathered and they dug together at the same time. One foot underground, they found the rotting head of a deity statue.

When they inquired of the elders, all of them said, "People once took part in a funeral in the rain, and when they arrived at this place they met robbers. The people scattered, but the head of a deity statue fell into the mud."[38]

(*GXSGC*, #23. 356–57; *TPYL*, 552. 2501a–b)

96. A NIGHTMARE

Lady Guo, the maternal grandmother of Bi Xiuzhi, was once sleeping alone at night. When she summoned her maids, they replied but did not show up. Lady Guo called them several times, but they still did not appear. Later, she heard the loud sound of someone stepping on the bed. She berated the maiden in a severe voice, and she replied with "Yes, yes," but still did not arrive.

In a moment, Lady Guo saw that on the screen there was a face resembling a deity statue. Each of its eyes was as big as a jar, and their light spread all over the room. Its palms were as big as winnowing fans, and its fingers were several inches long. Furthermore, its ears and eyes moved back and forth vigorously. Lady Guo had vigorously practiced the Way, and now she wholeheartedly concentrated on chanting the scripture. The creature left.

For quite a while, all the maidens came, saying, "Previously we intended to respond, yet it seemed we were pressed down by something. Now our bodies are light, so we have come."

(*GXSGC*, #162. 399–400; *TPGJ*, 359. 2848)

37. Guangling 廣陵, present-day Yangzhou 揚州.

38. As a practice, the deity statue was used in funerals.

97. THE FRAME OF A TILT HAMMER

There was a guest who came from afar to lodge at the home of Xu Jian, a native of Hongnong Commandery.[39] The guest had a horse that was startled and jumped at night. The guest felt upset, so he mounted the horse and left. A creature more than a *zhang* long followed the horse. The guest shot it and heard the sound of his arrow hitting wood.

The next day, he retraced the road he had passed and saw that his arrow had hit the frame of a treadle-operated tilt hammer.

(*GXSGC*, #186. 406; *TPYL*, 762. 3385a)

98. *RAKSASAS*

During the Song reign there was a state that was close to *raksasas*.[40] The *raksasas* entered its territory several times, eating countless people. The king made an agreement with the *raksasas* that said, "From today each of the families in this state will have a special day of duty. On that day, the family on duty should send [a boy] to you. Please do not kill people randomly anymore."

A family of Buddha devotees had an only son aged ten who was the next boy to be sent [to the *raksasas*]. At the time of his departure, his parents wailed bitterly, and then chanted the name of Buddha

39. Hongnong 宏農 Commandery, seat in modern Lingbao 靈寶, Henan.

40. *Raksasas* is one of the most noted Buddhist demons, transmitted into China along with Buddhist teachings. *Yiqiejing yinyi* 一切經音義 [Pronunciation and meaning of all the scriptures] says, "*Raksasas* are evil demons. They eat the flesh of people. Some of them fly in the air while some walk on the ground. Both types are nimble, quick, and terrible." "*Raksasa* is the name of violent and evil demons, which are extremely ugly as males and extremely beautiful as females. But both of them eat people. In addition, there is a state of female *raksasas* that is located on an island in the ocean." See Huilin 慧琳 (fl. 5 century), *Yiqiejing yinyi* (Taibei: Datong shuju, 1970), 25. 510, 7.130; cf. *Taishō Tripitaka*, 54. 464. For a study of the evolution of *raksasas* in both India and China, see Zhenjun Zhang, "Buddhist Impact on the Creation of New Fictional Figures and Images in the *Youming lu*," 145–168.

wholeheartedly. Because Buddha's power was great, the *raksasas* could not get close to the boy. The next morning, the parents found that their son was still alive and they went back home together happily.

From then on, the calamity of the *raksasas* ceased completely. [Lives of] people in the state had indeed depended on this family.

(*GXSGC*, #254. 430; *TPGJ*, 112. 773; *FYZL*, 50. 1514)

99. QIAN TENG

Qian Teng was the Governor of Pei Commandery in the third year of the Xianhe reign (328),[41] and he was never moderate in his traveling. He dreamed of a man in black who told him, "Why do you go on outings endlessly? I should cut off the legs of your horse!"

Later, Teng went out, and the legs of his horse broke for no reason. When he walked to a place outside the outer wall of the city, it suddenly became dark. A man who was more than a *zhang* tall and wore a black cap and white clothes shouted at the driver of Teng's cart, to tell the driver to avoid him. In a moment the tall man arrived. He hit the cart driver with a whip, and the driver fell down right then.

When dawn arrived, Teng's followers saw that the cart was empty, and they tried to find him. After walking sixty to seventy steps, they found Teng leaning against a small table, sitting on the ground in luxuriant vegetation. Teng said, "I myself don't know what has happened."

Fifty days later, Teng was sentenced and put to death.

(*GXSGC*, #86. 377; *TPGJ*, 321. 2543–44)

41. Qian Teng 牽騰, a general of Eastern Jin under Zu Yue 祖約 (d. 330), the General Conquering the West and Governor of Yuzhou 豫州. In 328 Zu Yue joined Su Jun's 蘇峻 rebellion and captured Jiankang, yet soon was defeated and surrendered to Shi Le 石勒, the emperor of Later Zhao 後趙 (319–351). Qian Teng also surrendered to Shi Le.

Pei 沛 Commandery; its seat was in modern Xiang 項 County, Anhui, from Han to Jin.

100. THE PRINCE OF MOUNT DOU

The family of Shen Zong, a native of Yuhang,[42] was constantly poor. Once he entered the mountain with his father. On their way back home, they saw a man with about four hundred attendants around him. The front carriage carried impedimenta with horsemen holding whips on both sides of the road, and the honor guards before and after him were like those of an officer with an emolument of two thousand bushels of grain.

From the distance they saw Zong and his father, asked them to stop, and approached Zong and asked him to light their fire for them. Thereupon Zong asked, "What noble man is this?" The reply was, "He is the Prince of Mount Dou to the south of Yuhang." Zong knew that he was a spirit; therefore he kowtowed and said, "I hope to be protected and helped."

Later when Zong entered the mountain, he obtained a jade pig.[43] From then on his affairs all came out as he wished. He prospered in both farming and silkworm raising. Consequently, his family became wealthy.

(*GXSGC*, #178. 403; *TPYL*, 359. 1653b & 472. 2166b; *TPGJ*, 294. 2342)

101. THE DEITY OF HOUGUAN COUNTY

In Houguan County there was a deity of the official residence.[44] At the end of each year, the officials would slaughter an ox as sacrifice to him.

When Wu Zeng of Pei Commandery was appointed the magistrate of the county, he stopped doing so. A year later Zeng was transferred to the position of Adjutant of the General Who Establishes Might. The deity came at night to ask Zeng, "Why don't you give me my food?"

42. Yuhang, TPGJ (294. 2342) reads *Yuyao* 余姚.

43. *TPGJ* reads *yuzhen* 玉枕, "a jade pillow."

44. Houguan 侯官 County, modern Minhou 閩侯, Fujian.

The deity was rude in voice and countenance, blaming him severely. The officials then purchased an ox on the way as sacrifice and at the same time offered him apologies; then the deity left.

(*GXSGC*, #207. 411; *TPGJ*, 294. 2343)

102. RIVER DEITY

Zhao Bolun, a native of Moling,[45] once went to Xiangyang. The boatman prayed to the river spirit, promising a pig. When the boatman made the sacrifice, however, he offered only a pig shoulder.

That night, Bolun and others dreamed of an old man and an old woman with hoary temples. Both of them wore cloth garments, held oars in their hands, and showed anger toward them. The next morning as soon as they set out, their boat struck sand and stones that could not be avoided by human strength.

Then they offered sumptuous food to the deities and they were able to get through.

(*GXSGC*, #209, 413; *TPGJ*, 318. 2514)

103. THE DEITY OF GONGTING MONASTERY

Gongting Temple in Nankang Commandery was proved especially effective in its divine power.[46]

In the period of Emperor Xiaowu (373–396) of Jin, a monk arrived at the temple. When the statue of the deity saw him, tears streamed wildly down its face. Accordingly the deity displayed his own name; it turned out that he was the monk's old friend.

The deity said, "I am deeply sinful. Can you help me transcend the painful transmigration?"

Thereupon the monk started fasting and reciting sutras on his behalf, and said, "I want to see your real physical form." The deity

45. Moling 秣陵, present-day Nanjing.

46. Nankang 南康 Commandery; its seat was modern Ganzhou 贛州, Jiangxi.

replied, "The physical form with which I was endowed is extremely ugly and cannot be shown."

The monk pleaded bitterly. Thereupon the deity transformed into a snake with a body several *zhang* long. Hanging its head on the beam, it listened to the reading of sutras wholeheartedly, blood dripping from its eyes.

By the night of the seventh day of the seventh month, the snake died, and the temple was closed as well.

(*GXSGC*, #133. 392; *TPGJ*, 295. 2346)

104. THE DEITY OF HARSH FROST

Yangqi of Henan, styled Shengqing, contracted malaria when he was young. From a shrine he got a book regarding the ways of exorcising hundreds of types of demons, and whenever he used it to drive out demons, it proved to be effective.

When he was the Governor of Rinan,[47] his mother went to the privy and saw a ghost whose head was several feet long, and she told Shengqing about it.

Shengqing said, "This is the Deity of Harsh Frost." Then he drove it out, and had it transformed into a slave servant. To send a letter to the capital, the deity could set out in the morning and return in the evening. In doing physical labor, it had the strength of a thousand men.

There was someone who contracted enmity with Shengqing. Shengqing sent the deity to the man's home at night. The deity approached the head of his bed, held both of the man's hands, opened its red eyes, and stretched its tongue down to the ground. The man was almost scared to death.

(*GXSGC*, #192. 407; *TPGJ*, 292. 2320; & *TPYL*, 883. 3924b–25a)

47. Rinan 日南 Commandery, in modern Vietnam.

105. EXORCISING DEMONS

In the middle of the Yongchu reign (420–422) under Gaozu of the Song,[48] Zhang Chun was the Governor of Wuchang. Once, someone was marrying off his daughter, and the daughter had not yet entered the carriage when she lost control of herself. She dashed out to hit people and the carriage, saying that she disliked marrying a vulgar man.

A sorcerer said the girl was befuddled by evil demons, so he took her to the side of a river, drummed drums, and treated her with magic and prayer. Zhang Chun assumed that the sorcerer was deceiving and confusing the commoners, so he set a deadline for the sorcerer and requested the evil demon to be caught by then.

Later, a green snake came to the sorcerer's place. Right then the sorcerer pierced its head with a nail. At noon, he saw a big turtle coming from the river and lying prostrate in front of him. The sorcerer drew magic figures on its back with crimson ink, then sent it back into the river.

When it was dark, a big white alligator appeared from the river, now sinking, now emerging. The same turtle was behind it, urging it to go quickly. The alligator assumed itself that it would be put to death, so it made bold entering the curtains to bid farewell to the girl.

The girl wept bitterly, saying that she had lost her good match. Then she gradually recovered from losing her composure.

Someone asked the sorcerer, "What was the cause of the demonic phenomenon?" The sorcerer replied, "The snake was a messenger, the turtle was a go-between, and the alligator was the match of the girl. All of the three creatures that I caught are demons."

From this moment Zhang Chun knew that the sorcerer was effective.

(*GXSGC*, #235. 421; *TPYL*, 932. 4145a)

48. Gaozu 高祖, named Liu Yu 劉裕 (r. 420–422), the founder of [Liu] Song dynasty (420–479).

106. SHAMAN LI

During the Taiyuan reign, in Linhai Commandery there was a shaman surnamed Li.[49] No one knew where he was from. He was able to tell fortunes by divination and reading faces. He made magical water to treat patients, and many of them were healed. He also worshiped Buddha and read sutras.

He told others, "Next year there will be a great plague and this area will be the worst place. After another two dozen years, in the big commandery to the northwest of this place, stiff corpses will block the road."

At that time Zhou Shudao of Runan had resigned from the position of Magistrate of Linhai, and he was temporarily staying at home. The shaman said, "This time when Magistrate Zhou leaves, it is inappropriate to go southward; otherwise he will certainly suffer a sudden death." Then he pointed to the northern mountain, saying, "There will be unusual things to be seen." After more than ten days, a huge stone dropped one hundred *zhang* down from the mountain, with a thump resembling thunder.

Yu Kai was the Governor of Linhai Commandery. While passing by Runan, he visited Zhou. Zhou gave a feast with girl singers to treat him. When night came, Yu returned to his boat. At dawn, Yu pushed open the wind screens himself, shouting loudly, "Shudao, why are you so silly that you still have not got up?" The attendants felt their master's body and looked at his face, and found that he had stopped breathing quite a while ago.

The next year, several thousand people in the county died of illness.

(*GXSGC*, #128. 390; *TPYL*, 735. 3258b–59a)

107. NORTHERN DIPPER SAVED MR. GU FROM DEMONS

A man of Wuzhong by the name of Gu set out for a farmhouse[50] in the daytime. When a little more than ten *li* away from the farmhouse, he

49. Linhai 臨海 Commandery, modern Linhai County, Zhejiang.

50. Wuzhong 吳中, modern Wu County, Jiangsu.

heard an indistinct sound coming from the northwest. Lifting his head, he found that four to five hundred people, wearing red clothes and measuring twenty feet tall, had arrived swiftly and encircled him in three rings. Gu's breathing almost ceased, and his body could not move.

When it was near evening, the siege had still not ended. He could not move his mouth to speak, so he chanted the name of the Northern Dipper in his mind. Within the period of time it takes to eat a meal, the demons said to each other, "He holds his mind toward gods; we should release him." Suddenly it was as if the fog had been removed.

Gu went back to his house and lay down in exhaustion. That night, in front of his door was a fire that was raging yet not burning. The ghosts approached him in succession. Some left and some came. Some summoned Gu to talk with them, some entered to remove his quilt, and some stood on his head yet were as light as a goose feather. At dawn they disappeared.

(*GXSGC*, #212. 413–14; *TPGJ*, 319. 2526–27)

4

THE REALM OF GHOSTS

108. RESTORING THE *PO* SOUL[1]

Cai Mo (281–356) sat in the hall of his government office.[2] Suddenly he heard the sound of his neighbor on the left calling back the *po* soul. He went out of the front hall to watch, and saw an old woman dressed in a short-sleeved yellow silk shirt and a light green skirt ascending to heaven slowly and lightly from the home where someone had just died. On hearing the call, she looked back. This was repeated several times, and she ascended and descended with the calls for quite a while. When the calling stopped, the old woman vanished.

Cai Mo inquired of the dead woman's family, and they told him that she was dressed in exactly the same clothes he had seen on the figure.

(*GXSGC*, #77. 374; *TPGJ*, 320. 2533)

109. THE GREEN SUBSTANCE OF CORPSES

Zhu Zongzhi, the grand judge of Guiji State,[3] frequently saw that when a dead body was placed into a coffin, a green substance resembling an

1. For the *hun* soul and *po* soul in Chinese religion, see footnote 8 in chapter 1.
2. Cai Mo, see footnote 7 in chapter 2.
3. Guiji 會稽 State, the area of modern Shaoxing 紹興, Zhejiang, covering the same area under the administration of Guiji Commandery. "Grand Judge," translation of *sili* 司理.

inverted urn in shape would appear about three feet away from the head of the corpse. When a person stood at that place the green stuff disappeared, yet when the person left it appeared again.

It was also said that, "When a dead body is placed into a coffin, its ghost will come back to face it."

(*GXSGC*, #223. 417–18; *TPGJ*, 360. 2854)

110. A TALL GHOST

At the beginning of the Long'an reign (397–401), Mr. Yin of Chen Commandery was the Magistrate of Linxiang.[4] A ghost in this county was more than three *zhang* tall. When he sat on the roof of a house, his feet could still touch the ground.

As soon as Yin entered his office, the ghost came. Each time Yin ordered him to leave, he would shake the screen and rattle the windows. Yin's annoyance grew.

His younger brother observed the ghost, and he also saw this. He always drew his knife at his brother's side to quarrel with the ghost.

The ghost said, "Don't curse me. Otherwise I'll hit you and break your mouth!" Suddenly the ghost hid its form, hitting his mouth until it was bleeding.

Later his jaw went askew, and he became disabled.

(*GXSGC*, #142. 394; *TPGJ*, 319. 2526)

111. A HAIRY GHOST

Yin Zhongzong entered Shu at the beginning of the Long'an reign (397–404) to be an adjutant of Mao Qu.[5] After entering Fuling Commandery,[6] he lodged in an official inn for the evening. Suddenly, a ghost appeared before him, its whole body covered in hair. Through

4. Chen Commandery, see note 20 in chapter 3. Linxiang 臨湘 County, modern Changsha 長沙, Hunan.
5. Mao Qu 毛璩, Governor of Yizhou 益州 of Jin from 394 to 405.
6. Fuling 涪陵 Commandery; its seat was modern Fuling, Sichuan.

the window he seized Zhong's arm and pulled Zhong toward him. Zhongzong yelled loudly. People nearby came to save him, and then the ghost left.

(*GXSGC*, #145. 395; *TPYL*, 883. 3924b)

112. A GHOST STRETCHES HIS TONGUE

At the end of the Wu Kingdom (222–280), a gentleman attendant in the Palace Secretariat,[7] whose name has been forgotten, read books at night.

His home had multiple gates. Suddenly he heard all the outer doors open. He feared there would be an urgent imperial edict.

Furthermore, the inner door opened as well. A man about eight feet tall, wearing black clothes and a black cap and holding a stick, sat on the bed. They looked at each other for quite a while, then the man stretched his tongue down to his knee. The gentleman attendant was greatly terrified, and he tore his books to make a fire.

When it was dawn and the rooster crowed, the ghost left. All the doors were closed as before, and the man was safe and sound.

(*GXSGC*, #59. 368; *TPYL*, 469. 2157b)

113. EVIL GHOST IN A TOWERING TOMB

During the time of Wu, Chen Xian took business as his profession. Once, driving a donkey on his way, he passed an empty residence with broad buildings and a red gate, where nobody was to be seen. Xian led his donkey in to lodge there for the night.

At night, he heard someone say, "This petty man has no fear, he ventures to make trouble here!" Then a man came to Xian and blamed him by saying, "How did you dare enter this official residence without permission?"

7. Translation of *zhongshu lang* 中書郎.

At that time the moonlight was hazy. Xian saw that the man's face had a dark birthmark, eyes without pupils, and upturned lips with teeth exposed, and his hands held a yellow silk rope.

Xian quickly ran to a village behind the residence, and told people there what he had seen. The elderly said, "In the old days, there were evil ghosts there."

The next day, Xian looked at the place where he had seen the residence. He found that there were both towering tombs and deep ditches.

(*GXSGC*, #58. 368; *TPGJ*, 317. 2512)

114. A NEW GHOST SEARCHES FOR FOOD

There was a new ghost, whose form was thin and spirit tired. Suddenly, he saw a ghost friend he had known when he was alive, who was fat and strong. After exchanging greetings, his friend asked, "Why do you look like this?" The new ghost replied, "I am so hungry that I almost cannot hold myself together. You know a variety of ways to live better, you should teach me." The ghost friend said, "This is extremely easy. You need merely to haunt people, then they will be terrified and shall offer you food."

The new ghost went to the east end of a big village and entered the house of a family worshiping Buddha and vigorously observing the Dharma. In their western wing room there was a millstone. The ghost approached and turned it in the way a human would. The head of this family said to his children, "Since our family is poor, the Buddha takes pity on us and lets the ghost turn the millstone for us." Then they husked some wheat and gave it to him to grind. When dusk arrived, he had ground several *hu* of wheat. Feeling tired, he left.

Afterward he cursed his ghost friend, "How come you deceived me?" The ghost friend said, "Just go again, and you will naturally get food."

Again the ghost entered a house at the west end of the village. This family practiced Daoism. At the gate there was a stone mortar. The ghost sat on the mortar and pounded with a pestle, as though he were human. The man said, "Yesterday, the ghost assisted someone else, today he came again to help me. We may prepare some unhusked rice to gave him." He also gave his serving maid a winnowing fan and a sifter. At dusk, the ghost was exhausted. Yet the host did not give the ghost food to eat.

The ghost returned in the evening, saying angrily, "Since I have a relationship with you by marriage, no others could be compared with you. Why did you cheat me? I assisted others for two days, yet did not get a single bowl of food." The ghost friend replied, "You yourself did not meet the right people. Those two families worshiped Buddha or served the Dao; it is naturally hard to move them with feeling. Now go to a commoner's home to haunt them, and you will certainly get food."

The ghost left again and found another home. By its gate there was a bamboo pole. The ghost entered the door, seeing that there was a crowd of women eating together in front of the window. When he arrived in the courtyard, there was a white dog. The ghost held the dog and let it walk in the air. Seeing this, the family was surprised, saying, "There has never been such a strange thing." The diviner said, "There is a guest seeking food. You may slaughter the dog, together with sweet fruit, wine, and rice, and offer it as a sacrifice in the courtyard. Then you will be able to avoid abnormal disasters." The family followed the diviner's words, and the ghost indeed had a big meal.

Afterward, the ghost constantly haunted people, because his ghost friend had taught him how.

(*GXSGC*, #255. 431; *TPGJ*, 321. 2544)

115. A GHOST LIVING WITH HIS FAMILY

Yu Chong drowned at Jiangzhou in the middle of the Jianyuan reign (343–344).[8] On the same day he returned home, showing his form as usual. Mostly he stayed in the room of his wife, Nee Yue.

8. Jiangzhou 江州, established in the first year of the Yuankang 元康 reign (291) of Jin, covering most of modern Jiangxi province during the Jin. See Tan Qixiang, *Zhongguo lishi dituji*, 4. 3–4.

At first his wife was fearful, and she frequently called her nieces to accompany her. Because of this the ghost gradually came less.[9] Sometimes he came temporarily, then cursed angrily, "You are fond of associating with living persons, yet that causes you to suspect me and dislike me. How could this be fair to my intention of returning?"

Her nieces were spinning and weaving inside when they saw the loom rise into the air, with a creature spinning it in disorder and throwing it to the ground. Her nieces were terrified and all left. Afterward the ghost appeared more frequently.

They had a three-year-old boy who approached his mother, asking for food. His mother said, "I have no money, where would I get food?" Then the ghost felt sorrowful.

The ghost put his hands on his son's head, saying, "It was unfortunate that I died this early, and it now causes you to be needy. I wronged you, yet I care for you. What a vexing feeling!" Suddenly he showed his form and put two hundred cash before his wife, saying, "You can buy food for our son now."

Things like this happened for years, yet his wife became more impoverished and could not even support herself. The ghost said, "You have kept chaste, yet you are in such a poor condition. I should indeed take you away from here."

Not long afterward, his wife died of an illness, and the ghost was never seen again.

(*GXSGC*, #88. 378; *TPGJ*, 322. 2552)

116. WANG MING'ER MANIFESTS HIS PHYSICAL FORM

Wang Ming'er, a native of Donglai Commandery,[10] once lived in Jingxi. One year after his death, he showed up in his physical form, returned

9. The original words 作伴 (Accompaniment) in *TPGJ* was replaced with 鬼來 (The ghost came) here based on the Huang Pilie edition. Cf. Zheng Wanqing, *YML*, 4. 124.
10. Donglai 東萊 Commandery, the area of modern Yandai 煙臺 and Weihai 威海 in Shandong.

to his home for a whole day, and requested that his relatives and friends be summoned to chitchat. He said, "The heavenly government allowed me to temporarily return home."

While saying that he was about to depart, he started shedding tears. By greeting his fellow villagers, he expressed his deep feeling to them. He said to his son, "Since I left the human world, it has been a whole year. I have longed to see my hometown again." He ordered his son to visit the village with him.

When they passed the temple of Deng Ai (197–264),[11] he ordered his son to burn it down. His son was astonished, saying, "Ai was the General of Pacifying the East when he was alive and has been numinous after his death. Commoners offer sacrifices to him for blessing. Why do you want to set his temple on fire?"

Ming'er became angry, saying, "Ai is now polishing armor at the imperial store, and his ten fingers will be gone very soon. How can he be numinous?" He said further, "Also, the Grand General Wang [Dun] is now an ox;[12] he is driven back and forth and is about to die. Huan Wen is but a soldier.[13] All of them are in hell. In such inexplicable dilemmas, how could they bring disaster or blessing to others? If you intend to seek blessing, you should just be respectful, submissive, and loyal, and love your parents. In addition, don't be angry at others. This will be extremely good for you."

He also ordered, "You may collect fingernails, which can be used to redeem your crimes." He asked people as well to make tall thresholds, so that when a ghost came and entered their rooms to record their crimes, they would stumble over it and then forget everything.

(*GXSGC*, #215. 414–15; *TPGJ*, 320. 2537)

11. Deng Ai 鄧艾 was General Pacifying the West of the Cao Wei 曹魏 Kingdom (220–265), instead of General of Pacifying the East as in the next sentence of this story.

12. Wang Dun 王敦 was the younger brother of the Counselor-in-Chief Wang Dao 王導 (276–339), son-in-law of Emperor Wu 武 (r. 265–290) of Jin, and Regional Inspector of Jiangzhou and Jingzhou respectively under Emperor Yuan (r. 317–322). He captured the capital of Jin, Jiankang, and named himself Counselor-in-Chief in 322, but he died of illness in 324. His biography is in *Jin shu*, 98. 2553–66.

13. Huan Wen, see footnote 18 in chapter 3.

117. RUAN ZHAN[14]

Ruan Zhan (fl. 307–312) persistently believed that ghosts do not exist,[15] and nobody in the world was able to refute him. He himself always thought that his theories were sufficient to distinguish and justify things in both this world and the netherworld.

Suddenly a ghost appeared. He reported his name and went to see Ruan as a guest. After greetings, they discussed how to distinguish right from wrong. The guest had unmatched ability in this area.

At the end of their talk, they spoke of ghosts and spirits. They had a bitter debate, and the guest yielded. Then he suddenly became angry, saying, "Ghosts and spirits have been talked about by the sages and worthies from ancient times to the present. Why do you alone say that they do not exist? I myself am a ghost!" Thus he suddenly changed his form into something not human, and a moment later he dissolved.

Ruan was terrified, and both his mood and his look were very bad. A little over a year later, he died of sickness.

(*GXSGC*, #67. 371; *TPYL*, 617. 2774a–b; *TPGJ*, 319. 2526)

118. THE DEITY OF YANGSHA

Peng Huzi was young and strong, possessing great muscular strength. He frequently said that there are neither ghosts nor spirits.

---

14. Beginning in the Eastern Han (25–220), some scholars questioned the idea that the spirit has a physical existence. In the Eastern Jin (317–420) there was also debate about whether the spirit or soul has a physical form (*xing* 形) or not. The "immortality of spirit" became an important doctrine for Buddhists in the Southern and Northern Dynasties period (386–589). Chinese Buddhists used every possible means to make this viewpoint convincing. One means was inventing stories about spirits manifesting themselves in physical form. For this reason, stories concerning the transformation of spirit or soul became widespread (see Zhenjun Zhang, *Buddhism and Tales of the Supernatural in Early Medieval China*, 18–21). This is one of them.
15. Historically, Ruan Zhan 阮瞻 (styled Qianli 千里) was an official of the Jin, the eldest son of Ruan Xian 阮咸 (234–305), one of the famous "Seven Worthies of the Bamboo Grove" 竹林七賢. He was a man of placid disposition and few attachments, and noted for his ability to get the essence of a work without close study. His biography is in *Jin shu*, 49. 1363.

After his mother's death, a vulgar shaman admonished him, saying, "Someday the deity of Yangsha will return and kill someone again. It is proper for you to leave home and yield to him." Then all those who were young or weak in his family fled and hid, and Huzi was left alone in the house.

At midnight, someone pushed down the door and entered. He searched the east room and west room respectively, but failed to find anyone. Then he entered the main room and rushed toward the mourning hall. Huizi was terrified and did not know what to do, so he entered an earthen jar, which had been placed there previously, and covered his head with a wooden board. He felt that his mother was on the board, and someone asked her, "Is anybody under the board?" His mother replied, "No one." Then they left together.

(*GXSGC*, #259. 432–33; *TPGJ*, 318. 2521)

119. ADJUTANT HE

When Commander-in-Chief Huan was garrisoned at Zheqi Ridge,[16] Adjutant He went out in the morning, talked in the field, and urinated on a skeleton. After returning, he slept in the daytime and dreamed of a woman who said, "You are a decent man, why did you defile me? I'll let you know me this evening!"

At that time there were fierce tigers around that area, so nobody dared to walk outside at night. Adjutant He often dug a hole in the wall as his urinating pit. That night, he approached the pit intending to urinate. Enraged by his urinating, a tiger bit his penis off, and he died right then and there.

(*GXSGC*, #106. 384; *TPYL*, 892. 3961a)

16. Commander-in-Chief Huan, Huan Wen. Zheqi 赭圻 Ridge, located west of modern Fanchang 繁昌, Anhui.

120. SUO YUAN

When Suo Yuan was at Liyang,[17] he contracted an illness. From the western border came a young girl with a certain surname, who said herself that she was sent down by spirits and came to inform Suo Yuan, and promised to treat and take care of him.

By nature Yuan was upright and outspoken; he considered her a bewildering demon. He detained her, put her in jail, then killed her and displayed her corpse in the market. Before death the girl said, "Seventeen days later, I'll let Suo Yuan know [the consequence of] his crime."

By the expected time, Yuan truly died.

(GXSGC, #120. 387; annotation in "Shangshi" of *SSXY*, 17. 647)

121. WUHUAN

Yu Hong was an assistant in the official residence of the Prince of Jingling,[18] and his home was at Jiangling.[19] Yu Hong asked Wuhuan, his servant, to deliver some rice to support his family.

Having walked no more than three *li*, Wuhuan met robbers and was killed. His corpse floated down a river and stopped alongside Chakou Village.

At that time, a man named Wen Xin lived by the side of the river, and his mother was ill. A doctor told him, "She needs to take some human skull powder. After taking it, she will fully recover." Xin promised a handsome reward for the powder. His neighbor, Mrs. Yang, saw the corpse of Wuhuan, so she cut off his head and sent it to Wen Xin.

Xin set it on fire, intending to get rid of the skin and flesh. Three days passed, yet the head was not burned, and the eyes opened and scanned the area. Even though he felt it was strange, Wen Xin still treasured the head and did not throw it away. Accordingly, he scraped

17. Suo Yuan 索元, a general of Jin under Huan Xuan 桓玄, the usurper of Jin. Liyang 歷陽, modern He 和 County, Anhui.
18. For Yu Hong 庾宏 and the Prince of Jingling 竟陵 here, no further information has been found.
19. Jiangling 江陵, northwest of modern Shashi 沙市 city, Hubei.

some powder from its ear and cheek bones and gave it to his mother to take.

Immediately his mother felt the bones choke her throat, and after seven days she passed away. Shortly thereafter, Mrs. Yang fell ill, and her body was all red and swollen, resembling an ox or a horse. She saw Wuhuan's head come and curse her, "How could you avoid the retribution for good and evil?"

Mrs. Yang told this to her son. When she finished speaking, she died.

(*GXSGC*, #165. 400; *TPGJ*, 119. 838)

122. DISASTERS FROM STEALING COFFIN BOARDS

Mr. Xu of Dongwei,[20] whose forename has been forgotten, returned to his own commandery to be the governor. After he died, his tomb was built at Lingshan of Dong'an.[21]

Previously, someone opened his tomb, and the coffin was destroyed. When Xie Xuan was the Governor of Pengcheng,[22] the generals under him included Sima Long of the Qi Commandery,[23] his brother Xie Jin, Wang Xiang of Andong,[24] and others. All of these men fetched the destroyed coffin and divided the pieces to make their carriages. Shortly afterward, the three men all met with disasters, and the series of disasters never stopped.

The soul of Wang Xiang's mother passed word to her sons and grandsons, saying, "In the past Xiang and the brothers of Sima Long fetched the coffin in the tomb of Governor Xu to make carriages. The deaths and ruination of Long and others were all because of this."

(*GXSGC*, #231. 420; *TPGJ*, 320. 2540–41)

20. Dongwei 東魏 Commandery was not yet established when Xie Xuan was alive, so Zheng Wanqing suggests that it should be Dongguan 東莞 Commandery in modern Shandong.
21. Dong'an 東安 Commandery, seat in modern Yishui 沂水 County, Shandong.
22. Pengcheng 彭城, modern Xuzhou 徐州, Jiangsu.
23. Sima Long 司馬隆 (d. 276), member of the royal house and Prince of Anping 安平 of Western Jin.
24. Should be Dong'an, since there was no Andong 安東 County during the Jin and Song. Cf. Zheng Wanqing, *YML*, 5. 178.

123. LÜ SHUN'S WIFE

Lü Shun's wife died, so he remarried his wife's younger cousin. Accordingly he tried to build three tombs. Each time, when the construction was almost done, the tombs abruptly collapsed.

One day when Lü was lying in bed in the daytime, he saw that his wife had come. She came and shared the quilt with him, and her body was as cold as ice. In order to maintain the division between the living and the dead, Shun talked with her and asked her to leave.[25] Later, his wife saw her cousin and said angrily, "There is no limit to [the number of] men in the world, yet you share a single husband with me! You made the tombs but could not finish them. I caused it to be so."

Not long after, both the husband and his [second] wife dropped dead.

(*GXSGC*, #218. 415; *TPGJ*, 322. 2551–52)

124. OLD YAO

In Xiang County,[26] there was a boy by the name of Yao Niu. When he was just over ten years old, his father was killed by a villager. One day Niu sold his clothes and purchased a knife and a halberd, intending to avenge his father. Later he met the villager in front of the county government and stabbed him to death among a crowd of people.

The officials caught him, [but] the magistrate was sympathetic with him for his integrity of filial piety and postponed [the date to deal with] his case. It happened that there was an amnesty; he was able to avoid the punishment. Furthermore, the magistrate spoke with someone in [the government of] the commandery and the region so as to save him; finally he was able to avoid trouble.

Afterward, the magistrate went hunting. While chasing a deer, he entered the grass, among which there were several deep old wells. His

25. Chinese people believe that people and ghosts belong to different realms, so they should be separated.

26. Xiang 項 County, east of modern Xiangcheng 項城 County, Henan. *TPGJ* (320. 2539) reads *Xu xian* 須縣.

horse was about to approach them when he saw an old man who lifted a stick to hit the horse. The startled horse evaded him and could not reach the deer.

The magistrate became angry. He drew his bow and was about to shoot him. The old man said, "There are wells there, I was afraid that you would fall into them."

The magistrate asked, "Who are you?"

The old man kneeled down and replied, "Father of Yao Niu, the commoner. I'm grateful to you for saving Niu; therefore I came to repay your favor." Then he disappeared.

Having experienced this event related to the netherworld, the magistrate granted many favors to the commoners for several years while he was in an official position.

(*GXSGC*, #179. 404; *TPYL*, 482. 2207b, 479. 2196b, & 353. 1622a; *TPGJ*, 320. 2538–39)

125. A DECEASED MOTHER TAKES CARE OF HER SON

In recent years a man hired a young clerk who frequently requested to return home, yet didn't fulfill his wish.

Quite a few days later, when the clerk was sleeping under the southern window, the man saw an old, fat, and large woman around the age of fifty or sixty walking in the door with great difficulty.

While sleeping, the clerk failed to cover himself with his quilt. The woman went to the side of his bed, took the dropped quilt, covered him with it, and then went out the door and left.

Then the clerk turned over and his coat fell off. The woman returned and covered him with it again just like she had previously.

The man felt strange, so he directly asked the clerk why he constantly requested to return home. The clerk replied, "My mother has been ill."

Then the man asked for his mother's appearance and age. Both resembled what he had seen. The only difference was that the clerk said his mother was thin.

The man asked again, "What is your mother's illness?"

The clerk replied, "Her illness is merely edema, that's all."

The man immediately gave the clerk a vacation, and asked him to leave right away. Yet at that moment the clerk received a letter from his home, saying that his mother had died.

Thinking back to the fatness he had seen, the man realized that it was her appearance when she was swollen.

(*GXSGC*, #250. 428; *TPGJ*, 323. 2561)

126. CHENG BIAO AND HIS DECEASED BROTHER

Cheng Biao's elder brother passed away. Cheng was grieving and had an obstruction in the circulation of his vital energy, crying and weeping day and night.

Carrying two liters of wine and a plate of pears, his elder brother appeared and approached him, and they drank to please each other. Biao asked him a question, yet his brother did not reply.

Biao, choked with sad sobs, asked, "Now you, my brother, are up in heaven. Is there more good fortune or more bitterness?"

For a long while his brother did not respond. In silence, he poured the rest of the wine into a cup and left, holding the wine jar.

Later, [Biao] was fishing on the lake. When he passed by the place where he had drunk together with his brother, he released his fishing line and felt sad. A big fish jumped into the boat and looked down at the small fish. Facing heaven, Biao cried bitterly. Looking down, he saw the big fish, and he released all the small fish. Then the big fish leaped out of the boat itself and swam away.

(*GXSGC*, #168. 401; *TPYL*, 936. 4158b; *YWLJ*, 86. 1473)

127. A LAME GHOST

Zhao Ji, the previous commandant of Ye County,[27] often stayed in the field.

Previously, a crippled man had died and was buried by the footpath. More than twenty years later, a man from afar passed by the door of

27. Ye 鄴 County, modern Linzhang 臨漳, Hebei.

Zhao's residence. After walking more than ten steps, the man suddenly pretended to be crippled.

Zhao Ji immediately asked him the reason. The man from afar replied with a smile, "There was a lame ghost before. I imitated him for fun, that's all."

(*GXSGC*, #214. 414; *TPGJ*, 320. 2540)

128. AVOIDING A DISASTER

Wang Biaozhi (305–377) of the Jin,[28] a young man who was not yet an official, once sat alone in his studio, in front of which there were some bamboo stalks.

Suddenly he heard a sigh. Biaozhi became cautious and was astonished that the voice resembled his deceased mother's. Thus he went forward to have a look, and saw his mother wearing the same clothes as she had before her death. Biaozhi kneeled down to greet her and sobbed.

His mother said, "You are going to have an enormous calamity. From today, when you see a white dog, if you can walk eastward for one thousand *li* [and stay there for] three years, you will be able to avoid the disaster." Then his mother disappeared. Biaozhi felt sad and upset until the next morning.

At dawn, he noticed a white dog constantly following him. Then he prepared his luggage, and was about to go to Guiji. When he had walked for one thousand *li*, the disturbances he had seen all disappeared. He stayed there for three years, then returned to his studio.

Again he heard the voice and saw his mother as she had appeared before. She said, "You were able to follow my words, so I come to congratulate you. From now on, you will live to an age over eighty, and hold the position of prime minister and duke."

Later, everything occurred exactly as his mother had predicted.

(*GXSGC*, #103. 383; *TPYL*, 883. 3924b; *TPGJ*, 320. 2538)

---

28. Wang Biaozhi 王彪之, styled Shuhu 叔虎, was the nephew of Wang Dao (276–339) and the Director of the Imperial Secretariat of Eastern Jin. After Huan Wen's death he shared the administration of Jin with Xie An 謝安 (320–385).

129. DEAD FRIEND GUAN SHUANG

Both Hu Zhang of Shan County and Guan Shuang of Shangyu County were fond of fighting with weapons.[29] After Shuang died, Hu Zhang dreamed of Shuang, who jumped back and forth with a knife in front of him. When he awoke, Zhang felt extremely unhappy. The next day, he pasted a talisman onto the wall.

Zhang intended to travel to a distant place and had untied his boat and taken out his paddles when he saw Shuang coming. To urge Zhang to stay on, Shuang said, "When two people know each other's mind, their feeling may last for a thousand years. Yesterday night when I approached you to play, you were just sleeping. Therefore I left. Now why did you use the talisman to reject me? As a man you don't understand the ways of the world. Do you think I am afraid of the talisman?"

(*GXSGC*, #211. 413; *TPGJ*, 319. 2528)

130. CAI KUO'S DEAD SON

Cai Kuo (379–425) was appointed Governor of Yuzhang Commandery and had not yet set off to assume office.[30] His eldest son was waiting for his bride while lodging on an island. He intended to pull his bride's boat through, but his shirt got caught on the bow and he fell into the water and sank immediately.

Xu Xianzhi (364–426) was the Governor of Yangzhou,[31] and he ordered the officials on both sides of the river to offer handsome rewards to fishermen and the Kunlun (southeast Asia) servants for finding his corpse, but they could not find it until the second watch.

While his bride was weeping, she heard her husband telling her as if in a dream, "I am now under your boat."

29. Shan County, see footnote 2 in chapter 1. Shangyu 上虞 County, east of modern Shaoxing, Zhejiang.

30. Cai Kuo 蔡廓, styled Zidu 子度, was the grandson of Eastern Jin Minister of Education Cai Mo (281–356), Editorial Director Assistant (著作佐郎) of Eastern Jin, Governor of Yuzhang Commandery (modern Nanchang, Jiangxi), Palace Aide to the Censor-in-Chief (御史中丞), and Minister of Personnel (吏部尚書) of Liu Song. His biography is found in *Song shu*, 57. 1569–85.

31. Xu Xianzhi, see footnote 21 in chapter 2.

She told her maid, and her maid told others.

Xu ordered the boatmen to dive in search of him and, as expected, they discovered he was sitting under the boat. When he was first dragged out of the water, his color was the same as when he was alive.

(*GXSGC*, #248. 427; *TPYL*, 396. 1829a)

131. GHOSTS PLAYING MUSIC

When Huan Baonu of the Jin was the Governor of Jiangzhou,[32] there was an overseer surnamed Gan whose home was under the Linchuan Commandery. At the age of thirteen, his son died of illness and was buried among the tombs east of his home.

Approximately ten days later, people suddenly heard drums and music on the east road. About one hundred people directly went to Gan's home, asking: "Is Overseer Gan home? We come especially to visit you, and your worthy son is among us."

People could only hear their voices, yet could not see their forms. They laid out several long-necked jars of wine for them, and in a short while two jars were empty.

When he first heard the drumming, the Governor of Linchuan thought it was someone making fun of him who would certainly come to visit him as well. Yet later it became silent and nobody had arrived. When Gan told him what had happened, he was astonished.

(*GXSGC*, #97. 381; *TPGJ*, 319. 2527)

132. A GHOST STOPS FIGHTING

Li Jing, a native of Guiyang Commandery,[33] battled Zhu Ping, and Ping ran after him with a halberd. After running for more than a hundred

32. Huan Baonu 桓豹奴, named Huan Si 桓嗣, was the oldest son of Huan Chong 桓沖 (328–384), the famous general of Eastern Jin and the brother of Huan Wen (312–373). He was appointed General Governing the West in 377 and later stationed at Xiakou 夏口 (west of Wuchang) as Governor (太守) of Xiyang 西陽 and Xiangcheng 襄城. His biography is in *Jin shu*, 74. 1953.

33. Guiyang 桂陽 Commandery; its seat was in the modern city of Chenzhou 郴州, Hunan.

steps, Ping suddenly saw a ghost more than ten feet tall who stopped him, saying, "Li Jing's life span is not yet exhausted. How could you kill him? Don't do it! Otherwise, it will certainly hurt your hand."

Being drunk, Zhu Ping rushed directly to Jing's home. The ghost followed him. Ping saw Jing. As he was about to cut him with his halberd, he suddenly froze, as if he was tied, and his left-hand fingers were indeed wounded.

Then Ping stood still in the courtyard. At dusk, he was freed and left. The ghost said to him, "I told you in advance. Why didn't you listen?" After speaking these words, the ghost disappeared.

(*GXSGC*, #210. 413; *TPGJ*, 318. 2520)

133. A GHOST DISTINGUISHES HIS CORPSE THROUGH A DREAM

In the early period of the Taiyuan reign (376–396) of the Jin, Fu Jian (338–385) sent General Yang An to encroach on Xiangyang.[34] A soldier in the army died. One of his fellow townsmen escorted his coffin back home, and was about to arrive at his house the next day.

The dead man told his wife in a dream, "The corpse being sent to you is not mine. The one under the cabin is mine. The chignon you previously knotted for me is still there. Uncover it and look at it, then you will know which one is mine."

On the following day, the man who escorted the coffin arrived as expected. The woman told her mother so and so, but her mother was not convinced. Then the woman went to Nanfeng herself and carefully

34. Fu Jian 苻堅 (styled Yonggu 永固), from a *di* 氐 family of Shanxi, was the founder of the Former Qin 秦 State (351–394). He ascended the throne in 357 and conquered all of north China by 370, but was defeated at the Fei River 淝水 (in Anhui) by Eastern Jin troops in 383 in his attempt to annex the south and unify China and died two years later (see Richard Mather, *Shih-shuo Hsin-yü* [Minneapolis: University of Minnesota Press, 1976], 520; M. C. Rogers, *The Chronicle of Fu Chien* [Berkeley and Los Angeles, 1968]). His biography is found in *Jin shu*,113–114. 2883–2929.

Xiangyang 襄陽, modern Xiangfan 襄樊, Hubei.

examined the other corpses. She found one with a chignon exactly in the style as she had previously knotted.

(*GXSGC*, #122. 388; *TPGJ*, 322. 2551)

134. DRUMBEATS AND HORN MUSIC FROM AN OLD TOMB

Xi Fanghui, the Minister of Works of the Jin,[35] was burying his wife in Mount Li, and he sent Shi Ze, the official of Guiji Commandery,[36] to build the tomb. Shi Ze razed many old tombs to the ground.

Later, he tore down a tomb with an extremely grand structure and numerous splendid utensils and precious items. When the tomb was unearthed, drumbeats and horn music were heard from it. Since then, this has recurred numerous times.

(*GXSGC*, #80. 375; *TPYL*, 338. 1550a–b)

135. GHOST FIGHTING

Whenever Yu Jing, a native of Jiande,[37] went to the privy, there would be someone who put grasses into his hand, yet he could never see that person's form. This had occurred many times.

Later, when he went to the privy again, after quite a while nobody gave grass to him, and he heard the sound of fighting outside. Peeping at them, he saw that his deceased servant and maid were striving to give him the grass. Since the servant was just ahead of the maid, the maid punched him from behind, and because of this they fought.

After the time it takes to eat a meal, Yu Jing intended to go out, yet the servant and the maid were still fighting. Jing berated them in an

35. Minister of Works is Xi Fanghui's 郗方回 posthumous title, to which he was indeed appointed yet that he never assumed when he was alive.

36. Guiji, see footnote 21 in chapter 3.

37. Jiande 建德 County, established in the forth year of the Huangwu 黃武 reign of Wu Kingdom (225), with its seat in Meicheng zhen 梅城鎮 of present-day Jiande city, Zhejiang.

irritated voice. They vanished like an extinguished fire and never appeared again.

(*GXSGC*, #172. 402; *TPYL*, 186. 905a)

136. GHOSTS STEAL MILLET

The Zhuge family of Langye, two brothers, lodged at Jinling.[38] Their family was very poor, and they often supported themselves by borrowing money or begging. They put millet in a grain bin and consumed a set portion each day, but it became empty before it should have. At first they thought it was because there was a thief in their family, so they sealed the grain bin and marked the seal. However, the millet was consumed as soon as it had been.

Later, an old friend came to visit from afar. Arriving at the entrance to the lane when it was about dusk, he saw several people, coming out the gate, shouldering millet.

The guest asked, "Is Mr. Zhuge in?"

The reply was, "Both are here."

The guest entered. Having finished exchanging greetings, the guest asked, "How can you sell so much millet?"

The host said, "We rely on loans and begging for millet to fill our hungry mouths. How could we sell it?"

The guest said, "When I came, I met several men at the gate who went out with millet on their shoulders. If you did not sell millet, what was that for?"

The host brothers looked at each other, and they felt that it was strange. Entering to look at the seal, they found it exactly as it had been. They tried to open the grain bin to measure the millet, and found there was barely any more than ten *hu*. They knew then that what they had lost from beginning to end was not stolen by humans.

(*GXSGC*, #191. 407; *YWLJ*, 85. 1447; *TPYL*, 837. 3741b)

38. Jinling 晉陵, modern Changzhou 常州, Jiangsu.

137. LAUGHING AT A GHOST

In a restroom Ruan Deru once met a ghost[39] who was more than ten feet tall, black, and with big eyes. The ghost was in a single-layer white shirt, wearing a flat headdress, and was only inches away from him.

Deru was at ease and calm, saying to the ghost with a smile, "People say that ghosts are disgusting. It is so true."

The ghost was ashamed and withdrew.

(*GXSGC*, #66. 371; *TPGJ*, 318. 2521; *TPYL*, 186. 905a)

138. TYING UP A GHOST

A boy of an immigrant family from the north, accompanied by several partners, was herding oxen in the wild field. They saw a ghost hidden deep in the grass to set up nets everywhere, intending to trap people in them. Before the ghost finished setting up the nets, the shepherd from the north stole a net and used it to catch him, immediately tying up the ghost.

(*GXSGC*, #190. 407; TPYL, 832. 3714b)

139. STABBING A GHOST

Liu Daoxi and his younger cousin, Kangzu,[40] did not believe in ghosts, while his older cousin Xingbo had seen ghosts when he was young. Neither could convince the other that they were correct.

Once it was said that east of the residence at Changguang Bridge in Jingkou, there was a killer ghost on the eastern twig fence. Daoxi asked where the place was, and dragged Xingbo there.

39. Ruan Kan 阮侃, styled Deru 德如, was a native of Chenliu 陳留 (present-day Qi 杞 County). He was the governor of Henei 河內 of Jin and a close friend of Xi Kang 嵇康 (223–262).

40. Liu Daoxi 劉道錫 was governor of Guangzhou of the [Liu] Song. His biography is in *Song shu*, 65. 1720.

Holding a long knife, Daoxi intended to hack the ghost. Xingbo shouted behind him, "The ghost is hitting you!"

Before reaching the residence of the ghost, Daoxi heard a big stick hitting something and fell to the ground. He did not wake until the next morning, and it took him over a month to recover.

Later, Xingbo said again, "East of the government office there is a ghost on the mulberry tree.[41] It looks young, yet it will certainly harm people when it grows up." Kangzu did not believe him. He asked Xingbo the height at which the ghost was located, and Xingbo pointed it out clearly to him.

After more than ten days, it was a dark night at the end of the month. Hidden in the dark, Daoxi pierced the place where the ghost lived with a halberd and returned home right away, and no one knew what he had done.

Early the next morning, Xingbo suddenly came and said in astonishment, "The ghost was stabbed by someone last night, and it is almost dead. It cannot move at all and will die in no time."

Kangzu laughed loudly.

(*GXSGC*, #213. 414; *TPGJ*, 320. 2540)

140. GHOST HERB MORTAR

Liu Song was at home when suddenly he saw a ghost. He drew his sword to cut it and the ghost ran away. Song stood up and ran after it.

Seeing the ghost lying on a rock on a high mountain, Song approached and rushed toward it. A crowd of ghosts strove to flee, discarding an herb mortar with herbs inside it. Accordingly, Song brought the items back home.

When preparing medicine for patients, Song always put in a tuft of herb that had been pounded in this mortar, and all of his medicine was effective.

(*GXSGC*, #187. 406; *TPYL*, 762. 3384a)

41. "Government office," rendition of *tingshi* 廳事.

141. DRUNK GHOSTS

In the first year of Jianwu (25–56) of the Han, a native of Donglai Commandery surnamed Mie,[42] whose family ran a bar, once entered the bar and saw three strange customers who had arrived together with cooked rice in their hands, scooping wine to drink. Mie was suspicious, and by moving their food holders he changed their dining place. Finally the three ghosts got drunk in the forest.

(*GXSGC*, #37. 361; Zheng, *YML* 4. 113; *BTSC*, 148. 327a)

142. THE SERVANT JIAN

Jian was a household servant of Li Xian, a native of Gaoping in the [Later] Qin dynasty (384–417).[43] Once when Jian arrived at Rocky Hill, he suddenly saw a man, who said to him, "My wife committed adultery with another man, and then I was murdered by them. I want to seek revenge. Can you help me?"

The servant followed his words, and truly saw someone come. The ghost held the man's head and asked the servant to give him a hand [in fighting the man].[44] Right then they pushed the man down to the ground. When they left, the man was half dead.

The ghost sent the servant one thousand cash, one *pi* of yellow-green silk, and a coarse gown, and then exhorted him, saying, "This gown is from the Ding family [who lived] at the western gate of the market. You may wear it yourself, but don't sell it under any circumstance."

(*GXSGC*, #232. 420; *FYZL*, 67. 2004)

---

42. Donglai 東萊 Commandery; its seat was in modern Ye 掖 County, Shandong.
43. The surname of a servant follows his owner's, and that is why only his given name, Jian 健, is mentioned here. Information about Li Xian 李羨 is not available. Gaoping 高平, modern Guyuan 固原, Shanxi.
44. Originally it reads *nu huan* 奴換; Zheng Wanqing changed it into 奴喚. Neither of them makes much sense.

143. THE MAGISTRATE OF PINGYU

Wang Ping of Nandun of the Jin built a new house.[45] When he had just moved in, he dreamed of a man who said to him, "Magistrate Wang of Pingyu intended to bribe Pu Shengzhi with a jar of gold but was executed by Pu.[46] The gold was buried on top of me, and I have been pressed so harshly. Furthermore, you built a house on it. I will not even have a crack to come in and out now."

The next morning Wang immediately dug up the earth under the wall. After he had dug down five feet, he found the gold as expected.

(*GXSGC*, #81. 375; *TPYL*, 811. 3604a–b)

144. MOVING A TOMB

An adjutant of Xunyang Commandery dreamed of a woman who approached him and kneeled down in front of him,[47] saying, "The tomb I was buried in is near water and has been submerged. If you can truly save me, I will let you avoid a minor disaster, though you will not be able to become rich and noble."

The adjutant responded, "What is the mark [of your tomb]?"

The woman said, "When you see a fish-shaped hairpin on the shore of an islet, it is exactly my tomb."

The adjutant searched the next morning, and he found a tomb on which there was a hairpin. Thus he moved the tomb to a higher and drier place.

More than ten days later, the adjutant reached the eastern bridge and his ox started to run directly toward the river. Just as his cart was about to drop off the bridge, the ox suddenly changed direction and the adjutant was exactly able to avoid the calamity.

(*GXSGC*, #184. 405; *TPYL*, 718. 3182)

---

45. Nandun 南頓, modern Xiangcheng 項城, Henan.

46. Pingyu 平輿, modern Ru'nan 汝南, Henan.

Pu Shengzhi 暴勝之, Embroidered-Uniform Censor, or Bandit-Suppressing Censor, under Emperor Wu of Han.

47. Xunyang 尋陽 Commandery; its seat was in Jiujiang 九江, Jiangxi.

145. A GHOST BESTOWS TREASURE

During the Long'an reign (397–404) of the Jin, Yan Cong built a house. At night he dreamed of a man who asked him, "Why did you destroy my tomb?"

The next day, Yan dug through the earth in front of his bed and consequently found a coffin. Then he offered sacrifices to the dead man in the coffin, saying, "Now I'll move you to a good place and build another small tomb for you."

The next morning, a man arrived at his door, requesting to see him. The guest was named Zhu Hu. After they sat down, the guest said,[48] "I have lived here for forty years. For your handsome offer yesterday, I feel endlessly grateful. Today is an auspicious day. You may dig my coffin out right now.[49] In my suitcase I have gold mirrors to assist you."

Consequently he lifted the suitcase from the front part of the coffin, took out three gold mirrors, and bestowed them upon Yan Cong.

(*GXSGC*, #146. 395; *BTSC*, 135. 237b)

146. GHOSTS STRIVING FOR A TOMB[50]

Wang Boyang died. While building a tomb for him, his son obtained three painted coffins, which he moved to the southern hill and placed there. At night he dreamed of Lu Su,[51] who said to him angrily, "I'll kill your father."

---

48. *Biezuo shenglie* 別坐生列 is replaced with *Liezuo naiyan* 列坐乃言 based on the quotation of *BTSC* in *Tang leihan* 唐類函 (see *GXSGC*, #146. 395).
49. Here the six characters, 仆以寒暑衣手, are deleted based on the quotation of *BTSC* in *Tang leihan* 唐類函 (see *GXSGC*, #146. 395).
50. *TPGJ* (389. 3105) credits this story and a variant to *SSJ*. The variant is a longer version, in which Lu Su appears to beat Wang Boyang, and is also found in volume 6 of *Xu Soushen ji* 續搜神記.
51. Lu Su 魯肅 (172–217), styled Zijing 子敬, was a politician and military general of Wu (222–280) during the Three Kingdoms period. He played an important role diplomatically in forming an alliance with Shu (221–263) to defeat the troops of Cao Wei (220–265) in the famous Red Cliff Battle.

Not long afterward he dreamed of his father, who said to him, "Lu Su was contending with me for the tomb."[52]

Later, he saw several liters of blood on the cushion and he suspected that it was because of the killing by Lu Su. The tomb is now located one *li* east of the long, broad bridge.

(*GXSGC*, #176. 403; *TPYL*, 375. 1733a)

147. HUAN GONG REPAID BY A GHOST

Huan Gong was an adjutant of Huan Shimin (d. 389).[53] In front of his bed in his official residence in Dantu there was a dented cave. He looked at it carefully and found it was an old tomb, in which the coffin had rotted. While eating, Huan often threw some of his meal into the cave, and he did this for years.

Later, when he awoke from a nap, he found a man in front of his bed, saying, "It has been seven hundred years since I passed away. My offspring have been extinguished and sacrificial offerings discontinued. While eating, you have always shared your food with me. My gratitude to you is endless. According to the record of your position, you should be the Governor of Ningzhou."[54]

Later, Huan truly became the governor, as the man had told him.

(*GXSGC*, #164. 400; *TPGJ*, 320. 2539)

148. A DIVINE BIRTH

Hu Fuzhi of Qiao Commandery took a wife from the Li family.[55] For more than ten years they had no sons; then the wife passed away.

52. The original text reads *yudi* 與弟, "with [your] younger brother." It makes no sense. *TPGJ* (389. 3105) reads *yuwu* 與吾, "with me."

53. Huan Shimin 桓石民, nephew of the Grand Marshal Huan Wen, was military governor of Jingzhou, Jiangzhou, and Yuzhou 豫州 of Jin. *GXSGC* reads *Anmin* 安民 for *Shimin*.

54. Ningzhou 寧州, the area of modern Yunnan. Its seat was in Wei 味 County (present-day Qujing 曲靖, Yunnan).

55. Qiao 譙 Commandery; its seat was in modern Bo 亳 County, Anhui.

Hu wept bitterly over her, saying, "You did not leave me even a single son, yet you died. How cruel is this!"

Suddenly the woman sat up, saying, "Touched by your bitter grief, I will not become rotted right away. You may come to me after dusk, as you usually did; then I will give birth to a boy for you." After finishing, she lay down again.

Following what she said, Fuzhi approached her to make love in the dark, without fetching a light or candle. Further, he said with a sigh, "It is impossible for a dead woman to give birth to a baby. We can just make a side room to put her in, wait for ten months, and then encoffin her for the funeral."

After that, he felt that the woman's body was slightly warm, as if she had not died. After ten months, the woman truly gave birth to a baby boy. The boy was named Lingchan, meaning divine birth.

(*GXSGC*, #175. 403; *TPYL*, 360. 1660b; *TPGJ*, 321. 2548)

149. REN HUAIREN'S DEATH

In the first year of the Shengping reign (357–361) of the Jin, Ren Huairen was thirteen, and he became an administrative clerk in the Department of State Affairs. His fellow villager Wang Zu, who became a director in the same department for the second time, constantly bestowed favors [sexually] on him.

When Huairen was fifteen or sixteen, he tended to be rebellious. Harboring hatred toward him, Zu arrived in Jiaxing, killed Huairen, encoffined him, and buried him by the edge of Xu Zuo's farmland.[56]

Zuo lodged at his farm at night and saw the tomb. He offered sacrifice separately to the soul in the morning, at noon, and in the evening, yelling, "Ghost in the field, come to me to have some food." When it was dusk, the time for sleep, he would say, "Come accompany me to sleep." Zuo did this for quite a long time.

56. According to the "Treaties of Five Elements" in *Jin shu*, since the Taikang 太康 reign (280–289), buggery and keeping gigolos had become popular among scholar officials. The tragedy described in this story occurred in such a milieu. Cf. Zheng Wanqing, *YML*, 4. 124.

Later, the ghost suddenly showed himself, saying, "Tomorrow, my family shall take off the mourning clothes and offer me sacrifice, which will be extremely sumptuous. You may go together with me."

Zuo replied, "I am a stranger, I should not see them."

The ghost said, "I will conceal your form from them."

So Zuo went together with the ghost. After walking for the time needed to have a meal, they arrived at his home.

There were many guests in his home. The ghost took Zuo to the seat of the soul. After his gobbling, the food was all gone. All of his family wailed and could not control themselves, assuming their son had returned.

Seeing that Wang Zu was coming, the ghost said, "This is the man who killed me!" Since he was still afraid of him, he walked out right then, and thus Zuo's form was revealed.

Everyone in the family was terrified, and they all asked Zuo for the truth. Accordingly Zuo told them the story from beginning to end. They then followed Zuo to take the coffin away, and the ghost stopped appearing.

(*GXSGC*, #260. 433; *TPGJ*, 320. 2536–37)

150. ROMANCE OF A GHOST

There was a nobleman. After his death, Wang Fengxian, the Magistrate of Yongxing County,[57] dreamed of talking with him face to face, as they usually had before.

Fengxian asked him, "Do you still have sex with women?"

The noble replied, "Sometime later, you may go to my home to ask my maid."

After waking up later, Wang Fengxian went to ask the nobleman's maid. She replied, "Last night I dreamed of an incubus, my master."

(*GXSGC*, #237. 422; *TPGJ*, 276. 2183)

57. Yongxing 永興, Yuji 余暨 of Han; it was changed to Yongxing by Sun Quan (r. 222–252). Its seat was west of modern Xiaoshan 蕭山 County, Zhejiang.

151. ZHONG YOU'S GHOST GIRLFRIEND

Zhong You (151–230) suddenly stopped having audiences with the sovereign,[58] and both his consciousness and his temperament became abnormal. When his colleague asked why, he replied, "A woman often comes to me, and she is exceptionally beautiful." The man who asked said, "She must be a ghost. You should kill her."

Later, when the woman came, she stopped outside the door and asked, "Why are you intending to kill me?"

Zhong You said, "I won't." Then he called her in earnestly. He had a heart that could not bear to kill her, so he only slightly wounded her.

Then the woman ran out, rubbing the blood with new cotton all the way.

The next day, Zhong You sent someone to look for her by following the traces of blood on the ground. When he reached a big tomb, he saw a woman inside a coffin, whose body was like a living person's, wearing a white silk shirt and a red embroidered cotton sweater. One of her thighs had been wounded, and she was rubbing the blood with the cotton from the sweater.

After that she disappeared.

(*GXSGC*, #51. 366–67; *TPGJ*, 317. 2509)

152. A GHOST NURTURES A CHILD

In the tenth year of Taiyuan of Jin (385), Ruan Yuzhi lived in front of a Buddhist temple in Shixing.[59] He was fatherless, poor, and could not support himself. He cried all the time.

Suddenly he saw a ghost writing on a brick while approaching him.[60] It read,

58. Zhong You 鍾繇, styled Yuanchang 元常, a famous calligrapher and Grand Tutor of Cao Wei during the Three Kingdoms period.
59. Shixing 始興; its seat was southeast of modern Shaoguan 韶關, Guangdong. See Tan Qixiang, *Zhongguo lishi dituji*, 3. 58.
60. *Zhuan* 塼 was originally *bo* 搏, but the Zhonghua edition of *TPGJ* (320. 2539) changes it according to a Ming hand-copied edition.

Your father died and returned to the realm of darkness.
Why do you cry for so long?
Within three years from now,
your family will be supportable.
I shall lodge at your house
and not let you suffer any loss.
Do not fear that I will do you harm;
I will do good things for you.

From then on the ghost was always in his home and gave him what he needed. Two or three years later, Ruan's family was comparatively well off. He cooked a meal for the ghost, and talked and laughed together with him. When Ruan asked him for his surname, he replied, "My surname is Li, my name is Liuzhi, and I was your brother-in-law."

Ruan asked, "Where are you from?"

The ghost said, "I have already received punishment [in hell] and was temporarily born into the realm of ghosts. For the time being I lodge at your home, and in four or five years I will leave."

Ruan asked, "Where will you go?"

He replied, "I will be reborn into the world of human beings."

When the time came, the ghost bid him farewell and left, as expected.

(*GXSGC*, #125. 389; *TPGJ*, 320. 2539)

153. A CHILD IN RED

During the fifth year of the Yixi reign of the Jin (405–418), Liu Cheng of Pengcheng frequently saw ghosts.[61] When he became the Commander of the Left Guard, his official residence was connected to that of Chao Ying, the general. When Cheng approached Chao to sit and talk, they saw a little boy in red who held a round red flag, resembling a lily flower. A few days later, Chao's residence was set ablaze.

(*GXSGC*, #136. 393; *TPGJ*, 320. 2539–40)

61. Pengcheng, see footnote 22 in chapter 4.

154. CHILDREN STRIVING FOR A POT

At the beginning of the Yuanjia reign, Senior Recorder Liu Jun's home was located at Danyang.[62] One day when it was raining heavily, he saw three children in front of his gate, all about six to seven years old, playing games, yet their clothing was not wet at all. Jun suspected that they were not human beings.

Shortly thereafter, he saw that the children were fighting over a targeting pot. Jun pulled his bow to hit it with a ball and exactly hit the pot. Suddenly the children disappeared. Jun obtained the pot, then hung it by his attic.

The next day, a woman entered his door, holding the pot and sobbing. Jun asked her the reason, and she replied, "This is my son's belonging, I wonder why it is here?" Jun told her what had happened. The woman took the pot and buried it in front of her son's grave.

One day later, Jun saw one of the children again, who held the pot and came to his door. Lifting it, the child told Jun with a smile, "I got the pot again!" After finishing his words, he disappeared.

(*GXSGC*, #241. 423; *TPGJ*, 324. 2571; *TPYL*, 350. 1613a)

155. A GHOST PAYS A DEBT

Zhou Jing, a native of Anding Commandery,[63] was planting watermelon.

During a severe drought, a ghost lifted water from the well using a waterwheel, to water the watermelons for him. The watermelons became big and their stems luxuriant.

Zhou Jing asked the ghost his name, yet the ghost did not reply. After returning home, Zhou Jing told his father what had happened and asked, "Have you ever done a favor for someone?"

His father said, "Fan Ying, who lived in the western suburbs, previously worked as an official in [the government of] the commandery,

62. Danyang 丹陽 County, modern Danyang, Jiangsu.

63. Anding Commandery centered around the modern city of Jingchuan 涇川 in Gansu. See Tan Qixiang, *Zhongguo lishi dituji*, 4. 55.

and he had to pay several hundred *hu* of rice back to the government. At that time, I assisted him with one hundred *hu* [of rice]. The man has already died."

(*GXSGC*, #202. 410; *TPYL*, 978. 4335b)

156. EXCHANGING A GIRL WITH A BOY

In the first year of the Shengping reign (357–361) during the Jin, Chen Su of Shan County was wealthy.[64] Yet ten years after he took a wife, he had no sons. The husband intended to take a concubine. His wife prayed in front of a spirit and was suddenly pregnant.

The wife of his neighbor, a humble man, was pregnant at the same time. Therefore, Chen Su's wife bribed the wife of her neighbor, saying, "If I give birth to a boy, it is the will of heaven. If my baby is a girl and yours a boy, we should exchange them." Thus both sides agreed. Later, the neighbor's wife gave birth to a boy, and Chen's wife gave birth to a girl three days later. Then they exchanged them, and Chen Su was delighted.

When the boy was thirteen, he took the duty of offering sacrifices. An old servant woman of the family, who could often see ghosts, said [to Chen Su], "I found that when your ancestors came, they always stopped at the gate. I saw only a group of petty men who came to the seats and enjoyed the offering."

The father was astonished. He invited others who could see ghosts and asked them to observe when the sacrifice was offered. Their words were the same as the old servant woman's.

Then Chen Su confronted his wife. She was scared and told him the whole story. Then they sent the boy to his own home and asked for their daughter back.

(*GXSGC*, #92. 379; *TPGJ*, 319. 2527)

---

64. Shan 剡 County, see footnote 2 in chapter 1.

157. DEMONIC MAGIC

In the third year of the Yongchu reign (420–422) of Song, a ghost suddenly appeared at the home of Zhang Feng,[65] a man of Wu Commandery,[66] saying, "If you share your food with me, I shall protect and assist you." Then he ate with the ghost, placing a mat on the ground, spreading rice on the mat, and serving him wine, meat, and five other dishes. In this way the ghost obtained what he wanted and no longer offended people.

Later, taking advantage of cooking for the ghost, Feng cut the spot where they ate. Then he heard the cries of more than ten people, and the cries were sorrowful, all saying, "I am dying, yet how will I get a coffin?" He heard also, "Our host has a boat that he loves very much. I should take it as my coffin."

He saw the boat arrive, followed by the sound of wood being cut with a saw. When they finished cutting the boat, he heard someone calling to lift the corpse and place it into the coffin. Feng could not see anything, he only heard the voice arranging and directing, but without the sound of nails being driven into the coffin.

Then he saw the boat being gradually lifted into the air and entering the clouds. After a long while it disappeared, and the boat fell from the sky and shattered into a hundred pieces. Then he heard the wild laughter of several hundred people, saying, "How could you kill me? Do you think I should be stranded by you? I know your evil heart, and I hate what you did, therefore I broke your boat."

Feng changed his mind and served this ghost again. He asked his fortune and what to do in the future. The ghost told Feng, "You can place a big jar in the corner of the house; I'll find something for you."

Every ten days, he poured things out of the jar, including gold, silver, copper, iron, fish, and the like.

(*GXSGC*, #234. 420; *TPGJ*, 323. 2559; *FYZL*, 67. 2004–05)

65. For Zhang Feng 張縫, *TPGJ* (323. 2559) reads Zhang Long 張隆.
66. Wu Commandery; its seat was in modern Suzhou, Jiangsu.

5

THE NETHERWORLD AND THIS WORLD

158. A NU

When Chen Zhongju (ca. 95–168) was lowly and humble,[1] he often lodged at the home of his master, Huang Shen.[2]

One night, a baby was born to that family, but Zhongju did not know. Around the third watch at midnight, someone knocked on the door. After quite a while, someone replied from inside, "Inside my door there is a nobleman whom you cannot approach. It is more appropriate for you to come in through the back door."

After a little while, the visitor returned to the front door, and the one from inside asked him, "What kind of baby did you see? What name? What age will she or he live until?"

The one who returned replied, "It is a boy, called A Nu, and he will live until the age of fifteen."

The one inside asked again, "Why will he die [at such a young age]?"

The one who returned replied, "He will be building a house for someone. He will fall down and die." Zhongju heard this and memorized it secretly.

---

1. Chen Fan 陳蕃, styled Zhongju 仲舉, grand tutor during the regency of the Empress Dowager Dou 竇 (147–167). He joined the regent marshal Dou Wu 竇武 (d. 168) to curb the power of eunuchs yet was killed by them. Cf. *Hou Han shu* (History of Later Han), 96.
2. Another version reads *Huang Jia* 黃甲 for *Huang shen* 黃申 (*TPGJ* 316. 2502).

Fifteen years later, Zhongju became the governor of Yuzhang Commandery.[3] He sent an official to ask where the boy (A Nu) was. His family replied, "When he assisted your host in building a house, he fell down from it and died."

Afterward, Zhongju became a great man of rank as expected.[4]

(*GXSGC*, #41. 363; *TPGJ*, 137. 984 & 316. 2502)

159. WANG ZHI

A native of Langye,[5] surnamed Wang 王 and named Zhi 志,[6] lived in Qiantang.[7] His wife, from a Zhu family, died of illness during the ninth year of Taiyuan and left two children. Furthermore, Wang died of a sudden illness in the fourth month of the same year. Three days later, the area beneath his heart was still warm, and he awoke after seven days.

He said that right after his death, there were more than twenty men, all in black garments, who held life span records. After being questioned and recorded, he left and arrived at a building with a red door and white walls, resembling a palace. One official wore a red garment, white belt, black cap, and kerchief. The garments some officials wore were all connected with pearls and pieces of jade, differing from the garments of the human world.

He walked ahead farther and saw a large, tall man, whose bearing resembled a cloud. Wang kowtowed toward the official, saying to himself, *My wife has already died, and my orphan children are still young; I don't know what to do!* Then he shed tears.

---

3. Yuzhang 豫章 Commandery, the area west of modern Nanchang, Jiangxi. See Tan Qixiang, *Zhongguo lishi dituji*, 4. 25–26.
4. *TPYL* (361. 1665a) quotes this story (a bit different at the end) from *SSJ* and notes, "It is the same in the *Youming lu*." For an English translation of that item, see DeWoskin and Crump, *In Search of the Supernatural*, 236.
5. Langye 琅邪 Commandery, the area of modern Linyi 臨沂 and Zhecheng 諸城, Shandong (see Tan Qixiang, *Zhongguo lishi dituji*, 3. 51). Eastern Jin established Langye Commandery at Baixia 白下 (north of modern Nanjing).
6. *TPGJ* (383. 3051) reads ming Zhi 名志, "named Zhi," for *wangming* 忘名, "his name forgotten."
7. Qiantang 錢塘, modern Hangzhou.

At this, the official's countenance changed, and he said, "According to [the record of] your life span, you should have come here; but because of your orphans, I specially grant you three more years of time [to live in the human world]."

Wang said further, "Three years are not enough to keep my son alive."

A man near him said, "How stupid, you vulgar dead! Three years here are thirty years in the mortal world."

Then they sent him out.

After another thirty years, Wang died as expected.

(*GXSGC*, #124. 389; *TPYL*, 887. 3941; *TPGJ*, 383. 3050–51)

160. BORROWING A LIFE SPAN

During the period of the Taiyuan reign,[8] a Daoist master came from afar and nobody knew where he was from. He said, "When one's life should end but a living person is willing to die in his or her stead, then one can continue living. If one urges someone to replace him or her by force, it works for only a short while." When people heard this, all considered his words false and absurd.

Brothers Wang, Ziyou (d. 388), and Zijing (344–388) lived in great harmony.[9] When Zijing became terminally ill, Ziyou told the master, "My capability is not as good as my younger brother's, and [the promotion of] my position is blocked. Please exchange my life span with my younger brother's."

The master replied, "The case in which a living person may replace the dying one is only if the living person's life span still has time left,

8. Taiyuan 泰元 should be Taiyuan 太元 (376–396), reign of Emperor Xiaowu 孝武 (r. 373–396) of Eastern Jin.

9. Ziyou 子猷, named Huizhi 徽之, was the fifth son of Wang Xianzhi 王羲之 (390–c. 365), the well-known calligrapher of Eastern Jin. He was known as an eccentric and undisciplined man. Zijing 子敬, named Xianzhi 獻之, was the seventh son of Wang Xizhi and a famous calligrapher. He was the *Zhongshu ling* 中書令, president of the Central Secretariat, before his death. For their biographies, see *Jin shu* 80. 3103–06).

so that the time can be added to the life span of the dead. Yet now when your worthy younger brother's life should be ending, your life span should be exhausted as well. Then, what are you going to use to replace his life span?"

Ziyou had previously had a carbuncle on his back. After Zijing became terminally ill, they were constantly forbidden to visit each other. When Ziyou heard that his brother had passed away, he stroked his heart with his hands in deep sorrow. He did not even utter a single sound; thereupon his carbuncle burst and broke.[10]

Thinking over the words of the master, they seem convincing and had a solid basis.

(*GXSGC*, #129. 391; footnote in "Shangshi" [Grieving for the departed] of *SSXY*, 17. 645)

161. CHEN LIANG REVIVES FROM DEATH

During the Taiyuan reign period (376–396) [of Jin], Chen Liang, a man of Beidi Commandery,[11] was on good terms with Liu Shu, a native of

---

10. This paragraph is quoted in *TPYL* (371. 1712a) as from *YML*. But the death of Ziyou depicted in the *SSXY* (17. 645) is totally different:

> Wang Hui-chih and his younger brother, Wang Hsien-chih, were both critically ill at the same time, but Hsien-chih died first (388). Hui-chih asked his attendants, "Why don't I hear any news at all? This must mean he's already dead." As he spoke he showed no hint of grief. Immediately ordering a sedan chair, he came to Hsien-chih's house to offer condolences, still without weeping at all. Since Hsien-chih had always been fond of the seven-stringed zither (*ch'in*), Hui-chih went directly in and sat on the spirit bed (*ling-ch'uang*). Taking Hsien-chih's zither, he started to play, but the strings were not in tune. Throwing it to the ground, he cried out, "Tzu-ching! Tzi-ching! You and your zither are both gone forever!" Whereupon he gave himself up utterly to his grief for a long while. In a little more than a month he, too, was dead. (Mather, *SSXY*, 17. 328)

11. Beidi 北地 Commandery covers the area around modern Yao 耀 County, Shanxi (see Tan Qixiang, *Zhongguo lishi dituji*, 3. 43–44).

the state of Pei.[12] In addition, he did business with Li Yan, who was from the same commandery. Once, they gained a handsome profit and purchased some wine to drink together to celebrate. Consequently, Yan murdered Liang. He wrapped his corpse in reeds and threw it into the wild grass.

After ten days or so, Liang was revived and returned home. He said that when he died, he saw a man who wore a red kerchief and led him to the gate of a city. Under the gate there was a stand, and [by the stand] he saw an old man who held a red pen to check a record book.

The man who wore a red kerchief said, "Down below was a man by the name of Chen Liang. He is only a roaming soul, so there is no department that deals with his circumstance. It is for this reason that I brought him here."

The man who checked the record book replied, "You may let him leave right away."

After he came out of the gate, Liang suddenly saw his old friend Liu Shu. Liu said to him, "I never expected that we would meet in this place. Luckily, you have been released by an honorable deity now. In the mulberry tree that grows behind the side house of my home, there is a wild cat that frequently makes trouble, and my family has been excessively vexed by it. After you return, would you please speak to my family for me?"

Liang promised him.

After he regained consciousness, he went to the officials to bring a lawsuit against Li Yan, and Li pleaded guilty. Then Chen Liang specially told [Liu] Shu's family what Shu had said.[13]

His family cried, saying, "All is like what he said." Therefore, they cut down the tree, caught the wild cat, and killed it. The abnormality was finally gone.

(*GXSGC*, #131. 391–92; *TPGJ*, 378. 3010)

---

12. Pei 沛 was a state in the Western Jin period, but it became a commandery during the Eastern Jin. The seat of Pei Commandery was located northwest of the modern city of Huaibei, Jiangsu. See Tan Qixiang, *Zhongguo lishi dituji*, 4. 7–8.

13. *Reng* 仍, "still," in the text should be *nai* 乃, "then."

162. THE THUNDER GOD

In the first year of the Jingping reign (423–424) [of Song], a native of Qu'e died of an illness and met his father in heaven.[14]

His father said to him, "Your life span has exactly eight years left. When this period is up, you will be subject to guilt and punishment after death. I want to find you a proper job, but there is no vacant position except the Thunder God. I shall report [to the official] so as to let you fill the position."

Right then he sent in a report, so his son was able to fill the position.

Being ordered to go east of the Liao River to give rain, his son rode on the dew carriage that contained water,[15] spraying water from the east to the west. Before finishing the task, he again received a tally that transferred him west of Liao River.

Having finished the task, he met his father and bitterly requested to return, saying that he was unhappy to be in that position. His father sent him away; thus he was able to revive.

(*GXSGC*, #240. 422; *TPGJ*, 383. 3052–53)

163. XU YOU

Xu You (d. 204) dreamed of an official wearing black clothes.[16] Holding a painted tablet with six official dispatches, the official in black kneeled down, saying, "You, the governor, will be the Lord of the Northern Dipper in the seventh month of the upcoming year." Furthermore, there was another tablet with four official dispatches, stating, "Chen Kang will be the Recorder."

14. Qu'e was located at the modern city of Danyang 丹陽, Jiangsu. See Tan Qixiang, *Zhongguo lishi dituji*, 3. 55.

15. *Zhong you* 中有 was originally *niu yi* 牛以, and it has been changed here according to a hand-copied version of the Ming.

16. Xu You 許攸, styled Ziyuan 子遠, was a native of Nanyang 南陽 and a noted military advisor in the Three Kingdoms period. Being arrogant because of his achievement, he was killed by Cao Cao 曹操 (155–220), the posthumous Emperor Wu of Wei.

After he awoke, by chance Chen Kang arrived, saying, "Today I come to visit." Hearing this, Xu You felt even more terrified. He asked Kang the reason for the visit. Kang said, "I am a Daoist mentor. I should be no more than a local deity; now I have the position of Recorder under the Northern Dipper. I feel I do not deserve it."

In the seventh month of the next year, both of them died on the same day.

(*GXSGC*, #204. 410–11; *TPGJ*, 276. 2176)

164. WANG JU

Wang Ju,[17] the prefect of Hengyang,[18] was going to be the Governor of Guangzhou.[19]

When Ju reached Changsha, he saw a man who was more than ten feet tall, wearing a white single-layered cotton shirt, holding a tablet, and yelling to his attendants on the bank, "Come to me!"

Ju examined the tablet; it was from Du Lingzhi. He entered the boat to speak with him, and they talked about their parting and gathering in the old days.

Ju asked, "You are a native of Jingzhao.[20] When did you start your journey to come here?"

Du replied, "I set off this morning."

Ju was surprised and asked him again.

Du said, "It is the Jingzhao in heaven, and I myself am a ghost. I was sent to see you, that's all."

17. Wang Ju 王矩, styled Lingshi 令式, was the prefect of Nanping 南平 of Jin. He was appointed the Governor of Guangzhou of Jin in 360 and died not long after that. See *Jin shu*, 100. 2625.
18. Hengyang Commandery, see note 58 in chapter 2.
19. Guangzhou in Western Jin covered most areas of modern Guangdong and Guangxi. Its seat was Fanyu 番禺, modern city of Guangzhou. See Tan Qixiang, *Zhongguo lishi dituji*, 3. 57–58.
20. Jingzhao 京兆 Commandery, the area northwest of present-day Xi'an, Shanxi, in the Western Jin dynasty. See Tan Qixiang, *Zhongguo lishi dituji*, 3. 33–34.

Ju was terrified. Accordingly, Du asked for a brush and paper [to write], saying, "You must not know a single word from heaven." Then he wrote on the paper, folded and rolled it, put it in a small box he got from Ju, sealed it, and handed it to Ju, saying, "Don't open it now. When you arrived at Guangzhou, you can look at it."

Ju stayed [at Guangzhou] for several months, and he became melancholic; then he opened the box and looked at the letter. It read, "This is the order to summon Wang Ju as Recorder of the Left Fate Controller."

Ju felt terribly upset; accordingly he died of an illness.

(*GXSGC*, #219. 416; *TPGJ*, 322. 2554)

165. WANG WENDU SUMMONED TO BE A GHOST OFFICIAL

Wang Wendu (330–375) of the Jin garrisoned at Guangling.[21] One day, he suddenly saw two attendants with swan-head style imperial tablets in their hands who came to summon him.

Greatly startled, Wang asked the attendants, "What type of official am I going to be?"

The attendants said, "General of the North and Governor of both Xuzhou and Yanzhou."[22]

Wang said, "I have already been in such a position, why do you summon me again?"

The ghosts said, "That is in the world of humans. Now the positions you will take are official titles in heaven."

Wang was frightened. Then he saw the welcoming officials in black clothes and numerous minor clerks in white garments. A short while later, Wang became sick and died.

(*GXSGC*, #157. 398; *TPYL*, 606. 2727b; *FYZL*, 56. 1692)

---

21. Wang Wendu 王文度, named Tanzhi 坦之, was president of the Central Secretariat and Governor of Xuzhou and Yanzhou of Eastern Jin. See *Jin shu*, 75. 1964. Guangling 廣陵, modern Yangzhou 揚州, Jiangsu.

22. In Eastern Jin, Xuzhou 徐州 covered the area around modern Yangzhou, while Yanzhou 兗州 covered the area northwest of Yangzhou. See Tan Qixiang, *Zhongguo lishi dituji*, 4. 5–6.

166. LIU QINGSONG

When Liu Qingsong of Guangling got up in the morning, he saw a man wearing an official's garment. The man gave him a tablet, saying, "You are summoned to be the Governor of Lu Commandery."[23] After finishing his words he left, and did not return.

The next day, the man came again, saying, "You should assume your position immediately."

Qingsong knew that he must die. He went home to tell his wife, deal with domestic affairs, and take a bath. In the late afternoon, he saw carts and horses with officials on both sides.

Qingsong suddenly died. His family all witnessed the cart rising into the sky. It went out southward for more than a hundred steps and gradually rose higher until it finally disappeared.

(*GXSGC*, #216. 415; *TPGJ*, 321. 2545)

167. JI QUESHI

Ji Weihan's younger brother [within his clan] was called Queshi, and was previously the adjutant of Tan Daoji (d. 436).[24] He had been ill, and he saw a man in red who came and bowed to him with hands clasped, saying, "I came especially to pick you up."

In order to avoid the summons, Queshi offered the man handsome gifts and a sumptuous feast. The ghost said, "Moved by your welcome of boundless hospitality, I shall stop a little while for you." Then he disappeared, and Queshi gradually recovered.

Later, during his mourning period for his parent, Queshi returned to Shouyang.[25] Again he met the ghost, who said to him, "The envoy who comes to welcome you is arriving soon. You should dress up right now."

23. Lu 魯 Commandery, the area of modern Qufu 曲阜, Shandong.

24. Tan Daoji 檀道濟, a famous general under Liu Yu 劉裕 (r. 420–422), Emperor Wu 武 and the founder of the [Liu] Song dynasty. He was killed by Emperor Wen 文 (407–453) during the thirteen years of Yuanjia (436). See his biography in *Song shu*, 43. 1341–44.

25. Shouyang 壽陽, modern Shou 壽 County, Anhui.

Queshi pleaded, "Previously you showed mercy to me. Could you take pity on me again?"

The ghost replied, "The previous summons was just intended to enslave you; therefore I stopped it. Now the lord of Mount Tai has offered you the position of Recorder and furthermore, the envoy will arrive soon. There is no way to refuse anymore."

At that moment they saw the carts and horses, with halberds displayed in front. Queshi pointed this out to his family, yet none of them could see.

After leaving a letter at home, Queshi summoned his relatives and friends to bid farewell. While talking and laughing, he suddenly passed away.

(*GXSGC*, #246. 424; *TPGJ*, 323. 2559–60)

168. OXEN EPIDEMIC

During the period of the Huan Xuan reign (402–404),[26] when oxen were stricken by an epidemic, there was a man who ate the meat of a dead ox and thus became ill and died.

After he died, he saw someone who, holding a notebook, took him up to heaven. An honorable man asked, "What crime did this man commit?" The netherworld official replied, "This man committed the crime of eating the meat of a dead ox."

The honorable man said, "Now we need oxen for transportation. Since they are not able [to do it],[27] their meat is being taken as food by common people. Why kill him further?" [So the honorable man] urged him to allow the man to return [to the human world].

26. Huan Xuan 桓玄, the youngest son, by a concubine, of Huan Wen (213–373), commander-in-chief of the Jin. He became the Governor of Jiangzhou and the Army Commander of Jingzhou and seven other commanderies under Emperor An (397–402), yet usurped the Jin in 403 by capturing the capital Jiankang and establishing the short-lived Chu. In the following year he was defeated and killed by Liu Yu (356–422), founder of the Song.

27. "Since they are not able to" 既不能 is not found in the Zhonghua edition of *TPYL* or in *TPGJ*.

Having been revived, the man told the story in detail. Thereupon none of those who ate ox meat had any trouble.

(*GXSGC*, #116. 386; *TPYL*, 887. 3942a, 900. 3995a; *TPGJ*, 383. 3053)

169. GAN QING

During the Jin dynasty there was a man by the name of Gan Qing, who passed away without any illness.[28] At that time the Magician Wu Meng told Qing's son, "Marquis Gan's life span is not yet exhausted. I'm requesting to prolong it,[29] so you cannot encoffin his body and send it to the grave."

Qing's dead body lay in a quiet room, and only beneath his heart was still a bit warm. Qing lay there for seven days. It was just in midsummer and Qing's body was about to decay;[30] then Meng came at dawn and dashed water on him. Around noon, Qing awoke, and at once tried to speak. Before he uttered any words, all of his family felt grief as well as joy. Meng asked someone to spray water on him by mouth, and thereupon Qing got up. After vomiting several liters of rotten blood, he was gradually able to speak. After three days, he recovered his former condition.

He said that at the beginning he saw several dozen people coming, and he was tied up, shackled, and then brought to a prison. More than ten people in the same circumstances answered questions in turn. Before his turn arrived, he saw Master Wu, facing north, stating that he should be released. Thereupon the king ordered his men to take off his shackles and let him go back home. All the officials he saw welcomed Master Wu, and Wu greeted them as his fellows. It was not clear what deity he was.

(*GXSGC*, #72, 373; *TPGJ*, 378. 3009–10; *TPYL*, 887. 3942a)

---

28. Gan Qing 干慶, elder brother of Gan Bao 干寶 (d. 336), Eastern Jin scholar and the compiler of *Soushen ji*.
29. For *fang wei qingming* 方為請命, *TPGJ* (378. 3010) reads 我為試請命, "I'm trying to request to prolong his life span."
30. 時盛暑，慶形體向壞 is added from *TPYL* (887. 3942b).

170. SHAMAN SHU LI[31]

In Baqiu County there was a shaman called Shu Li.[32] He died of an illness in the first year of the Yongchang reign (322–323) of the Jin. The local earth god escorted him to Mount Tai.

The laymen usually addressed a shaman as Daoist. When they first passed by the Houses of Good Fortune in the netherworld,[33] the local earth god asked the official, "What kind of place is this?" The official replied, "The Houses of Daoists." The local earth god said, "This man is a Daoist." Then he handed him over.

Li entered the gate. He saw hundreds and thousands of tile-roofed houses, all hung with bamboo curtains and naturally fitted with beds and couches.[34] Men and women stayed separately. Some were chanting sutras, some were singing hymns, and some were eating leisurely. All of them were happy beyond expression.

Shu Li's document and name reached the gate of Mount Tai, yet he himself did not. The local earth god was investigated and questioned.

The god said, "On the way here we saw several thousand tile-roofed houses. I asked the official, who said that they were for Daoists, and so I handed Li over."

Thereupon a spirit was sent to bring him again.

At that time Shu Li had not yet finished looking over all the places when he saw a man with eight hands and four eyes. With gold pestles in his hands the man ran toward Shu, intending to crash into him. Terrified, Shu ran back out of the gate. The spirit was already waiting for him, and he caught Shu and brought him to Mount Tai.

---

31. This is one of the noted "netherworld adventure" narratives, in which many aspects of the Chinese netherworld have been changed to reflect Buddhist beliefs. The trial and physical tortures described here, for example, are not at all indigenous. Sacrificial offerings made in traditional Chinese culture were also challenged. From this story we can see the Buddhist conquest of China in literature as well as the critical conflict between Buddhism and Confucianism.
32. Baqiu 巴丘 County, modern Xiajiang 峡江, Jiangxi.
33. *Mingsi* 冥司 (the netherworld) is added from *TPGJ*.
34. *TPGJ* (283. 3253) reads *xuan lian zhi ta* 懸簾置榻 (hung with bamboo curtains and fitted with couches).

The Governor of Mount Tai asked Shu, "When you were in the world of human beings, what did you do?"

Shu replied, "I served thirty-six thousand spirits, exorcised evil demons for people, and presided over temple sacrifices. Sometimes I slaughtered cows, calves, pigs, sheep, chickens, and ducks."

The governor said, "You flattered spirits by killing living creatures, so you are guilty of a crime for which you deserve to be put on a hot grill."[35]

The governor had an official lead Shu to the place featuring the hot grill. There he saw a creature with an ox head and a human body. The creature held an iron fork, pierced Shu with it, and placed him onto the iron grill. After tossing and turning on the grill, his body was scorched and mashed; he pleaded in vain for death. Tortured for two days and one night, he experienced the most intolerable suffering.

The governor asked the supervisor [of record keeping], "Should Shu Li's life be ended? Or did someone deprive him of the rest of his years?"

They checked the record, and it turned out that eight years still remained in his life span. The governor said, "Bring him over here." The man with the ox head skewered Shu again with the iron fork and placed him by the side of the grill.

The governor said, "Now I will send you back to live out the rest of the years in your life span. Never again kill creatures and engage in licentious sacrifices!"

All of a sudden, Shu Li was revived, and subsequently he did not work as a shaman anymore.

(*GXSGC* #82. 376; *FYZL* 62. 1849–50; *TPYL* 735. 3259a; *TPGJ* 283. 2253–54)

171. KANG ADE

Kang Ade had been dead for three days, and then he returned to life. He said, "When I first died, two people supported me with their hands under my armpits, and an official on a white horse ran after us.

35. 佞神殺生，其 (flattered spirits by killing living creatures, so) are added from *TPGJ* (283. 3254).

"Not knowing how many *li* we walked, I saw a black gate facing north. Entering from the south, I saw a black gate facing east; entering from the west, I saw a black gate facing south; and entering from the north, I saw more than ten tile-roofed houses. There was a man wearing a black garment and towering cap, with more than thirty officials by his side, all calling him governor; to the southwest there were also forty or fifty officials."

Then Ade went forward to greet the governor. The governor asked, "What did you do to serve?"

Ade replied, "I built a Buddhist tower and a monastery at home to support Buddhist monks."

The governor said, "You achieved grand fortune and merit." Then he asked the Emissary of Record Keeping: "Is this man's life span exhausted?"[36]

Ade saw an official holding a book and lowering his head to the ground to check the records; the words were very small. The official said, "There are still thirty-five years left."

The governor was furious, saying, "How could you, a minor official, dare to suddenly deprive others of their lives?" Then he had the white-horse officer tied to a pillar and punished him with one hundred blows until his blood overflowed.

The governor asked Ade, "Do you want to go back home?"

Adereplied, "Yes."

The governor said, "Now I'm going to send you back home, yet I intend to let you travel in hell right now." He gave Ade a horse and an attendant, and they went out from the northeast.

Not knowing how many *li* he had passed, Ade saw a city that was several square *li* in area. There were numerous earth houses. Then he saw his deceased elder uncle, elder aunt, younger uncle, and younger aunt, who had died before he began to worship Buddha. All of them were wearing fetters and rags. Their bodies were covered with mucus and blood.

---

36. Dulu shizhe 都錄使者 is rendered here as Emissary of Record Keeping. The duty of the officials in this position can be different, though all of them are related to record keeping of people's life spans and the deeds in their current lives, which relate to karmic retribution through physical transformation into their next lives.

While going forward farther, he saw a city in which someone was lying on a burning metal bed, which was just becoming red. In total he saw about ten hells, and each had its own horrible torture. The names of the hells were Red Sand, Yellow Sand, and White Sand, a total of seven; and then there were Knife Mountains, Sword Trees, and Red Bronze Pillars for people to embrace. Then they returned.

Further, he saw seventy or eighty houses roofed with tube-shaped tiles, both sides of which were planted with Chinese scholar trees. They were called The Houses of Good Fortune. Various disciples of the Buddha lived inside. Those who had more blessings would ascend to heaven, and those who had fewer blessings stayed in these rooms.

From a distance Ade saw more than twenty big palaces, and a man and two women coming down from one of them. They were his father's elder brother and younger brother, each with his wife, who had died after Ade started worshiping Buddha.

In a moment a Buddhist monk came and asked Ade, "Do you know me?" Ade replied, "No!" The monk said, "How come you don't know me? You and I have been the host of Buddha." Thereupon Ade remembered it.

When they returned to the governor's office, the governor dispatched the two men to send Ade back home, and suddenly he revived.

(*GXSGC*, #264. 434–35; annotation in *Bianzheng lun* 辯證論, 8)

172. SE LUZHEN'S EXPERIENCE IN THE NETHERWORLD

Se Luzhen, the Attendant of the Mansion of the Northern Palace, was originally a clerk of Xun Xian (322–359), the Inner Gentleman.[37] In the middle of the sixth month during the fifth year of Taiyuan of the Jin, he died of an illness. After one night he awoke, saying that he had met Cui, Xian's son.

Cui said to him in happy astonishment, "The years of your life span are not yet up, but this bureau needs to get three generals. For this

37. Xun Xian 荀羨 was a general of the Jin and had been the *Bei chonglang jiang* 北中郎將 (Northern Leader of Court Gentleman) and Governor of Xuzhou. See *Jin shu*, 75. 1980.

reason I cannot let you go. If you know someone who is as capable and efficient as you are, I will replace you with him."

Luzhen recommended Gong Ying immediately. Cui asked, "Is Ying capable of shouldering the task?" Luzhen replied, "Ying is not inferior to me."

At first, Cui asked Luzhen to write down his name, but the words he wrote could not be used by ghosts. Then Cui found a pen and wrote it down himself. Thus Luzhen was able to come out.

Suddenly he saw a former neighbor, who had died seven or eight years earlier and was then a gatekeeper of Mount Tai. He asked Luzhen, "Is Inspector Se the only one who is able to go back?" Then he entrusted Luzhen with this: "After you go back, please tell my wife that before I died, I buried fifteen thousand coins under the large bed in our residence. I originally intended to purchase bracelets for my daughter, yet I did not expect that I would die suddenly and so was not able to tell my wife." Luzhen promised him.

Right after he was revived, he sent someone to report to his neighbor's wife, but she had already sold the house and moved to Wujin.[38] Then he went there to tell her, and also told the owner of the house and asked him to dig the cash up. As expected, they found as much money there as they had been told they would. Se Luzhen urged the gatekeeper's wife to purchase bracelets for her daughter.

In a short while, Gong Ying also died. People of that time all took the story as a marvel.

(*GXSGC* #123. 388–89; *TPGJ* 383. 3050)

173. EXCHANGING FEET

During the reign of Emperor Yuan of Jin (317–322), a certain man from a noble clan died of a sudden illness. He saw a man who brought him up to heaven, and visited the Controller of Fate. The Controller of Fate double-checked his records; his life span was not up yet, and he had been summoned by mistake. The supervisor sent an order to let him go back.

38. Wujin 武進, modern Wujin County, Jiangsu.

The man's feet were still painful. He could not walk and thus had no way to return to the mortal world. Several supervisors became anxious. They said to each other, "If this man cannot return in the end because of the pain in his feet, we will be punished for detaining an innocent person." Consequently they told the Controller of Fate one after another.

The Controller of Fate deliberated for quite a while, then said, "By chance there is a newly summoned foreigner, surnamed Kang, who is outside the western gate. This man deserves the punishment of death right away, yet his feet are extremely healthy. Exchange them, it wouldn't hurt any of them."

The supervisor accepted the order and went out, and was about to exchange them. Yet the foreigner's body was extremely ugly and his feet were awful, thus the man was reluctant to accept them. The supervisor said, "If you do not exchange, then you have to choose to stay here forever."

Having no other choice, the man obeyed him. The supervisor asked both of them to close their eyes. In a moment, their feet had been exchanged.

Then they sent the man to return home, and he was suddenly revived. He told his family everything. He exposed and looked at his feet; they were truly the foreigner's feet, which were all covered with hairs and emitted an unpleasant odor. The man was a scholar, who was fond of embellishing his fingers and feet. However, he now suddenly had such feet. He did not want to see them at all. Even though he was able to be alive again, from time to time he became melancholic and almost suicidal.

Others saw the foreigner who was dead but not yet encoffined, and his home was at the Eggplant Riverside. The man went there himself to see the foreigner's corpse, and he saw that his feet were attached to the foreigner's body. When the foreigner was encoffined and sent to the graveyard, the man faced him and wept.

The foreigner's sons all possessed the natural disposition to love their father. Whenever it was a festival or first day of a month, all his sons missed their father sadly. They ran to the man and embraced his feet to cry loudly. When they suddenly met on the way, they would hold his feet and wail. Because of this, every time he went out or came in, he asked people to guard the gate against the sons of the foreigner.

He hated the dirty feet for the rest of his life and never looked at them. Even during the three hottest ten-day periods of the year in the midsummer, he always covered them with multiple layers of cloth, not allowing them to be exposed at any time.

(*GXSGC* #70. 372–73; *TPGJ* 376. 2993–94)

174. SHI CHANGHE

Shi Changhe died, yet four days later he revived, saying that when he first died he walked toward the southeast. He saw two people fixing the road ahead, who always kept fifty steps away from him; when Changhe walked faster, they walked faster as well so that the distance between them remained the same. On both sides of the road were shrubs with thorns, all of which were like falcon talons. He saw a crowd of people, old and young, walking in the thorn bushes, as if they were being pursued. Their bodies were wounded by the thorns, and congealed blood was seen on the ground.

Seeing that Changhe walked alone on the smooth road, the people in the thorn bushes sighed, saying, "Only the disciples of Buddha are happy—they can walk on the main road."

Walking forward, Changhe saw seventy or eighty tile-roofed houses; among them there were more than ten attics with windows. A man with a face three feet wide, wearing a long-sleeved black gown, was sitting by the window. Only the upper part of his gown could be seen.

Changhe bowed to the man. The man said to him, "Worthy Shi, you have come? It has been more than twenty years since we parted."

Changhe replied, "Yes." Then, in his mind, it seemed that he recalled the moment of parting.

Meng Cheng, Governor of Pingyi Commandery,[39] and his wife had died previously. The man in the attic asked, "Worthy man, did you know Cheng?"

Changhe replied, "I knew him."

39. Pingyi 馮翊 Commandery; its seat was in present-day Dali 大荔, Shanxi, during the Jin dynasty.

The man in the attic said, "When he was alive, Meng Cheng did not make a great effort [in religious pursuits]; now he is constantly doing the cleaning for me. His wife made a great effort; now she lives leisurely without being bothered by affairs of the government authority."

He lifted his hand and pointed to a house to the southwest, saying, "Now Meng Cheng's wife lives there."

Right then Meng Cheng's wife opened the window and saw Changhe. She asked, "Worthy Shi, when did you come?" Then she asked about each of his sons and daughters by name, old and young, and if they were doing well. Finally she said, "Before returning home, please drop in. I rely on you to bring a letter to them."

In a moment, Changhe saw Cheng coming from west of the attic with a broom and a manure basket in one hand and a walking stick in the other. He also asked about his family. The man in the attic said, "I heard that Yulongchao is making a great effort in his practice. Do you believe? What do you practice?"

Changhe replied, "I don't eat fish or meat, never drink wine, constantly practice chanting the honorable sutras, and save those who experience various illnesses and sufferings."

The man in the attic said, "It looks like what others have said about you is not false." Then he asked the Supervisor of Record Keeping,[40] "Is Worthy Shi's life span exhausted, or did someone absurdly deprive him of his life?"

The supervisor replied, "According to the record, there are still forty years left [in his life span]."

The man in the attic ordered the supervisor: "Please prepare one carriage, two horses, and two officials to escort Worthy Shi home."

Just a moment later, from the east the carriage, horses, and attendants came, and the number was exactly as dispatched. Changhe kowtowed, bid farewell, mounted the carriage, and started the trip home. By the side of the road he had previously passed, there were post houses with beds, couches, and cooking and dining utensils used by the officials and commoners.

---

40. Dulu Zhuzhe 都錄主者, Supervisor of Record Keeping, sometimes called simply *zhuzhe* 主者, Supervisor, is the head of the department that keeps records of people's life spans.

Abruptly, they arrived at his home. Walking forward, Changhe saw his parents sitting by the side of his corpse.

Seeing his corpse as big as an ox and smelling the bad odor from it, Changhe was reluctant to enter it anymore. He walked around the corpse three times and sighed. When he passed by the head of his dead body, he noticed his late elder sister pushing him from behind. He fell down onto the face of his dead body and, due to this, revived.

(*GXSGC*, #265. 435–36; annotation in *Bianzheng lun*, 8)

175. ZHAO TAI TRAVELS IN HELLS[41]

Zhao Tai, styled Wenhe, was a native of Beiqiu of Qinghe.[42] The government summoned him to take office, but he did not accept. He devoted himself to the study of books and documents and became famous in his village. At the age of thirty-five, Zhao Tai suddenly felt a pain in his heart and died at midnight on the thirteenth day of the seventh month in the fifth year of the Taishi reign of the Jin (265–274).[43] His heart remained somewhat warm and his body flexible. After the corpse had been kept for ten days, a breath that sounded like thunder

41. This is one of the earliest "netherworld adventure" narratives, which shows a heavy influence of Buddhist concepts of hell with great detail. In addition, the depiction of the "City of Transformation" is creative and not found anywhere else, including in Buddhist sutras. This story has been translated into English previously; see Kao, *Classical Chinese Tales of the Supernatural and the Fantastic*, 162–71. A variant of this story is found in Wang Yan's *Mingxiang ji*, a collection of Buddhist miracle tales that appeared some fifty years later; see Campany's rendition in *Signs from the Unseen Realm*, 77–82.

    For studies of the "netherworld adventure" motif, see Maeno Naoaki, "Meikai yugyo"; *Chugoku shosetsu shi ko*, 112–49; and Campany, "Return-from-Death Narratives in Early Medieval China."

42. Beiqiu 貝邱, southeast of the modern city of Linqing 臨清, Shandong. During the Jin, it belonged to the Qinghe region at the border of modern Hebei and Shandong. See Tan Qixiang, *Zhongguo lishi dituji*, 3. 39–40.

43. The "Song Taishi" (465–471) in *TPGJ* (190. 740) is a mistake for "Jin Taishi," since it was much later, even after the death of Liu Yiqing (d. 444), the compiler of this collection. *Bianzhen lun* reads "Jin" for "Song." *Mingxiang ji* (quoted in *TPGJ* 377. 2996) also reads "Zhao Tai of the Jin."

erupted from his throat. Opening his eyes, he asked for water to drink. Having finished drinking, he got up right away.

He said that when he first died, there were two men who rode yellow horses and were followed by two soldiers. They simply said, "Catch him and take him away." The two soldiers supported him under his arms from both sides and proceeded toward the east.

Not knowing how many *li* they had passed, he then saw a big city wall, which resembled tin and iron in color and was extremely tall. Entering from the western gate, he saw the official residence, which had a black double gate and included several dozen tile-roofed buildings. There were about fifty or sixty men and women. The major official, wearing black clothing, listed Zhao Tai's name as the thirtieth. After a moment he was taken in. The prefect sat facing westward and double-checked his name and surname.

Then Zhao Tai was taken southward through a black gate. There was a man wearing scarlet clothing, sitting in a large room, calling out names in order, and asking the people what they had done during their lives: what crimes they had committed, what merits they had achieved, and what good deeds they had done. Each person replied differently.

The supervisor said, "Please make sure what you say is true. From the six ministries we always dispatch Emissaries of Record Keeping,[44] who reside permanently in the human world, recording the good and evil one has done, so as to verify it. There are three bad realms for the dead, and killing creatures or using them as sacrifices results in a rebirth in the worst realm.[45] Following Buddhist Dharma, observing the Five Precepts and Ten Virtues,[46] and distributing alms with a merciful

44. For 六師督錄使者, a *BZL* note reads 六部都錄使者 (Emissaries of Record Keeping from the six ministries), which is what I follow here.

45. The three bad realms for the dead are ghosts, animals, and hell. Hell is considered the worst.

46. "Five Precepts" refers to the first five of the Buddhist "Ten Commandments" against killing, stealing, adultery, lying, and intoxicating liquors. The observance of these five ensures rebirth in the human realm. "Ten Virtues" is defined as not committing the ten evils—killing, stealing, adultery, lying, double-talk, coarse language, filthy language, covetousness, anger, maintaining perverted views.

heart, one will be reborn in the House of Good Fortune and live peacefully without anything to do."

Zhao Tai replied, "I did neither anything good nor anything evil."[47]

After all the trials had finished, Zhao Tai was assigned to work as the Inspector of Waterworks, taking more than one thousand people to transport sand and shore up riverbanks. He worked assiduously day and night, and wept with regret, saying, "I did not do good things, and now I have fallen into this place."

Later he was transferred to the position of Supervisor of Waterworks, in charge of the affairs of various hells. He was given a horse and sent east to inspect the hells.

Farther on, he arrived at the *Nili* hell,[48] where six thousand people lived. There was a fire tree, fifty paces in circumference and ten thousand feet tall. All around the tree were swords, and fire was burning on the tree. Beneath it people in tens or in fives fell onto the fire swords, which pierced their bodies. [The prison official] said, "These people cursed others, robbed others, and by doing so hurt those who are good and kind."

Tai saw his parents and a younger brother weeping in this hell, and also saw two men come with documents in hand. They ordered the prison officials, saying, "There are three people whose families serve Buddha. On their behalf,[49] their families hung streamers and canopies in the temple, burned incense, chanted the *Lotus Sutra,* and promised to redeem the sins they committed when they were alive. Let them go out to live in the House of Good Fortune."

Having dressed in ordinary clothing, those released headed to a gate named Great House of Opening Light. It was a black gate of three layers,[50] each of which consisted of white walls and red pillars. The three men then entered the gate, and they saw in the palace the precious treasures dazzling under the sun. In front of the hall stood a pair of

47. For上不犯惡, *BZL* reads 亦不犯惡.
48. *Nili* is the Sanskrit pronunciation of hell. It has been translated as hell as well as Taishan 泰山, Mount Tai.
49. According to *Mingxiang ji* and the note in *Bianzheng lun*, *weiyou* 為有 here should be *weiqi* 為其, "for them" or "on their behalf."
50. *Hei* 黑 (black) here is added from BZL.

statues of crouching lions, shouldering a bed made of gold and jade.[51] It was called the Seat of Lions.

They saw a great man, ten feet tall, whose face was golden-colored and whose neck radiated sunlight, sitting on the bed. Numerous Buddhist monks were standing by to wait on him. Noted Daoist priests and bodhisattvas sit all around him. The Governor of Mount Tai came to greet him.

Zhao Tai asked an officer, "Who is this great man?"

The officer said, "He is the Buddha, master of converting and saving people in heaven and this world."

Then he heard the Buddha say: "Now I want to save beings in the evil paths of existence as well as those in various hells and let all of them out of the hells to accept salvation."

It was said that at that moment nineteen thousand people were able to come out, and then the hells were empty.[52] It was seen that ten people who should go up to heaven were summoned while the carriages and horses waited for them, and they rose into the void and left.

Further, Zhao Tai saw another city that was more than two hundred square *li*, and its name was City of Receiving Transformation. It was said that those who had never heard of the teaching of Buddha and whose interrogation in hell was finished would receive their karmic retribution through transformation in this city.

Zhao entered the city from the northern gate and saw that there were hundreds and thousands of earthen buildings. In the middle there was a tile-roofed house; its width was more than fifty steps. In the basement of the house were more than five hundred officials who faced each other and recorded people's names and the good or bad deeds they did.

The kind of transformations each person would receive followed what each had done: those who killed living creatures were said to become mayflies, which are born in the morning and die in the

51. *Xiang* 象 (resembling) is replaced by *fu* 負 (shouldering) according to the hand-copied version.

52. *Jishi* 即時 is replaced by *jihong* 即空 (then became empty) according to the Ming dynasty hand-copied version.

evening;[53] if they were to become human beings, they would die young. Those who stole and robbed were to become pigs or sheep, to be slaughtered and given to people for food. Those who had committed acts of sexual wantonness were to become cranes, ducks, or snakes. Those who had instigated trouble between people were to become owls that make evil cries; people who hear them all curse them and wish that they would die. Those who refused to pay their debts were to become species such as donkeys, horses, oxen, fish, or turtles. Under this big house there was a basement facing north with one door facing south. People were summoned and entered through the northern door. All those who went out the southern door had their shapes transformed into those of animals.

He saw another city that was one hundred square *li*. In it were peaceful and pleasant tile-roofed houses. It was said that people who, while alive, did not do evil things or good things would stay in this ghost realm, and after one thousand years they would be able to go out and become human beings.

He saw another city that was five thousand steps wide and was called Center of the Earth. Those who were punished there could not bear the suffering. There were around fifty or sixty thousand men and women, all naked; they helped each other in hunger and fatigue. Seeing Zhao Tai, they kowtowed to him and cried.

Having finished inspecting the hells, Zhao Tai returned. The supervisor asked him, "Aren't the hells as the dharma says? You committed no sins, so you were invited to be Supervisor of Waterworks. Otherwise, you and the others in this hell would be treated in the same way."

Tai asked, "What should a person do while he is alive in order to be happy after his or her death?"

The supervisor replied, "Only the followers of Buddha who make great efforts in practice and never violate the precepts will be happy."

Tai asked further, "If the piled-up sins committed by a person before he believed in Buddha were as high as a mountain, but then he began to follow the dharma, would those sins be wiped out?"

53. For *shazhe* 殺者 (killers), BZL reads *shashengzhe* 殺生者 (those who kill living creatures).

The supervisor replied, "All of the sins would be wiped out."

The supervisor again summoned the Emissary of Record Keeping and asked, "What was the cause of Zhao Tai's death?"

The emissary opened a rattan box and examined the old records, saying, "He still has another thirty years to live. His life was absurdly taken by an evil ghost. Now he should be sent back home."

From then on, Zhao's family, old and young, determined to serve Buddha. To seek good fortune on behalf of his grandparents, his parents,[54] and his two younger brothers, Zhao Tai hung streamers and canopies, and he chanted the *Lotus Sutra* as well.

(*GXSGC*, #247. 424–27; *TPGJ* 109. 739–41)

176. SCHOLAR WANG ZIZHEN'S GHOST FRIEND[55]

In the past there lived Wang Zizhen, a native of Taiyuan.[56] Loving him greatly, his parents once sighed, saying, "Our son has not yet been well educated." So they sent him to study with Mr. Bian Xiao, the Erudite of Dingzhou.[57]

Mr. Bian was a native of Xinyi in Chenliu.[58] He broadly involved himself in the study of ancient ways and had answered numerous scholarly inquiries. After Confucius's death, Mr. Bian was the only one who had three thousand disciples.[59] He was peerless, so scholars within the Four Seas all went to Bian to study with him.

54. *Fumu* 父母 (parents) is added according to *BZL*.

55. This piece has not been included in any previous editions of the *Youming lu*. I found it in the *Dunhuang bianwen ji* 敦煌變文集 after having finished all the translations for this book. Because of its unique depiction of the netherworld and how the trial in the netherworld affects life in the human world, it is put here instead of in chapter 4 about the realm of ghosts.

56. Taiyuan, see footnote 9 in chapter 3.

57. Dingzhou 定州, the area around the modern city of Dingzhou, Hebei. It belonged to Zhongshan State 中山國 during the Han dynasty.

58. Chenliu, see footnote 39 above in this chapter.

59. Following this sentence there are four characters, 莫如歸伏; the meaning is unclear.

Having walked thirty *li* after entering the territory of Dingzhou, Zizhen took a rest under a locust tree by the side of the road. A ghost who had changed into the form of a living man also rested under the same tree.

Zizhen believed that he was a living man, not a ghost, so he asked, "Where are you from?"

The ghost also asked Zizhen, "Where is this young man from?"

Zhen replied, "My parents thought I lack knowledge, so they sent me to study with Mr. Bian of Dingzhou. That is all."

The ghost asked Zizhen further, "What is your name?"

Zizhen replied, "My surname is Wang and courtesy name Zizhen, a native of Taiyuan."

The ghost said, "I am a native of Bohai, surnamed Li and named Xuan. My parents died early, and I live together with my older brother. Considering that I have never studied in school, my older brother sent me to study with Mr. Bian. From now on, I'll study together with you as your classmate."

Seeing that Li was older, Zizhen stood up to bow to him, and they became brothers. After walking together and arriving at the host's home in Dingzhou, they drank wine and pledged to be friends and would never break the vow under any circumstances.

During the three years of learning, Li Xuan's talent and skill surpassed Mr. Bian's. Mr. Bian asked Li Xuan, "Are you a sage? Why are you so smart, differing greatly from others? In the past, I considered myself talented. Now I am not as talented as scholar Li. Do you have any other skills? I wish you would tell us."

Li Xun bowed to Mr. Bian twice, saying, "It was destined for me, your disciple, to meet you and receive your instruction, but I don't know why I have been able to achieve so much."

Thus Mr. Bian appointed Li Xuan his teaching assistant. All of his disciples were in awe of Li Xuan.

In the school, nobody ventured to disobey the regulations—if any did, he would be punished. In his private room, Li Xuan taught Zizhen to understand the meaning of the classics. Whenever Zizhen could not understand, he would be punished. Zizhen took Li Xuan's words as his master's, and he never made a decision himself. Because of this, Zizhen achieved success in his learning.

Later, Wang Zhongxiang, a retainer of the Heir Apparent and a native of Taiyuan, joined them. Zhongxiang was a distant relative of Zizhen, so he came to him to study briefly as a visiting scholar. One night, when he lived together with Zizhen, he noticed that Li Xuan was a ghost.

On his way back the next day, when the two men were holding each other's hands to bid farewell, Zhongxiang said to Zizhen, "As your relative and friend, I cannot but tell you the anomaly I have seen. Your current friend is not a good man."

Zizhen questioned him, "In terms of learning, Li Xuan is a Confucian scholar and a gentleman; in terms of appearance, he is matchless. Why do you say that he is not a good man?"

Zhongxiang replied, "What I speak of is not about general human affairs and his appearance. You, my younger brother, are a living man, but Li Xuan is a ghost. The living and the dead go different ways. How can he be your friend? If you don't believe me, you may fetch a bundle of thatch and spread it to sleep on. You may lie on the thatch together, with heads facing opposite directions. When you get up in the morning and look at the thatch, you will find that the thatch you slept on is solid but the thatch he slept on is still fluffy and bulky."

Later, when Zizhen picked up thatch, spread it, and observed it after rising the next morning, it was truly as Zhongxiang had said. Zizhen then knew that Li Xuan was a ghost.

At a proper time, Zizhen asked Li Xuan, "There is gossip, saying that you are a ghost. Is this true?"

Xuan replied, "I am a ghost. Last night Wang Zhongxiang came and noticed. Therefore I let you, my younger brother, know that I am a ghost in the form of a man, as well as who else knows it. Seeing that I was young, the King Yama appointed me Department Clerk. The king thought that my knowledge was not broad enough, so he sent me to study with Mr. Bian. If I reached my goal in three years, he would appoint me Assistant Magistrate of Taishan; if I could not reach the goal, I would be sent back as a commoner. Thanks to the instruction of Mr. Bian, I reached the learning goal within a year. I was appointed Assistant Magistrate of Taishan, and it has been two years since then. I am only here because you are not going home yet; my bond with you has prevented me from leaving this place. Now that you know I am a ghost, you will be afraid of living closely with me. I also don't have to travel with you anymore. It is the proper time for me to return.

"Previously I suffered back pain. It was because someone who sued your father said that I was forming a clique to pursue selfish interests and should not have been involved in the trial. Not even asking whether I had done right or wrong, the king directly decided to punish me by flogging me a hundred strokes. That was why I suffered back pain. Recently the king even dealt with trials himself. Your father showed up today. The king truly intended to put him on the list [of condemned]. You should go home right away. If your father still has breath, please offer wine and jerky as sacrifice to me at an intersection and call my name three times. Then I will come to save him, and he will surely live. If he has already has no breath, there will be no way to save him. Then what can we do? What can we do?

"Now you have achieved success in learning. You should try your best to establish yourself and behave cautiously. I can prolong your life span and, by entreating the High God's approval, offer you the positions of Prefect of Taiyuan Commandery and Governor of Guangzhou."

Consequently, Zizhen parted with him and arrived at home. Seeing that his father still had breath, he carried pure wine and venison jerky to an intersection and offered them as sacrifice to Li Xuan, while calling his name three times. Wearing a tall cap and surrounded by numerous horsemen and attendants, Li arrived in time on the back of a white horse. It was extremely magnificent. Besides, two boys in blue led him to meet Zizhen, in the same way they had met previously as classmates.

Li Xuan immediately asked about Zizhen's father's illness. Zizhen replied, "My father lost his voice and cannot speak. There is little breath left. I hope you can save his life."

Li Xuan told Zizhen, "My younger brother, just close your eyes. I'll bring you to see your father."

Then Zizhen closed his eyes. In a moment, Li Xuan brought Zizhen to the gate of the palace of King Yama, and they both stood facing the north. Xuan said to Zizhen further, "Previously I intended to bring you to see your father, but your father is now fettered in jail, wan looking. It would be unbearable to see him, so you don't have to meet him. Now there will be a man in white pants, walking barefooted, wearing a purple silk cap, and holding a document. This is the man who sues your father. He will walk toward us from the back of the court. Now I have a bow and some arrows for you to wait especially for him. When you see that he is coming in the distance, shoot and kill him; then your father's illness will vanish. Otherwise, your father will be put on the death list and in the end will not live."

Before Li Xuan finished speaking, the man had come. Xuan reminded Zizhen, "This is the man. You should shoot him carefully. I have to go see the head judge, so I cannot stay here for long to avoid being blamed by others."

After Xuan left, the man approached to pass Zizhen. Zizhen then drew his bow to shoot and hit him in his left eye. The man dropped his document and, covering his eyes with his hands, ran away.

Zizhen picked up the document and looked at it. He found it was only two pieces of paper, both bearing the name of his father.

Xuan said to Zizhen, "King Yama smelled the breath of a living person. You should not stay here for long. Please leave as soon as possible. Where did you shoot your enemy?"

Zizhen replied, "In his left eye."

Xuan said, "You didn't hit the fatal place. When his eye heals, he will come back to harm your father again. Your father now has a while to relax. When you get home, you should find your enemy and kill him. Only then will your father escape calamity."

Zizhen replied, "I really don't know who my enemy is."

Xuan said further, "Just kill those who have an old grievance with you."

Zizhen parted from Li Xuan with worry.[60]

Then Zizhen arrived at home. He found nobody who had an old grievance with him. It was only that he had lost a white rooster. It had not crowed for seven days, and nobody knew where it was. He searched for it everywhere, and finally found it lying in a cage with a blinded left eye.

Zizhen said, "My enemy is precisely this creature. Its left eye was shot by me. The white pants were its body, the bare feet were its claws,

60. Following this sentence, the fourteen characters, 更審借問怨家姓名, 弟但到家思維，seem unreadable.

and the purple silk cap was the crest on its head. This is my family's enemy."

Thereupon, he killed the rooster and cooked it into soup to feed his father. Consequently, his father's illness healed.

Later, Zizhen became the Prefect of Taiyuan Commandery. During the reign period of Emperor Jing of the Han, Zizhen was appointed Governor of Guangzhou. He lived to 138 years old and passed away in a natural death.

Among those who were helped by a ghost, nobody has surpassed Wang Zizhen. Therefore, there is a saying:

A white rooster is not suitable to be raised;
If it is raised, its host will be harmed.
A white dog is unable to be raised;
If it is raised, it brings disaster to its host.

It is talking about the case in this story.

(From Wang Zhongmin 王重民 et al., eds., *Dunhuang bianwen ji* 敦煌變文集 [Beijing: Renmin wenxue chubanshe, 1984], 879–82)

6

ANIMALS AND MEN

177. THE NAKED CREATURES

In the mountains of Dongchang County,[1] there are such creatures. Their figures are like those of human beings, their length four or five feet; their bodies are naked; their hair, four or five inches long, hangs down loosely. They often live among the stones in the towering mountains. They have a husky voice but cannot speak, though they can summon each other by whistles. They often conceal themselves in the dark, so cannot be seen frequently.

Once, some people went to cut wood and camped in the mountains. After they went to sleep at night, the creatures appeared. Holding their children in their arms, they started a fire with stones, caught lobsters and crabs from the ravine, approached the fire beside the people, and roasted the lobsters to feed their children.

One man had not fallen asleep. He secretly awoke the others and told them what had happened, and consequently they stood up together and made a surprise attack against the creatures. Thus the creatures ran away and left their children there. Their voices resembled the cries of human beings. The creatures urged a group of their fellows, male and

1. Dongchang 東昌 County, established at the end of Wu under Luling Commandery; its seat was in modern Ji'an 吉安 County, Jiangxi.

female, to hit the people with stones. They approached the people, got their children, and then stopped attacking.

(*GXSGC*, #256. 431–32; *TPYL*, 883. 3925a)

178. WOOD GUESTS[2]

Wood guests are born in the mountainous areas of the south. Their heads, faces, and speech are not completely different from those of human beings, but their hands and feet are as sharp as hooks. They live among the precipices, and after death their corpses are also encoffined and carried to a grave. They are able to exchange goods with people without revealing their shapes. Now in the south there is a ghost market, where ghosts exchange goods with humans in a similar way.

(*Gujin tushu jicheng*, 514.37a)

179. THE YOUNG OF BIG PENG

As a teenager, King Wen of Chu (689–676 BCE) was fond of hunting. A man offered him a falcon. King Wen looked at it. Both of its claws and spurs were marvelous and neat; surely it was not an ordinary falcon.

Thus the king went hunting in the Yunmeng marsh. Nets were set like spreading clouds, smoke and fire stretched up to the sky, the hounds were striving to bite, and falcons were competing to pounce. Lifting its head and opening its eyes, this falcon watched the distant edge of the clouds,[3] with no intention to fight or bite. The king said, "What my falcons have caught reached a hundred creatures, yet your falcon has showed no intention of exerting itself. Are you deceiving me?"

---

2. This piece was not included in Lu Xun's *GXSGC* edition of *Youming lu*. It is added from *Gujin tushu jicheng* 古今圖書集成 (Shanghai: Zhonghua, 1934), ed. Chen Menglei 陳夢雷 (b. 1651– 1752) et al., 514.37a.
3. For 遠視雲際, "Watched the distant edge of clouds," *TPGJ* (460. 3770–71) reads 遠瞻雲際. Both are missing in the *GXSGC* version.

The man who presented the falcon replied, "If it served merely to hunt pheasants and hares, how could I venture to present it to your majesty?"

After a little while, a creature was flying near the edge of clouds. Its color was white yet its shape was beyond recognition. Then the falcon lifted its wings and dashed up like lightning. In a moment, feathers fell like snow and blood like rain. A huge bird fell onto the ground. Its two wings were measured several dozen *li* in width, and nobody knew its name.

At that time an erudite man said, "This is the young of a big bird, *peng*."

Then King Wen offered this man a handsome reward.

(*GXSGC*, #26. 357; *TPYL*, 926. 4114b; *TPGJ*, 460. 3770–71)

180. THE BREATH OF TURTLES (1)

Once there was a man who, while walking in the mountains, fell into a ravine. Since there was no way to get out, he was almost starved to death. He saw numerous turtles and snakes stretching their necks toward the four directions. Therefore the man imitated them, so he was not hungry anymore. His body became extremely light and nimble, and he was able to climb the stone bank.

Several years later, he lifted his body and raised his arms, climbed out of the ravine, and was able to go back home. His face was happy and lustrous, and he was much smarter. When he could eat food, he ate different dishes. One hundred days later, he recovered his original condition.

(*GXSGC*, #171. 402; *TPYL*, 69. 326a)

181. THE BREATH OF TURTLES (2)

At the end of the Han there was chaos. A man of Yingchuan was about to go to another commandery to avoid the disasters.[4] He had a

4. Yingchuan 穎川, modern Yu 禹 County, Henan.

daughter around seven or eight years old, who could not walk a long distance. It was difficult to preserve both their lives. By the road there was a broken tomb; the man tied his daughter with a rope and put her down into it.

More than a year later he returned and went to the tomb to search for his daughter, intending to bury her in another place. But he found that his daughter was still alive.

The father was startled, and he asked his daughter how she had survived. The girl said, "In the tomb there was a turtle. In the mornings and evenings it stretched its head to inhale air. I tried to imitate it, and as expected, I felt no hunger and thirst."

Her family searched for the creature in the tomb, and it turned out that it was a big turtle.

(*GXSGC*, #47. 365; *TPYL*, 559. 2526b–27a)

182. THE DOG DIWEI

In the second year of Taixing (318–321) of Jin, Hua Long of Wu was fond of archery and hunting. He raised a dog, called Diwei, that always followed him. One day when Long reached the side of a river,[5] his whole body was twined by a big snake. Consequently, his dog bit the snake to death, but Hua Long fell prostrate and lost consciousness. The dog walked back and forth, howling, barking, and roaming around the area.[6]

Surprised at its behavior, Long's family followed the dog to the spot, and they found Long dead on the ground. They brought him back home in a cart. He awoke two days later.

Until Long awoke, the dog refused to eat. Long loved it even more, the same as he loved his family and relatives.[7]

(*GXSGC*, #84. 377; *TPGJ*, 437. 3552; *TPYL*, 905. 4015a)

5. *TPYL* (905. 4015a) reads 至江邊伐荻, "went to the side of river to cut reeds."
6. *TPYL* reads 犬髣髴涕泣, "he seemed to weep tears."
7. The end of the *TPYL* version adds, 後忽失之，二年尋求，見在顯山 (Later it was lost suddenly. Long looked for it for two years, and then found it in a noted mountain).

183. A PARROT

When Huan Huo (320–377), Minister of Works of Jin, was at Jingzhou,[8] an adjutant cut the tongue tip of a parrot on the fifth day of the fifth month, and taught it to speak.

Consequently, there was nothing it could not name, and it could exchange greetings with people.

Adjutant Gu was good at playing zither. The parrot often stood listening for hours. It was also good at imitating people's voices and laughter.

The minister once gathered all of his officials and assistants and asked the parrot to imitate the voices of everyone who was seated; none of the parrot's imitations was inaccurate.

There was an assistant who spoke with a twang, so his voice was harder to imitate and the parrot's effort initially did not work well. Therefore the parrot stretched its head into an earthen jar, and then its voice was not different than that of the man who spoke with a twang.

Once the manager of a ceremony stole something in the parrot's presence. When the adjutant went to the privy and nobody else was there, the parrot told him what the manager had stolen. The adjutant kept it in mind but did not tell anyone.

Later the manager stole some beef, and the parrot told the adjutant again.

The adjutant said, "You said he stole beef; you should have evidence."

The parrot said, "He wrapped it with a new leaf of lotus and put it behind the screen."

When the adjutant looked, he indeed found it. He severely punished the manager. However, being troubled by the parrot, the thief killed it by pouring boiling water onto it.

The adjutant felt sorrow for the parrot for many days, and he requested to kill the man for vengeance.

8. Huan Huo 桓豁, the younger brother of the Grand Marshal Huan Wen (312–373), was the Governor of Jingzhou from 365 to 377. Minister of Works was his posthumous title.

The Minister of Works said, "Based on the pain caused by his killing the parrot, he truly should be sentenced to death. Yet we cannot punish him with the most severe penalty because of a bird."

Finally, he sentenced him to only five years in jail.

(*GXSGC*, #95. 380–81; *TPYL*, 923. 4096; *TPGJ*, 462. 3793)

184. A MOLE CRICKET REPAYS A FAVOR

Pang Qi, the Governor of Luling Commandery of Jin,[9] was styled Ziji. His ancestor was involved in an incident and was imprisoned, though he was not really guilty.

Seeing that a mole cricket was crawling around, he addressed it: "If you are numinous and are able to save me from death, wouldn't that be great?" Then he threw food to the mole cricket. The mole cricket ate all the food and left.

After a while it came back, and its body became a little bigger. The man felt that this was strange, and gave it food again. In several days, it was as big as a young pig.

When the time came for the man to receive the death penalty, the mole cricket dug a big hole at the foot of the wall. Thus the man was able to get out and flee. Later, he received an amnesty and was able to stay alive.

(*GXSGC*, #158. 398; *TPYL*, 643; *CXJ*, 20. 493)

185. GOLDEN GEESE

In the Yixi reign period, when the Lord of Qiang, Yao Lue, fetched bricks by digging the [bank of] Yingou River at Luoyang,[10] he obtained a pair of male geese that were both golden in color. Crossing their necks, they cackled and hissed for a long while, and the sound was heard all

9. Luling 盧陵 Commandery covered the region around modern Yongfeng 永豐 County, Jiangxi (Tan Qixiang, *Zhongguo lishi dituji*, 4. 25–26).

10. Yao Xing 姚興 (366–416), styled Zilue 子略, was the Emperor of Later Qin from 394 to 416. He seized Luoyang in 399.

over the highland on the banks of the river. Then he raised them in this river.

(*GXSGC*, #141. 394; *YWLJ*, 91. 1580; *TPGJ*, 462. 3788)

186. A SNAKE MOURNS FOR ITS MOTHER

The wife of Xie Zu, a native of Guiji,[11] first gave birth to a boy and then gave birth to a snake about two feet long. The snake slithered directly out of the door and left.

Several decades later the woman passed away at an old age, and Xie Zu suddenly heard the sound of wind and rain from the northwest. A moment later he saw a snake, its length more than ten *zhang* and its belly more than ten arm spans around, entering the door and reaching the spirit seat. Then it arrived at the place where Xie's wife's coffin was placed, coiled around the coffin several times, and hit it with its head until blood and tears flowed out of its eyes. After quite a while, the snake left.

(*GXSGC*, #197. 408; *TPYL*, 934. 4151b)

187. A WHITE TURTLE

In the middle of the Xiankang reign period of the Jin (335–342), Mao Bao, the Governor of Yuzhou,[12] was defending Zhucheng.[13] A soldier in the army bought a white turtle in the market of Wuchang. It was four to five inches long. He placed it in a jar and fed it. The turtle grew bigger and bigger before he released it in the Yangzi River.

Later [the troops in] Zhucheng were defeated by Shi [Le], and all the people who ran into the river drowned. The person who had nurtured the turtle entered the water with his armor on, and felt as if he had fallen onto a stone. In a moment he saw that it was the white turtle that he had previously released.

11. Guiji, see footnote 21 in chapter 3.
12. Mao Bao's 毛寶 biography is found in *Jin shu*, 81. 2122. Defeated by Shi Jilong 石季龍 (r. 335–349) of the Later Zhao (328–351), Mao Bao fell into the river and drowned.
13. Zhucheng 邾城 was located 20 *li* northwest of modern Huanggang 黃崗, Hubei.

After he was able to reach the [opposite] bank, he looked back, but the turtle had left.

(*GXSGC*, #87. 377; *TPGJ*, 118. 823–24)

188. MEN IN BLACK

When Huan Miao governed Runan Commandery, someone sent him four black ducks as gifts. His eldest son dreamed of four men in black requesting that he save their lives. When he awoke, he suddenly saw the ducks that were about to be killed. Then he saved them by purchasing meat to replace them. After returning, he dreamed of the four men, who came to thank him and then left.

(*GXSGC*, #163. 400; *TPGJ*, 276. 2187–88)

189. RED WORDS ON A FISH'S BELLY

During the Yuanxi reign (304–308) of the Jin, there was an old man who lived in the Guiyang Commandery and had always taken fishing as an occupation.[14] Once he went out fishing in the early morning; he encountered a huge fish eating the bait. He pulled the fishing line so quickly that both the man and the boat suddenly fell into the water. His family looked for his corpse at the site and saw that both the old man and the fish were dead and entangled in the fishing line. On the belly of the fish there were some red words, which read,

I heard that Zeng Pool is a delightful place,
therefore I came here from Yan Pool.
I killed this old man,
who bullied me with a fishing pole several times.
He liked to eat red carp,
and today he got what he deserved.

(*GXSGC*, #148. 396; *TPYL*, 66. 316a)

14. Guiyang 桂陽 Commandery, the region centered on the modern city of Chenzhou 郴州, Hunan. See Tan Qixiang, *Zhongguo lishi dituji*, 3. 54.

190. THE ARCHERY MASTER

During the time under Fu Jian (r. 357–385),[15] an archery master passed by Mount Song. He saw a pair of white birds on a pine tree, each resembling a swan yet a bit larger.

Further, when he arrived under the tree he saw a snake, its length about five *zhang,* climbing up the tree to catch the birds. When it was merely one *zhang* from the birds, they intended to fly away. The snake opened its mouth to suck them in, so the birds could not leave. Struggling to move up and down for the time of finishing a meal, the birds were almost tired out.

The archery master drew his bow and shot three arrows. The snake fell down and the birds were able to fly away, stopping to comb out their feathers with their beaks one hundred steps away from the tree.

In a moment, the clouds became dark and thunder boomed shockingly. Terrified, the archery master was not able to move a step. He saw those two birds flying back and forth above him and their feathers falling in profusion. It seemed that they were rescuing him. This happened several times; then the thunder stopped and the lightning ceased. The archery master was able to avoid disaster and the birds flew high as well.

(*GXSGC*, #94. 380; *TPYL*, 479. 2196 & 914. 4052)

191. AN OX SENDS A MESSAGE THROUGH A DREAM

Wang Hua of Langye,[16] the protector general, had an ox. It walked very fast, and Wang Hua often rode on it.

Later the ox became old, and Wang dreamed of it talking to him, saying, "I am feeble and old, and I cannot be loaded heavily. It would be okay to carry two people, but I will definitely die if I carry more than two."

15. Fu Jian, see footnote 34 in chapter 4.

16. Langye, see footnote 4 in chapter 2.

Hua thought it was a chance dream, and he rode it with two other people returning home. The ox really died.

(*GXSGC*, #194. 408; *TPYL*, 900. 3995b)

192. JI HAN'S BLACK BULL

During the Yuanjia reign period, the Governor of Yizhou, Ji Han (372–431), was transferred to govern Southern Xuzhou.[17] Previously, he had transported a black bull from Shu. He rode on it from time to time and raised and constantly took care of it himself.

When Han suffered from an illness for many days, the bull was also reluctant to eat. When he died, the bull shed a flood of tears.

Before Mr. Ji's coffin returned to the capital, the advance party drove the bull to the previous residence. The bull was reluctant to move. They knew that this was abnormal, so they waited for the coffin. As soon as the coffin was unloaded from the boat, the bull followed them to leave.

(*GXSGC*, #245. 423–24; *TPYL*, 900. 3995b)

193. AN OX KOWTOWS IN TEARS

When Huan Chong (328–384) was governing Jiangling, it was New Year's Eve, on which an ox was supposed to be boiled.[18] After gazing at the guard commander for a long while, the ox suddenly shed tears.[19]

The guard commander took an oath, saying, "If you can kowtow to me, I will report to [the governor to] let you live."

---

17. Ji Han 吉翰, styled Xiuwen 休文, was appointed governor of Yizhou 益州 (modern Sichuan) in the third year of the Yuanjia reign (426), and he was in that position for three years with good reputation before he returned because of illness.

    Southern Xuzhou 南徐州, modern Zhenjiang 鎮江, Jiangsu.
18. Huan Chong, a younger brother of Huan Wen.
19. Guard commander, translation of 內帳都督.

No sooner had he finished his words than the ox kowtowed to him. Everyone felt it was odd.

The guard commander told the ox again, "If you really want to live and you kowtow to everyone, I will go directly [to report]."

The ox shed tears like rain, and then it kowtowed endlessly.

By chance Chong was drunk, so the commander was not able to report to the governor. Consequently the ox was butchered. When he awoke from drunkenness, Chong received the report. Hearing of this, he sighed, and the guard commander was severely punished with flogging.

(*GXSGC*, #96. 381; *TPYL*, 900. 3995b)

194. THE BIRD IN A HONEY LOCUST TREE

In the yard of Yu Wan, a native of Qu'e,[20] there was a honey locust tree more than ten arm spans around and more than ten *zhang* tall. Its branches were luxuriant and well spaced, shading the houses of several families. A variety of birds lived in it.

Once, Yu Wan asked his servant to cut the upper branches of the tree, and the servant fell off and was almost dead. In the air, someone cursed, "Wan, why do you cut my home?" Then the person pushed and threw tiles and stones at him. All his family, old and young, became exhausted.

This lasted for a year, and then gradually stopped.

(*GXSGC*, #199. 409; *TPYL*, 960. 4259b)

195. A RIVER DRAGON'S REVENGE

At the beginning of the Long'an reign period (397–401) of Jin, Xie Sheng of Qu'e entered a lake in a boat to pick water chestnuts. Seeing that a river dragon was coming toward his boat, he avoided it. The river

20. Qu'e, see footnote 27 in chapter 1.

dragon then followed him from behind, so Sheng killed it with his pitchfork. Terrified, he returned home.

Several years passed, yet he encountered no calamities.

In the middle of the Yuanxing reign period (363–365), there was a worldwide drought. Sheng walked together with several fellow travelers to the middle of the lake. He saw his old pitchfork there and picked it up, saying, "This was mine."

The others asked for the reason; Sheng told them the truth. After walking several steps, he then had a pain in his heart. Only one night after he returned home, he died.

(*GXSGC*, #144. 395; *TPYL*, 930. 4135b; *TPGJ*, 131. 927)

7

ANECDOTES OF NOTABLE FIGURES

196. GUEST STAR

Emperor Wu of the Han (r. 140–87 BCE) once dressed as a commoner to travel secretly. When passing by the house of a family, he saw a maid with "beauty that could ruin a state." The emperor liked her, so he took lodging there and slept together with the maid at night.

There was a young scholar lodged also in the same home, who was good at astrology. Suddenly he saw a guest star moving, overshadowing the seat of the emperor and approaching it aggressively.

Startled, the scholar jumped up and shouted continuously, "Ah, tut-tut! Tut-tut!"

Unconsciously he raised his voice. Then he saw that a man, holding a knife, was about to break down the door. Hearing the scholar's urgent shouting, the man lowered his knife and ran away. At the same time the guest star disappeared.

Hearing his strange voice, the emperor summoned him and inquired about it. The scholar gave him a detailed account of what he had seen. Realizing what had happened, the emperor said to himself, *This man must be the husband of the maid, and he intended to kill me*. Then he summoned his bodyguards and revealed to the host, "I am the Son of Heaven."

Thereupon the servant man [lover of the girl] was caught and put to death, and the emperor handsomely rewarded the scholar.

(*GXSGC*, #27. 357–58; *KYZJ*, 83. 596–97)

197. THE JADE GIRL

When Emperor Wu of the Han lived in the Sweet Spring Palace,[1] a jade girl descended from heaven and frequently played chess with him for entertainment.

The girl was graceful and pretty, so the emperor liked her and tried to force her to have an affair with him. Thereupon the girl spat in the emperor's face and left. Consequently, he suffered from a skin ulcer for over a year.

The *History of Han* says, "To prevent sunstroke, [the emperor] lived in the Sweet Spring Palace." That was exactly the time when he met the jade girl.

(*GXSGC*, #29. 358; *TPYL*, 88. 421b & 387. 1790a)

198. LADY FENG

Lady Feng was the Worthy Lady of Emperor Huan (r. 147–167) of the Former Han. Her beauty was matchless.

More than thirty years after her death, a group of robbers opened her tomb and found that the beauty of the lady was the same as before. Striving to rape her, the robbers consequently attacked one another and all died.

(*GXSGC*, #44. 364; *Diaoyu ji* 雕玉集, 14)

199. A FOX INTERPRETS CLASSICS

Dong Zhongshu (179–104 BCE) once lowered his curtain and was chanting the classics to himself,[2] when a guest arrived. His bearing, manner, voice, and tone were all extraordinary.

1. Sweet Spring Palace (甘泉宮), located in Mount Ganquan at Chunhua 淳化 County, Shanxi, was built under Emperor Wu of Han.
2. Dong Zhongshu 董仲舒, a scholar instrumental to Emperor Wu of Han (r. 140–87 BCE) in proscribing non-Confucian schools of thought and espousing Confucianism as the orthodox state ideology, which lasted for around

The guest talked with him about the five classics, exploring their subtle and profound aspects.

Zhongshu had never heard of such a man, and thus he suspected that he was an anomaly.

The guest said further, "It is going to rain."[3]

Then Zhongshu teased him, "Those who live in a nest know when there is wind, and those who live in a hole know when it is raining. If you are not a fox, then you are a rat."

Hearing these words, the guest turned pale and lost control of himself. He transformed into a fox and left in a hurry.

(*GXSGC*, #33. 360; *TPGJ*, 442. 3611–12; *TPYL*, 912. 4041a)

200. A ROOSTER TALKS ABOUT METAPHYSICS[4]

Song Chuzong of Pei State, Governor of Yanzhou of the Jin,[5] once purchased a constantly crowing rooster. He loved and raised it in an exceptional way, and always doted on it, placing it on the window sill.

Then the rooster uttered human words, talking with Chuzong. Its talk was extremely metaphysical and it never paused all day long.[6]

Because of this, Chuzong's ability to talk was greatly improved.

(*GXSGC*, #156. 398; *YWLJ*, 91. 1585; *TPYL*, 918. 4073; *SLFZ*, 18. 387)

---

two thousand years. It is said that when he was a diligent young scholar during the time of Emperor Jing (r. 157–141 BCE), he did not find time to look at the garden outside for three years.

3. *TPGJ* (442. 3611–12) does not include these five characters: 客又曰："欲雨。"
4. Since the Zhengshi reign of Cao Wei (240–248), discussing metaphysics had become a fad among scholars of Wei and Jin. It seems this tale is a satire on this phenomenon (see Zhang Wanqing, *YML*, 3. 64).
5. Song Dai 宋岱, styled Chuzong 處宗, was Governor of Jingzhou of the Jin and author of *On the Classic of Changes*.
6. For *xuanzhi* 玄致 (*GXSGC* quotes from *SLFZ*), *YWLJ* reads *yanzhi* 言智, while both *TPYL* and *SLFZ* read *yanzhi* 言致. It seems that Lu Xun saw a different version of *SLFZ*.

201. WANG FUSI

Wang Fusi (226–249) annotated *The Classic of Changes*,[7] then laughed at Zheng Xuan (127–200) for being a Confucian,[8] saying, "That old man made no good points."

At night, Wang suddenly heard the sound of wooden clogs. In a short while, a man entered, calling himself Zheng Xuan. He reproached Wang, saying, "You are still young, how could you give strained interpretations and draw far-fetched analogies, and absurdly ridicule Laozi?" He looked extremely angry, and after finishing his words he withdrew.

Wang Fusi was terrified and upset. Not long after that, he died of pestilence.[9]

(*GXSGC*, #98. 381–82; *YWLJ*, 79. 1349; *TPYL*, 883. 3924b)

202. WEN WENG

Wen Weng was once felling a big tree,[10] intending to cut it at the point eighteen feet above the ground. He made a vow to the gods first, saying, "If I can eventually have a salary of two thousand bushels [of grain],[11]

---

7. Wang Fusi 王輔嗣, named Bi 弼, was the founder of metaphysics of Wei and Jin. His synthesis of Confucian and philosophical Daoist thought, epitomized in his commentaries on *Laozi* and the *Book of Changes*, has colored all subsequent interpretations of these works (see Mather, *SSXY*, 593).
8. Zheng Xuan 鄭玄, a great master of Confucian classics of the Eastern Han.
9. Another interpretation of his death is that he was executed in 249 in his twenty-fourth year because of his involvement with the clique of Cao Shuang 曹爽 (d. 249) (see Mather, *SSXY*, 593). In fact, Wang Bi only lost his position in the incident of Cao Shuang, but soon afterward died of pestilence.
10. Wen Weng 文翁, named Dang 黨 and styled Zhongweng 仲翁, was the Governor of Shu 蜀 Commandery (the area around present-day Chengdu 成都, Sichuan) under Emperor Jing 景 of Han (r. 188–141 BCE).
11. The salary of the governor of a commandery, *jun* 郡.

my axe will hit that point." Then he threw his axe at the tree, and it precisely hit the point.

Later he truly became governor of a commandery.[12]

(*GXSGC*, #34. 360; *TPYL*, 763. 3387)

203. HE BIGAN

He Bigan of the Han dreamed of a noble guest, and his residence filled with carriages and horses.[13] After awaking, he told his wife.

Before he finished talking, an old woman, who was about eighty or more, asked to take shelter from the rain. The rain was very heavy, yet her clothes were not at all wet.

Bigan went forward to let her in and gave her a courteous reception. Then she said, "Your ancestor was from [the clan of] Hou Ji, and assisted Yao. The inward effect [of his deeds] will reach down to the Jin era. Today heaven grants you these records [of their deeds]."

The records were like bamboo slips, nine inches long, and totaled nine hundred and ninety. She gave them to him, saying, "His offspring who are able to put on such a slip will be rich and honorable."

Having said that, she went out of the gate and disappeared

(*GXSGC*, #36. 361; *TPGJ*, 137. 982)

204. DIVINING FOR A GRAVEYARD

The father of Yuan An (d. 92) of the Han died.[14] His mother sent him to call on a diviner with chicken and wine to inquire about a graveyard.[15]

---

12. The "Wen weng" in *TPGJ* (137. 982; credited to *Xiaoshuo* 小說) reads 後果為蜀郡守, "Later, he truly became the governor of Shu Commandery."
13. He Bigan 何比干, styled Shaoqing 少卿, was Supervisor of Law Enforcement (廷尉正) under Emperor Wu of Han.
14. Yuan An 袁安 (styled Shaogong 邵公), a native of Ruyang 汝陽 (modern Shangshui 商水, Henan), was the Minister of Works and Minister of Education of Eastern Han.
15. For *bugong* 卜工, *TPGJ* (389. 3101) reads *bugong* 卜貢.

On the way Yuan An met three young scholars who asked him, "Where are you going?" Yuan An told them everything. The scholars said, "We know a good graveyard." Yuan An treated them with the chicken and wine.

After that, they told Yuan An the place, saying, "You should bury your father at this place.[16] By doing so your family will be nobles from generation to generation." Then they said good-bye to him. After they had walked away several steps, Yuan An looked back yet could not see any of them.

Yuan An suspected that they were spirits, so he buried his father at the place they suggested. Consequently, he ascended to the position of Minister of Education. His sons and grandsons were prosperous, and five dukes appeared in his family within four generations.

(*GXSGC*, #40. 362; *TPGJ*, 137. 984)

205. THE SEAL OF THE MARQUIS OF LOYALTY AND FILIALITY

Zhang Hao,[17] a native of Changshan Commandery,[18] was the Prime Minister of the State of Liang.[19] Once immediately after a rainstorm, a mountain bird resembling a magpie flew down and dropped to the ground. While people were striving to pick it up, it became a ball of stone.

Hao broke it with a stick and obtained a golden seal, which read, "The Seal of the Marquis of Loyalty and Filiality."

16. These four characters, 當葬此地, are added from *TPGJ* (389. 3101).
17. Zhang Hao 張顥, styled Zhiming 智明, was the younger brother of Zhang Feng 張奉, the Palace Attendant-in-Ordinary (中常侍) of Eastern Han. He was promoted from Chamberlain for Ceremonials (太常) to Grand Commandant (太尉) in the first year of Guanghe 光和 (178) under Emperor Ling 靈帝 (r. 168–189) but was deposed within half a year.
18. Changshan 常山 Commandery; its administrative seat was in modern Yuanshi 元氏 County, Hebei.
19. State of Liang 梁, capital Xiayi 下邑, modern Dangshan 碭山 County, Anhui.

Hao reported this to the royal court. The emperor took it and hid it in a secret chamber. Hao reached the position of Defender-in-Chief in the reign of Emperor Ling of Han (r. 168–189).[20]

(*GXSGC*, #42. 363–64; *YWLJ*, 46. 819; *CXJ*, 27. 646)

206. PURPLE AIR ABOVE A TOMB

Sun Zhong was a native of Fuchun of Wu Commandery and a descendant of Sun Wu (c. 575–470 BCE).[21] Zhong made a living by growing watermelon. When his watermelons began to ripen, three men approached him,[22] begging for watermelons to eat. Thereupon Zhong led the three men to his thatched cottage, prepared food, and plucked watermelon to feed them.[23]

Having finished eating, the three men told Zhong, "We have accepted your great kindness, yet have nothing to repay you with. Please allow us to find a graveyard for you."

Then they led him to a hill.

The men asked him, "Do you want to be enffeoffed from generation to generation, and be the Son of Heaven for several generations?"

Zhong replied, "Yes."

Thereupon they pointed to a place, saying, "You should bury your parents there."

The three men said further, "We are the Controllers of Fate. When you walk down this hill, don't look back within a hundred steps."

20. This happened in the first year of Guanghe (178).
21. For Sun Wu zhi hou 孫武之後, *TPYL* (978. 4335b) reads 堅之父也，與母居，至孝篤信.

    Fuchun 富春, modern Fuyang 富陽 County in Zhejiang, which belonged to Wu Commandery during the Han and Jin.

    Sun Wu 孫武, styled Changqing 长卿, also known as Zunzi 孫子, was an ancient Chinese military general, strategist, and philosopher during the Spring and Autumn period (770–476 BCE) and the author of *Sunzi bingfa* 孫子兵法 [The art of war].
22. For *sanren laijiu* 三人來就, *TPYL* (978. 4335b) reads 三少年容服妍麗，詣鐘.
23. For 設飯摭瓜以食之, *TPYL* (978. 4335b) reads 為設食出瓜，禮敬殷勤.

Zhong looked back after walking thirty steps and saw the three men become white cranes and fly away.

Zhong later buried his parents at the place they had pointed to, where purple air often connected to the sky and spread over the ground. The elders said, "The Sun clan is rising!"

Zhong begot Jian (155–192),[24] styled Wentai, who served under Emperor Ling [of Han] as General Who Eliminates Barbarians and Governor of Changsha.

Jian begot Quan (182–252),[25] styled Zhongmou, who occupied east of the Yangzi River at the end of Han, established the Wu Kingdom, became the Son of Heaven, took Yangzhou as his capital, and named his reign Jianye; later he moved his capital to Wuchang.

Quan begot Liang (243–260),[26] Liang begot Xiu (235–264),[27] and Xiu begot Hao (242–284).[28] Hao was attacked by the Jin and surrendered to Jin; Emperor Wu [of Jin] enfeoffed him as Marquis Guiming [returning the Heavenly Mandate].[29]

They were truly the Son of Heaven, the emperor, for four generations. Sun Quan was called Grand Emperor; Liang was dethroned; Xiu was Emperor Jing. Hao was the Last Emperor. Their rule lasted continuously for sixty-eight years.[30]

(*GXSGC*, #48. 365–66; *LLZS*, 7. 332b)

207. LU SU

Sun Quan (182–252) fell ill. A shaman reported to him, saying, "There was a ghost wearing a silk kerchief. It seemed to be an old general or

24. Sun Jian 孫堅, styled Wentai 文臺, was General Who Eliminates Barbarians (破虜將軍) and Governor of Changsha 長沙 of the Eastern Han.
25. Sun Quan 孫權 (r. 222–252), see footnote 1 in Chapter 2.
26. Sun Liang 孫亮, Prince of Guiji (r. 252–258).
27. Sun Xiu 孫休, Emperor Jing 景帝 (r. 258–264).
28. Sun Hao 孫皓, Emperor Mo 末帝 (r. 264–280).
29. Emperor Wu 武帝 of Jin, Sima Yan, 司馬炎 (r. 265–290).
30. Instead of following Lu Xun's new version of this story (based on *TPYL* 559 & 978, *SLFZ* 27, *CXJ* 8, and *YWLJ* 86), this translation is based on the more informative and complete one from *LLZS* (7. 332b), which Lu Xun puts in his note in *GXSGC*, #48. 366.

prime minister. At first I scolded him loudly, yet he did not respond, and he directly entered the palace."

That night, Quan saw Lu Su coming,[31] and his clothes were exactly as the shaman described.

(*GXSGC*, #54. 367; *TPGJ*, 317. 2513)

208. THE THREE BROKEN-ARMED DUKES

Someone appraised the tomb of Yang Shuzi's (221–278) father,[32] saying that there was the air of emperors above it. Thereupon Shuzi dug a ditch behind the tomb himself. The diviner said later, "There should still be a broken-armed duke [among the three] coming from [the geomancy of] this tomb."[33]

Yang Hu (Shuzi) was good at riding, and he had a son about five or six years old. After he dug the tomb, his son died right away. Yang was the Commander-in-Chief of Xiangyang at that time. While riding around and around in training he fell down and broke his arm.

At the time all the scholars admired and praised his loyalty.[34]

(*GXSGC*, #61. 61; *TPYL*, 369. 1701b; annotation in *SSXY*, 20. 705)

209. JIAOZHOU SCISSORS

When Yuan Cong was the Governor of Xin'an Commandery,[35] at the southern border of the commandery there was an engraved stone slab. Once when Yuan arrived there to feast and carouse, someone obtained a pair of scissors from under the stone; everyone was surprised.

31. Lu Su, see footnote 51 in chapter 4.
32. Yang Shuzi 羊叔子, see footnote 26 in chapter 2.
33. The three sentences above are added from *TPYL* (369. 1701b). The last sentence reads 由（猶）當出折臂三公 instead of 尚當出折臂三公 (*GXSGC* #61. 61).
34. This story is also found in Yang Hu's biography in *Jin shu* (34. 1024).
35. Xindu 新都 Commandery was renamed Xin'an 新安 in the first year of Taikang 太康 (280) of Jin. Its seat was west of modern Chun'an 淳安 County, Zhejiang.

Cong inquired of the recorder. The recorder replied, "In the past Prince Huan of Changsha drank and feasted at Sunzhou,[36] but the elders said, 'This islet is narrow and long. Does it indicate that you will be the Governor of Changsha [long sand]?' This had been proven to be true. Three vertical knives (刂) form a region (*zhou* 州); so if you get a Jiaozhou [clipping] knife, you will be the Governor of Jiaozhou as well."[37]

Later, Cong really governed Jiaozhou.

(*GXSGC*, #189. 406; *TPYL*, 830. 3703a–b quotes from *SSXY* and says, "It is the same in the *YML*.")

210. THE SORCERER DU YAN

Dong Zhuo (d. 192) believed in sorcery.[38] The sorcerer Du Yan was always in his army, praying for blessings on his behalf.

One day, Yan asked Zhuo for a piece of cloth. In haste, Zhuo had no cloth, but did have a towel. Yan said, "It can be used."

Having taken the towel, Yan began to write on it. The character he wrote seemed to have two mouths, one big and the other small, and one was on top of the other. He raised the towel with his writing and told Zhuo, "Be careful with this!"

Later, Zhuo was killed by Lü Bu (d. 199), and then people in later times realized that the character Yan wrote hinted at Lü Bu.[39]

(*TPYL*, 735. 3258b; *GXSGC*, #49. 366)

---

36. Prince Huan of Changsha 長沙桓王 is the posthumous title of Sun Ce 孫策 (175–200), the elder brother of Sun Quan (182–252), the founder of Wu.
    Sunzhou 孫洲, present-day Wangzhou 王洲, is in the middle of the Fuchun 富春 River in Fuyang 富陽 County, Zhejiang.
37. Jiaozhou 交州 covered modern Guangdong, Guangxi, and northern Vietnam during the Han. During the Three Kingdoms period it was divided into Guangzhou and Jiaozhou, which covered Leizhou 雷州 peninsula in Guangdong, southern Guangxi, and northern Vietnam with administrative seat Longbian 龍編 (in present-day Vietnam).
38. Dong Zhuo 董卓, the usurper of the throne of Eastern Han. He seized control of the capital Luoyang in 189 after the death of Emperor Ling, yet was killed later by his foster son, Lü Bu 呂布.
39. Two *kou* 口, mouth, forms Lü 呂 in Chinese writing.

211. THREE HORSES SHARE ONE MANGER

Emperor Wu of Wei (155–220) suspected that the sons of Emperor Xuan [of Jin] (179–251) were not loyal subjects of the Cao clan.[40] Furthermore, he once dreamed of three horses sharing one manger. He hated the sons even more. Thus he summoned Emperor Wen (Cao Pi, r. 220–226) and Emperor Ming (Cao Rui, r. 227–239) and told them what he had seen in the dream. Both said, "There are numerous ways to guard against them. Please don't worry about it groundlessly." Emperor Wu agreed.

Later, the sons of Emperor Xuan really destroyed the Cao clan and took the throne from them, all similar to what was seen in the dream.

(*GXSGC*, #50. 366; *TPYL*, 400. 1850a)

212. THE MELODY OF GUANGLING

He Siling, a native of Guiji,[41] was good at playing zither. One night he sat in the moonlight, playing a zither in the wind. Suddenly came a man who was very tall, with fetters and a wretched face. The man reached the middle of the courtyard and praised Siling's playing. Then he talked with Siling, and called himself Xi Zhongsan.[42]

40. Emperor Wu of Wei 魏武, posthumous imperial title of Cao Cao 曹操, a powerful warlord at the end of the Eastern Han (25–220) and the father of Cao Pi 曹丕, the founder of Wei State during the Three Kingdoms period (220–280).

Emperor Xuan 宣 of Jin, posthumous imperial title of Sima Yi 司馬懿, a general of Cao Wei and grandfather of Sima Rui 司馬睿, the founder of Jin.

41. Guiji, see footnote 21 in chapter 3.

42. Xi Zhongsan 嵇中散 refers to Xi Kang 嵇康 (223–262), styled Shuye 叔夜, the *Zhongsan dafu* 中散大夫 (Grand Master of Palace Leisure) of Jin. He was a famous philosopher, musician, and poet, as well as one of the noted "Seven Worthies of the Bamboo Grove" (竹林七賢). His unbending personality and uncooperative attitude toward Sima Zhao 司馬昭 (211–265), the posthumous Emperor Wen of Jin, brought him disaster—being sentenced to death. Cf. *Jin shu*, 49. 1369–74.

He told Siling, "Your playing was pretty facile, yet did not follow the old methods." Therefore he offered him the "Melody of Guangling."

He Siling took it, and it has stayed extant until today.

(*GXSGC*, #221. 417; *TPGJ*, 324. 2569 quotes from *YML*; *TPYL*, 579. 2615b, quotes from *SSXY*, yet this is not found in its extant version)

213. XI KANG

Xi Kang was playing a zither under the lamp when he saw a man more than ten feet tall, black faced, and wearing an unlined garment with a leather belt. Kang looked at him closely, then blew out the light, saying, "I'm ashamed to vie with an evil spirit for light!"

(*Leishuo*, 11. 189a)[43]

214. FA ZU AND WANG FU[44]

Li Tong, a native of Pucheng,[45] came back to life from death, saying, "I saw Fazu (fl. 300), the Buddhist monk, explaining the *Sutra of Suramgama* to King Yama; I also saw the Daoist priest Wang Fu (fl. 300), in fetters,

43. This piece was not included in *GXSGC*. It is found in Zeng Zao (1091–1155), *Lei shuo*, 11. 189a.

44. Fazu 法祖, named Boyuan 帛遠, a native of Henei 河內 (Qin 沁 County of Henan) and a famous Buddhist monk in the reign of Emperor Hui 惠 (r. 290–306) of Jin. Emperor Hui treated him as both a mentor and a friend. His biography is found in the *Liang gaozeng zhuan*. See Huijiao 慧皎 (497–554), *Gaoseng zhuan heji* 高僧傳合集, 327a.

Wang Fu 王浮 was a Daoist priest and a contemporary of Fazu, noted for writing the anti-Buddhist treatise *Huahu jing* 化胡經 [On the conversion of the barbarians], in which he says that Buddha was an incarnation of the founder of Taoism, Laozi. This story exposes the conflict between Buddhism and Daoism in early medieval China.

45. Pucheng 蒲城, the modern city of Changyuan 長垣 in Henan. See Tan Qixiang, *Zhongguo lishi dituji*, 3. 37.

begging Fazu to listen to his confession of sins, yet Fazu was not willing to do that."

(*GXSGC*, #265. 434; annotation in *Bianzheng lun*, 6)

215. THE PRINCE OF ANXI'S THREE LIVES[46]

An Shigao, the marquis, was the Prince of Anxi State (Parthia). He became a monk together with the son of a great patron and studied the way [of enlightenment] in a city in Shewei.[47] Every time a host refused to help them, the son of the great patron would become angry. Shigao always admonished him.

Having roamed for twenty-eight years, Shigao decided that he should go to Guangzhou. It happened that there was a revolt. A man met Shigao and drew his knife without a hitch, saying, "I have really got you now!" Shigao replied with a laugh, "I owed you a debt in a previous life; thus I came from afar to repay you." Then the man killed him.

A teenager said, "This stranger, who came from a state far away, could speak our language and did not show any sign of reluctance. Could he be a deity?" The people all laughed in astonishment.

---

46. This tale describes the three lives of the Prince of Anxi 安息. It is the earliest literary work in China to express the Buddhist idea of rebirth and transmigration. It also gave rise to a new popular motif in Chinese literature.

An Shigao 安世高, also known as An Qing 安清 (fl. 148–171), was a productive Buddhist sutra translator and a great master of Buddhism in the late Han period. According to the conventional viewpoint, he was a crown prince of Parthia who abandoned his right to the throne in order to devote himself to religious life. His biography is found in Huijiao's (497–554) *Gao seng zhuan* [Biographies of eminent monks], included in Huijiao et al., *Gaoseng zhuan heji*, 1–4, which follows mainly the story we are reading. For a comparison of the two works, see Zhenjun Zhang, "Buddhist Impact on the Creation of New Fictional Figures and Images in the *Youming lu*." An English account of An Qing can also be found in Zürcher's *The Buddhist Conquest of China*, 32–33.

47. Shewei 舍衛, an old state in India.

The soul of Shigao returned and was reborn in the state of Anxi, becoming the son of the prince, again with the name Shigao. At the age of twenty, the Marquis of Anxi gave up the lordship again so as to learn the Way [of enlightenment]. Ten and some more years later, he said to those who studied with him, "I shall go to Guiji Commandery to repay my debt."[48]

As he passed by Mount Lu,[49] he visited his friends; then he passed by Guangzhou. Seeing that the teenager was still alive, he went directly to his home and talked about the events in the past with him. The young man was greatly delighted and followed him to Guiji.

While passing by the Monastery of Mount Ji, Shigao summoned the deity of the mountain and talked with him. The shape of the god of Mount Ji was like a python; his body was several dozen feet long, and he shed tears. Shigao spoke to him; the python then left. Shigao returned to his boat. There was a young man who got onto the boat, kneeled down, and went forward to receive an incantation; then he disappeared. Shigao said,[50] "The young man you saw a moment ago was the deity of the temple, and he is now able to get rid of his ugly form."

It was said that the deity of the temple was the son of the great patron. Later the temple attendant noticed a bad smell and saw a dead python. From then on the deity disappeared.

Shigao went on to Guiji and entered the gate of a market. It happened that there were some people fighting, and someone hit Shigao's head by mistake. Thus he passed away.

Consequently the guest from Guangzhou worshiped Buddha more diligently.[51]

(*GXSGC*, #254. 430; *TPGJ*, 295. 2346–47)

48. Guiji, see footnote 21 in chapter 3.
49. Mount Lu 廬山, a noted mountain located south of Jiujiang 九江, Jiangxi. It is also a famous Buddhist holy site.
50. Originally *Guangzhou ke* 廣州客 (the man from Guangzhou), it is corrected here according to a hand-copied edition of the Ming.
51. For *shifo jingjin* 事佛精進, "worshiped Buddha more diligently," a Ming dynasty hand-copied version of *TPGJ* reads *yizhi yu foshe* 瘞之於佛舍, "buried him in the Buddhist monastary" (*TPGJ*, 295. 2347).

216. FOTU CHENG, THE WESTERN MONK

Shi Le (r. 319–332) asked Fotu Cheng,[52] "Can Liu Yao (d. 329) be caught?[53] Is there any portent in which this can be seen?"

Cheng ordered his servant boy to practice abstinence [from meat and wine] for seven days. Then he put some sesame oil in his palm, rubbed it, set a piece of sandalwood on fire, and chanted incantations.

After a while, he raised his palm toward the boy, and in it was something distinctly unusual. Cheng asked, "Did you see anything?"

The boy replied, "I only saw a military man who was tall, large, and white, with an unusual appearance. His arms were tied up with a red silk thread."

Cheng said, "This was none other than Liu Yao."

In that very year, [Shi Le] captured Liu Yao alive as expected.

(*GXSGC*, #89. 378; *TPYL*, 370. 1705a)

217. TIGER DISASTER

Dowager Li, mother of Emperor Xiaowu (r. 373–396) of the Jin,[54] was originally a humble palace girl. Emperor Jianwen (r. 371–372) had no sons, and he had ordered all the masters of physiognomy to read the faces of the palace girls.[55] Dowager Li was then doing humble labors,

---

52. Shi Le 石勒 was the founder of the Later Zhao 後趙 (319–351) in the Sixteen States period (303–436). His biography is found in the *Jin shu*, 104. 2707–33, 105. 2735–59.

    Fotu Cheng 佛圖澄 (232–348) was a famous Indian monk of the Jin, noted for his magical arts. He came to Luoyang in the fourth year of Yongjia 永嘉 (307–312) of the Jin and was trusted by Shi Le, emperor of the Later Zhao. Fotu Cheng had a large number of disciples who were devoted to the Buddhist dharma. Owing to him and Shi Le, Buddhism flourished in Luoyang, and 893 Buddhist monasteries were built. His biography is found in *Jin shu*, 95. 2484.

53. Liu Yao 劉曜 was the founder of the Former Zhao (318–329) in the Sixteen States period.

54. Emperor Xiaowu 孝武, named Sima Yao 司馬曜, was the ninth emperor of Eastern Jin.

55. This happened when Emperor Jianwen 簡文帝, Sima Yu 昱, was still the Prince of Guiji, a long time before he was enthroned in 371.

so she did not participate in the selection. However, the fortune-teller pointed to her and said, "This woman should give birth to a noble son, yet will face a tiger disaster." The emperor thus favored her, and she gave birth to Emperor Xiaowu and the Prince of Guiji, Sima Daozi (364–403).[56]

After ascending to the noble position of dowager, she was convinced of the effectiveness of the fortune-teller, yet surprised at the prediction that there would be a tiger disaster. Moreover, she had never seen a tiger, so she ordered someone to create a statue of one. She stroked the tiger with her hands and intended to make fun of it by hitting it. Then her hands became swollen and painful, and consequently she died of the disease.

(*GXSGC*, #121. 387–88; *TPYL*, 892. 3961a)

218. GUO JINGCHUN

Counselor-in-chief Wang met Guo Jingchun and asked him to predict his fortune through divination.[57]

When the divination was finished, Guo's mood was very bad. He said, "There will be a disaster from thunder. If you order your driver to drive a cart westward for several *li*, obtain a cypress tree, cut it into logs as long as you are, and put them in the place where you sleep, then the disaster can be averted."

Wang followed this counsel. Within several days, it thundered as expected, and the cypress logs all became small pieces.

(*GXSGC*, #74, 374; *TPYL*, 954. 4236a)

---

56. Sima Daozi 司馬道子 served as regent during his nephew Emperor An's 安 reign period (397–418).

57. Counselor-in-Chief Wang here refers to Wang Dao 王導, styled Maohong 茂弘, one of the most famous figures in the Eastern Jin. He was originally the Prince of Langye under Emperor Yuan 元 (317–322), and later he became the Counselor-in-Chief of Emperor Yuan, Emperor Ming 明 (323–325), and Emperor Cheng 成 (326–342). His power overwhelmed almost all the powerful ministers at the time, and the Wang clan became one of the two most distinguished clans, Wang and Xie, in southern China. See his biography in *Song shu*, 42.1311–27; *Nan shi*, 21.569–72.

219. WANG MAOHONG'S DREAM

Wang Maohong (276–339), the Counselor-in-Chief [of Eastern Jin], once dreamed of someone trying to buy his eldest son, Changyu, with a million cash. The Counselor-in-Chief was fairly disgusted with it. In secret, he prayed for his son in every possible way.

Later, while building a house, he dug into a cave full of cash. He estimated the amount; it was around a million. He became extremely unhappy and hid all of the money.

In a little while, Changyu passed away.

(*GXSGC*, #75. 374; *TPYL*, 406. 1850a)

220. MARQUIS JIANG REQUESTS FOOD[58]

Wang Changyu, the Secretariat Attendant, had a good reputation, and he was the dearest son of his father, Wang Dao, the Counselor-in-Chief of Jin.

When the illness that Changyu contracted became critical, the Counselor-in-Chief arrived, very worried about the illness. He sat on the bed for several days without eating. Suddenly he saw an extremely strong man wearing armor and holding knives.

"Who are you, sir?" Wang asked.

---

58. Marquis Jiang 蔣侯 was a historical figure who became a deity after his death. Based on Gan Bao's *SSJ*, "Jiang Ziwen 蔣子文 was a man from Guangling given to wine and lust, as well as being frivolous and dissipated. However, he would often say of himself, 'My bones are pure; I shall be a god when I die.' Toward the end of Han, he was made Commander of Moling (Modern Nanjing). In this capacity one day he pursued bandits to Mount Zhong, where they smote him and wounded him on the brow. He took off his seal and bound himself up with its ribbon. Notwithstanding, he died soon after. When the First Ruler of Wu (Sun Quan) took the throne, one of Wen's former officers met Wen on the road riding a white horse, carrying a white feather fan, and followed by the retinue he always had." Later Sun Quan offered Jiang the posthumous title of Marquis of Zhongdu 中都侯 (see *SSJ*, 5. 57; DeWorskin and Crump, *In Search of the Supernatural*, 5. 53–54). Jiang was worshiped widely from then on.

The man replied, "I am Marquis Jiang. Your son is not in good health, and I intend to request that his life be prolonged. Therefore I have come. Please don't worry anymore."

Wang was overjoyed and his countenance changed. Right then he ordered food to be brought, and consequently the food Jiang ate reached several *dou*. No one within or outside the family understood the reason.

Having finished eating, Jiang suddenly became sad. He told Wang, "The life span of the Secretariat Attendant is exhausted. He cannot be saved." After finishing these words, he disappeared.

(*GXSGC*, #76. 374; *FYZL*, 95. 2752; *TPGJ*, 293. 2331)

221. MAGICIAN AN KAI

An Kai, a lay sorcerer of Ancheng Commandery,[59] mastered the magical arts. Every time he offered sacrifice to the spirits, he drummed drums, slaughtered the three domestic animals,[60] piled firewood, lit a fire, and waited until the flames were raging. Then he put a belt around his waist and entered the fire. When the sacrificial papers [with elegiac address] were all burned, however, Kai's body and clothing were the same as before.

At that time Wang Ningzhi (334–399) was the Governor of Jiangzhou,[61] and Kai served him on a trip. Pretending to comb Wang's hair, Kai pinned lotus leaves together to make a cap and handed it to Wang to wear. At that time Wang did not feel that the cap was abnormal, yet after he sat down the lotus leaves transformed into their original form. All of the people who sat there with him were startled.

(*GXSGC*, #101. 382; *FYZL*, 61. 1823; *TPYL*, 687. 3066b & 737. 3270a–b)

---

59. Ancheng 安城 Commandery belonged to Jiangzhou during Eastern Jin. Its seat was in modern Anfu 安福, Jiangxi.
60. Also known as the three sacrifices: ox, goat, and pig.
61. Wang Ningzhi 王凝之, styled Shuping 叔平, was the second son of Wang Xizhi 王羲之 (303–361), the most famous calligrapher in the history of China. His biography can be seen in *Jin shu*, 80.2102–03.

    Jiangzhou, see footnote 8 in chapter 4.

222. WANG NINGZHI'S WIFE[62]

Lady Xie, wife of Wang Ningzhi, the General of the Left Army of the Jin and Prince of Langye, suddenly lost her two sons. Being extremely regretful, she shed tears for six years.

Later she suddenly saw her two sons return, both in fetters. They consoled their mother, saying, "You should end the pain of losing your sons. Both of your sons are sinful. It is appropriate for you to create good fortune on our behalf."[63]

Thereupon she was able to stop grieving, and instead, she diligently prayed for them.

(*GXSGC*, #102. 382; *TPGJ*, 320. 2538)

223. THE BUDDHIST NUN[64]

Huan Wen (312–373) harbored the mind of a usurper.[65] At that time, a Buddhist nun came from afar. It was in summer, the fifth month of the year. The nun was bathing in another room. Wen spied on her stealthily and saw the naked nun cut her belly with a knife to get her five internal

---

62. Wang Ningzhi's wife, Xie Daoyun 謝道蘊, was the granddaughter of Xie An 謝安 (320–385), another bigwig comparable to Wang Dao in the Eastern Jin. She has long been considered one of the most famous talented women in the history of China. Stories about her talents in literary critique and writing have been passed down by word of mouth as approbation. Yet her life in her later years was miserable. Her sons, as well as her husband, were killed during the Sun En 孫恩 rebellion (399–402); after that she lived as a widow. See her biography in *Jin shu*, 96.2516; *SSXY*, 2. 131; and Mather, *SSXY*, 2. 64.
63. *Zuofu* 作福 (create good fortune) is rendered by Robert Campany as "perform acts for [the generation of] fortune." See his *Signs from the Unseen Realm*, 137.
64. This tale describes a Buddhist nun's magic art, the ability to recover from the extraction of five organs and the amputation of her body parts, including the head.
65. Huan Wen 桓溫 was the son-in-law of Emperor Ming of the Jin. At first he was the Governor of Jingzhou, later he wielded power arbitrarily as the Commander-in-Chief. He schemed to replace the Jin himself, but died before he succeeded. See note 18 in chapter 3.

organs (the viscera) out first; next she cut off her two legs, head, and hands as well.

After a long while she finished bathing. Wen asked her, "Earlier I saw you. How could you mutilate yourself like that?"

The nun replied, "When you become the Son of Heaven, you should also be like that." Wen felt disconsolate.

(*GXSGC*, #107, 384; *TPYL*, 395. 1826a)

224. JIANG ZIWEN

When Huan Xuan's (369–404) ambition to usurp became unbridled, he sent the Censor to Ancheng Commandery to murder Sima Daozi, the Grand Mentor.[66]

Xuan was in Nanzhou[67] when he saw a man wearing a flat-top kerchief and holding a horse whip, who informed him, "Marquis Jiang has come."

Xuan was startled. Then he saw by the steps a servant driving a curtained carriage and a scholar official who called himself Jiang Ziwen.

"Why did you murder the Grand Mentor?" Jiang said. "Your fate is similar to his."

In the twinkling of an eye, he disappeared.

(*GXSGC*, #118, 387; *TPYL*, 359. 1653b)

225. A MA

When Yuan Zhen of Chen Commandery was at Yuzhou,[68] he sent three courtesans, A Xue, A Guo, and A Ma, to Huan Xuanwu (Wen). Quite a while after their arrival, three of them went to the front of the

66. Huan Xuan, see footnote 26 in chapter 5.

67. Nanzhou 南州, another name of Gushu 姑孰, modern Dangtu 當塗 County, Anhui.

68. Yuan Zhen 袁真, a native of Chen 陳 Commandery (seat in modern Huaiyang 淮陽 County in Henan), was Governor of Yuzhou 豫州 (seat in Shouchun 壽春) of Eastern Jin.

courtyard to watch the sky and saw a shooting star fall directly into the water of a basin. Xue and Guo each tried to scoop it out with a gourd ladle, but both failed to retrieve it. When A Ma was scooping, the star entered the gourd ladle by chance. She drank the water and then felt she was pregnant. Consequently she gave birth to Huan Xuan.

(*GXSGC*, #108. 384; *KYZJ*, 71. 522)

226. XIE ANSHI

When Xie Anshi (320–385) lived under the rule of Huan Wen,[69] he constantly feared that he would not be able to protect himself.

One night, he suddenly dreamed that he traveled sixteen *li* in Huan's carriage, stopped while he saw a white rooster, and was not able to go forward anymore. Nobody could interpret this dream.

When Huan Wen died, Xie replaced him as prime minister. Sixteen years later when he fell ill, Xie Anshi realized the clue in the dream, saying, "Taking Huan's carriage indicates replacing his position, sixteen *li* indicates I have only sixteen years in his office, stopping when I saw the white rooster indicates that, now that the God of the Year, *Tai sui,* is at the position of the cock, my illness will never be cured."

In no more than a few days, he died.

(*GXSGC*, #99. 382; *TPYL*, 398, 774; *BTSC*, 140. 280b)

227. THE DAOIST PRIEST XU XUN (1)

Xu Xun's (239–374) father died when he was young, and he did not know where his ancestral grave was. Touched by his sincere admiration,

69. Xie An 謝安, styled Anshi 安石, accepted the position of Sergeant-at-Arms under Huan Wen at the age of forty, yet refused to cooperate with him when Huan intended to usurp the throne of Jin. Later Xie An became the Governor-General of Military Affairs in five regions and Vice Director of the Department of State Affairs of Jin. In the year of 383, under his direction his brother Xie Shi 謝石 (327–388) and nephew Xie Xuan 謝玄 (343–388) defeated the invasion of the Former Qin in the battle of Fei River. He was posthumously entitled Grand Tutor. His biography is in *Jin shu*, 79. 2072–77.

one day his grandfather suddenly showed up, saying, "I died thirty-one years ago. Now I will be able to receive a formal funeral. It is because of your filiality." Accordingly, he raised a tablet, saying, "You may search for me under this sign." Thereupon Xu Xun went to welcome the coffin of his grandfather to a grave in his hometown. The gravediggers said, "From [the geomancy of] this grave a marquis and a magistrate of a small county should come."

(*GXSGC*, #114. 385; *TPYL*, 519. 2360a)

228. THE DAOIST PRIEST XU XUN (2)

Huan Wen (312–373) went northward to attack Yao Xiang (331–357) across the Yi River.[70] Xu Xun told him, "I didn't see the sign that you will catch Xiang, yet you will still achieve great deeds. I saw Xiang walking into the Great Subtlety."

Huan Wen asked, "What is the Great Subtlety?"

Xun Replied, "The south is the Red Wild, and the north is the Great Subtlety. He will certainly go northwest."

It happened just as Xu Xun said.

(*GXSGC*, #105, 384; *YWLJ*, 6. 102)

229. AUNT JIANG

Liu Cong was good at playing the zither. Suddenly he contracted an illness of fatigue. Xu Xun said, "Recently I saw the female ghost of the Jiang family seize you among the mountain stones and specially ask you to play the zither to entertain her. I'm afraid this will give rise to disasters."

70. Yao Xiang 姚襄 was once the Governor of Bingzhou 并州 of the Jin, and he later declared himself Da Chanyu 大單于. In 356 he was defeated by Huan Wen, and he was killed during the following year by the army of Former Qin (351–394) (see *Jin shu*, 116). His younger brother Yao Chang 姚萇 (330–393) was the founder of the Later Qin 後秦 (384–417).

The Yi 伊 River starts from Luanchuan 欒川 County and enters the Luo 洛 River at Yanshi 偃師 County, Henan.

Cong said, "I often dreamed of a girl who took me to a feast to play; I'm afraid I cannot avoid it."

Xun laughed and said, "Aunt Jiang adores you so much, I am afraid she won't release you. I have presented a dirge to her on your behalf. When you go there today, there should be no disaster."

Gradually, Cong healed.

(*GXSGC*, #112, 385; *TPYL*, 577; *BTSC*, 109. 104b)

230. A DRAGON CARRIES A BOAT ON ITS BACK

Wang Dun (266–324) sat next to Wu Meng,[71] and in his seat Wang showed his detestation of Wu. Thus Wu suddenly disappeared, and he took a boat and traveled one thousand *li* in one night. The travelers who went with him saw that there were two dragons carrying the boat on their backs, and the whole boat did not touch the water at all.

(*GXSGC*, #72, 373; *BTSC*, 137. 257b)

231. WALKING ON WATER

Wang Dun summoned Wu Meng. Meng arrived at the mouth of the river, entered the water, and ordered the boatmen to go forward together with him.

When the boat arrived at Dalei, they saw Wu Meng walking on the water, returning from the northeast to welcome the boat. When his disciple asked him why he was there, Meng replied, "The river deity raised the waves several times to harm travelers. I sent him an order and have just come back." He showed them a pearl as verification.

(*GXSGC*, #71, 373; *YWLJ*, 84. 1438; *TPYL*, 803. 3567b)

71. Wang Dun 王敦, see note 12 in chapter 4. Wu Meng 吳猛, styled Shiyun 世云, a native of Fengning and a noted Daoist priest. He was also known as one of the twenty-four filial sons. Cf. tale 169, "Gan Qing" (p. 123).

232. THE FIVE-COLORED EGG

Luo Junzhang (303–380) of Guiyang had no intention [of learning] even when he was about twenty years old. He had no interest in scholarship.

Once, while he was sleeping during the day, he dreamed of a bird egg glittering with five colors, unlike any object in the human world. In the dream he fetched and swallowed it.

Thereupon he gradually had aspirations. He studied diligently, read the nine classics, and thereby was known for his "pure talent."[72]

(*GXSGC*, #115. 386; *TPYL*, 928. 4127a)

233. XU XIANZHI'S DREAM

When Xu Xianzhi (364–426) was the Recorder of Wang Ya (334–400),[73] the Junior Mentor, he dreamed of his father, Zuozhi,[74] who told him, "From now on please don't cross the scarlet Bird Floating Bridge. Then you should become noble."

When Xianzhi was halfway across the floating bridge later, he thought of the dream in which his father cautioned him and turned the head of his horse back. A moment later, the bridge collapsed behind him.[75] Because of this, he was able to be appointed the recorder, and eventually, he really became the Chief Overseer of the Department of State Affairs.[76]

(*GXSGC*, #238. 422; *TPGJ*, 276. 2185)

72. Luo Han 羅含, styled Junzhang 君章, was Lieutenant Governor under Huan Wen. His *Gengsheng lun* 更生論 (On reincarnation) is included in the *Hongming ji* (*Taisho* 52. 27bc). His biography is found in *Jin shu*, 92. 2403–04.

73. Ya 雅 was mistaken as Xiong 雄 in *TPGJ* (276. 2185) as well as in *GSSGC* # 238. Here I follow Zheng Wanqing's correction (*YML*, 2. 45) based on Xu Xianzhi's biography in *Song shu*.

74. *Zuozhi* 祚之 is mistaken as *Zuo* 作 in *TPGJ* and *GXSGC*.

75. *Er qiaozhe* 而橋折, "and the bridge was broken," were added based on the block-printed edition of Huang Pilie (1763–1825). See Zheng Wanqing, *YML*, 2. 45.

76. Xu Xianzhi's biography is found in *Song shu*, 43. 1329–35; and Li Yanshou, *Nan shi*, 35. 432–35.

234. A FOREIGN MONK

When Yao Hong's (r. 415–417) uncle Shao,[77] the General-in-Chief, was in charge of all military affairs, he summoned a foreign Buddhist monk and inquired whether [his future] would be auspicious.

Thus the monk made [something] from flour shaped like a large pancake, ten feet in diameter. The monk sat on it, ate the western side first, then the northern side, then the southern side, and then rolled up the rest and swallowed it. When he finished the monk got up and left without a single word.

In the fifth month of that year, Yang Sheng (r. 395–425) defeated Yao's troops at Qingshui.[78] In the ninth month, Jin troops launched an expedition northward and recovered and pacified Ying and Luo.[79] Finally they swept the Feng and Gao,[80] and captured Yao Hong alive there.

(*GXSGC*, #152. 397; *TPYL*, 860. 3819b)

77. Yao Hong 姚泓 (388–417) was the last emperor of the Qiang 羌 state Later Qin. After Later Qin was conquered by the Jin general Liu Yu, he was delivered to the Jin capital Jiankang and executed. See his biography in *Jin shu*, 119. 3007. Yao Shao was the brother of Yao Hong's father, Yao Xing 姚興 (366–416).

78. Yang Sheng 楊盛 (r. 395–425) was the Lord of Qiuchi 仇池, a state in modern Gansu. Qingshui 清水 was a city northwest of modern Qingshui in Gansu. See Tan Qixiang, *Zhongguo lishi dituji*, 3. 43–44.

79. The Ying 穎 River rises southwest of Mount Song in Henan and enters the sea at Shouyang 壽陽, Anhui; the Luo River originates at Mount Hua 華 and flows through Luoyang (Tan Qixiang, *Zhongguo lishi dituji*, 4. 9–10). Ying and Luo here refer to the area of central China south of the Yellow River.

80. Both the Feng 豐 River and the Gao 鎬 River are branches of the Wei 渭水 River, west of the modern city of Xi'an. See Tan Qixiang, *Zhongguo lishi dituji*, 4. 54–55. Feng and Gao refer to the area around modern Xi'an, Shanxi.

8

LOCAL LEGENDS

235. THE HUSBAND-WATCHING STONE

On the mountain north of Yangxin County,[1] Wuchang Commandery, there is a "Husband-Watching Stone." Its shape resembles a standing person.

According to folklore, there was a chaste woman whose husband joined the army and went to a place far away because of a national calamity. His wife, carrying their little son, gave a farewell dinner for him on this mountain. She stood watching her husband until she became a piece of standing stone.[2]

Therefore "Husband-Watching Stone" was given as its name.

(*GXSGC*, #12. 355; *CXJ*, 5. 108; and *SLFZ*, 7. 146, credits to *SSXY*)

236. PENG E

During the rebellion of Yongjia (311) of the Jin,[3] the commanderies and counties had no constant lords, and the powerful bullied the weak.

1. Yangxin 陽新 County, modern Yangxin, Hubei.
2. For 立望夫而化為立石, *TPYL* (440. 2025a) reads 立望而死，形化為石, "She stood watching until she died, and her body became a piece of stone."
3. The Upheaval of Yongjia occurred in the fifth year of the Yongjia reign (307–312) under Emperor Huai 懷, during which the *Xiongnu* 匈奴 (Huns) army crushed Jin troops, captured Luoyang, and massacured 30,000 people.

In Yiyang County there was a girl by the name of Peng E.[4] Her parents and brothers, more than ten in total, were attacked by the rebels from Changsha.

At that time Peng E carried a bucket on her back and went out to fetch water from a river. Hearing that the rebels had arrived, she ran back. Seeing that the blockhouse was broken, she could not endure the sadness and fought against the rebels barehanded. The rebels tied her up, drove her to the side of the river, and were about to kill her.

By the side of the river there was a big mountain, and the height of the cliff was several dozen *zhang* high. Peng E looked up at the sky and shouted, "How could there not be a spirit in heaven? What crime have I committed that I deserve to be treated like this?" She then ran toward the mountain. The mountain opened several *zhang* wide immediately, with an even road leading inside as smooth as a whetstone.

Running after Peng E, the rebels entered the mountain too. Then the mountain was closed as it had been before and the rebels' bodies were all crushed to death inside while their heads were exposed outside.

The water bucket that Peng E had discarded became a stone with a shape resembling a rooster. Thus the local people named the mountain Stone Rooster Mountain, and the river E Pool.[5]

(*GXSGC*, #69. 372; FYZL, 32. 1012; *TPYL*, 888. 3946b)

---

4. Yiyang 宜陽 County, modern Yichun 宜春, Jiangxi.
5. In traditional Chinese culture heaven has been described as an omnipotent high god who supervises and dominates the world of creatures. It responds to the affairs of human beings by sending down calamities, bestowing good fortunes, and acting as the savior. This story is beyond doubt from this tradition, yet the way the girl is saved is unique compared with prior depictions of heavenly retribution in the historical texts. A typical example of such depictions can be found in Sima Qian, *Shi ji*, 38.1631; cf. Zhenjun Zhang's English translation in Nienhauser Jr., ed., *Grand Scribe's Record*, 5. 1, 288–89. For discussions of heavenly *bao* (retribution), see Kao, "Bao and Baoying"; and Zhenjun Zhang, "From Demonic to Karmic Retribution"; also see *Buddhism and Tales of the Supernatual in Early Medieval China*, 82–106.

237. LOCAL INSPECTORS STRIVE FOR TERRITORY AT THE BORDER

At the border of the Yidu and Jianping commanderies,[6] there are five to six mountain peaks that are uneven and intertwined with one another. Above the peaks are two stones leaning against each other, resembling statues of two people who are pushing up their sleeves and confronting each other. As the saying goes, they are the local inspectors of the two commanderies striving for territory there.

(*GXSGC*, #11. 355; *CXJ*, 5. 107; *YWLJ*, 6. 109; *SLFZ*, 7. 149)

238. THE STATE OF KING GAO

In Shixing County (in Guangdong) was the State of King Gao.[7] It stretched up and down along the mountain for more than ten *li*. Pits and moats were set up in several layers, and footpaths connected with each other. Inside the city, in the ruins of ancient halls shattered tiles and crumbling posts still exist.

To the east, there is a tomb for King Gao. As for King Gao, he has never been heard of.

(*GXSGC*, #4. 353; *TPYL*, 193. 931a)

239. THE TOMB OF KING GAO

In Shixing County there is a city called King Gao. To the east of the city there is a tomb. In the past someone excavated the tomb and fell into it, but the resonant sound of horns could be heard coming from inside. The grave robber was afraid and refilled it with earth.

(*GXSGC*, #5. 354; *BTSC*, 121. 151a)

---

6. Yidu 宜都 Commandery; its seat was in the modern city of Yichang, Hubei; Jianping 建平 Commandery, its seat was in modern Wushan 巫山 County, Sichuan. Both were established in the Three Kingdoms period.
7. Shixing 始興, modern Shixing County, Guangdong.

240. HOT WATER SPRING AT SHIXING

At the Divine Water Source of Shixing, there is a hot water spring. Whenever there is frost or snow, the steam above it, as high as several *zhang*, can be seen. When raw stuff is thrown into the water, it becomes cooked in a second. In the spring small red fish often swim, yet nobody has ever caught one.

(*GXSGC*, #6. 354; *TPYL*, 940. 4178 & 71. 334b)

241. WARM AND COLD WATER SPRINGS

At Fushan of Ai County there are two springs,[8] a warm water spring and a cold water spring. Both come out from the foot of one mountain, and the origins of the two springs are only several feet apart. The hot water spring can boil chicken and pigs, and the cold water spring often appears to be made of ice. After flowing several *zhang*, the two streams merge as one.

(*GXSGC*, #7. 354; *CXJ*, 7. 145; *TPYL*, 71. 334b)

242. WELLS IN THE TEMPLE OF LAOZI

Nanlai Village of Xiangyi County is Laozi's hometown.[9] In the village there is a temple of Laozi in which there are nine wells. For the people who can fast and bathe before entering the temple, the water in the wells will become warm or cool according to their wishes.

(*GXSGC*, #8. 354; *CXJ*, 7. 154; *TPYL*, 189. 916b)

243. OLD WELL BY THE DIVINE ALTAR

On the Mountain of Nine Marquis Deities in Shanyin County, there is a divine altar. In front of the altar there is an old well, in which there is

8. Ai 艾 County, seat in modern Xiushui 修水, Jiangxi.
9. Xiangyi 襄邑 County, modern Sui 睢 County, Henan.

never any water. When people offer sacrifices to the deities and pray for it, water will pour out. After providing enough water for use, it will then gradually stop.

(*GXSGC*, #18. 356; *TPYL*, 189. 916b)

244. TIDE POND

To the east of Xiping County,[10] Shi'an Commandery, there is a mountain. The shape of the western part of the mountain is long and narrow, under which water pours into a pond. Every day the water fluctuates twice. Therefore, it was named the Tide Pond.

(*GXSGC*, #9. 354; *TPYL*, 74. 346a quotes from a note in Sheng Hongzhi, *Jingzhou ji*)

245. REED POND

To the northeast of Leiyang County (in Hunan) there is a reed pond covering 800 acres of land, its depth unfathomable. In the pond is a big fish that vigorously jumps out of the water every five days. Its length is around three arm spans, and its shape is abnormal. Each time it jumps out of the water, small fish swim ashore with the waves; their number is seemingly infinite.

(*GXSGC*, #10. 354; *TPYL*, 74. 346a–b)

246. ROOSTER MOUNTAIN

More than ten *li* south of Mount Lu, there is a mountain called Rooster Mountain. On the mountain there is a stone cock. Its crest and spurs are lifelike.

Daoist priest Li Zhen resided there, treasuring and enjoying the stone cock from time to time. One day the stone cock was suddenly

10. Xiping 熙平 County, modern Yangshuo 陽壽, Guangxi.

broken. Zhen told others, "It happened so suddenly to the cock. Is my life going to end?"

Thereupon he bid his old friends farewell, and more than a month later he passed away.

(*GXSGC*, #15. 355; *TPGJ*, 142. 1018)

247. THREE PEAKS OF MOUNT HENG

The three peaks of Mount Heng are the most towering and prominent peaks. One is not able to see them until there is a clear sky after morning rain.

Under the peaks there is a spring that resembles an unrolled bolt of white silk. While separating and casting light onto the green forest, its waters swiftly fall to the bottom of the mountain. Though not a speck of dust moves, a free, clear wind constantly flows above it.

(*GXSGC*, #16. 355; *TPYL*, 71. 334a)

248. GOLDEN TERRACE IN THE SEA

In the sea there is a golden terrace, sitting a hundred *zhang* above the water. Its structure is artful and pretty, exhaustive superlative craftsmanship. It casts light onto mountains and islets along the horizon and shines alongside the Milky Way in the heavens above.

Inside the terrace there is a golden stool with a variety of engraved patterns, on which there are a hundred tastes of food. The four deities with great strength constantly stand there to protect it. Once, an immortal who mastered the five supernatural powers came, intending to enjoy the food.[11] The four deities hit him, and he withdrew gradually.

(*GXSGC*, #2. 353; *TPYL*, 849. 3796b; *YWLJ*, 62. 1119; *BTSC*, 133. 226a)

11. Wutong 五通, the five supernatural powers, including: 1) *shenzu tong* 神足通, the power to be anywhere at will; 2) *tianyan tong* 天眼通, the power to see anything anywhere; 3) *tian'er tong* 天耳通, the power to hear any sound anywhere, 4) *taxin tong* 他心通, the power to know the thoughts of all other minds, and 5) *suming tong* 宿命通, the power to know past lives.

249. A PHOENIX HEAD FLIES INTO THE ZHANG RIVER

Fengyang Gate of Yecheng was a five-story building,[12] twenty *zhang* above the ground, forty *zhang* long, and twenty *zhang* wide. Two golden phoenix heads were built onto it. When Shi Jilong was about to decline,[13] a phoenix head flew into the Zhang River and was seen clearly at its bottom. The other phoenix head still exists.

(*GXSGC*, #3. 353; *YWLJ*, 63. 1130; *CXJ*, 24. 573)

250. THE TERRACE OF QIAO COUNTY

To the east of Qiao County,[14] a terrace was built next to the city wall. It was twenty square *zhang* and eight feet tall. Some say that it was a grave in the old times. Emperor Wu of Wei built a terrace there.[15]

Once the eastern wall was broken, and gold and jade leaked out. Many people who tried to pick up the treasure died. Accordingly, the broken wall was built again.

(*GXSGC*, #19. 356; *TPYL*, 811. 3604b)

251. BATHING IN WARM ORCHID WATER

The temple had an area of four square *zhang*, with no walls built around it. The path to the temple was five feet wide, and orchids were planted on both sides. Those who practice fasting would boil the orchids to bathe, then offer sacrifices in person. This is called "bathing in warm orchid water."

(*GXSGC*, #1. 353; *YWLJ*, 38. 677; *CXJ*, 13. 318)

12. Yecheng 鄴城 was the capital of Shi Jilong 石季龍 in this story (see next footnote), located in present-day Linzhang County, Henan Province.
13. Shi Jilong, agnomen of Shi Hu 石虎 (295–349), the third emperor of Later Zhao and a notorious tyrant.
14. Qiao 譙 County, present-day Bo 亳 County, Anhui.
15. Emperor Wu of Wei, Cao Cao (155–220), was a native of Qiao County.

252. DONGLAI WINE

The people of Donglai are clever by nature.[16] The wine they make is mostly pure, changing from turbid to clear. Two people said, "Because of this it is aromatic."

(*GXSGC*, #25. 357; *BTSC*, 148. 322a)

253. GHOST HOWLING

The old town of Le'an County has experienced famine and turmoil.[17] Its people died of starvation, and dry skeletons sprawl across the ground. Each time it is overcast and about to rain, the sounds of howling and sighing grate on people's ears.

(*GXSGC*, #20. 356; *TPYL*, 486. 2228a)

254. THE GHOST WRESTS A FISH

To the south of Pingdu County,[18] there was a tomb on the bank of a river. A traveler caught a carp by the bank. On his way he met a man from the tomb who said to him, "How dare you fetch my fish?" Then he grabbed it, put it on his cart, and left.

(*GXSGC*, #21. 356; *TPYL*, 936. 4160b)

255. THE PRINCE OF JIANGDU'S TOMB

In Guangling there is a tomb said to be that of the Prince of Jiangdu of the Han, [Liu] Jian.[19]

Once when a villager passed by the tomb, he saw several dozen sets of millstones on the ground, and he took one and brought it home. It was just dusk when someone knocked on his door urgently, requesting him to return the millstone.

---

16. Donglai Commandery, see footnote 42 in chapter 4.
17. Le'an 樂安 County, modern Boxing 博興, Shandong.
18. Pingdu 平度 County, modern Anfu 安福, Jiangxi.
19. Liu Jian 劉建, the grandson of Emperor Jing (r. 157–141 BCE) of Han, inherited the title Prince of Jiangdu 江都.

The next morning, the villager sent the millstone back and placed it at the same spot.

(*GXSGC*, #22. 356; *TPYL*, 762. 3385b)

256. THE QUEEN MOTHER

The Queen Mother once descended into the Sweet Spring Palace.

(*GXSGC*, #30. 358; *BTSC*, 12. 61b)

257. LAMP IN THE RAIN

Emperor Wu of Han ground green tin filings with black leopard white phoenix ointment, and then mixed them in butter to make lamps. The lamps would not extinguish even in the rain.

(*GXSGC*, #32. 360; *LLZS*, 13. 351a)

258. CAO E

Cao E's (130–143) father drowned. After seeing a floating watermelon, E obtained his corpse.[20]

(*GXSGC*, #39. 362; *YWLJ*, 87. 1503)

259. CRANE GATE

Duke Tao once caught fish at a border path southwest of Xunyang.[21] He called his pond "Crane Gate."

(*GXSGC*, #113. 385; annotation in "Xianyuan" of *SSXY*,)

---

20. This is an abstract of the story of Cao E 曹娥, a Han dynasty girl who drowned herself in order to find her father's lost corpse in the river. In the first year of the Yuanjia reign of Eastern Han (151), Du Shang 度尚, the magistrate of Shangyu 上虞, built a tomb and a temple on her behalf. Since then, Cao E has been venerated as an exemplar of filial piety in the history of China.
21. Duke Tao 陶, named Tao Kan 陶侃 (259–334), Duke of Changsha, Minister of Defense and Governor of Jingzhou and Jiangzhou of Jin. He was also the great-grandfather of Tao Qian 陶潛 (365–427), the famous poet of Eastern Jin.

260. CHENG JI

Cheng Ji, a native of Wuxuan,[22] was born of a concubine, so he was not recommended [to be an official]. His family often asked him to plant onions. Later, two trees grew in his garden with their branches intertwined.

(*GXSGC*, #174. 403; *TPYL*, 824. 3673b)

261. MALE AND FEMALE TREE

In Hu Wan's home there is a miraculous honey locust tree. On the other side of the road is a big elm tree. A saying passed down from old times says that they are a pair of male and female trees. One night the elm tree was cut down, and subsequently the honey locust tree withered and died.[23]

(*GXSGC*, #200. 409; *YWLJ*, 88. 1525)

262. A GOLDEN BULL (1)

Twenty *li* up from the Gold Hill in Baqiu County is the Golden Pond;[24] its depth is unfathomable. A rapid called Golden Rapid is there as well.

In the ancient time, someone was fishing on the pond and obtained a golden chain. When he pulled the chain, it came out continuously and filled the whole boat; then out came a golden bull, its body strong and its bellow wild. While the fisherman was shocked, the bull jumped desperately back into the pond. Before the chain completely vanished, the fisherman cut it with a knife and thus got several feet of it.

The names of the pond and rapid were given according to this story.

(*GXSGC*, #13. 355; *YWLJ*, 83. 1424–25)

---

22. Wuxuan 武宣, present-day Wuxuan County, Guangxi.
23. The *GXSGC* edition takes the *Wan* 晚 in 晚被斫 (at night [the elm tree] was cut down) as the man, Hu Wan, by underlining it. It is a mistake.
24. Baqiu, see footnote 32 in chapter 5.

263. A GOLDEN BULL (2)

The Bull Islet Ford of Huainan is extremely deep and unfathomable. Once, someone saw a golden bull there, its shape extremely splendid and strong, with a golden chain.

(GXSGC, #14. 355; YWLJ, 83. 1424)

264. THE DIZZYING POOL

In the lower reaches of the river in Shuo County there is a Dizzying Pool,[25] so named because it dizzies those who look at it. By its side there is a dam.

In the past someone passed by on a boat and saw a dead dragon on the dam, and it seemed that it was stranded.

Shortly afterward, he saw a tall, strong man in black, standing beside the bank and speaking to him: "While getting off the dam yesterday, I could not pass it and thus died. You may report this for me to the Dizzying Pool."

The passerby said, "There is no one on the Dizzying Pool. How could I report it?"

The man in black said, "When you arrive at the pool, just speak aloud."

The passerby did as he instructed. In a moment, a sound of weeping from the pool was heard.

(*GXSGC*, #23. 357; *TPYL*, 66. 316a)

25. Shuo 碩 County, information is not available.

APPENDIX

265. WANG DONGTING

Wang Dongting once dreamed of someone giving him a big writing brush, with a shaft as big as a raster.[1] After awaking, he told others, "I'll do something as a well-known writer someday."

A little while later, Liezong passed away.[2] Both the elegy and posthumous title proposal for him were written by Wang.

(*TPYL* 399. 1843b quotes from *SSXY*, yet this is not in the extant version)

266. ZHENG ZICHAN

Zichan (d. 522) of Zheng had a good reputation for taking care of his mother.[3] Once he visited the state of Jin as an envoy under an order, and on the way he felt a pain in his heart. Then he sent someone back to his home to ask how his mother was. His mother said, "I suddenly

---

1. Wang Dongting 王東亭, named Wang Xun 王珣 (349–400), was Marquis of Dongting and Minister of Education of Eastern Jin. He was the grandson of Wang Dao and a noted calligrapher. A similar story is found in Wang's biography in *Jin shu*, 65.1756–57.
2. Liezong 烈宗, the posthumous title of Sima Yao, Emperor Xiaowu of Eastern Jin.
3. Zichan 子產 was a vassal of Zheng 鄭 in the Spring and Autumn period.

felt that my heart and body were not harmonious, and I missed you. That is all."

(*TPYL* 411. 1897b quotes from *SSXY*, yet this is not in the extant version)

267. XU GANMU

When Xu Ganmu (364–426) was young,[4] he dreamed of a crow flying down from the sky with a long-handled umbrella in its mouth and standing it in front of his yard. The crow flew up into the sky again and came down with another umbrella. In total it stood three umbrellas there, and then cried loudly, made an angry noise, and left.

Later, Xu really contracted a foul disease, and consequently died of it.

(*TPYL* 920. 4083a quotes from *SSXY*, yet this is not in the extant version)

268. SALTED DRAGON MEAT

Someone sent some salted meat to Zhang Hua. When Hua saw it, he told his guest, "This is salted dragon meat. Inside it there is a light of five colors." The guest examined it, and it was just as Hua said. Later he heard from his host that it was made from the white fish obtained under reeds 茅积.

(*TPYL* 862. 3832a quotes from *SSXY*, yet this is not in the extant version)

269. THE DILU HORSE

When Liu Bei first went to Liu Biao for shelter,[5] he stationed his troops at Fancheng. Those under Liu Biao intended to take advantage of their conference to catch Liu Bei.

4. Xu Ganmu 徐干木, named Xianzhi 羡之, Minister of Education of the [Liu] Song.
5. Liu Bei 劉備 (r. 221–223), styled Xuande 玄德, the founder of Shu. Liu Biao 劉表 (142–208), styled 景升, was Governor of Jingzhou at the end of Eastern Han.

Bei noticed this, so when he went to the privy he left. The Dilu horse he rode fell and sank in the Tanxi stream west of the city and could not get out.

Bei urgently told the Dilu horse, "This is a strategic point for me. Why don't you try your best?"

The horse understood his words, so it jumped over three *zhang* and was able to cross the river.

(*YWLJ*, 93. 1619 [Animal, a] quotes from *SSXY*, yet this is not in the extant version)

270. THE GHOST OF FANGFENG

In Guiji was the ghost of Fangfeng, who had been seen frequently in the nearby cities and towns. It often sat on the Leimen Gate[6] with two legs touching the ground. The magistrate of Hengyang, He Taoyi, was good at playing the zither. Hearing the sound of the zither, Fangfeng danced in He's atrium.

(*YWLJ* 44. 782 quotes from *SSXY*, yet this is not in the extant version)

271. CHEN ZHUANG

During the time of Huan Cheji,[7] there was a man called Chen Zhuang who entered Mount Wudang to learn the Daoist doctrine. White smoke always drifted from the place where he lived, and fragrance was smelled everywhere.

(*TPYL* 981. 4343a quotes from *SSXY*, yet this is not in the extant version)

6. The gate of Shaoxing 紹興.
7. Huan Chong, the *Cheji jiangjun* 車騎將軍 (Chariot and Horse General) and governor of Jingzhou of Eastern Jin.

272. CAO SHUANG

When Cao Shuang (d. 249) was about to be put to death,[8] he dreamed of two tigers with the Thunder God, resembling two jars, in their mouths and put him in the courtyard.

(*TPYL* 13. 66a quotes from *SSXY*)

273. TOMB OF WANG ZIQIAO

The tomb of Wang Ziqiao is in Jingling. During the Warring States period, a robber excavated it but found nothing; there was only a sword hanging in the open grave. When the robber intended to fetch it, the sword emitted a sound resembling the roar of a dragon and a tiger. Therefore he dared not approach it. In a moment, it flew up directly into the sky.

The *Classic of Immortals* says, "When a true man passes away,[9] a sword will mostly take his place. Five hundred years later, the sword can also make a numinous transformation." This story is the verification of it.

(*TPGJ* 229. 1755 quotes from *SSXY*)

274. ZHANG HENG AND CAI YONG

A month after Zhang Heng's death,[10] Cai Yong's mother became pregnant. The talents and appearance of Heng and Yong were similar. Their contemporaries conjectured that Yong was the reincarnation of Heng.

(*Xutan zhu* 續談助 13 quotes from *SSXY*)

8. Cao Shuang 曹爽, Marquis Wu'an 武安 of Wei, was killed by Sima Yi (179–251), the founder of Jin.
9. A true man is a man who has achieved enlightenment.
10. Zhang Heng 張衡 (78–139), styled Pingzi 平子, was a writer and astronomer of the Eastern Han. Cai Yong 蔡邕 (132–192), styled Bojie 伯喈, was a writer of Eastern Han.

275. SUN HAO

On the eighth day of the fourth month, Sun Hao (242–284) urinated on a golden statue [of Buddha], and he called it "bathing Buddha."[11] Later, his penis contracted a disease, and only recovered after he confessed his sin.

(*BKLT* 3. 65a quotes from *SSXY*)

276. FOOD BECOMING SPIRAL SHELLS

During the Yongxi reign (290), the family of Wei Guan (220–290) was cooking.[12] Their food dropped onto the ground and morphed into spiral shells that all stretched out their feet to walk. Later, Guan was put to death.

(*TPYL* 885. 3931a quotes from *SSXY*, yet this is not in the extant version)

277. WEI FAJI

Wei Faji was a native of Yixing. At the age of twelve, his son contracted an illness that lasted for years.

Once a spirit came to talk to him, saying, "Your bed mat is not clean. Where should I sit?"

Faji replied, "There is a painted kerchief box that is very clean. Why don't you enter it?" Accordingly, he put fresh fruit in the box.

When he heard a sound inside, he covered the box. Hearing something shaking inside, he then wrapped the box with his cloth. It was as heavy as five *sheng* of millet.

Then his son recovered from the illness.

(*TPYL* 711. 3168a quotes from *SSXY*, yet this is not in the extant version)

---

11. Sun Hao was the last Emperor of Wu during the Three Kingdoms period.
12. Wei Guan 衛瓘, styled Boyu 伯玉, a general and Minister of Works of Jin.

278. IRON HAMMER

In the third year of Yongjia, in the flower bed under the terrace of the old Prince Rencheng of Wei in Zhongmu County,[13] there was an iron hammer of the Han. It was six feet long and buried three feet underground, with its head pointed toward the southwest.

(*TPYL* 763. 3389a quotes from *SSXY*, yet this is not in the extant version)

279. WHITE JADE OF CHANGSHAN

Prince Changsha moved his fief to Changshan. When he arrived, he dug a well. At the point four *zhang* under the ground, he obtained a piece of white jade three to four square feet in area.

(*TPYL* 805. 3579a quotes from *SSXY*, yet this is not in the extant version)

280. DU YU

When Du Yu (222–285) was Governor of Jingzhou and guarded Xiangyang,[14] from time to time there were feast gatherings. When he was drunk, he would close the door of his study and lie down alone, not allowing others to approach him.

Once when he was drunk, he was heard throwing up in his study, and his voice cried out in great pain. All of his attendants were terrified. Then a clerk opened the door and had a look. He saw there was a big snake on the bed, lowering its head by the side of the bed to vomit, yet not a single man in sight.

(*TPYL* 388. 1793a–b quotes from *SSXY*, yet this is not in the extant version; *TPGJ* 456. 3727 quotes from *Liu shi xiaoshuo*)

13. Prince Rencheng 任城, the second son of Cao Cao, named Cao Zhang (d. 223). After his death, his son was enfeoffed at Zhongmu 中牟.
14. Du Yu 杜預, a famous general of Western Jin and Governor of Jingzhou.

281. THE IMMORTAL RESIDENCE[15]

At the bottom of Songgao Mountain there was a big cave. During the Jin dynasty, a man fell into the cave by mistake. He saw two people playing chess there; by their side was a cup of white liquid. They gave it to the man to drink, and his strength increased ten times.

The chess players asked, "Do you want to stay here?"

The man who had fallen replied, "I don't want to stay."

The chess players said, "To go westward from here, there is a big well. Inside it is a flood dragon. Please throw yourself into the well, and you will be able to get out yourself. If you are hungry, take the stuff in the well to eat."

The man who had fallen just followed what they said. After around half a year, he came out at central Shu and returned to Luoyang. He inquired of Zhang Hua about what he had experienced. Hua replied, "That is the Immortal Residence.[16] What you drank was carnelian juice, and what you ate was stone marrow from the dragon cave."

(*GXSGC*, #63. 370; *CXJ* 5. 103–04 and *TPYL* 39. 185a–b)

282. BREAKING A PROMISE CAUSES LOSS OF MAGIC FIGURES

Xu Chang and Bao Liang of Wuxing had long been close friends. Bao intended to teach Xu secret magical arts, but he told him first, "It is proper to make a pledge." Xu pledged that he would never be an official in government. Then Bao gave him the magic figures. Consequently, Xu could constantly see eight grand deities around him. He was able

15. Both *CXJ* 5 and *TPYL* 39 quote this piece from *SSXY*. Yet Lu Xun notes, "The present edition of *Shishuo* does not include this tale. When the collectanea of the Tang and Song quote from the *Youming lu*, they sometimes also say that this is from *Shishuo*." See his *GXSGC*, #63. 370.

16. Zheng Wanqing made a mistake in punctuation, so he took *xianguan* (immortal residence) as *xianguan fu* (a man of immortal residence). See his *YML*, 24–25. The correct punctuation should be as follows: 此仙館，夫所飲者玉漿 instead of 此仙館夫，所飲者玉漿。

to see everything in the past as well as in the future, and his ability and insight increased daily.

People in the county and village all talked about Xu with approval, and the authority intended to hire him as Assistant Magistrate of the county. Xu was delighted with it.

The next morning, however, seven of the eight deities disappeared, and the one left was arrogant, different from his usual behavior. When Xu asked him why, he replied, "You broke your promise, so we won't work together with you. The reason I was asked to stay here alone was to guard the magic figures, and that is all."

Thus Xu returned the magic figures and withdrew.

(*GXSGC*, #258. 432; both *TPYL*, 882. 3919b–40a and *TPGJ*, 294. 2340 quote from *SSXY*, yet this is not found in the extant version)

283. ZHANG HUA

When Zhang Hua was about to decline, blowing wind brought six to seven cloth rods leaning against the wall.

(*GXSGC*, #64. 370; *TPYL* 830. 3703b quotes from *SSXY*)

284. JIA YONG LOST HIS HEAD

The Governor of Yuzhang, Jia Yong, possessed divine power. When leaving the commandery to launch a punitive expedition against the rebels, he was killed by them and beheaded.

He mounted his horse to return to his camp, saying through his chest, "I was defeated in battle and wounded by the rebels. Everybody, please look: is it better to have a head or not to have one?"

The officials wept, saying, "It is better to have a head."

"No!" said Jia Yong. "It is also nice without a head."

After finishing his words, he immediately died.

(*GXSGC*, #217. 415; *TPGJ* 321. 2548, no source given)

285. THE MOLE CRICKETS

Shi Ziran of Guiiji said, there was a man wearing an unlined white silk garment and a silk hat who went directly to his mat, held his hands, and talked to him. When Ziran asked his name, he replied, "My surname is Lu, and my name is Gou. My home is by the river, close to Tanxi."

Five days later, when his craftsman dug in the old hill by the west ditch in the field, he found a big pit full of mole crickets—about a *dou* (ten pints) or so. Among these mole crickets, several were very strong, and one was huge. Ziran suddenly realized what had happened, saying, "My recent guest called himself Lu Gou, which became Lou gu (mole crickets) by exchanging the finals of the two characters while keeping their initials. The guest said his home was in Tanxi, which means west pit."

Then he filled the whole pit with boiling water. Since then the mole crickets have been extinct.

(*GXSGC*, #257. 432; *TPYL* 948. 4209b, no source given)

TALES APPEARING IN OTHER RENDITIONS

1 AGM 186. 107–08; *CCT* 40. 137
2 *CCT* 43. 143–44; *ST* 278–81
3 *CCT* 44. 145–46; *ST* 292–95
4 *CCT* 47. 149–50; *ST* 296–97
6 *CCT* 42. 141–43; *ST* 282–87
9 *CCT* 45. 146–47; *ST* 266–69
11 *AGM* 207. 119
14 *CCT* 41.139–40; *ST* 262–65
17 *AGM* 205. 118
26 *AGM* 189. 110
46 *AGM* 200. 116
57 *AGM* 206. 118–19
59 *AGM* 191. 111
64 *AGM* 193. 112–13
65 *AGM* 203. 117
74 *AGM* 201. 116
81 *AGM* 208. 119–20
90 *AGM* 196. 114–15
91 *ST* 274–77
113 *AGM* 192. 111–12
114 *ST* 298–303
115 *AGM* 197. 115
136 *AGM* 194. 113–14
139 *ST* 188–91

170 *CCT* 46. 147–49
180 *AGM* 187. 109
181 *AGM* 195. 114
182 *ST* 270–73
187 *AGM* 204. 117–18
194 *AGM* 202. 117
206 *AGM* 190. 110–11
209 *AGM* 188. 110
226 *AGM* 198. 115
253 *AGM* 184. 107
254 *AGM* 185. 107

WORKS CITED

WORKS IN CHINESE AND JAPANESE

Bai Juyi 白居易 (772–846) and Kong Chuan 孔傳. *Bai Kong liutie* 白孔六帖 [Bai's classified encyclopedia enlarged by Kong]. Taibei: Xinxing shuju, 1969.

Ban Gu 班固 (32–92). *Han shu* 漢書 [History of Han]. Beijing: Zhonghua shuju, 1962.

Cao Xueqin 曹雪芹 (1715–1764) and Gao E 高鶚. *Honglou meng* 紅樓夢 [Dream of the Red Chamber]. Beijing: Renmin wenxue chubanshe, 1982.

Chen Guishi 陳桂市. "*Youming lu xuan yan ji* yanjiu" 幽明錄宣驗記研究 [A study of the *Records of the Hidden and Visible Realms* and the *Records of Manifest Miracles*]. M.A. thesis, Gaoxiong Normal University, 1987.

Chen Guying 陳鼓應, ed. *Zhuangzi jinzhu jinyi* 莊子今注今譯 [Modern commentary and translation of *Zhuangzi*]. Beijing: Zhonghua shuju, 1983.

Chen Menglei 陳孟雷 (b. 1651–1752) et al., eds. *Gujin tushu jicheng* 古今圖書集成 [Chrestomathy of illustrations and writings ancient and modern]. Shanghai: Zhonghua shuju, 1934.

Chen Shou 陳壽 (233–297) *Sanguo zhi* 三國志 (History of the Three Kingdoms). Beijing: Zhonghua shuju, 1959.

Duan Chengshi 段成式 (803–863). *Youyang zazu* 酉陽雜俎 [Miscellaneous morsels from Youyang]. Beijing: Zhonghua shuju, 1981.

Fang Xuanling 房玄齡 (578–648). *Jin shu* 晉書 [Jin history]. Beijing: Zhonghua shuju, 1974.

Fan Ye 范曄 (398–445) and Sima Biao 司馬彪 (d. 306). *Hou Han shu* 後漢書 [Eastern Han history]. Beijing: Zhonghua shuju, 1962.

Fan Ziye 范子燁. *Shishuo xinyu yanjiu* 世說新語研究 [Study of the *New Account of Tales of the World*]. Harbin: Helongjiang jiaoyu chubanshe, 1998.

Feng Youlan 馮友蘭. *Zhongguo zhexue shi* 中國哲學史 [History of Chinese philosophy]. Hong Kong: Kaiming shudian, 1970.

Gan Bao 干寶 (fl. 335–349), ed. *Shoushen ji* 搜神記 [In search of the spirits]. Beijing: Zhonghua shuju, 1979.

Hao Yixing 郝懿行 (1757–1825), ed. *Shanhai jing jianshu* 山海經校疏 [*The Classic of Mountains and Seas* with collations and commentary]. Taibei: Yiwen yinshuguan, 1965.

Hu Ting 胡珽 (1822–1861), ed. *Linlang mishi congshu* 琳琅秘室叢書 [Book series from the secret room *linlang*]. Taibei: Yiwen chubanshe, 1967.

Hu Yinglin 胡應麟 (1151–1602). *Shaoshi shanfang bicong* 少室山房筆叢 [Collected notes from the study of Shaoshi Mountain]. Taibei: Shijie shuju, 1963.

Huijiao 慧皎 (497–554), et al. *Gaoseng zhuan heji* 高僧傳合集 [A synthesized collection of biographies of eminent monks]. Shanghai: Shanghai guji chubanshe, 1991.

Huilin 慧琳 (fl. fifth century). *Yiqiejing yinyi* [Pronunciation and meaning of all the (Buddhist) scriptures]. Taibei: Datong 大通 shuju, 1970; *Taishō Tripitaka*, 54. 464.

Huiyuan 慧遠 (334–416). "Sanbao lun" 三報論 [On the three types of retributions]. In Shi Jun's 石峻 *Zhongguo fojiao sixiang ziliao xuanbian* 中國佛教思想資料選編 [Selected materials on the history of Chinese Buddhist thought]. Beijing: Zhonghua shuju, 1981.

Jiang Liangfu 姜亮夫, ed. *Chongding Qu Yuan fu jiaozhu* 重訂屈原賦校注 [Revised Qu Yuan's *Rhapsodies* collated and annotated]. Tianjin: Tianjin guji chubanshe, 1987.

Kong Yingda 孔穎達 (574–648). *Zuozhuan zhushu* 左傳注疏 [*Zuo zhuan* with commentary and subcommentary]. *SBBY*. Taibei: Taiwan Zhonghua shuju, 1965.

Li Daoping 李道平. *Zhouyi jijie zuanshu* 周易集解纂疏. Beijing: Zhonghua shuju, 1994.

Li Fang 李昉 (925–996) et al., eds. *Taiping guangji* 太平廣記 [Extensive records from the Taiping reign period]. Beijing: Zhonghua shuju, 1961.

——, ed. *Taiping yulan* 太平禦覽 [Taiping reign period imperial encyclopedia]. Beijing: Zhonghua shuju, 1960.

Li Fengmao. *Xianjing yu youli: shenxian shijie de xiangxiang* 仙境與遊歷：神仙世界的想像 [Immortal land and traveling: the image of the immortal world]. Beijing: Zhonghua shuju, 2010.

Li Jianguo 李劍國. *Tang qian zhiguai xiaoshuoshi* 唐前志怪小說史 [A history of pre-Tang *zhiguai* stories]. Tianjin: Nankai daxue chubanshe, 1984.

——, ed. *Xinji Soushen ji* 新輯搜神記 [Newly compiled *In Search of the Supernatural*]. Beijing: Zhonghua shuju, 2007.

Li Yanshou 李延壽 (seventh century). *Nan shi* 南史 [History of the south]. Beijing: Zhonghua shuju, 1975.

Liu Xu 劉昫 (877–946). *Jiu Tang shu* 舊唐書 [Old Tang history]. Beijing: Zhonghua shuju, 1975.

Liu Yeqiu 劉葉秋. *Wei Jin nanbeichao xiaoshuo* 魏晉南北朝小說 [Fiction of the Wei Jin Northern and Southern dynasties]. Bejing: Zhonghua shuju, 1961.

Liu Yiqing劉義慶, ed. *Youming lu* 幽明錄 [Records of the hidden and visible realms]. In *Guxiaoshuo gouchen* 古小說鉤沉 [Collected lost old stories]. In *Lu Xun quanji* 魯迅全集 [Complete works of Lu Xun], v. 8. Beijing: Renmin wenxue chubanshe, 1973.

Liu Yuanru 劉苑如. *Shenti, xingbie, jieji: Liuchao zhiguai de changyi lunshu yu xiaoshuo meixue* 身體、性別. 階級—六朝志怪的常異論述與小說美學 [Body, sex, and class: discourse of the normal and abnormal and fictional aesthetics in the anomaly accounts of the Six Dynasties]. Taibei: Zhongyang yanjiuyuan Zhongguo wenzhe yanjiusuo, 2002.

Lu Qinli 逯欽立, ed. *Xian Qin Han Wei Jin Nanbeichao shi* 先秦漢魏晉南北朝詩 [Poetry of pre-Qin, Han, Wei, Jin, and the Northern and Southern dynasties]. Beijing: Zhonghua shuju, 1983.

Lu Xun 魯迅, ed. *Gujixuba ji* 古籍序跋集. *Lu Xun quanji* 10. Beijing: Renmin wenxue chubanshe, 1981.

——. *Guxiaoshuo gouchen* 古小說鉤沉 [Collected lost old stories]. In *Lu Xun quanji* 魯迅全集 [Complete works of Lu Xun], 8. 353–436. Beijing: Renmin wenxue chubanshe, 1973.

——. *Zhongguo xiaoshuo shilue* 中國小說史略 [A brief history of Chinese fiction]. Beijing: Renmin wenxue chubanshe, 1973.

Luan Baoqun 欒保群 and Lü Zongli 呂宗力, eds. *Rizhilu jishi* 日知錄集釋 [Collected notes on *Record of Knowledge Gained Day by Day*]. Shanghai: Shanghai guji chubanshe, 2006.

Luo Zhufeng 羅竹風, ed. *Hanyu da cidian* 漢語大辭典 [Great Chinese dictionary]. Shanghai: Shanghai cishu chubanshe, 1986–1979.

Ma Zhefang 馬振方. *Zhongguo zaoqi xiaoshuo kaobian* 中國早期小說考辨 (A textual study of early Chinese fiction). Beijing: Beijing daxue chubanshe, 2014.

Maeno Naoaki 前野直彬. *Chugoku shosetsu shi ko* 中國小說史考 [Study of the history of Chinese fiction]. Musushino: Akiyama Shoten, 1975.

——. "Meikai yugyo" 冥界遊行 [Traveling in the netherworld]. In *Chugoku bungakuho* 中國文學 [Chinese literature] XIV (April 1961): 38–57; *Chugoku shosetsu shi ko,* 112–49.

Makoto Mekada 目加田誠, *Sesetsu shingo* 世說新語 1–3. Tokyo: Meiji shoin, 1975–78.

Ouyang Xiu 歐陽修 (1007–1072) and Song Qi 宋祁 (998–1061). *Xin Tang shu* 新唐書 [New Tang history]. Beijing: Zhonghua shuju, 1975.

——. *Yiwen leiju* 藝文類聚 [Compendium of arts and letters]. Shanghai: Zhonghua shuju, 1965.

Pu Muzhou 蒲慕洲. *Muzang yu shengsi—Zhongguo gudai zongjiao zhi xingsi* 墓葬與生死—中國古代宗教之省思 [Burial and the matter of life and death: pondering ancient Chinese religion]. Taibei: Jinglian chuban gongsi, 1993.

Pu Songling 蒲松齡. *Liaozhai zhiyi* 聊齋志異 [Strange tales from Make-do Studio]. Shanghai: Shanghai guji chubanshe, 1979.

Qutan xida 瞿曇悉達, ed. *Kaiyuan zhanjing* 開元占經 (Divination classic of the Kaiyuan reign period). Beijing: Zhongyang bianyi chubanshe, 2006.

Ruan Yuan 阮元 (1764–1849). *Chongkan Songben shisanjing zhushu* 重刊宋本十三經註疏 [Reengraved Song edition of the commentaries and subcommentaries to the Thirteen Classics]. Taibei: Yiwen yinshuguan, 1960.

Saoye shanfang 掃葉山房. *Wuchao xiaoshuo dagun* 五朝小說大觀 [Grand spectacle of the five dynasty stories]. Taibei: Guangwen shuju, 1979.

Shen Yue 沈約. *Song shu* 宋書 [Song history]. Beijing: Zhonghua shuju, 1974.

Shi Baochang 釋寶唱 (fl. 465). *Biqiuni zhuan* 比丘尼傳 [Bhikshuni biographies]. In Huijiao et al., *Gaoseng zhuan heji*, 963–77.

Sima Biao 司馬彪 (d. 306). *Xu Han shu* 續漢書 [Continuation of the history of Han]. Beijing: Zhonghua shuji, 1965.

Sima Qian 司馬遷 (145–86? B.C.). *Shi ji* 史記 [Record of the historian]. Beijing: Zhonghua shuju, 1959.

Sun Changwu 孫昌武. ed. *Guanshiyin yingyanji* 觀世音應驗記 [Records of miracles concerning Avalokiteśvara]. Beijing: Zhonghua shuju, 1994.

Sun Yirang 孫詒讓 (1848–1908). *Mozi xiangu* 墨子閒詁 [Intermittent glosses on *Mozi*]. Taibei: Shijie shuju, 1962.

Tan Qixiang 譚其驤. *Zhongguo lishi dituji* 中國歷史地圖集 [The historical atlas of China]. Beijing: Ditu shubanshe, 1982.

Tao Qian 陶潛 (365–427). *Soushen houji* 搜神後記 [Sequel to *In Search of the Spirits*]. In Wang Genlin, *Han Wen Liuchao biji xiaoshuo daguan*.

Tao Zongyi 陶宗儀 (fl. 1360–1368), ed. *Shuo fu* 說郛 [The city of talks]. Taibei: Xinxing 新興 shuju, 1963.

Wang Genlin 王根林 et al., eds. *Han Wei liuchao biji xiaoshuo daguan* 漢魏六朝筆記小說大觀 [Grand spectacle of Han Wei and Six Dynasties *zhiguai* stories]. Shanghai: Shanghai guji chubanshe, 1999.

Wang Guoliang 王國良. *Liuchao zhiguai xiaoshuo kaolun* 六朝志怪小說攷論 [Study of Six Dynasties *zhiguai* stories]. Taibei: Wen shi zhe chubanshe, 1988.

——. *Wei Jin Nanbeichao zhiguai xiaoshuo yanjiu* 魏晉南北朝志怪小說研究 [Study of Wei Jin Northern and Southern dynasty fiction]. Taibei: Wen shi zhe chubanshe, 1984.

Wang Ming 王明, ed. *Baopuzi neipian jiaoshi* 抱朴子內篇校釋 [Inner chapters of the *Master Who Embraces Simplicity* with collations and explanations]. Beijing: Zhonghua shuju, 1980.

—— ed. *Taiping jing hejiao* 太平經合校 [*Taiping jing* synthesized and collated]. Beijing: Zhonghua shuju, 1960.

Wang Shoupeng 王壽朋, ed. *Chongkan zengguang fenlei Leilin zashuo* 重刊增廣分類類林雜說. 15 v. No. 1219 of *Xuxiu siku quanshu* 續修四庫全書. Shanghai: Shanghai guji chubanshe, 2002.

Wang Yao 王瑤. *Zhonggu wenxueshi lunji* 中古文學史論集 [On the history of medieval literature]. Taibei: Chang'an chubanshe, 1982.

Wei Zheng 魏徵 (580–643) et al. *Sui shu* 隋書 [Sui history]. Beijing: Zhonghua shuju, 1973, 980.

Wu Cheng'en 吳承恩 (1500–1582). *Xiyou ji* 西遊記 [Journey to the west]. Hong Kong: Shangwu yinshuguan, 1961.

Wu Shu 吳淑 (947–1002). *Shilei fu zhu* 事類賦注 [Commentary on the *Rhapsody of Classified Matters*]. Taibei: Xinxing shuju, 1969.

Wu Zengqi 吳曾祺 (b. 1852). *Jiu xiaoshuo* 舊小說 [Old fiction]. Shanghai: Shanghai shangwu yinshuguan, 1957.

Xian Hong 蕭虹. "*Shishuo xinyu* zuozhe wenti shangque" 世說新語作者問題商榷 [A discussion on the authorship of the *New Account of Tales of the World*]. In *Guoli Zhongyang tushuguan guankan* 國立中央圖書館館刊 14, no. 1: 8–24.

Xiao Dengfu 蕭登福. *Xian Qin liang Han mingjie he shenxian sixiang tanyuan* 先秦兩漢冥界和神仙思想探源 [Exploring the origins of concepts of the netherworld and immortals in the pre-Qin and Han period]. Taibei: Wenjin chubanshe, 1990.

Xie Mingxun 謝明勳. *Liuchao zhiguai xiaoshuoyanjiu shulun: Huigu yu lunshi* 六朝志怪小說研究述論：回顧與論釋 [A review of the studies of Six Dynasties *zhiguai* stories: retrospection and interpretation]. Taibei: Liren shuju, 2011.

Xie Zongwan 謝宗萬, ed. *Quanguo zhong-caoyao huibian* 全國中草藥匯編. Beijing: Renmin weisheng chubanshe, 1975. http://zhongyaocai360.com/G/gupiteng.html.

Xu Shen 許慎 (30–124). *Shuowen jiezi* 說文解字. Beijing: Zhonghua shuju, 1963.

Xu Shuofang 徐朔方 and Yang Xiaomei 楊笑梅, ed. *Mudan ting* 牡丹亭 [Peony pavilion]. Beijing: Renmin wenxue chubanshe, 1963.

Yan Kejun 嚴可均 (1762–1843), ed. *Quan shanggu sandai Qin Han sanguo liuchao wen* 全上古三代秦漢三國六朝文 [Complete prose of Antiquity, the Three Dynasties, Qin Han, Three Kingdoms, and Six Dynasties]. Beijing: Zhonghua shuju, 1965.

Ye Qingbing 葉慶炳. "Liuchao zhi Tang de tajie jiegou xiaoshuo 六朝至唐的他界小說 [Stories about the other world in the Six Dynasties and the Tang]. *Taida zhongwen xuebao* 臺大中文學報 [Chinese journal of Taiwan University] 3 (1989): 9.

Yu Jiaxi 余嘉錫, ed. *Shishuo xinyu jianshu* 世說新語箋疏 [Annotated new account of tales of the world]. Beijing: Zhonghua shuju, 1983.

Yu Shinan 虞世南 (558–638), ed. *Beitang shuchao* 北堂書抄 [Extracts from the north hall]. Taibei: Wenhai chubanshe, 1961.

Yu Yingshi 余英時. "Zhongguo gudai sihou shijieguan de yanbian 中國古代死後世界觀的演變 [The changing conceptions of the afterlife in ancient China]." In his *Zhongguo sixiang chuantong de xiandai quanshi* 中國思想傳統的現代詮釋 [Modern interpretation of traditional Chinese thought], 123–43. Taibei: Jinglian chuban shiye gongsi, 1987.

Yue Hengjun 樂衡軍. "Zhongguo yuanshi bianxing shenhua chutan" 中國原始變形神話初探 [Preliminary exploration of protometamorphoses myth of ancient China]. In Gu Tianhong 古添洪, ed., *Cong bijiao shenhua dao wenxue* 從比較神話到文學 [From comparative myth to comparative literature], 159–72. Taibei: Dongda tushu gongsi, 19772.

Zang Lihe 臧勵龢. *Diming dacidian* 地名大辭典 [The big Chinese gazetteer]. Hong Kong: Shangwu yinshuguan, 1982.

Zeng Zao曾慥 (1091–1155). *Lei shuo* 類說 [Talks on classified matters]. Beijing: Beijing tushuguan guji zhenben congkan, 1988.

Zhang Chang 張萇, "Luelun Gudai xiaoshuo zhong de renshenlian gushi" 略論古代小說中的人神恋故事 [Brief remarks on the love stories between man and goddess in ancient Chinese fiction]. *Xinan shifan daxue xuebao* 西南師範大學學報 1 (1991): 94–99.

Zhang Zhenjun 張振軍. *Chuantong xiaoshuo yu Zhongguo wenhua* 傳統小說與中國文化 [Traditional fiction and Chinese culture]. Guilin: Guangxi shifan daxue chubanshe, 1996.

——. "Shi bai xueyuan shuolue: jianlun Zhongguo chuantong xiaoshuo de shizhuan tezheng" 史稗血緣說略：兼論中國傳統小說的史傳特徵 (Brief remarks on the consanguinity between history and fiction). *Zhongguo renmin daxue xuebao* 中國人民大學學報 6 (1995): 93–99.

Zhao Yi 趙翼 (1727–1814). *Gaiyu congkao* 陔餘丛考 [Collection of miscellaneous studies]. Taibei: Shijie shuju, 1965.

Zheng Wanqing 鄭晚晴, ed. *Youming lu*. Beijing: Wenhua yishu chubanshe, 1988.

Zhou Shujia 周叔迦 and Su Jinren 蘇晉仁, eds. *Fayuan zhulin jiaozhu* 法苑珠林校注 [*Fayuan zhulin* with collations and annotations], 1–6. Beijing: Zhonghua shuju, 2003.

WORKS IN WESTERN LANGUAGES

Allen, Sarah. *Shifting Stories: History, Gossip, and Lore in Narratives from Tang Dynasty China.* Cambridge, MA: Harvard University Asia Center, 2014.

Belpaire, Bruno. *Anthologie chinoise des 5e et 6e siecles: le Che-chouo-sin-yu par Lieou (Tsuen) Hiao-piao.* Paris: Éditions universitaires, 1974.

Cai, Meghan. "The Social Life of Texts: Reading Zhuang Chuo's 莊綽 (fl. 1126) *Jilei bian* 雞肋編 [Chicken Rib Chronicles]." Ph.D. diss., Arizona State University, 2016.

Campany, Robert Ford. *A Garden of Marvels: Tales of Wonder from Early Medieval China.* Honolulu: University of Hawai'i Press, 2015.

——. *Making Transcendents: Ascetics and Social Memory in Early Medieval China.* Honolulu: University of Hawai'i Press, 2009.

——. "Return-from-Death Narratives in Early Medieval China." *Journal of Chinese Religions* 18 (Fall 1900): 91–125.

——. *Signs from the Unseen Realm: Buddhist Miracle Tales from Early Medieval China.* Honolulu: University of Hawai'i Press, 2012.

——. *Strange Writing: Anomaly Accounts in Early Medieval China.* Albany: State University of New York Press, 1996.

Chan, Leo Tak-hung. *The Discourse on Foxes and Ghosts: Ji Yun and Eighteenth-Century Literati Storytelling.* Honolulu: University of Hawai'i Press, 1998.

DeWoskin, Kenneth J. "The Six Dynasties *Chih-kuai* and the Birth of Fiction." In *Chinese Narrative Critical and Theoretical Essays,* ed. A. H. Plaks, 21–52. Princeton: Princeton University Press, 1977.

DeWoskin, Kenneth J. and J. I. Crump Jr. *In Search of the Supernatural.* Stanford: Stanford University Press, 1996.

Dien, Albert E. "The *Yuan-hun Chih* (Accounts of Ghosts with Grievances): A Sixth-Century Collection of Stories." *Wen-lin: Studies in the Chinese Humanities,* ed. T. T. Chow, 211–28. Madison: University of Wisconsin Press, 1968.

Ding Wangdao, ed., *100 Chinese Myths and Fantacies.* Hong Kong: Shangwu yinshuguan, 1988.

Dudbridge, Glen. *Religious Experience and Lay Society in T'ang China: A Reading of Tai Fu's* Kuang-i chi. Cambridge University Press, 1995.

Encyclopedia Britannica Inc., ed. *Encyclopedia Britannica.* Chicago: Encyclopedia Britannica Inc., 1998.

Gjertson, Donald Edward. *Miraculous Retribution: A Study and Translation of T'ang Lin's "Ming-pao chi."* Berkeley: Centers for South and Southeast Asian Studies, University of California, 1989.

Gu Ming Dong. *Chinese Theories of Fiction: A Non-Western Narrative System.* Albany: State University of New York Press, 2006.

Hawkes, David. *The Songs of the South.* New York: Penguin, 1985.

Inglis, Alister D. *Hong Mai's Record of the Listener and Its Song Dynasty Context.* Albany: State University of New York Press, 2006.

Kao, Karl S. Y., ed. *Classical Chinese Tales of the Supernatural and the Fantastic.* Bloomington: Indiana University Press, 1985.

—. "Bao and Baoying: Narrative Causality and External Motivations." *CLEAR* 11 (1989): 115–38.

Lau, D. C. *The Analects of Confucius.* London: Penguin, 1979.

Legge, James (1815–1897). *The Chinese Classics.* Hong Kong: Hong Kong University Press, 1960.

Mair, Victor, ed. *The Columbia Anthology of Traditional Chinese Literature.* New York: Columbia University Press, 1994.

Marney, Johe. "The 'Other World' in Chinese Literature." *Literature East and West* 18, no. 2–4 (1974, actually 1978): 158–65.

Mather, Richard B. *A New Account of Tales of the World.* Minneapolis: University of Minnesota Press, 1976.

Matsunaga, Daigan and Alica. *The Buddhist Concept of Hell.* New York: Philosophical Library, 1972.

Nienhauser, William H. Jr., ed. *Grand Scribe's Records,* v. 1, 2, 5. 1 and 7. Bloomington and Indianapolis: Indiana University Press, 1994–2006.

—, ed. *The Indiana Companion to Traditional Chinese Literature.* 2nd ed. Taipei: SMC Publishing., 1987.

—. "Origins of Chinese Fiction." *Monumenta Serica* 38 (1988–89): 191–219.

Plaks, Andrew. "Toward a Critical Theory of Chinese Narrative." In Plaks, *Chinese Narrative: Critical and Theoretical Essays.* Princeton, NJ: Princeton University Press, 1977.

Sterckx, Roel. *The Animal and the Daemon in Early China.* Albany: State University of New York Press, 2002.

Swartz, Wendy, et al., eds. *Early Medieval China: A Sourcebook.* New York: Columbia University Press, 2014.

Yang Xanyi and Gladys Yang, trans. *Selected Tales of the Han, Wei and Six Dynasties Periods.* Beijing: Foreign Languages Press, 2006.

Yu, Anthony. "Rest, Rest, Perturbed Spirit! Ghosts in Traditional Chinese Fiction." *HJAS* 47 (1987): 397–434.

Yu Ying-Shih. "O Soul, Come Back! A Study in the Changing Conceptions of the Soul and Afterlife in Pre-Buddhist China." *HJAS* 47 (1987): 363–95.

Zeitlin, Judith T. *History of the Strange: Pu Songling and the Chinese Classical Tales.* Stanford: Stanford University Press, 1993.

Zhang Zhenjun. *Buddhism and Tales of the Supernatural in Early Medieval China: A Study of Liu Yiqing's* Youming lu. Leiden and Boston: Brill, 2014.

——. "Buddhist Impact on the Creation of New Fictional Figures and Images in the *Youming lu.*" *Sungkyun Journal of East Asian Studies* 10, no. 2 (2010): 145–68.

——. "From Demonic to Karmic Retribution: Changing Concepts of *Bao* in Early Medieval China as Seen in the *Youming lu.*" *Acta Orientalia* 66, no.3 (2013): 267–87.

——. "Observations on the Life and Works of Liu Yiqing." *Early Medieval China* 20 (2014): 83–104.

——. "On the Origins of Detached Soul Motif in Chinese Literature." *Sungkyun Journal of East Asian Studies* 9, no. 2 (2009): 167–84.

——. "A Textual History of Liu Yiqing's *You Ming Lu.*" *Oriens Extremus* 48 (2009): 87–101.

Zürcher, Erik. *The Buddhist Conquest of China: The Spread and Adaptation of Buddhism in Early Medieval China.* Leiden: E. J. Brill, 1959.

——. "Perspectives in the Study of Chinese Buddhism." *Journal of the Royal Asiatic Society* 2 (1982): 161–76.

INDEX

TRANSLATIONS FROM THE ASIAN CLASSICS

Major Plays of Chikamatsu, tr. Donald Keene 1961

Four Major Plays of Chikamatsu, tr. Donald Keene. Paperback ed. only. 1961; rev. ed. 1997

Records of the Grand Historian of China, translated from the Shih chi of Ssu-ma Ch'ien, tr. Burton Watson, 2 vols. 1961

Instructions for Practical Living and Other Neo-Confucian Writings by Wang Yang-ming, tr. Wing-tsit Chan 1963

Hsün Tzu: Basic Writings, tr. Burton Watson, paperback ed. only. 1963; rev. ed. 1996

Chuang Tzu: Basic Writings, tr. Burton Watson, paperback ed. only. 1964; rev. ed. 1996

The Mahābhārata, tr. Chakravarthi V. Narasimhan. Also in paperback ed. 1965; rev. ed. 1997

The Manyōshū, Nippon Gakujutsu Shinkōkai edition 1965

Su Tung-p'o: Selections from a Sung Dynasty Poet, tr. Burton Watson. Also in paperback ed. 1965

Bhartrihari: Poems, tr. Barbara Stoler Miller. Also in paperback ed. 1967

Basic Writings of Mo Tzu, Hsün Tzu, and Han Fei Tzu, tr. Burton Watson. Also in separate paperback eds. 1967

The Awakening of Faith, Attributed to Aśvaghosha, tr. Yoshito S. Hakeda. Also in paperback ed. 1967

Reflections on Things at Hand: The Neo-Confucian Anthology, comp. Chu Hsi and Lü Tsu-ch'ien, tr. Wing-tsit Chan 1967

The Platform Sutra of the Sixth Patriarch, tr. Philip B. Yampolsky. Also in paperback ed. 1967

Essays in Idleness: The Tsurezuregusa of Kenkō, tr. Donald Keene. Also in paperback ed. 1967

The Pillow Book of Sei Shōnagon, tr. Ivan Morris, 2 vols. 1967

Two Plays of Ancient India: The Little Clay Cart and the Minister's Seal, tr. J. A. B. van Buitenen 1968

The Complete Works of Chuang Tzu, tr. Burton Watson 1968

The Romance of the Western Chamber (Hsi Hsiang Chi), tr. S. I. Hsiung. Also in paperback ed. 1968

The Manyōshū, Nippon Gakujutsu Shinkōkai edition. Paperback ed. only. 1969

Records of the Historian: Chapters from the Shih chi of Ssu-ma Ch'ien, tr. Burton Watson. Paperback ed. only. 1969

Cold Mountain: 100 Poems by the T'ang Poet Han-shan, tr. Burton Watson. Also in paperback ed. 1970

Twenty Plays of the Nō Theatre, ed. Donald Keene. Also in paperback ed. 1970

Chūshingura: The Treasury of Loyal Retainers, tr. Donald Keene. Also in paperback ed. 1971; rev. ed. 1997

The Zen Master Hakuin: Selected Writings, tr. Philip B. Yampolsky 1971
Chinese Rhyme-Prose: Poems in the Fu Form from the Han and Six Dynasties Periods, tr. Burton Watson. Also in paperback ed. 1971
Kūkai: Major Works, tr. Yoshito S. Hakeda. Also in paperback ed. 1972
The Old Man Who Does as He Pleases: Selections from the Poetry and Prose of Lu Yu, tr. Burton Watson 1973
The Lion's Roar of Queen Śrīmālā, tr. Alex and Hideko Wayman 1974
Courtier and Commoner in Ancient China: Selections from the History of the Former Han by Pan Ku, tr. Burton Watson. Also in paperback ed. 1974
Japanese Literature in Chinese, vol. 1: *Poetry and Prose in Chinese by Japanese Writers of the Early Period*, tr. Burton Watson 1975
Japanese Literature in Chinese, vol. 2: *Poetry and Prose in Chinese by Japanese Writers of the Later Period*, tr. Burton Watson 1976
Love Song of the Dark Lord: Jayadeva's Gītagovinda, tr. Barbara Stoler Miller. Also in paperback ed. Cloth ed. includes critical text of the Sanskrit. 1977; rev. ed. 1997
Ryōkan: Zen Monk-Poet of Japan, tr. Burton Watson 1977
Calming the Mind and Discerning the Real: From the Lam rim chen mo of Tsoṇ-kha-pa, tr. Alex Wayman 1978
The Hermit and the Love-Thief: Sanskrit Poems of Bhartrihari and Bilhaṇa, tr. Barbara Stoler Miller 1978
The Lute: Kao Ming's P'i-p'a chi, tr. Jean Mulligan. Also in paperback ed. 1980
A Chronicle of Gods and Sovereigns: Jinnō Shōtōki of Kitabatake Chikafusa, tr. H. Paul Varley 1980
Among the Flowers: The Hua-chien chi, tr. Lois Fusek 1982
Grass Hill: Poems and Prose by the Japanese Monk Gensei, tr. Burton Watson 1983
Doctors, Diviners, and Magicians of Ancient China: Biographies of Fang-shih, tr. Kenneth J. DeWoskin. Also in paperback ed. 1983
Theater of Memory: The Plays of Kālidāsa, ed. Barbara Stoler Miller. Also in paperback ed. 1984
The Columbia Book of Chinese Poetry: From Early Times to the Thirteenth Century, ed. and tr. Burton Watson. Also in paperback ed. 1984
Poems of Love and War: From the Eight Anthologies and the Ten Long Poems of Classical Tamil, tr. A. K. Ramanujan. Also in paperback ed. 1985
The Bhagavad Gita: Krishna's Counsel in Time of War, tr. Barbara Stoler Miller 1986
The Columbia Book of Later Chinese Poetry, ed. and tr. Jonathan Chaves. Also in paperback ed. 1986
The Tso Chuan: Selections from China's Oldest Narrative History, tr. Burton Watson 1989
Waiting for the Wind: Thirty-Six Poets of Japan's Late Medieval Age, tr. Steven Carter 1989
Selected Writings of Nichiren, ed. Philip B. Yampolsky 1990

Saigyō, Poems of a Mountain Home, tr. Burton Watson 1990
The Book of Lieh Tzu: A Classic of the Tao, tr. A. C. Graham. Morningside ed. 1990
The Tale of an Anklet: An Epic of South India—The Cilappatikāram of Iḷaṅkō Aṭikaḷ, tr. R. Parthasarathy 1993
Waiting for the Dawn: A Plan for the Prince, tr. with introduction by Wm. Theodore de Bary 1993
Yoshitsune and the Thousand Cherry Trees: A Masterpiece of the Eighteenth-Century Japanese Puppet Theater, tr., annotated, and with introduction by Stanleigh H. Jones Jr. 1993
The Lotus Sutra, tr. Burton Watson. Also in paperback ed. 1993
The Classic of Changes: A New Translation of the I Ching as Interpreted by Wang Bi, tr. Richard John Lynn 1994
Beyond Spring: Tz'u Poems of the Sung Dynasty, tr. Julie Landau 1994
The Columbia Anthology of Traditional Chinese Literature, ed. Victor H. Mair 1994
Scenes for Mandarins: The Elite Theater of the Ming, tr. Cyril Birch 1995
Letters of Nichiren, ed. Philip B. Yampolsky; tr. Burton Watson et al. 1996
Unforgotten Dreams: Poems by the Zen Monk Shōtetsu, tr. Steven D. Carter 1997
The Vimalakirti Sutra, tr. Burton Watson 1997
Japanese and Chinese Poems to Sing: The Wakan rōei shū, tr. J. Thomas Rimer and Jonathan Chaves 1997
Breeze Through Bamboo: Kanshi of Ema Saikō, tr. Hiroaki Sato 1998
A Tower for the Summer Heat, by Li Yu, tr. Patrick Hanan 1998
Traditional Japanese Theater: An Anthology of Plays, by Karen Brazell 1998
The Original Analects: Sayings of Confucius and His Successors (0479–0249), by E. Bruce Brooks and A. Taeko Brooks 1998
The Classic of the Way and Virtue: A New Translation of the Tao-te ching of Laozi as Interpreted by Wang Bi, tr. Richard John Lynn 1999
The Four Hundred Songs of War and Wisdom: An Anthology of Poems from Classical Tamil, The Puṟanāṉūṟu, ed. and tr. George L. Hart and Hank Heifetz 1999
Original Tao: Inward Training (Nei-yeh) *and the Foundations of Taoist Mysticism*, by Harold D. Roth 1999
Po Chü-i: Selected Poems, tr. Burton Watson 2000
Lao Tzu's Tao Te Ching: *A Translation of the Startling New Documents Found at Guodian*, by Robert G. Henricks 2000
The Shorter Columbia Anthology of Traditional Chinese Literature, ed. Victor H. Mair 2000
Mistress and Maid (Jiaohongji), by Meng Chengshun, tr. Cyril Birch 2001
Chikamatsu: Five Late Plays, tr. and ed. C. Andrew Gerstle 2001
The Essential Lotus: Selections from the Lotus Sutra, tr. Burton Watson 2002
Early Modern Japanese Literature: An Anthology, 1600–1900, ed. Haruo Shirane 2002; abridged 2008
The Columbia Anthology of Traditional Korean Poetry, ed. Peter H. Lee 2002

The Sound of the Kiss, or The Story That Must Never Be Told: Pingali Suranna's Kalapurnodayamu, tr. Vecheru Narayana Rao and David Shulman 2003
The Selected Poems of Du Fu, tr. Burton Watson 2003
Far Beyond the Field: Haiku by Japanese Women, tr. Makoto Ueda 2003
Just Living: Poems and Prose by the Japanese Monk Tonna, ed. and tr. Steven D. Carter 2003
Han Feizi: Basic Writings, tr. Burton Watson 2003
Mozi: Basic Writings, tr. Burton Watson 2003
Xunzi: Basic Writings, tr. Burton Watson 2003
Zhuangzi: Basic Writings, tr. Burton Watson 2003
The Awakening of Faith, Attributed to Aśvaghosha, tr. Yoshito S. Hakeda, introduction by Ryūichi Abé 2005
The Tales of the Heike, tr. Burton Watson, ed. Haruo Shirane 2006
Tales of Moonlight and Rain, by Ueda Akinari, tr. with introduction by Anthony H. Chambers 2007
Traditional Japanese Literature: An Anthology, Beginnings to 1600, ed. Haruo Shirane 2007
The Philosophy of Qi, by Kaibara Ekken, tr. Mary Evelyn Tucker 2007
The Analects of Confucius, tr. Burton Watson 2007
The Art of War: Sun Zi's Military Methods, tr. Victor Mair 2007
One Hundred Poets, One Poem Each: A Translation of the Ogura Hyakunin Isshu, tr. Peter McMillan 2008
Zeami: Performance Notes, tr. Tom Hare 2008
Zongmi on Chan, tr. Jeffrey Lyle Broughton 2009
Scripture of the Lotus Blossom of the Fine Dharma, rev. ed., tr. Leon Hurvitz, preface and introduction by Stephen R. Teiser 2009
Mencius, tr. Irene Bloom, ed. with an introduction by Philip J. Ivanhoe 2009
Clouds Thick, Whereabouts Unknown: Poems by Zen Monks of China, Charles Egan 2010
The Mozi: A Complete Translation, tr. Ian Johnston 2010
The Huainanzi: A Guide to the Theory and Practice of Government in Early Han China, by Liu An, tr. and ed. John S. Major, Sarah A. Queen, Andrew Seth Meyer, and Harold D. Roth, with Michael Puett and Judson Murray 2010
The Demon at Agi Bridge and Other Japanese Tales, tr. Burton Watson, ed. with introduction by Haruo Shirane 2011
Haiku Before Haiku: From the Renga Masters to Bashō, tr. with introduction by Steven D. Carter 2011
The Columbia Anthology of Chinese Folk and Popular Literature, ed. Victor H. Mair and Mark Bender 2011
Tamil Love Poetry: The Five Hundred Short Poems of the Aiṅkuṟunūṟu, tr. and ed. Martha Ann Selby 2011
The Teachings of Master Wuzhu: Zen and Religion of No-Religion, by Wendi L. Adamek 2011

The Essential Huainanzi, by Liu An, tr. and ed. John S. Major, Sarah A. Queen, Andrew Seth Meyer, and Harold D. Roth 2012

The Dao of the Military: Liu An's Art of War, tr. Andrew Seth Meyer 2012

Unearthing the Changes: Recently Discovered Manuscripts of the Yi Jing (I Ching) *and Related Texts*, Edward L. Shaughnessy 2013

Record of Miraculous Events in Japan: The Nihon ryōiki, tr. Burton Watson 2013

The Complete Works of Zhuangzi, tr. Burton Watson 2013

Lust, Commerce, and Corruption: An Account of What I Have Seen and Heard, *by an Edo Samurai*, tr. and ed. Mark Teeuwen and Kate Wildman Nakai with Miyazaki Fumiko, Anne Walthall, and John Breen 2014; abridged 2017

Exemplary Women of Early China: The Lienü zhuan *of Liu Xiang*, tr. Anne Behnke Kinney 2014

The Columbia Anthology of Yuan Drama, ed. C. T. Hsia, Wai-yee Li, and George Kao 2014

The Resurrected Skeleton: From Zhuangzi to Lu Xun, by Wilt L. Idema 2014

The Sarashina Diary: *A Woman's Life in Eleventh-Century Japan*, by Sugawara no Takasue no Musume, tr. with introduction by Sonja Arntzen and Itō Moriyuki 2014; reader's edition 2018

The Kojiki: *An Account of Ancient Matters*, by Ō no Yasumaro, tr. Gustav Heldt 2014

The Orphan of Zhao *and Other Yuan Plays: The Earliest Known Versions*, tr. and introduced by Stephen H. West and Wilt L. Idema 2014

Luxuriant Gems of the Spring and Autumn, attributed to Dong Zhongshu, ed. and tr. Sarah A. Queen and John S. Major 2016

A Book to Burn and a Book to Keep (Hidden): Selected Writings, by Li Zhi, ed. and tr. Rivi Handler-Spitz, Pauline Lee, and Haun Saussy 2016

The Shenzi Fragments: *A Philosophical Analysis and Translation*, Eirik Lang Harris 2016

Record of Daily Knowledge *and* Poems and Essays: *Selections*, by Gu Yanwu, tr. and ed. Ian Johnston 2017

The Book of Lord Shang: Apologetics of State Power in Early China, by Shang Yang, ed. and tr. Yuri Pines 2017

The Songs of Chu: An Ancient Anthology of Works by Qu Yuan and Others, ed. and trans. Gopal Sukhu 2017

Ghalib: Selected Poems and Letters, by Mirza Asadullah Khan Ghalib, tr. Frances W. Pritchett and Owen T. A. Cornwall 2017

Quelling the Demons' Revolt: A Novel from Ming China, attributed to Luo Guanzhong, tr. Patrick Hanan 2017

Erotic Poems from the Sanskrit: A New Translation, R. Parthasarathy 2017

The Book of Swindles: Selections from a Late Ming Collection, by Zhang Yingyu, tr. Christopher G. Rea and Bruce Rusk 2017

Monsters, Animals, and Other Worlds: A Collection of Short Medieval Japanese Tales, ed. R. Keller Kimbrough and Haruo Shirane 2018

GPSR Authorized Representative: Easy Access System Europe, Mustamäe tee 50, 10621 Tallinn, Estonia, gpsr.requests@easproject.com

www.ingramcontent.com/pod-product-compliance
Lightning Source LLC
Chambersburg PA
CBHW020933310726
48980CB00007B/751/J

* 9 7 8 0 2 3 1 1 8 7 1 6 9 *